10 DAYS TO RUIN

OZEROV BRATVA
BOOK 1

NICOLE FOX

10 DAYS TO RUIN

OZEROV BRATVA BOOK 1

I'm arranged to be married...

To the devil himself.

Unless I find a way out.

Here's how to lose a mob boss in ten days:

DO act like the biggest brat the world has ever seen.

Sasha's face when you send dishes back at a five-star restaurant will be priceless.

DON'T ask your dad for help.

He's the one who arranged this wedding in the first place.

He won't—*can't*—save you now.

DO put on your hottest "naughty secretary" outfit and drop in unannounced to tease your fiancée wild in his office.

But DON'T let him touch.

DO keep him guessing.

DON'T let him close.

DO drive him crazy.

DON'T let him kiss.

Most of all…

DO keep your heart locked up and your hands to yourself.

Because if Sasha Ozerov gets one tiny glimpse at weakness…

He'll do the unthinkable.

Make you fall head over heels for him.

And you'll be left wondering one thing, like me.

I had ten days to make a mob boss hate me.

What happens if I start to love him instead?

***10 Days to Ruin** is Book 1 of the Ozerov Bratva duet. The story concludes in Book 2, **10 Days to Surrender**.*

1

ARIEL

I blame Superman for the way my life turned out.

If The CW hadn't cast Tom Welling as Superman in *Smallville,* it would've been different.

If Tom Welling didn't have cinnamon roll eyes and the bone structure of a sex god, it would've been different.

If I hadn't been a hyper-impressionable twelve-year-old girl caught deep in the vicious chokehold of puberty when the season four premiere of *Smallville* aired, then I wouldn't have been so jealous of Lois Lane getting to see Tom Welling naked that my crush on him immediately and violently transferred to a girl crush on her, and then I wouldn't have wanted to be a reporter, and then I wouldn't have gotten this job at The New York Gazette, and my editor wouldn't have sent me to this gala, and I wouldn't be in this situation I'm in.

But The CW *did* cast Tom Welling.

Tom Welling *did* have cinnamon roll eyes and the bone structure of a sex god.

And Lois Lane *did* get to see him naked in season four.

And so all of the other things did happen, one domino colliding into the next, shit rolling downhill, and so now, I'm cloistered in the men's bathroom at the New York Metropolitan Museum of Art, hyperventilating and bleeding from a cut on my hand and wondering just how the fuck I'm supposed to go back out there and do my job.

The woman in the mirror doesn't have any more of an idea than I do. She's staring back at me helplessly. Green eyes, auburn hair, punching well above her weight class in a Diane von Furstenberg dress she stole from her best friend's closet.

"What're we gonna do?" I try asking my reflection. She just mouths the question back to me, that useless tramp.

I sigh and look down at my hand. If you thought the Met would be ritzy enough to ensure their door handles were free of jagged, rusted edges, you'd have thought wrong. I just opened up a good two-inch gash in my hurry to slam the stupid thing behind me after I charged in here, because the women's bathroom had a line two dozen deep, because of course it did.

I've got my other hand clamped on top of it to stop my life juice from splurting everywhere. But the blood is starting to well up between my fingers and it's making me a teensy bit queasy.

I don't do blood. I don't do stitches. I don't do grievous wounds or even particularly bad bruises.

When you grow up the way I did, you see enough of that stuff to last a lifetime.

But I'm by myself in here and no one is coming to my rescue.

So with a big, brave inhale, I peel away my good hand and take a look at–

"Nope. Nuh-uh. Nooo thank you." My reflection agrees with me—that's a nasty cut. If I spend even a millisecond longer looking at it, I might pass out.

Wouldn't that be a headline? *Reporter Faints in Men's Bathroom While On-Duty; Cracks Head Open On Sink; Funeral Sparsely Attended.* Honestly, I'd have to laugh—it would be undeniably hilarious if my obituary got a byline before I ever actually got one myself.

In my defense, I haven't had many opportunities to actually, like, *do the job I was hired for.* My six months at the Gazette have thus far been spent primarily going back and forth to the Starbucks on the corner. I'm not sure if it's an intern thing, or a rookie hazing thing, or just a *Hey, you're a woman, therefore you're on coffee run duty* thing. But whatever the cause, I've had precious little opportunity to do what I took this job for.

Reporting. Telling stories. Shining little lights into the dark, cramped corners of the world, because I know better than almost anyone what goes on in those corners.

That in itself is a little bit ironic, if only because I've worked like hell to get *out* of those corners. Didn't I leave home the first chance I could? Didn't I change my name? Didn't I sever (almost) all contact with the man who raised me in those corners?

I did. I did. I did.

The *real* irony, though, is that the very first chance I get to do some real reporting... is on that man himself.

That's right: Leander Makris, New York's infamous crime boss and head honcho of the city's Greek mafia, is the star of my article.

He's also my dad.

I didn't know he'd be hosting this gala until I showed up tonight, but when that slap from reality landed, it did so with a *vengeance.* Thus the tears, and the fleeing into the wrong bathroom, and the hyperventilating, and the reminiscing about how Tom Welling led me all wrong and if I ever get my hands on him I'm gonna kiss him and then kick him, possibly not in that order.

"Breathe," cautions my reflection. "You're starting to look a little crazy."

She's not wrong. Gina, the best friend from whom I stole the DVF dress I'm wearing, did my hair in fancy braids for the night (albeit only after I bribed her into it). One is starting to come loose, though, and I lost an earring at some point in my flight to the bathroom. Between those things and the blood starting to trickle down my fingertips, I really do look like a nutcase.

At least nobody else is here to witness my—

"Shit."

The door handle that sliced me starts to turn. I move faster than I've ever moved in my entire life as I sprint into the nearest stall, slam the door, and hike my feet up on the toilet so no one sees that there's a woman in heels and painted toenails creeping her way around the men's bathroom.

The door creaks inward.

Footsteps ring out. Male—I mean, obviously, they're male, given the fact that we're in the men's bathroom, but there's a heavy *thump* and a kind of power in the stride that can only come attached to a Y chromosome.

Thump.

Thump.

I stare at the gap underneath the stall door. My breath is held hostage in my lungs and I'm doing the best I can to get my heart to stop beating so damn loudly as those feet come into sight.

And then they stop right in front of me.

I used to play a game with my mom when I was little—before she left, before she told Baba, *I can't do this anymore* and kissed me on the cheek and took her one duffel bag with her—where we'd sit outside coffee shops and make up stories about the people who passed by.

Little old lady in a pillbox hat that Jackie O. would've been jealous of? *Secretly a fairy princess,* my mom would whisper in my ear. *She's been hiding out in our world while her one true love fights a war to make their kingdom safe for her again.*

A young, scruffy man busking on the corner for dollar bills dropped into his guitar case? *That's an angel,* she'd tell me. *He accidentally fell off a train in heaven and he's gotta earn enough money to buy his ticket back home.*

The hot dog vendor was a genie. The breakdancers on the subway were forest nymphs. Every rat scurrying past on the sidewalk was a poor little boy under a witch's spell who just had to find a way to break the curse.

But *these* shoes? *This* man?

That can only be a devil.

It's in the flawless gleam of the oxblood leather loafers. The way the charcoal gray pants cuff, ironed to razor-blade perfection, floats above his ankle. Those socks, black as midnight.

And when he speaks, I know it for sure, because the voice those ankles belong to is like anointing oil poured over broken granite.

"*Mne plevat'*," he growls in a harsh, ice-cold rumble. "*Ya khochu, chtoby ty nashel yego i ubil.*"

The bathroom is graveyard quiet, but I can hear only mumbled squeaking from the other end of the phone call. The man in the oxblood shoes doesn't let his friend finish before he interrupts.

"Should I repeat myself in English so the message is clear? '*I don't give a fuck. I want you to find him and kill him.*' Don't call back until it's done."

The beep that follows ends the call.

I realize when the edges of my vision start to burn and blacken that I haven't breathed since the man walked in. I can feel sweat beading up on my temples and my armpits. But I just have to hold out a little longer, a little longer, *a little fucking longer,* because if the man will just leave, then I can…

Oh, no.

I see it as it's happening—fast enough to understand, but too slow to do anything about it.

The blood that's been leaking down my knuckles forms a diamond at the tip of my pointer finger. Wells up. Swells up. Stretches…

And then it falls to the checkerboard tile floors with a tiny, a soft, but an utterly undeniable *plip.*

Silence follows.

Then: slowly, slowly… those oxblood shoes turn to face me.

"Whoever's in there," the devil snarls, "open the door before I break it down."

2

ARIEL

I never knew that the expression *"When one door closes, another opens"* could happen quite so literally. I thought that was the kind of thing a lazy copywriter puts on Chinese takeout fortune cookies.

But scarcely two minutes after the bathroom door closes on one chapter of my life, the stall door swings open to begin another.

My first thought when I see him is, *Damn—I really nailed it.*

Because the man standing framed in the stall entryway is exactly how I pictured him to a freaking T.

My gaze starts at his feet, which I've already spent an exhaustive amount of mental energy analyzing. It rises up the streamlined pleat of his ash-gray suit pants, past strong thighs and a lean waist, grazing over how his white shirt clings to six very clearly defined abs, up to where the narrow V of his tieless collar reveals a smattering of dark chest hair and the briefest glimpse of a tattoo etched into the tan skin just beneath his throat.

From there, it keeps going. It drinks in the blunt, brutal cliff of his chin. The sloping jawline stubbled with the beginnings of a beard. A proud, jutting noise, cheekbones that Tom Welling would slay for, and eyes so blue that I can feel the cold burn of their stare. His hair is dark, curly, and tousled where it falls over his forehead.

My second thought is, *The CW fucked up. They should've cast* him.

Even now, after hearing him casually order some subordinate to commit murder, I can't help but feel that girlish giggle bubbling up inside me. Same as twelve-year-old me felt when Superman rose out of that cornfield in his birthday suit, like, *Golly gee, you sure are handsome!*

I wouldn't dare say that out loud, though.

Because Superman here looks like he's ready to commit some murder of his own.

His hands are flexing at his sides. I see more tattoos stamped into his knuckles—letters in Cyrillic, which immediately makes it click in my head that it was Russian he was speaking into the phone a moment ago. Thin, white scars run between the ink. Those hands look highly capable. I'd very much like to not find how just *how* capable.

"I'd say *'Take a picture; it will last longer,'* but you've been staring at me long enough that I'm pretty fucking sure you have it all memorized by now," he spits. The voice matches his eyes: cold as the grave, rough, relentless.

I start to squeak, "Sorry," then I stop and scold myself for the girly uptalk intonation and for even daring to apologize in the first place. Then I remember that I am in fact in the wrong bathroom and I start to say it again. Then I stop and scold myself for stuttering like a buffoon. Then I—

"For God's sake, spit it out," the man snaps.

I frown and squint. "You're kind of an asshole."

Gotta give credit where it's due: that's certainly not a meek, simpy apology. Is it a smart thing to say, though?

Probably not.

To my surprise, the man blinks placidly. He doesn't smile—I'd worry about the structural integrity of his broodiness if he even tried—but some imperceptible portion of his frigid rage fades away.

"'Kind of' doesn't even begin to cover it."

"An honest asshole, at least," I concede.

He shakes his head. "Definitely not that." Then he eyes me and holds out a hand. "Are you going to squat on that toilet like a gargoyle for our entire conversation, or would you like help down?"

I eye the hand he's offering. It's even more intimidating up close. I know some girls are into guys' hands, and I get that, and it really is a very nice hand, aesthetically speaking.

But something about the scars in combination with the easy, breezy, beautiful murder threat he issued in the very recent past is giving me pause.

Carefully, using the handrail attached to the stall wall instead of the male hand attached to the devil in the gray suit, I lower myself from my toilet perch and assume a quasi-normal human posture.

"It's fine; I can do it mys—"

I promptly collapse.

It's my knees that betray me. Thirty-three doesn't seem that old in the grand scheme of things, but I'm a New Yorker born and bred, so I've put a lot of miles on these joints of mine, walking up avenues and down streets since I was old enough to put one foot in front of the other. Apparently, five minutes of holding a power squat on the Met's toilets is asking too much of what cartilage remains.

I'm hurtling towards a hot date with the floor when the man moves. He's fast and languid at the same time, and I could almost swear I see him roll his eyes as he intervenes.

Then that same hand that I turned down a moment ago loops around my waist and stops me from concussing myself with my own pride. Effortlessly, without losing so much as a hair out of place, he drags me back to my feet and settles me there.

The hand, though, stays plastered to my hip.

"You're kind of an idiot," he says matter-of-factly.

He's kidding—I think he's kidding, at least, because he's using my own words to mock me and those eyes of his are gleaming in a mischievous sort of way—but the cement-mixer-churning-glaciers quality of his voice doesn't really change.

Playing along, I reply, "'Kind of' doesn't even begin to cover it." I glance down at his hand, huge and splayed across my waist. "But thank you for saving me."

He nods, once, briskly, then peels his hand away. The heat and pressure of it lingers long after it's gone.

"I think it's safe to assume you're not a spy," the man drawls. "Either that or you're the worst one in the history of the profession."

I force out a wheezy, panicked laugh. "I'm a professional spy, actually. In a manner of speaking."

His forehead wrinkles, those thick, dark brows arrowing downward. "You can't be ser—"

"Reporter," I blurt before the murdery glint in his eyes comes roaring back to life. "I was making a joke. Not a very good one, apparently."

He keeps frowning, but the wrinkles smooth away enough to let me breathe again. "You're a reporter," he repeats, stroking his jawline. "Hm. Here to report on…?"

I wave a hand in the general direction of the ballroom where tonight's gala is taking place. "The illustrious generosity of our fine host and his many important charitable causes, for which he cares quite deeply and genuinely and definitely not just for the PR and tax write-offs."

The man makes a short barking noise. It takes me a second to realize that that's what passes for a laugh from him. "I don't think Leander can even spell 'generous.'"

I do a double-take. There aren't many people in this world willing to talk shit about Leander Makris, much less to a complete stranger. The man has a sufficiently bloody reputation that it's just not worth the risk.

This man, however, couldn't possibly care any less. As I try to puzzle out just who he is that he'd dare speak so freely about a guy with more murder and racketeering allegations than Brooklyn has baristas, he rakes a hand through his hair and checks his watch.

"Somewhere to be?" I ask.

"No," he says. "Just trying to figure out how long I can hide in here before I have to go mingle with the vultures again."

It's my turn to laugh, though hopefully, I sound like less of a barking seal than my new friend here did. "You don't strike me as the kind of guy who's afraid of social obligations."

His scowl darkens. "It's them who should be afraid. If I have to endure one more conversation about Upper West Side brownstone renovations or the guest list of the mayor's New Year's Ball, I'm going to put a fucking bullet in someone's skull."

Again, I'm fairly sure he's making a joke, the same way I told Gina yesterday that *if I have to fetch one more nonfat iced mocha latte with extra whip for Sportswriter Steve, I'm going to commit seppuku on the Brooklyn Bridge.*

But also, I can't quite forget that he did just literally discuss murder on the phone, so the joke hits a little too close to home for comfort.

"Well," I say as nonchalantly as I can, "I wouldn't want to keep you from your duties for the evening. Sounds like your hands are full, and besides, I've really only been dying to talk about this new backsplash that my neighbor had installed in her..."

He holds up a hand to stop me. "Don't. Not even as a joke."

"Noted," I say, miming zipping my lips. "Backsplashes are off the table."

But as I make the motion, the man's eyes lock onto something. That furrow in his brow returns, carved deeper than ever.

I'm confused, until he says in a stern growl, "You're bleeding."

I look down and, yep, turns out that inconvenient speed bump in my evening hasn't magically disappeared. I feel the familiar lurch in my stomach, the seasick tingle of blood rippling down to the tips of my fingers and toes.

I wobble a bit. The man's hand flies out to steady me once again. "It's really not a big—"

"Hush," he orders, and I immediately fall silent like he just mashed the mute button on the Ariel Ward remote control. "Sink. Now."

Just like that, I'm a marionette in his grasp. He pilots me and my legs obey as we drift toward the sink together.

I'm suddenly powerless to do anything that he doesn't tell me to do. Can't wait, can't think, can't argue, can't flee. I can only receive things, isolated little sensations that come and go like passing clouds.

His hands are big.

He smells nice. Kinda minty.

He's tall, too. Very tall. Some might say too tall. Not me, though. I wouldn't say that. I'd say he's a very good height.

"Let go."

I follow his gaze down to realize I'm death-gripping my own pinky finger. It's going a weird purply-white at the end from lack of circulation. I let him uncurl one digit at a time until I've given up the grasp and he's got my sliced hand cradled in his palm.

He turns on the sink with his free hand and checks the water a few times until it's warm enough. He looks at me.

"Don't scream. They'll think I'm doing something I shouldn't be."

Before I can ask who "they" is and question whether maybe they'd be right and whether this whole situation is in fact a bad idea, he passes my hand under the faucet.

I have to bite the inside of my cheek to stop from screaming. White-hot pain flashes through me—but only for a second. Right on its heels is a warm ease.

I can unclench. I can breathe.

"I don't like blood," I explain sheepishly once I open my eyes again.

The man is looking at me, appraising, calm. "Could've fooled me."

I bite my lip so I don't laugh. "I'm a better reporter than I am an actress, I swear."

"Is that so?" He arches a brow. "Let's see it. I'll give you an exclusive."

Frowning, I look him up and down again. "Please don't hate me for asking this, but should I know who you are?"

"You wound me." He touches his chest playfully for a second, then shrugs. "Or maybe you flatter me. I'm used to fawning people blowing smoke up my ass. 'Willfully ignorant' is a nice change of pace."

I wrinkle my nose. "Was that supposed to be a compliment?"

Chuckling, he stoops down, opens the cabinet beneath the sink, and withdraws a first aid kit. How he knew it was there is beyond me, but he did it so casually that it's like he just expected the world to provide him what he needed and so it provided. I have to blink and knuckle my eyes until the amazement recedes.

"No," he replies as he unclasps the kit and starts to pull out bandages, gauze, and disinfectant. "A compliment would be me telling you that you look fucking stunning in that dress. Calling you ignorant was merely an observation."

I slap his chest with my good hand. "Ass!" I cry out.

"Now, it's my turn to ask if that's supposed to be a compliment."

I'm not sure whether I want to laugh, scream, strip, or escape. It's just that something about this man is too smooth to be real. He quips, but it's not quippy; he rescues, but he's no white knight; he reaches into empty cabinets and retrieves first aid kits that, logically, simply *should not be there.*

And yet they are.

My mouth opens and closes while I try and fail to process the gray-suited enigma who's currently pouring hydrogen peroxide over my cut. For a professional wordsmith, I'm really coming up short on insightful things to say here.

He doesn't seem to mind my goldfish impression, though. He just loops gauze around my finger, followed by a bandage. His touch is surprisingly tender.

"You still haven't told me who you are," I manage finally.

"No," he agrees, a ghost of a smile playing at the corners of his mouth. "I haven't."

"Do I have to beg?"

"I wouldn't mind if you did."

"But would it work?"

"Only one way to find out."

His eyes crinkle at the corners, the only sign that he might be smiling. That mouth remains a cruel slash of bourbon color nestled in the forest of dark beard surrounding it.

"Does this whole mysterious stranger act usually work for you?" I ask, aiming for sardonic but landing somewhere closer to breathless and giddy.

"I wouldn't know." His eyes meet mine, and there's that dangerous glint again. "I've never tried it before."

"Liar."

"Absolutely." He crowds me closer, still holding my hand. His hips kiss mine just as the small of my back kisses the sink behind me. "But you knew that already."

I should back away. I really, really should. Everything about this man is a red flag. Charisma is a red flag. Cleverness is a red flag. Being that stupidly good-looking is like a whole flagpole's worth of red flags.

But I've spent my whole life running from dangerous men, and something about that gets exhausting after a while.

Maybe that's why I don't move when he reaches up with his free hand and tucks a loose strand of hair behind my ear. Or maybe it's just because the bathroom lights are hitting his eyes in a way that makes them look like Arctic ice at midnight.

"Your friend did a nice job with these braids," he murmurs, fingers trailing down one plait. "Shame about the one coming loose."

I blink. "How did you—?"

"Your dress is safety-pinned in the back, which means it doesn't fit, which suggests you borrowed it from someone. The braids are too complex to do yourself, and they're actually even in the back, and I'm fairly certain you don't have eyes in the back of your head. So I took an educated guess."

"I… You… Are you showing off?"

"Maybe." His hand settles at the nape of my neck. I can feel my own pulse hammering against his palm. "Is it working?"

My throat is dry. "That depends on what you're trying to achieve."

The corner of his mouth quirks up, and I realize I've never been more aware of another person's lips in my entire life. "I thought that was obvious," he says.

I laugh deliriously. "There is not one single, solitary thing about you that is obvious."

"No? Then let me be clear."

His face is so close to mine. It's all I can see, all I can possibly bring myself to care about. I'm bathing in his scent as his lips draw closer and closer.

And closer still, and closer still, until—

The bathroom door creaks.

We spring apart like teenagers caught behind the bleachers. My mysterious stranger's face transforms instantly, that almost-softness hardening into marble as he turns toward the door.

He doesn't have to say a word. The newcomer takes one look at us—me with my bandaged hand and flushed cheeks, him with his thundercloud scowl and general aura of *Do not fuck with me*—and backs right out again.

When the door clicks shut, we both exhale. But the tension doesn't go away. Something lingers in the air between us, electric and unfinished and dangerous as all hell.

"You should go," he warns, though it sounds like it costs him something to say it.

I gulp. "Should I?"

"Yes." He runs a hand through his hair. "Because if you don't leave now, I'm going to kiss you. And once I start, I'm not going to want to stop."

He's right. I should go. I take a half-step toward the door, then pause and turn back. "What if I don't want you to stop?"

His face is half-shadowed. A dark pit where his left eye should be. "You should be very, very careful before you say things like that to a man like me."

I look at him. His head almost brushes the ceiling and his shoulders seem to span from wall to wall. I was spot-on the first time: he's a bad idea made real. Mama would've whispered a scary fairy tale about him. He's a beast, a golem, a dark prince who curses everything he touches.

I look at the door. It's there. I could grab the knob—avoiding cutting my hand on it this time, preferably—and twist. I could open it. I could leave.

But whether it's masochism or recklessness or just plain old stupidity, something compels me to turn back instead. To open my mouth, and to tell this demon…

"Or else what?"

3

ARIEL

In two strides, he's pinning me against the wall. One hand tangles in my hair, ruining what's left of Gina's handiwork. The other hand grips my waist and bunches my dress into a disaster of borrowed silk. His mouth crashes into mine like storm waves breaking on a levee.

I've been kissed before, but not like this. *Never* like this. He kisses me like I'm air and he's drowning. And God help me, that's exactly how I kiss him back.

When I gasp, he thrusts his tongue past my teeth and claims my mouth. I moan and let him.

"Last chance to run, *ptichka,*" he growls.

In answer, I drag him back down to me. The sink edge digs into my back as he lifts me onto it. My dress rides up my thighs and his hands follow, leaving trails of fire on my skin. When he breaks the kiss to trace a path down my neck with his lips, I have to bite back another moan.

"Someone could walk in," I manage to whisper, even as my fingers work at his shirt buttons.

He reaches past me to lock the door, the movement pressing him even closer. "Let me worry about that."

Then he's kissing me again and it's easy to do exactly that: let him handle the worrying. Some days, it feels like all I do is worry. So for him to pick me up and move me here and move me there and take all that burden off my plate? I feel light. I feel weightless.

I feel like I could fucking fly.

Time melts and skews as he gathers me against him and nips his way down the curve of my throat. I let my head drape backward as I gaze up at the ceiling through half-lidded eyes, fingertips clawing into his thick shoulders for dear life.

He keeps murmuring things against my skin—*"ptichka"* and *"I shouldn't"* and *"fucking hell, you taste good."* Every single one makes my toes curl.

When his fingertip ventures up to find the edge of my panties, I suck in a sharp gasp. "This is a—"

"—bad idea," he agrees. "Tell me something I don't fucking know."

But neither of us stop when that finger slides beneath the lace and strokes through my wetness. I bite down where his neck meets his shoulder so I don't scream. Stuttering half-syllables come pouring through my muffled mouth.

"P-pl-p-pl..." It never quite makes it all the way to a word.

It doesn't have to, though. He knows what I'm pleading for. Like the first aid kit, everything he touches is exactly where it's supposed to be.

When he parts me, I come so fast that my cheeks burn red with embarrassment. Scarcely a dozen pumps of two scarred fingers into me and I'm falling apart and quivering in his arms.

It gets messier from there. Clothes fumble. Belts unlatch. My underwear slides down my thighs and vanishes, heaven only knows where.

But when he lines his hard cock up with my pussy, he stops. His forehead is pressed to mine. Eyes huge and blue. Breath rattling in and out of his lungs. He's just this side of undone, like the humanity in him is thrashing against the steel bars of the cage he uses to keep it stowed away.

I, on the other hand, look absolutely ruined already, if my quick glance into the mirror is anything to go by. The braids are a distant memory. The straps of my dress have fallen down my shoulders to let my boobs peek over the neckline of my dress. My skin is flushed red everywhere he's touched and kissed and bit.

Of all the things about him that have brought me to this moment, though, this line in the sand, this one door closing and another opening, it's that look in his eyes that pushes me over the threshold.

He really doesn't do this.

Not "this" as in sex, because any man that handsome and that obviously wealthy and that supremely confident in his own skin can clearly have women in his bed at the snap of his fingers. What I mean is that he doesn't do "this" as in gaze down at the woman he's about to fuck like she might be the death of the self-control that defines him. He doesn't do "this" as in show that there is anything accessible within him that might charitably be called a soul. He doesn't do "this" as in let his bedmates look back and wonder just what it might take to crack him open for once in his grim, bloodsoaked life.

He doesn't do "this."

Neither do I.

But then he slides into me, and we both do something we've never done before.

For all the build-up, it's almost remarkable how fast the sex is. Brutal things can never last that long. And besides, I'm skittering in and out of awareness, too overwhelmed by how it feels like he's fucking my heart, splitting me wide open, wider, wider.

The thump and rattle of the sink touching the mirror glass times every thrust. I moan, broken, helpless. His hands carve divots in my bare waist.

"Spread for me," he orders. "Spread those fucking thighs and give me all of you."

But even as he orders it, he does it for me, molding me like putty. My hips are screaming with the strain and my throat is raw from the effort of holding back the kinds of moans that would draw attention from the partygoers on the other side of the wall. But I want so fucking badly to give him what he's asking.

Every twitch of his muscles drives him deeper into me than anyone's ever gone before. I'm a bouncing, sweaty disaster and I don't have the brain cells left to give a damn. Even as our mouths clash and our breath mingles and he keeps murmuring filthy nothings that are half-exhale and half-*fuck-you're-dripping-for-me,* all I can do is hold on and pray that the climax doesn't kill me.

He's not wrong—I am dripping for him. More broken syllables fall out of my mouth. "P-pl-pl… M-m-more…"

And just when I think he couldn't possibly give me more, he does. He drags me down onto his cock, crushing my waist between his palms, fucking harder and faster and more relentless.

Almost…

Almost…

Boom.

He growls, I whimper, and then we both explode, one on the heels of the next. Light fractures in my vision as the orgasm cleaves me in two. A few starlit, timeless seconds suck us in. For as long as those last, I'm soaring.

Then gravity reclaims us. Time reclaims us. Common sense reclaims us.

And all I can think as I float back down is, *That really was a bad idea.*

Returning to reality is an ugly affair. I'm suddenly aware of how unkempt my dress looks scrunched around my waist like that. How cold and sticky the sink countertop is. How what I just did—fucking a stranger while *literally on the job*—was so unbelievably rash that I should probably tender my resignation at the Gazette and go become a nun, because a lifetime of prayer and solitude is the bare minimum of what I'll need to redeem my soul after this idiotic stunt.

It would help if the stranger would say something. But as he straightens his clothes, shoots his cuffs, and steps back from me, it's as if he's pulling up the drawbridge and locking down the castle gates behind his eyes. Those glimpses of soul I saw swimming in the blue of his irises are long gone now. The shreds of humanity are hidden. He looks the way he did when he first opened the stall door.

Cold.

Cruel.

Merciless.

I open my mouth to tell him—I mean, shoot, *something,* if only because it feels like the silence is gonna swallow me whole if I don't. Should I ask his name? Should I give him my number? Should I see if he regrets this or if he maybe wants to do it again?

But he beats me to the punch.

He gives me one crisp, formal incline of the head, jaw clenched brutally tight. "Enjoy the gala," he says in that tar-on-rubble voice of his. "Try not to cut yourself again."

Then he's gone, leaving me leaking and lonely on a sink counter, wondering what in the fuck just happened.

4

SASHA

It's a fucking pity I'll never have that again.

I mourn the loss even as I stride away down the hall and leave the bathroom behind me—not looking back, not ever looking back, because looking back is the act of a fucking *ssyklo.* A pussy. A coward.

That doesn't mean I don't listen, though.

I hear the door close behind me. I hear my footsteps echo off the ceiling like a pulsing, thudding heartbeat. I hear the murmurs of the people I pass.

I hear it all.

But I never, ever look back.

The voice snarling in my head sounds like my father's—though, to be fair, everything sounds like my father's voice these days. Yakov Ozerov's ghost has been especially loud lately, ever since this arrangement with the Greeks started taking shape. I can almost smell the reek of cognac on his breath as he reminds me what matters: *Power. Control. Empire.*

Love is for children and fools. I am neither.

My phone vibrates in my pocket. Feliks. "The package is secured," he says in Russian when I answer. "But it's getting anxious about the delivery time."

Code for: the Serbian spy he caught snooping around an Ozerov warehouse earlier tonight is starting to panic.

"Keep it fresh," I reply. "I'm on my way."

I find a side exit and slip out into the December night. The cold bites through my suit jacket, but I barely feel it. St. Petersburg winters were far worse than anything New York can throw at me.

Still. Something about tonight's chill makes me long for what I left in my wake just now. Soft skin under my hands. Green eyes watching me like I might be worth saving.

She smelled like peaches. It's just now hit me that that's what that sweetness was. Ripe summer peaches, sweet ones, the kind that leave juice dribbling down your chin when you sink your teeth in. Peaches. Fucking pea—

So you're a fucking poet now? Forget her, Yakov bellows. *She's nothing. A distraction. Remember what happened the last time you let yourself get distracted?*

As a matter of fact, Father, I do remember.

The scars on my back remember, too.

My car waits at the curb, Klaus at attention behind the wheel. He doesn't speak as I slide into the back seat, just pulls smoothly into traffic.

Good man. He knows when I need silence.

As we drive, the city flows past my window in rivers of neon and shadow. Ten minutes to the abandoned restaurant where Feliks is holding our guest. Ten minutes to get my head in order. Ten minutes to forget the way that little *ptichka* whispered, "Or else what?" like she wasn't afraid of me at all.

I wonder if she's aware of how easily little birds like her get their wings broken.

It could've gone that way, after all. I could've clipped her feathers the moment I realized she'd overheard my conversation on the phone with Feliks. A quick twist of the neck and it would've been *bye-bye, birdy.* Another unfortunate mess easily swept under yet another bloodstained rug.

Wouldn't be the first time.

Won't be the last.

But one look at those wide green eyes told me what she truly was. Not a threat, not a spy, but a dove snared in the wrong trap.

So I did what I shouldn't have done: played with my food. I gave myself this little indulgence.

And why not? I deserve it. I fucking *deserve* one goddamn moment for myself before I hurl the last of my humanity into the gaping maw of this Bratva that always wants more, more, more from me.

It took my mother. It took my childhood. And now, it's taking my freedom.

Because once I return to the gala from this little errand, I'm going to meet the woman I have to marry.

That's the only reason I've bothered attending this bullshit dog-and-pony show in the first place. Fuck knows I don't usually make an appearance. Invites for these kinds of social torture sessions stuff my inbox on the regular. Everybody—civilian and criminal alike—wants Sasha Ozerov to darken the door of their little soirees. I'm a curioso, an oddity, a man who lives so far outside of the ridiculous lines into which they've boxed themselves that all they can do is gawk and whisper behind their hands.

There he goes, they tell themselves. *Don't get too close or he might bite.*

They're right—I might. And normally, that threat is enough to keep the gawkers at bay.

It wasn't enough for the reporter, though. That little bird flew close enough for me to snatch her out of the air and make a meal of her.

And fuck, what a meal it was. Her moans are still echoing in my head. She couldn't even spit out the word *Please*—that's how badly she wanted, needed me.

Fuck me if I didn't feel the exact same.

It was a lifetime's worth of impulse all distilled into one moment. Because I don't bend, I don't break, I don't waver, *ever.*

Except for once.

Except for tonight.

But as I said—that's behind me now. And I am no *ssyklo.*

The car stops. Klaus opens my door. The restaurant's broken sign casts sickly purple shadows across the cracked pavement.

Time to go to work.

Inside, the restaurant reeks of mildew, rust, and spoiled meat. Empty plates still sit on some tables, coated in years of dust, like the diners just got up and walked away mid-meal. The leather booths are cracked and peeling. Rats scatter at my approach.

Feliks emerges from the shadows with an unlit cigarette dangling from his lips. His scarred face twists into what passes for a smile. "He's in the kitchen. Been crying about his family for the last hour."

I grimace. They always cry about their families.

"Any complications?" I ask, shrugging off my jacket and handing it to him. No point in getting blood on good Italian wool.

"*Nyet*. Clean grab. No witnesses." Feliks follows me through the swinging doors. "Though he did try to swallow something when we caught him. Some kind of data chip."

I roll up my sleeves. "And?"

"Made him cough it up. Literally." He holds up a small plastic bag containing a bloody micro SD card. "Haven't checked what's on it yet."

"Give it to Roza. She'll have a field day."

The spy is zip-tied to a steel prep table, face mashed like a fucking eggplant and caked with dried blood. Remarkably, he's still conscious.

Young, too—younger than I expected. No doubt fresh out of whatever shithole the Serbs train their operatives in these days. Still soft with baby fat at the edges. His left eye swells shut; the right darts like a trapped roach.

The good eye widens when he sees me. "Y-y-y…"

"Yes," I agree. "Me. As always, I'm touched by my reputation." I grab a chair, spin it around, straddle it backwards. Feliks hands me a crowbar. The cold steel sings in my grip. "Let's talk."

The boy—because that's what he is, really; not a man, not even close—tries to look brave. "I have n-nothing to say to you."

Something tickles at the back of my mind. A flash of green eyes, defiant words: *Or else what?*

I shove the memory away. *Focus on the job.*

"Everyone says that in the beginning," I inform him sadly. My voice stays flat. Detached. A scalpel, not a sledgehammer. "But eventually, they all talk. The only question is how much it has to hurt first."

Many men say things like that. Few mean it. The Serbian boy knows that I do, because when he looks into my eyes as I speak, he flinches.

But that's just because he wasn't raised like I was. I don't flinch. I haven't flinched since the night my father held my fingers over the stove burner for tracking mud on his Persian rug. *"Pain is a language,"* he'd said, flames licking my skin. *"Learn it."*

This kid in front of me has no idea just how fluent I am. He doesn't know how deep the old scars go or how thick the callus is that's grown over them.

It's not his fault. But ignorance won't save him.

"Let's try questions. What's on the data chip?" I ask.

He whimpers but shakes his head, snot bubbling over split lips.

I sigh.

I stand.

I swing.

The crowbar cracks his kneecap—a wet *snap* of bone and tendon. His scream carves the room.

Ariel's face flickers in the aftermath—*green eyes blown wide, lips bitten raw.* I wrench my attention back to the present and grind my boot into the kid's shattered knee. He howls.

"Second opportunity. I cannot promise a third."

"F-fu-fuck you!"

Another swing. Ribs cave like rotten timber.

Her gasp against my mouth. The hitch in her breath when I slid inside her.

I drop the crowbar. It clatters, loud as a gunshot.

Feliks raises an eyebrow but says nothing.

The spy wheezes, pink foam on his chin. Lung puncture. He'll drown in his own blood soon.

I crouch to eye level. "Last chance to die useful."

In response, he spits. A weak arc of blood and saliva grazes my cheek.

I exhale and wipe it off. "Poor choice."

My knife finds his throat before he blinks. Steel parts flesh—a hot, red smile. He gurgles. Twitches. Stills.

And just like that, another little bird dies.

In the corner, I hear the rasp of gears and the burble of flame as Feliks finally lights his cigarette. "Messy," he comments.

"Efficient," I correct.

But my hands stutter as I clean the blade. *Her fingers, trembling as I bandaged her cut. The way she laughed—reckless, bright, a lit match in a oil well.*

I sheathe the knife, and with it, I put away those distractions.

Blood cools sticky between my fingers as I light a cigarette of my own off Feliks's flame. At our feet, the corpse leaks onto linoleum.

For a moment, I'm twelve again—watching my father gut a traitor in our kitchen. Mother scrubbed crimson from grout for days.

"Folks at the gala are whining," Feliks informs me, smoke curling around his jagged face. "They're asking when you'll make your rounds."

They. The vultures. The ones who'll clap like seals when I complete my deal with the Greeks tonight. They won't quite understand what it means, what will change, but they'll still applaud and cheer like the good little puppets they are.

I drag the smoke into my lungs until they burn. "Tell them to hold their standing ovation until after I sign my life away."

He snorts. "Don't sound too eager, *brattan*." He taps the ash off his cigarette. "Heard your bride-to-be's got fangs."

"Don't they all." The ember between my fingers pulses like a dying star. "The first Makris girl did, too. Look how it served her."

Something flickers behind his milky eye. "Leander is running out of spares."

My pulse hiccups. *Green eyes. Nips at her lower lip when she's seething. Orgasms like a wildfire catching. And when she moans, it's—*

The cigarette snaps between my fingers. I grimace, then drop it and crush it beneath my heel. "I don't keep track of their litter. As far as I'm concerned, one is as good as the next."

I start rolling my sleeves back down, smoothing my hair back in place. I walk a fine line between the shadow and the sunlight, and the civilians at the gala can only handle so much darkness before they shrink away in fear. Best to keep things buttoned-up.

Even when I'm reassembled, though, and Feliks has helped me back into my suit jacket, I feel filthy.

I need a shower. A scalding one. To strip this stink of fear sweat and cheap cologne.

"Leander's probably throwing a fit," I remark.

"Oh, let the old bastard get his panties in a twist. He's just a diva; always wants to be wined and dined and 69'd." Feliks barks a laugh. "The Greeks do love their pretty lies. Flowers. Champagne. A virgin bride."

"Put a bow on my head then," I mutter. "Though I'm no fucking virgin."

The farthest thing from it. But tonight felt different. Tonight, fucking into her, feeling her clench and pulse around me, took a thing from me that I've never given to anyone before.

"Sasha…"

Feliks catches my arm as I turn. For a moment, we're not *pakhan* and *soldat*. We're just two feral boys who clawed their way out of hell.

"Last chance to run, brother," he tells me. "There's no going back after this."

Once again, she flickers behind my eyelids. *Biting back moans. Clutching my shoulders. Wracking me. Ruining me.*

But sentiment is a *ssyklo's* indulgence.

I shake him off. "You know as well as I do we were never going back."

Fee sighs at the truth of it. Then he jerks his chin toward the cooling body sagging in its zip-ties. "Burn it all down?"

I glance around. The place is worthless—just another lifeless husk in a city full of them. "No. Dump the body, scrub the kitchen, but leave the building as it was."

He nods, grimly satisfied. That's a funny quirk of this best friend of mine: he'll gut strangers like landed fish, but he's strangely tender with how he handles the bodies. Maybe he's trying to pay some kind of atonement. Maybe he's just a neat freak. I don't ask and he hasn't volunteered the information.

Either way, I turn my back on him and step out into the night once again.

Klaus conveys me back to the gala, the second trip as silent as the first, and when I emerge from the car, it's like I never left.

As I step out, I leave behind Sasha Ozerov, *pakhan* of the Ozerov Bratva, man who breaks shins with crowbars and rinses blood from beneath his fingernails.

Here, I'm a cold, chiseled bastard in a Brioni suit and a bloodless tie. Here, I am a titan. Here, I am—

"Mr. Ozerov!" greets a spineless Greek crony whose name I forget. He's wearing a headset and clutching a clipboard. "Mr. Makris has been waiting for you. He urgently requests your presence."

"I bet he does," I mutter. "Lead the way."

In front of us, the Met glows like a poisoned jewel. Silk and diamonds and rotting hearts. The flash of paparazzi bulbs taking my picture casts it all in an eerie, fluorescent glow.

The clock strikes midnight right as I re-enter the ballroom. As promised, Leander Makris is waiting by the ice sculpture with a girl in white.

His daughter. My noose.

Her back is to me. Chestnut curls bound hastily into braids. Slender neck. Smells like peaches.

Then she turns.

5

ARIEL

THIRTY MINUTES EARLIER

The door clicks shut.

My knees hit the bathroom tile before I even realize I'm falling. But even when I land, it's with a pathetic "Oh." Just that sad sound, *Oh,* like a limp balloon letting go of its last breath of air.

The hem of my stolen dress pools around me like white melted wax. I stare at my reflection in the stall door's black lacquered steel—green eyes dilated wide, lipstick smeared into a clownish grin, that one braid still stubbornly determined to unravel all the way.

It's almost kinda artsy. Like, *disheveled, but make it fashion.* Someone alert *Vogue.*

The incense diffuser on the countertop coughs to life and starts oozing lavender smoke everywhere. Part of me wants to go unplug it, because with every wisp it releases, the smell of him goes away.

Less cedar.

Less mint.

Less dark, oiled machinery.

I can still taste him, though, hot and tingling on my tongue. And I can still feel him, both the ache and the stickiness he left behind in me.

My thighs throb. My hand throbs. My head throbs as it keeps replaying, again and again and in 4K Ultra HD, the moment of him grazing my earlobe with his teeth as he drove into me, complete with the Dolby Surround Sound of my own mortifying whimpers.

"You just had hate-sex with a man who probably uses human skulls as shot glasses," I tell the girl in the steel. "Congratulations. Your therapist's yacht fund thanks you."

I wince and tear my gaze away. Self-loathing is a bottomless pit and, in theory, I still have a job to do tonight, so I can't waste time wallowing.

I fish my phone out of my clutch. Three missed calls and a text from Gina: ***U alive????***

I try to type out a reply, but the letters on the keyboard start to swim and blur before my eyes.

This isn't me. The real Ariel Ward doesn't have panic attacks in Met bathrooms. The real Ariel Ward files FOIA requests at 2 A.M. and drinks cold brew strong enough to strip paint.

But the real Ariel Ward also hasn't seen her father in person since the night she climbed out her bedroom window with a backpack full of protein bars and a switchblade she'd stolen from his study.

Fifteen years, I think, pressing my forehead to the cool tile on the wall. *Fifteen years, and he's twenty feet away, hobnobbing with congressmen in the same building where I just let a Russian mobster's tongue—*

My stomach lurches. I run to the toilet and try to vomit, but nothing comes up.

When I finally stumble back to the sink, my reflection mocks me: Lois Lane cosplaying a *Real Housewife* after a bender. I splash water on my face, but the mascara streaks just smear into Rorschach blots. *What do you see here, Doctor? A woman who just came for a stranger on a bathroom sink? Hm, I think you might be right.*

The door whines open.

"Occupied!" I cry out, voice cracking.

"Not for long."

Leander Makris fills the doorway like a storm rolling over Brighton Beach. Black tuxedo, snowdrift beard, eyes the same poison-green as mine. As *hers*.

The air thickens with his cologne (Creed Aventus, four hundred and fifty dollars a bottle, the signature scent of every childhood car ride to "business meetings" that left blood on his cufflinks).

"Hello, *neraïdoula mou.*"

My little fairy. I used to think it was cute. When I got older, I started to wonder if he was mocking Mama, mocking me. A little fairy, not fit for this world, not brave enough or big enough to survive in it without his help.

Jasmine used to call me the same thing. But when she said it, it was never cruel or condescending. She'd whisper it to me in the darkness of our shared bedroom when the shouting downstairs got too loud. *Don't cry, neraïdoula mou. I'll sneak you Oreos once he passes out.*

"Hi, Baba."

His gaze flicks to my bandaged hand. "Still accident-prone, I see."

"A good father might ask if I'm okay."

He steps inside, rolling a cigar between his fingers—Cuban, unlit, another ever-present prop in the Leander Makris Production of *Gentleman Gangster*. In the brief instant before the door closes, I hear a snatch of sound from the ballroom. The string quartet is butchering Dvořák's American Quartet, which I only recognize because Mom used to play it on vinyl while she cleaned—back when we still had a mom, and vinyl, and things worth cleaning.

Then it closes, and quiet takes over again.

"Then tell me," he rumbles. "Are you okay, Ariana?"

"It's Ariel now. You know that."

He sighs and drums his fingers on the sink. When he looks down, his eyes narrow and I wonder for a moment if he can see the imprint of my ass on the marble. I'm so mortified by all of my terrible decisions tonight that I can't even find it in me to care if he does.

Then he sighs and looks at me. "I'd be a father to you if you'd let me, you know. You think I like being apart from my children? You think I want to see you hurt? You think I enjoy seeing you bleed?"

He reaches for me.

I flinch.

His hand freezes mid-air. Thick fingers, gold pinky ring. God, the things I've seen that hand do to people who displease him…

Then he withdraws it and I can breathe again.

"You look…" His voice softens, almost imperceptibly. "… tired."

"And you've lost hair," I fire back. "Guess the universe has a way of balancing itself out."

He chuckles and passes a palm over his thinning scalp. A beat passes. Two. A faucet drips. "You're here to report on the event, I assume?"

I nod, not trusting myself with words just yet.

"Would you like a quote? I can—"

"Got everything I need, thanks."

That's a lie, but I'll be damned if I let him claim some leverage over me that cheaply and easily.

Leander's face screws up in a pained grimace. "This doesn't have to be so hard, Aria—Ariel." He keeps rolling the cigar back and forth in his grasp. Back and forth, back and forth. "I *want* to be a part of your life. Let me help you."

I wobble to my feet, using the wall like a crutch, and glare at him. "After fifteen years under your roof, I got all the 'help' I needed. So did Jas. So did Mom. So I think I'm good in that regard, too."

"Very well." He sighs, the sound weary in a way I don't remember. "You'll stay for the midnight toast, at least."

"I have a deadline."

"You have a life." His eyes narrow. "One I've allowed you to play at long enough."

Allowed. As if my shitty studio apartment and my coffee-stained notebooks and the *Gazette* job I fought tooth and nail for are just unremarkable toys he's let me borrow.

"You don't 'allow' me anything." My voice shakes. "I walked away. I built—"

"A pseudonym. A house of cards. All for a paycheck that wouldn't even cover my dry cleaning." He steps closer, cigar tapping against his palm. "Tell me, *Ariel Ward*—do they know everything at your precious paper? Does your editor sip his latte wondering why a mousy little nobody knows so much about the docks? The warehouses? The shipping manifests?"

"I'm a reporter," I croak.

"You're a ghost." His laugh is bitter. "Chasing your sister's shadow."

The bathroom walls press closer. I see her everywhere now—in the auburn hair of strangers, in the smell of jasmine rice at the bodega, in the hollows of Leander's cheeks that deepen whenever someone mentions "daughters" in the plural.

"Don't." My throat burns. "Don't talk about her."

"You give me no choice, *neraïdoula mou!*" he roars suddenly, rearing up from his old man's stoop into the tall, grizzled bear who terrorized my adolescence. "Not in that. And not in what is coming next."

The first icy trickle of dread starts winding through my stomach. It's from something in his eyes, in the rasp of his voice, in the way that posture crumbles back down and he suddenly looks older than he's ever looked before.

Not in what's coming next.

I shouldn't ask. I won't ask. I can't ask. Asking the question implies wanting the answer, and ninety-nine-point-nine percent of me knows that that answer that Leander will give me is nothing I want to hear.

Fuck *one door closing and another opening.* This would be one cell door opening, throwing me inside, and shutting that same door again.

I shouldn't ask. I won't ask. I can't—

"What's coming next, Baba?"

He tucks the cigar into his breast pocket and scrubs both flat, wide, meaty palms over his face. Knuckles at his eyes like he's so tired he can barely stand. Then he looks at me again. "I will say it one more time, not because I think you'll believe me, but because—"

"—what's coming next, Baba?—"

"—but because I've always had your best interests at heart, whether you or your mother or your sister believed that or not—"

"—what's coming next, Baba?—"

"—and everything I do, everything I've done, it's always been for you, for my girls, my loves—"

"Tell me what the fuck is happening!" I scream.

He stops. His eyes are rimmed in red. "I've arranged for you to be married."

For a moment, all I hear is the drip of the faucet, the distant murmur of the gala's string quartet. They've left Dvořák behind and I don't recognize whatever they're playing now.

But I recognize this scene. A version of it, at least—because I watched Leander do this to Jasmine fifteen years ago.

"Married," I whisper, touching my swollen lip like that'll help make sense of the word. "You've arranged for me to be... married."

He steps closer, his shadow swallowing mine. "A union with the Ozerov Bratva. A merger of interests. Stability for both our families."

"What part of this is 'stable' for me?" I ask aloud, though I know he doesn't know the answer and couldn't care less about it.

"You'll want for nothing. You'll be wealthier than that gossip rag could ever make you, and free of that roach-infested apartment you call home. Most of all, you'll be *safe.* Safe from—"

"Go to hell." I back into the sink, the marble edge biting into my ass. Fifteen minutes ago, a man's hands held me there, hot and huge, strong and safe. Now, all I feel is cold, lifeless stone. "Go to fucking hell."

"In so many ways, I'm already there, *neraïdoula mou.*" He smiles, but it's a cracked thing. "You think I want this? You think I enjoy groveling to that Russian *malákas*?"

"Then don't! Call it off!"

"And lose the docks? The warehouses? The respect?" He barks a laugh even as he shakes his head sadly. "Your sister spat the same naïveté. Look where it got her."

"I told you not to talk about her."

"Why?" He crowds me, the cigar in his pocket crinkling.

"Because you'd rather pretend she's sipping mai tais in Miami? That she isn't rotting cold in some unmarked—?"

My palm cracks across his cheek before I realize I've moved. The sound echoes.

A slap thirty-three years in the making.

Baba doesn't flinch, though my handprint is red and stark on his bearded cheek. "Feel better?"

I'm quivering with rage. "Go. To. Hell."

"In due time, my daughter." He grips my wrist, pressing hard against the bandage Sasha wrapped. Blood blooms through the gauze as he squeezes. "But first, you'll walk out that door. You'll smile. You'll take Sasha Ozerov's hand. And you'll thank him for the honor."

I wrench free. "Or what? You'll kill me?"

"Kill you?" He tuts. "No, *koukla*. You are my daughter. But that little friend of yours—Gina, is it? The one who lent you this dress?" His smile widens as I freeze. "How long do you think she'd last in Hunts Point?"

That dread is back worse than ever, clutching my innards in its cold fingers and squeezing, squeezing. "You… you wouldn't."

Leander rises up as tall as he can. "There are no limits to what I would do to keep my family safe."

The walls close in. My reflection fractures in the steel stall doors—a dozen trapped Ariels, wide-eyed and trembling. *Fight*, they scream. *Fight!*

But every single one of them knows I lost this war a long time ago.

"I'll give you a moment to gather your thoughts," my father says. "Meet me by the ice sculpture when you are ready to proceed. And Ariana… don't try to run. I'd hate to have to chase you. This is hard enough on me already."

He leaves, the door sighing shut behind him.

In the mirror, the girl in the stolen dress stares back. Green eyes. Loose braid. A cut she can't stop reopening.

"Okay," she whispers.

"Okay," I echo.

Then I walk out to meet my cage.

Baba is standing by the ice sculpture in the middle of the ballroom when I emerge. It's a swan, wings spread wide, though they've started to look like they're drooping as they melt.

My dress and hair are mostly back in order. Not much I can do about my missing earring, but that's low on my list of concerns right now.

It's midnight. The clock begins to strike.

First toll: twelve sharp peals. A sound like a death knell. A sound like shattering cages.

Second toll: I feel him before I see him. A prickle across my skin. My blood remembers his hands better than my brain does.

Third toll: I turn.

Fourth: He's watching me. The man from the bathroom. Sasha Ozerov. Suit pristine, hair perfect, mouth set in that same brutal slash. But the tendons in his neck stand out like tension cables. His pupils swallow the Arctic blue of his eyes whole.

Fifth: My knees unlock. My stolen Valentino heels don't wobble. Small miracles.

Sixth: My father steps between us, grinning like this is *his* wedding day. "Sasha, meet my daughter, Ariel. Your fiancée."

Seventh: The ice sculpture weeps. I don't. Can't. Won't.

Eighth: Sasha's eyes darken to black.

Ninth: I want to laugh. Or scream. Or maybe book a one-way ticket to whatever dimension Lois Lane retired to after *Smallville* got canceled.

Tenth: Instead, I arch a brow. "We really need to stop meeting like this. People will talk."

Eleventh: His thumb brushes my bandaged palm—just a flicker, just enough to make my pulse hammer. "Our story's just getting started, *ptichka*."

Twelfth: The clock falls silent. The room holds its breath. And I realize, with the clarity of a bullet between the eyes, that happy endings are bullshit.

Some princesses get poisoned apples. Some get glass coffins.

Me? I get six feet of Russian nightmare wearing Brioni and a wedding ring.

"Well?" My smile could flay skin. "Ready to ruin each other's lives?"

He doesn't blink. "I was born ready."

6

ARIEL

The human heart is a traitorous little organ. It doesn't care about logic, or self-preservation, or the meticulously constructed walls you've wasted decades building up. It doesn't care that you've spent your whole life running from the very thing now standing in front of you, smirking like the devil who just won the last soul at the auction.

No—the heart does what it wants. It races when it should retreat. It softens when it should harden. It *aches* when it should burn with rage.

I'd know. Mine is currently trying to claw its way out of my ribcage like a caged animal.

Breathe, I tell myself, pressing a hand to my sternum as if I could physically shove the feeling back down. *Breathe, or you'll pass out in front of the man who literally ordered a hit over voicemail two hours ago. Breathe, or he'll see you break.*

But breathing requires oxygen, and the air in the Met's grand hall feels thick as syrup. Too much perfume, too many floral arrangements. My stolen DVF dress itches where sweat trickles down my spine. One stubborn curl clings to my cheek like a question mark. And my hand—the one he bandaged—throbs in time with the frantic rhythm of my pulse.

This isn't happening. This isn't happening.

But it is.

Sasha Ozerov—*the* Sasha Ozerov, heir to the Russian Bratva's throne, the man whose hands were literally inside of me less than an hour ago—stands before me, his ice-chip eyes widening a fraction as they lock onto mine.

For a second, the world narrows to the hitch in his breath, the subtle flex of his jaw, the way his knuckles whiten around the champagne flute he's holding. It's the first crack I've seen in his armor.

It's gone as quickly as it came.

Leander's voice booms beside me. "Sasha, meet my daughter, Ariel. Your fiancée."

Fiancée. It's just a word, theoretically speaking. In reality, it's a guillotine blade hurtling toward my throat.

Run, screams every survival instinct I've honed since childhood. But my feet are rooted to the marble floor, my lungs refusing to cooperate. The room wobbles. Memories crash over me in waves.

Twelve years old, hiding in a closet while Baba's enemies ransacked our apartment, their laughter sharp as gunfire.

Seventeen, stuffing my birth certificate into a backpack, stealing cash from his safe, slipping out the fire escape while he roared my name downstairs.

Twenty-two, scrubbing fake IDs until "Ariana Makris" was buried under layers of ink, becoming Ariel Ward—a name that didn't taste like blood on my tongue.

And now, this. A cosmic punchline. The universe laughing as it dumps me back into the lion's den, this time with a diamond collar around my neck.

Sasha's gaze flicks to Leander, then back to me. There's a flicker of something dangerous in his eyes—recognition, yes, but something hotter, darker. A challenge. A promise.

"A pleasure," he says, his voice that same rough heat that ignited something low in my stomach earlier. He extends a hand, the same one that had pinned me to the sink. I stare at it like it's a live wire.

Touch him, and you're lost.

But Leander is watching, his smile serrated.

So I take the devil's hand.

The contact sends a jolt through me, electric and unforgiving. His grip tightens. A silent question. A taunt.

"Likewise," I lie, pulling away too quickly.

Leander claps his hands, the sound like a judge's gavel. "Wonderful! Now, if you'll excuse me, I have philanthropic duties to attend to." He lingers on the words, the inside joke of a man who knows damn well that all of this is a puppet show for people too stupid to know better. "You two get acquainted."

He melts into the crowd, leaving me alone with the human embodiment of a double-edged sword.

Sasha steps closer, his cologne washing over me. "So," he murmurs, voice low enough to skirt the hum of the room. "Ariel Ward."

The way he says it—like he's peeling back a layer of my skin—makes me shiver. "Surprise."

His mouth twitches. "You could've mentioned you were the Makris spare."

"And ruin the mystery?" I force a smirk, though it feels brittle. "Where's the fun in that?"

He studies me, those blue eyes missing nothing: not the tremor in my hands, not the way my pulse flutters at my throat. "You're shaking."

"Adrenaline crash." I shrug, aiming for nonchalance. "Happens after you narrowly avoid death-by-murderous-stranger in a bathroom stall."

"Ah." He swirls his champagne. The liquid catches the light like liquid gold. "And here I thought it was my charm."

"Your 'charm' almost got me fired."

"But not killed."

"Not yet."

He hums, a sound that vibrates in my bones. "You're still standing, *ptichka*. That's more than most people manage."

The nickname—*little bird*—sinks its claws into me. I want to hate it. I want to hate *him*. So why can't I?

This isn't how it was supposed to go. Mama never told me this part of the fairy tale.

I wasn't supposed to *want* the monster.

"Why are you doing this?" I ask suddenly. "The Bratva doesn't need alliances. You could've taken the Greeks out years ago."

Something flashes in his eyes—a shadow, there and gone. "Careful, reporter. Curiosity killed the cat."

"And satisfaction brought it back." I tilt my chin up, defiant. "Don't avoid the question. Why marry me? Why not just put a bullet in my father's skull and take what you want?"

For a moment, I think he won't answer. Then he leans in, his breath grazing my ear. "Because bullets make martyrs, *ptichka*. But marriages? Those make empires."

The words slither down my spine. Before I can respond, he straightens, his mask of icy control back in place. "Dance with me."

It's not a request.

The orchestra swells as he tows me onto the floor, his hand settling at the small of my back like we've done this a million times before. We move in sync, this fucked-up parody of happily-ever-after-in-the-making. It's treacherously easy to let him lead me around.

"You're afraid," he observes, spinning me out before reeling me back in.

"Of you?" I laugh, bitter. "Please."

"Of what you'll become." His grip tightens. "Of how much you want to burn it all down."

There's not much in this world that stings more than the unvarnished truth—but the truth as told by Sasha Ozerov might be one of those things. Because he's right—I'm not just afraid of him, or Leander, or the shackles of this arrangement.

I'm afraid of the part of me that's still Ariana Makris, the girl who learned to lie before she learned to ride a bike. The part that knows how to survive in the dark.

"You don't know me," I whisper.

"Oh, I know enough. I know you taste like peaches and bad decisions. I know how it sounds when you come undone. And I know—" He dips me suddenly, his lips brushing my jaw. "—you'd rather die than let either of us win."

The music crescendos. Around us, the crowd applauds the band, oblivious to the war waging in the center of the dance floor.

When he pulls me upright, I'm trembling for real now. "What do you want from me?"

"Everything." His finger traces the line of my hip, possessive. "Starting with the truth you're hiding from yourself."

"Which is?"

"That when you said 'Or else what?' in that bathroom…" His grip tightens, sending electricity through my veins. "You weren't afraid I'd kill you."

The crowd melts away. There's only his breath on my collarbone, his lips grazing the hammering pulse at my throat.

"You were afraid I'd ruin you instead."

7

ARIEL

I used to have this recurring nightmare as a kid. In it, I'm standing at the edge of the roof of our brownstone in Brighton Beach, toes curled over the lip of the building. Ahead of me lies only empty space and a four-story drop to the concrete below. Behind me, something dark and hungry is slinking closer.

Jump or be devoured. Those are my options.

Story of my life, really. But standing here in this glistening ballroom with Sasha's words still burning in my ears, I finally understand what those nightmares were trying to tell me: sometimes, the monster behind you and the abyss in front of you are the exact same thing.

I ought to be scared—scratch that, fucking terrified—and to be sure, part of me is. I can feel that fear coiled up and quivering in my belly, an old, familiar terror that's never quite gone away.

But another part of me is *angry.*

I didn't spend twenty years scrubbing "Makris" off my skin like a stubborn wine stain just to let my father swap me for two cows and a fucking goat.

But therein lies the problem with men like Leander—they don't ask. They don't negotiate. They don't even have the decency to send a *"Hey, thinking of pimping you out to a Russian warlord. Thoughts?"* text. No, they just drop the bomb, light the fuse, and walk away whistling like they've done you a favor.

Case in point: the smug son of a bitch is already halfway across the ballroom, schmoozing with a senator whose hair plugs I could see from outer space. Meanwhile, I'm left standing here with his "gift"—a six-foot-two slab of Bratva monster who looks like he's two seconds away from either kissing me or slitting my throat.

Maybe both.

You weren't afraid I'd kill you. You were afraid I'd ruin you instead.

I snort, mostly to myself, and hustle off the dance floor. "This isn't happening."

Sasha arches a brow. "It quite literally is."

"No, see, 'literally' implies reality. And this?" I gesture wildly between us, from my borrowed dress to his oxblood leather shoes. "This is a network TV plotline. It's bad fan fiction. The kind where the writers ran out of ideas and started huffing glue."

"Reality is not quite as buttoned-up as your *telenovelas,*" he says with a dark chuckle. He crowds me close against a marble pillar as the other dancers go swirling past us, casting curious glances in our direction.

I plant a palm on his chest. "Back. Up. Unless you want my knee to make intimate friends with your groin."

His lips twitch. "Promises, promises."

"I'm serious."

"So am I." He catches my wrist, thumb skating over my racing pulse. "But by all means, scream. Cause a scene. Let your dear old dad explain to his esteemed guests why his long-lost daughter is assaulting his business partner in the middle of—"

"Shut up."

"I dare you to try and make me."

God, I want to. I want to claw that infuriating smirk off his face. I want to scream until the chandeliers shatter. But mostly, I want to run—far away from this gaudy, gilded nightmare. Back to my shitty Bushwick apartment with its IKEA furniture and persistent mold problem. Back to a life where my biggest worry was whether Sportswriter Steve would notice I swapped his oat milk for half-and-half.

Instead, I do what I've always done best: bluff.

"This marriage isn't happening," I say, chin lifted. "I don't care what deal you and Leander made. I'm not a bargaining chip."

Sasha tilts his head, studying me like a puzzle he's decided to solve out of boredom. "You think this is about you?"

"I think your ego's too big to share a room with my father's, so yes, this is absolutely about—"

"The only outsized ego here is yours, if you think that I give a single fuck about you or what you want," he snarls.

My mouth drops.

He's not done.

"This is not about you. This is not about your father. This is about power," he interrupts, voice sharpening, tightening "Control. A union that yokes together our organizations and ensures neither side gets... ideas." His grip tightens. "You? You're just collateral."

Collateral. I've seen what that looks like—and it looks like Jasmine. In my mind's eye, I see my sister's face the day she left home. That's been happening a lot tonight. Being back around these people makes it harder to find even a few minutes at a time where I don't think about her.

I ran to avoid exactly this, exactly what happened to her. Apparently, I didn't run far enough. I reached the roof edge, the abyss in front of me, and I hesitated.

This is what I get.

"Gee," I whisper hoarsely. "And here I thought you liked me for my personality."

"I don't know a thing about your personality," he retorts flatly. "I liked your mouth... When it wasn't spewing nonsense."

"And people say romance is dead."

"It's not just dead," he agrees. "It's six fucking feet under."

Before I can retort, a familiar voice cuts through the tension. "Ari! There you are!"

Uncle Kosti, my father's brother, pops up at my side, his salt-and-pepper beard crinkling with a smile. He's the human equivalent of a cashmere sweater—soft, worn-in, and tragically out of place in this den of wolves. If there's anyone I've missed since I ran away, it's Uncle Kosti.

Sasha's gaze flicks to him. "We're busy."

"And I'm her favorite uncle." Kosti loops an arm around my shoulders, steering me away. "I'm only borrowing her for a dance. *Yasou*, Mr. Ozerov."

For a heartbeat, I think Sasha might snap. His jaw clenches, eyes glacial. But then he dips his chin—a barely-there nod—and turns on his heel, melting into the crowd.

My father and fiancé are both busy now. I could run.

But they'd find me. The only reason Baba didn't do it sooner is because he didn't need me yet. Now that I have a purpose, I won't be getting away anytime soon.

"You okay, *koukla*?" Kosti murmurs as we shuffle awkwardly to a Viennese waltz.

"Peachy. Just found out I'm engaged to a human weaponized suit. How's the canapé selection?"

He sighs, the sound heavy with decades of Makris family baggage. There's no way he didn't know the plans for my future—not that he could've warned me, either way. He's just as trapped as I am. "Your father means well."

"He doesn't care about me. He wants to *control* me."

"Same thing, in his world." Kosti spins me gently, his hands calloused but kind. "He's missed you, you know. Talks about you like you're still six—his little girl, sneaking cookies before dinner."

A lump rises in my throat. Six-year-old me hadn't yet learned to check her shoes for tracking devices. Hadn't started sleeping with a knife under her pillow. Hadn't watched her mother walk out the door and known, deep down, she'd never come back.

"I'm not his little girl," I say roughly.

"No." Kosti's smile is sad. "You're a storm wearing his daughter's face. And storms? They don't bend. They break." He squeezes my hand. "So break it, *koukla*. Break it all."

Two hours and four martinis later, I'm slumped at a dive bar three blocks from the Met, picking at the label of a Brooklyn Lager while Gina side-eyes me like I've announced plans to join a cult. I'm passing through stages of grief that I didn't even know existed. All the standard stuff —denial, anger, bargaining—is long gone. I've moved onto cackling like a deranged hyena and drinking until the pain goes away.

"Let me get this straight," she says, waving her cosmo. "You hooked up with Jason Bourne's hotter cousin, then found out he's your mobster daddy's new BFF, and now, you're supposed to marry him?"

"In my defense," I say, "the hookup happened before the whole 'surprise, you're getting hitched' reveal."

How's that for a PSA against random hookups?

"Uh-huh. And the part where you didn't tell me you're, like, Greek mafia royalty?"

I wince. "In my defense again, I don't lead with that. It's not exactly LinkedIn material."

Gina rolls her eyes. "Maybe you should reconsider. I've seen your LinkedIn. The only thing on there is that sad internship at *Cat Fancy Monthly*."

"They were ahead of their time."

"They paid you in Friskies coupons! And you don't even have a cat!" She stabs her straw at me. "So what's the play here, Ari? You're really gonna let your dad marry you off to some Russian Terminator?"

"Fuck no." The words come out sharp, final. "I'd rather gargle broken glass."

"Then what's next? A scathing exposé? *'My One-Night Stand Is My Mobster Fiancé: A Love Story'* by Ariel Ward?"

"No. I'm going to do what my uncle said: burn it all down." I throw back the dregs of my beer. "Disappear. Fake my death. Join a convent in Saskatchewan. Whatever it takes."

Gina leans back, assessing me. "Saskatchewan's a vibe, but have you considered a girl's best friend instead?"

"Diamonds?"

"Arson," she says flatly.

"Gee!"

She rests a hand on my forearm. "Hear me out. We torch Leander's favorite yacht, blame it on Sasha, and then hop a flight to Bali. You can bang sexy surf instructors, I'll seduce Australian heiresses. It'll be iconic."

I smile sadly at her. "You'd really set a yacht on fire for me?"

"Babe, I'd steal a nuclear submarine for you." She grins back. "But only if you promise to name your firstborn in my honor."

"Deal." I clink my beer against her glass. "But first, I need leverage. Something to make both these psychos back off."

"Easy." She flags the bartender for another round. "Find Sasha's kryptonite. Does he have a secret family? A crippling fear of clowns? An OnlyFans?"

"He's a Bratva *pakhan,* Gina. His OnlyFans is probably just unboxing videos of human teeth."

"Hot." She pauses. "Wait, is that a thing?"

The bartender slides over two tequila shots. Gina downs hers in one gulp, licks the salt off her wrist, and smirks. "Relax, Ariel. We'll figure it out. You've survived worse than a six-pack with a murder kink."

I knock back my shot, the burn grounding me. "I'm not marrying him. Not ever."

"Atta girl." She slings an arm around me, her perfume—something aggressively floral she definitely shoplifted—filling my lungs. "Now, let's get shitfaced and key your dad's car."

"His car's bulletproof."

"Won't stop me from trying."

As we stumble into the neon-soaked night, I cling to the promise like a lifeline. *I'm not marrying him.*

But somewhere, in the darkest corner of my mind, Sasha's voice whispers back.

We'll see about that, ptichka.

8

SASHA

I watch Ariel vanish through the exit, her dress swishing like a battle flag as she goes. Every step she takes is defiance. Every sway of her hips is a middle finger to everything her father and I have planned for her.

She isn't going to make things simple.

Leander materializes beside me. "She'll need time," he says, squinting at the doors she'd stormed through.

"She'll need a leash."

"I tried that," he says with a braying laugh. "Then I barely saw the girl for almost two decades. She's not an easily broken filly, Sasha. Too much of her mother in her DNA for that."

"No, not a filly. She's feral. A stray. But even strays learn to heel."

Leander's jaw tightens, the vein at his temple throbbing. "Careful, boy. You're not dealing with some dockside whore. This is my blood."

I almost laugh. He wants to play Doting Daddy *after* offering me his daughter's unwilling hand in marriage? Hell of a time to pick up the parental slack.

"'Your blood'?" I step closer. "Your blood spent fifteen years running from you. You think she'll kneel now just because you've dangled a diamond ring in front of her?"

For a flicker, his mask slips. Raw, rotting pride bleeds through, and I wonder for a minute if the Leander Makris of old, the one they used to tell stories about, is back.

Then he sighs and it vanishes, and instead of the stony mask of a mob boss, I see the lined, wearied face of a father. "No," he concedes, "I know better than that. She won't kneel for a ring, for a man, for a marriage. Not even for her own father." His laugh is soaked through with misery. But when his eyes meet mine, they're calmer. Resigned. "But there are better ways to earn compliance."

"None so efficient as commanding it."

In the back of my head, I see the Serbian boy wailing as his bones shattered. After all, what's easier than taking what you need? What's easier than demanding it be given to you? If my father taught me anything, it's that the shortest distance between two points is a straight line drenched in blood.

But Leander just shakes his head. "There are better ways, Sasha. Take it from an old man who knows, who's tried, who's been in your shoes."

I roll my eyes. "What 'better ways'?"

"Time, for one. Patience, for another." He looks at me again, head cocked to the side, a curious kind of compassion on his face that has no place in a frank business discussion between two precarious allies. "And best of all, persuasion. Don't wrestle her. *Woo* her."

The laugh rips its way out of me. I never had a chance to stop it. "*Woo* her? You've lost your fucking mind, old man. Did catering to her feelings do a damn thing for you? Tell me: how many floral arrangements and boxes of *Sorry You Have A Fucking Beast For A Father* chocolates did you send to her door over the last fifteen years, hm? How many times did you try to mend fences? How did that work out?"

Leander rubs a hand over his face, looking suddenly exhausted. Even the bowtie of his tuxedo seems to be drooping. "Mock it all you want; heaven knows I deserve the scorn. And heaven knows I've heard enough of it from Ariana, when she deigns to talk to me. But…" He clasps my shoulder in a way that's so fatherly that I almost break his fingers just for the sheer audacity of it. "I can force her into this as well as you can, but we both know the mess that could be. There are… ten days until the New Year. Use them. Convince her this marriage isn't a cage. Convince her that it's… freedom. Power. A throne of her own."

"And if she still says no?"

"It won't come to that, will it? You've charmed harder targets."

I study him—the slight tremor in his hand as he smooths his lapels, the way his eyes linger on the exit Ariel fled through. The man is a paradox: a kingpin with a father's fraying nerves.

Pathetic.

Fascinating.

"Why the sudden mercy?" I ask. "The Leander I know would've sold her to the highest bidder by sunrise."

His throat bobs. "The Leander you knew buried a daughter."

Jasmine.

The name hangs unspoken between us. I keep my face stone, but memory flickers—Jasmine's hands shaking as she clutched her forged passport, her voice raw from begging. *Don't let him find me.*

Leander stares at his reflection in the melting ice swan, his voice hollow. "I won't lose another girl to pride. Not again."

There it is. The weakness. The rot beneath the varnish.

"Fine," I sigh. "Ten days. She'll be begging for the altar after one."

He doesn't smile. "See that she does. But *gently*, Sasha. She's not one of your Bratva rats. She's…" He hesitates.

"Yours?" I finish. "No, Leander. She stopped being yours the day she learned to spell *run*."

His knuckles whiten around the stem of his glass. For a second, I think he'll swing. But then he exhales, the fight draining out of him. "Just… make her want this. Make her believe it."

I turn toward the exit, my coat slicing the air behind me. "She will."

~

Ariel's scent clings to my jacket as I leave—peaches and panic. Even as the cold winter air of Manhattan rakes its talons over me, that summer smell lingers.

I shouldn't have touched her. Shouldn't have tasted her. Shouldn't have let her crawl under my skin like a fucking parasite.

But when she looked up at me in that bathroom, all fury and fear and fight, I saw *Jasmine*. Saw the girl I smuggled onto a cargo ship fifteen years ago, her delirious laughter echoing over the Brooklyn docks. *Thank you,* she'd whispered.

I didn't bother to reply.

A text lights up my phone. Feliks. ***Serbian problem handled. What next?***

I stare at the text, then at the glittering Met. ***Next***, I type, ***I play prince charming.***

Ariel wants a fairy tale? Fine.

I'll give her a goddamn epic.

9

ARIEL

The fluorescent lights in *The Gazette's* break room are doing their best impression of a medieval torture device. Honestly, hats off to them; they're really killing it.

Killing me, too.

I woke up with the hangover from hell after Gina drank me under the table last night. The blissful darkness of the drunken abyss was nice for a little while, as were the first few moments when I woke up in my own bed.

I blinked, grainy-eyed, as I stared up at the ceiling. Same old mold patches. Same old water stains. Same old popcorn ceiling that looks vaguely like Richard Gere if you squint just right.

Then I remembered.

Or else what?

What's coming next, Baba?

So break it, koukla. *Break it all.*

The weight of it all pinned me to the mattress. I was torn between screaming or sinking into denial, pretending I made it all up. I went with option three: I got up, got dressed, and went to work.

Now, I'm here, feeling like the wrong end of the Grim Reaper's GI tract, wondering if death might just be the cleanest solution to all my problems.

The coffee machine gurgles merrily. I lean in close to it and whisper, "If you give me decaf, I will end you."

"Talking to inanimate objects doesn't scream 'flourishing mental health.'" Gina sashays into the room. Unlike me, she looks infuriatingly put-together, per usual. Even now that we're in our thirties, she can drink half the bar and wake up looking like she's fresh out of a dermaplane facial.

"Very little in my life is flourishing right now, Gee."

"Do tell."

I turn to scowl at her. "I *did* tell. Last night. Do you really not remember?"

"Oh, yeah. Right. I remember." She licks PopTart frosting off her thumb. "But I also blacked out after the third shot, so just in case… tell me the whole thing again one more time?"

Before I can strangle her, our coworker Lora floats into the room like the rootless, carefree dandelion seed she is. Her polka-dot dress is inside-out, her hair defies gravity, and she's clutching a mug labeled *#1 Cat Aunt*.

I've never envied someone more.

"Good morning, ladies!" she chirps at a pitch and decibel that might very well summon every dog in the borough.

I wince and plug my ears. Lora does not notice.

"Did you see John's email?" Lora blows across her tea, sending plumes of steam toward the sagging ceiling tiles. "We're all supposed to pivot to the Mayor's new infrastructure bill. He wants six hundred words by three on community impact angles. Oh, and Ariel—he put you on the Brighton Beach team for interviews tomorrow. Yay, fieldwork!"

Gina chokes on her orange juice.

My fingers tighten around the scalding cardboard cup. The assignment should feel like a win—real reporting, finally. Instead, the words *Brighton* and *Beach* curdle in my gut. The last place I should go is anywhere near my father's domain.

Lora, meanwhile, has started humming.

It'd be nice to live in her world for a little while. Mostly because "her world" is a snow globe filled with rainbow sparkles, where everything is "yay" and "woo" and never-ending sunshine beams.

No room in a place like that for men like Sasha Ozerov.

"Yay, fieldwork," I grumble in a miserable monotone. "Can't wait."

Lora, in a shockingly perceptive move by her standards, looks over at me. "Is something the matter, buttercup?"

In response, I press my forehead to the cool laminate surface of the break room table. *Everything* is the matter.

"Ree here had a… let's call it a 'bad date,'" Gina answers for me.

"Bad date?" Lora's eyes go wide with sympathy. "Oh, no! Tell me everything. Was it one of those awful Hinge situationships? I had the worst experience last week with—"

"More like an arranged marriage situationship," Gina supplies helpfully.

I lift my head just enough to glare at her. "Thanks for that."

"Arranged marriage?!" Lora gasps, collapsing into the chair beside me. "That's so romantic! Like a fairy tale!"

And that is exactly why Lora falls in love with every man she meets. It's also why she writes the paper's dating advice column, though she's the last person on Earth anyone should take dating advice from. She's a romantic, naive enough to still have hope that things work out.

I gave that up years ago.

"Less fairy tale, more horror story. This guy is the farthest thing from Prince Charming."

"No man is," Lora sighs in a very un-Lora-like fashion. "But I thought Ethan was The One, you know?"

Gina perks up like a shark scenting blood in the water. I know that look. It's the same one she gets when someone mentions their cryptocurrency investments or healing crystals.

Pure, predatory delight.

"Tell us about Ethan," she says, leaning forward. "I need a distraction from Ariel's love life crisis."

Lora rests her chin on her hand and gazes into the distance. "He... He... H-h-he..."

Is she having a stroke? Gina mouths to me.

I'm wondering the same thing. Lora looks like she's malfunctioning. Sniffling, eyes welling up, cheeks flushing, shoulders starting to tremble…

"Oh, shit," I hiss. "She's…"

Crying.

No, not "crying"—she's straight-up ugly girl sobbing.

As per usual, Gina started this whole mess, but as per even more usual, I'm the one who feels obligated to pick up the pieces. "Lora," I venture, "are you okay?"

She sobs harder. "Yes! I'm fine! I'm— I'm just s-so happy for you—"

I find that hard to believe. Not because Lora wouldn't be happy for me—she's the single sweetest person on staff—but because these don't exactly look like happy tears.

This is sobbing-widow-at-a-funeral behavior. This is…

"Lora," I say carefully, "did Ethan break up with you?"

She blinks up at me. I can only watch in horror as her huge puppy dog eyes slowly fill to the brim with more and more tears… Then the dam bursts.

Lora hurls herself at me and starts full-on bawling. "I JUSD BISS HIM DO BUCH—"

"She turned German from trauma," Gina whispers.

I shoot Gina a withering glare and pat Lora stiffly on the back. "There, there. I'm so sorry. You deserve better."

I don't know any of that for sure. I've never even met Ethan, or Damian, or Connor, or Brett, or Alan, or whatever letter of the alphabet Lora's currently on. She is the kind of colleague we exchange gossip with, but not much else. We grab drinks after work if the stars align. And she does such a good job of keeping us up with her love life drama that we don't really have to go hunting for it.

Some unkind people—read: Gina—might call Lora a chronic oversharer. Me? I'm glad she spares me the trouble of talking about my own life.

"HE WAZ DE BEST THIG OB MY LIBE—"

I exchange a helpless look with Gina over Lora's heaving shoulders. "Fire escape?" I whisper. She gives me the thumbs up and we start to shepherd Lora that way.

The sign above the propped-open window says ***Emergency Exit***, and this definitely qualifies as an emergency. Emotionally speaking, if nothing else.

I settle Lora down on the nearest landing, and eventually, she takes enough calming breaths to speak English again. "It just happened so fast."

I frown. I was admittedly not paying very close attention when she first started talking about her "new beau," but I'm almost positive she met him less than six weeks ago. Her tear ducts have no sense of time, apparently. I've lent her my shoulder to cry on. I wish I was speaking metaphorically, but my jacket has now become the dry cleaner's problem. "I thought things were going great between you two?"

"They were! But then he started saying that he—that I—" Fresh tears well up and she dissolves again.

"It's okay, sweetheart," I say, patting her back. "We get it."

Gina frowns. "We do?"

"Yes," I snap, "we do. We all know the feeling of being dumped out of the blue. Isn't that right, Gina?"

"I mean..."

"I said, *Isn't that right, Gina?*"

Gee nods like a bobblehead on a dashboard. "For sure, yeah. Definitely been there. Happens to the best of us."

Luckily, Lora's lie detector skills aren't the sharpest. "You think I'm the best of us?"

"I wouldn't quite— Er, yeah, absolutely. Uh-huh." Gina adds a double thumbs-up for good measure.

"I gave him all these gifts," she sniffles. "Kept trying to surprise him, you know? Isn't that what loving couples do?"

I wince. "Surprises are..." *My nightmare.* "... always a good move."

"Right?" She sighs deeply. "I got him this huge ragu lasagna from Pacino's..."

I frown. "I thought you said Ethan was vegan?"

"Lasagna *is* vegan." Lora presses on. "I told him to close his eyes and spooned some into his mouth. I thought that was romantic."

It takes everything in me not to exclaim, *You hand-fed your vegan boyfriend pieces of dead cow!*

"So romantic," I agree.

"And I took him to this amazing show when the circus was in town. They even had lions!"

"But isn't he...?"

"An animal rights' activist?" Gina finishes for me.

"Exactly! He loves animals."

Gina and I exchange glances. I'm starting to see poor Ethan's side of the story.

Lora continues, blissfully unaware. "That was for our one-month anniversary…"

"Wait, you were together for a *month*?" Gina blurts out.

"Thirty magical days," Lora confirms wistfully. "I was going to be his wife."

"Did he tell you that?" Gina asks.

"No. I did."

"Alright!" I cut her off, afraid of where this is going. Suddenly, my life doesn't seem so bad. "It's getting late, so we should go back to the—"

"No, no," Gina insists. "I want to hear what happened. You told him you'd be his wife?"

"Yeah." Lora shrugs. "I planned a whole thing with the ringmaster and proposed."

Gina's jaw is hanging open in sheer glee. "This is the best day of my life."

"Let me get this straight," I interrupt. "You hand-fed your vegan boyfriend ragu, bought tickets to an animal circus, and proposed on your one-month anniversary? And then he broke up with you?"

God, who could blame him?

"You're right," Lora sighs. For a second, hope sparks in my

heart—the hope that I'm about to hear anything remotely self-aware. Then: "… I do deserve better."

Nope. Abandon all hope, ye who enter here.

She dusts herself off and rises. "Thanks, you guys. That actually made me feel a lot lighter."

"Anytime," Gina says. For once, I'm one-hundred percent sure she actually means it.

Lora gives us a smile and a wave, then disappears back through the window.

"You're an awful friend," I snap at Gina the minute Lora's footsteps fade.

"Are you kidding? We need to hang out with her more."

"I'm serious!"

She shrugs. "Didn't hear you take Evan's side, Mother Teresa."

"Ethan," I correct. But dammit, she's right. "If *that* is what the dating pool looks like, maybe I should take my dad and Sasha up on the offer. That was bleak." I sigh and crumple forward, head between my knees in the *this-plane-is-gonna-crash* position. "What am I gonna do, Gee?"

"Well, it sounds like Lora might have a contact at the circus, if you were thinking of joining up."

I twist around to glare at her. "This is my life you're mocking."

She sighs and leans back against the metal grates, mischief fading from her face. "Fine. You want serious? I can be serious. You seriously have almost no options."

"No, I have three." I tick them off on my fingers. "One, I run. But Leander will find me eventually. And if and when he does, he might actually follow through on his threats. To *both* of us." I glance meaningfully at her so she remembers she has skin in this game, too. "Two, I play along and try to find leverage like you suggested last night. But that could take months, and the wedding's probably got some insane accelerated timeline."

"What makes you think that?"

"Because that's how my dad operates. He doesn't give people time to think or plan. He just..." I wave my hand vaguely, trying to find the words. "Bulldozes. Steamrolls. Takes what he wants and leaves everyone else to deal with the aftermath."

Gina drums her fingers on the iron stairs. "So what's option three?"

"I tell him no. To his face. Make it clear this isn't happening."

"That's suicide," she says flatly.

"Maybe." I drain the last of my coffee. "But at least it's on my terms. And honestly? I'm tired, Gee. Tired of running, tired of hiding, tired of letting him dictate the terms of my life from afar."

She studies me for a long moment. "You're really going to do this, aren't you?"

"Yeah. I think I am."

"Then I'm coming with you."

"Absolutely not." I grab her hand. "This isn't your fight."

"Like hell it isn't. He threatened me, too, remember?"

"Which is exactly why you need to stay as far away from him as possible." I squeeze her fingers. "I've spent fifteen years keeping my distance from that world. I'm not dragging you into it now."

She opens her mouth to argue, but something in my face must stop her. Instead, she just asks, "When?"

"Now. Before I lose my nerve." I stand, gathering my bag. "Cover for me with the bosses?"

"Are you definitely a 'no' on arson? 'Cause I really do think fire might make this situation go away."

I laugh. "Glad to know you weren't too drunk to remember that. I'd hate for you to get yourself into trouble when I'm gone."

She catches my arm as I pass. "Seriously, Ari... Be careful, okay?"

I try to hold my smile. "Always am."

The drive to Brighton Beach feels like traveling backward in time. Every street corner holds a ghost: there's the bodega where I used to buy candy with Jasmine, the playground where Mama would take us after school, the church where Leander would parade us on Sundays like his perfect little family.

I park a block from his office. My hands are steady as I kill the engine, but my heart is doing its best to crack my ribs from the inside.

Come on, Ariel. You can do this.

As I walk around the corner, I see the warehouse looming. A lopsided, corrugated nightmare. Something your eyes would glaze right over—and that's intentional. Easier to do what you want when no one bothers looking in your direction.

But I know better.

I know that, somewhere in that building, Leander Makris is sitting in his leather chair, smoking his Cuban cigars, thinking he's already won. Thinking his prodigal daughter will fall in line like all the others.

I'm going to march in there and tell him to his face:

Not a fucking chance.

10

ARIEL

The warehouse door groans like a wounded animal as I enter. Classic Baba—why fix what still works, even if it sounds like a death rattle?

Inside, the smell hits me first: salt, motor oil, and the cigars he's smoked since I was old enough to steal them from his coat pocket. My throat tightens.

Two guards block the stairwell, carbon copy versions of the meatheads who used to lurk in our Brighton Beach kitchen, playing *xeri* and burning through one cigarette after the next until the dawn broke. One cracks his knuckles; the other smirks.

"Lost, princess?"

"Tell him I'm here."

The smirker taps his earpiece, muttering in Greek. A pause. Then he jerks his chin toward the freight elevator. "You know where to go."

The ride to the sixth floor takes a century. Scuffed mirrors line the elevator walls, reflecting a girl in a beat-up leather jacket and dirty boots, her hair a mess of curls she didn't bother to brush. I look like a feral cat. My mouth still tastes like last night's tequila. My thighs still ache from last night's sins.

Baba's office hasn't changed. Same mahogany desk, same floor-to-ceiling windows smudged with fingerprints. The godawful oil painting he commissioned of himself still hangs crooked behind him. He's bent over paperwork, gold pen in hand, but freezes when the elevator dings and spits me out.

When he looks up, his face does something I haven't seen in years: softens. Just for a heartbeat. Then it's gone.

"Ariana." He stands too quickly, knocking a file to the floor. "You're here."

"Ariel," I correct, lingering by the door. "I told you that."

He starts to round the desk, hesitates, then sinks back into his chair. His hands tremble as he straightens a stack of papers. I frown at the tremor—is it new, or have I just never noticed before? A bottle of pills peeks out from his top drawer. Beta-blockers, if the label's faded blue script is any clue.

"Sit," he says. Then he adds, "Please."

I stay rooted. "I'm not marrying Sasha."

He doesn't seem surprised. Just nods, slow. "I see."

"He's not a good man, Baba."

A flicker of something crosses his face—guilt? Annoyance?—before he masks it. "He's… direct. But he'll keep you safe."

"Safe?" I bark a laugh. "From who? You?"

He rubs his temple, the gesture so familiar it stings. I used to watch him do that at the kitchen table, late at night, while Mama slammed cabinets and muttered about *men and their wars*.

"You think I want this?" he asks quietly.

"You arranged it, so, yeah, if the shoe fits."

"Because I can't protect you forever!" The words burst out raw, startling us both. He clears his throat, stares at his hands. When he speaks again, it's quieter, but still shot through with that old, familiar steel. "Your shit job, your little apartment, your fake name—you think I don't know? That I haven't *let* you play house?"

The air leaves my lungs.

He leans forward, voice fraying as he continues. "My enemies want everything that's mine, darling. You're my daughter—that means you're included. You think they won't come for you? For her?"

I freeze. "'Her'?"

"The redhead. Your... friend." He says it like a dirty word. "Gina."

I'm across the room before I realize I've moved, palms slamming on his desk. "If you touch her—"

"*I* won't." He meets my glare, steady. "But others will. Unless you're untouchable."

"And marrying a Bratva psycho makes me untouchable?"

"Yes." He says it simply, like he's explaining rain. "Sasha's name is a shield. His people are wolves. They'll gut anyone who looks at you sideways."

I want to scream. To flip his desk, rip up his stupid painting, burn down this whole rusted morgue he calls his empire.

"I don't even know him," I say, my voice cracking. "Does that matter to you at all? Does… does love?" I hate myself for even saying it, for how pathetic it sounds. It's even worse out loud than it was in my head.

"'Love'?" He digs the heel of his hand into his eyes. "Your mother and I loved each other. For a while, at least."

The implication is that it didn't matter in the end. That fate destroyed them, so it can't possibly be his fault.

"And that worked out great for everyone involved," I spit with fifteen years' worth of sarcasm and resentment.

"Sometimes, the heart follows the head. Sometimes not."

I grit my teeth. "I don't give a fuck what follows what. No part of me is going into this willingly. You can't just sell me off like—"

"What if—" He stops and taps his fingers on the desk. "What if there was a compromise?"

I snort. "Since when do you compromise?"

"Since my daughter came back to me." His voice is soft, almost pleading. Something else I've never heard from him before. "Give it time. Just… a little time."

"I don't need time. I'll never change my—"

"Ten days," he says suddenly.

I blink in confusion. "What?"

"Spend ten days with him. Let Sasha show you... whatever it is young people show each other." He waves a hand, awkward, gruff. "If you still hate him after ten days, we'll talk."

"And Gina?"

Baba hesitates. In that hesitation, I see it—the man who taught me to ride a bike, who bandaged my knees after I jumped off the garage roof chasing Jasmine, who hummed *Nani Nani to Paidi mou* when thunderstorms kept me awake.

"Ten days," he repeats.

The silence stretches, thick with unsaid things. It's nowhere close to the promise I want, but it's all I'm going to get. Finally, I step back. "You're a bastard, Leander Makris."

He rises, slow and pained, and rounds the desk. For a wild moment, I think he'll reach for me. Instead, he stops an arm's length away, the scent of tobacco and burnt sugar wrapping around us.

"You have your mother's eyes," he murmurs. "Her stubbornness, too."

"Don't—"

But he's already leaning in, pressing a dry kiss to my cheek. The gesture is stiff, foreign—a ghost of the man who once spun me in the air until I shrieked with laughter.

And yet, goddamn him—I can't pull away.

The elevator ride down is a blur. At the foot of the stairs, the guards leer and chuckle. The smirker says something in Greek that sounds like *See you at the wedding,* but I ignore him.

I walk back to my car, putting that warehouse behind me one step at a time. But just before I turn the corner, I look back, because I'm sentimental and stupid and I never, ever learn my lesson. And as I do, I catch a flicker of movement in the sixth-floor window. A shadow, watching.

For a second, I almost wave.

11

SASHA

Date the girl.

What a fucking joke.

Leander wants me to wine and dine his spoiled little princess of a daughter for ten days straight. The old man is losing his edge.

My mood is black. But one of the perks of having ***CEO*** on your business cards is that I can clear an entire floor of the Ozerov Industries skyscraper for myself. No buzzing worker bees here to distract me. Just silence.

I prefer it that way. Silence allows me to sift through the gravel of my thoughts and dig out the gold. Both in this company and in the darker, bloodier business that lies beneath it, I'm the brains of the operation. If I'm not sharp as CEO, stocks plummet. If my head's not in the game as *pakhan*...

The costs get much, much higher.

So I can't afford to split my focus. Not now, not ever. That's a luxury for my employees downstairs, the ones who have no clue what kind of organization they're truly feeding. I, on the other hand, have to keep my eye on the ball at all times. That means no distractions.

And I won't let Ariel become a distraction.

Ten days. Fuck that. For a job like this, I don't need ten days. I don't even need five.

I just need one.

"Feliks," I growl into the intercom, "I want you to send something. ASAP."

"Sure thing," Feliks replies. "Name it."

"Flowers."

He wolf-whistles. "Sounds serious. Any preferences for the arrangement?"

"I don't give a shit."

"Romantic stuff, then."

I shake my head. *Romance* isn't what I'm after here—just the illusion of it. Grand gestures will get me halfway there. As for the other half…

I'll just pick up where I left off in that bathroom.

"Oh, and boss?" Feliks's voice pops back on the intercom.

"Yes?"

"They're here."

I don't glance up from my desk. "Send them in."

Seconds later, two figures enter: one nervous, the other calm. Feliks brings up the rear, preventing any escapes.

Not that they'd ever get that far.

"Brian, Peter. Sit."

The two men obey.

Feliks shuts the door and stations himself in front of it, arms folded across his chest.

"Gentlemen." I pick up the folder on top of my keyboard. "I believe you know this man."

Inside the folder is a single picture. I push it forward, letting the two employees take a good, hard look.

"Well?" I snap. "Speak."

"I don't know him, sir," Peter answers confidently, if quickly.

"I-I don't, either," Brian stammers. "Never seen him."

Pathetic. If this is the caliber of spies my rivals send me, it's no wonder they haven't managed to touch me yet. "He's Prabhat Gupta, our chief competitor. His company just launched a drug we've been developing for the past five years. He beat us to the market by six months." I push two small pink pills in front of them. "This is ours. This is theirs."

They both lean over the pills. Peter takes one in hand, holds it up to the light. Brian's eyes, however, don't seem to know where to settle. "That's… terrible. They must have one hell of an R&D depart—"

"It's the same."

Brian blinks. "S-Sorry?"

"I said it's the same. As in, *exactly* the same."

I crush one pill, then the other, and scatter the dust on my desktop. I do it bare-handed, if only to satisfy my slight flair for dramatics. Peter's brow rises, while Brian's gaze darts around wildly, at the pills, at the picture, at me.

Sometimes, it's almost too easy.

"And," I add, "the leak was traced back to *your* shared office."

Instant pandemonium. Peter's eyes just about fall out of his head. Brian, for his part, does a good job of looking shocked as well. He sags in his chair. "Th-that's impossible!" Brian splutters. "I swear, we didn't—"

"Yes, you did. One of you, at least. And now, I'm going to give the culprit a choice." I steeple my fingers and stare into their eyes. "Confess. If you do, I might show mercy. If you don't…"

There's no need to finish that sentence.

"You have ten seconds," I conclude. "Starting now."

I count them out by drumming my fingers on the desk: *Nine. Eight. Seven...*

"M-Mr. Ozerov, there must've been a mistake—"

Six, five, four... Feliks starts humming the *Jeopardy* theme from the doorway. He's got a sick sense of humor.

"I-I'm telling you the truth!"

Three... Two...

"Please you have to…!"

One.

"Time's up." I rise. "You're both fired. Feliks—"

"Okay, okay! It was me!"

I pause and look at the man who spoke. "So you admit it, Brian?"

"I-I do." He breathes in deeply, mustache trembling with every panicked inhale. "I'm sorry, Mr. Ozerov. I was in trouble. M-My debts, you see..."

I do see. I have a background check done on all my potential employees. His file is simple. Brian Fenner: deadbeat dad, prostitute enjoyer, and occasional Saturday night gambler. I didn't hire him out of ignorance and it sure as fuck wasn't out of pity—I thought his sins would be good blackmail and that his debts would make a strong incentive to put in overtime. I didn't think he'd be *this* stupid.

"Please don't fire me," he pleads. "I have kids, I have a family..."

"And your whores," I cut in as I open one of my desk drawers. "How will they ever cope without you?"

He goes white as a sheet. "M-Mr. Ozerov, please. I really need this—"

"I won't fire you."

His eyes light up. "Really?"

"Really."

"Oh, thank you! Thank you, Mr.—"

BANG.

Brian's body wobbles in place for a moment. Then, like a puppet with its strings cut, he falls over, staining the carpet red.

Peter doesn't move. His eyes follow the fall, the calm on his face giving way to mute horror.

Must be his first dead body.

"Got something to say?" I ask as I place the gun back in the drawer it came from.

He shakes his head so hard it's a miracle the damn thing doesn't fly off his neck. "No, sir. Nothing."

"Good. Then get lost."

He springs up from the chair and makes a beeline for the elevator, jamming his finger into the button like mad. It'll take a while to reach us up here on the top floor—Feliks always gets a kick out of sending it back to the lobby. His way of hazing guests.

Once Peter is in front of the elevator bank, shaking so hard he needs the wall as a crutch to stay upright, Feliks leans into my ear. "Was that wise or was it reckless?"

"Neither." I shrug. "No one gives a shit about him. He won't be missed."

"You could have fired him."

"I fired something."

A small smirk quirks his lips. I'm aware Feliks doesn't always approve of my methods, but he understands them. This man betrayed us. He turned mole against us. Bratva or not, that's unacceptable.

"I'll call the cleanup crew," he concludes.

"See that you do." He's walking away when I add, "Oh, and Feliks?"

"Yes?"

"No witnesses."

He gets what I'm saying immediately. With a nod, he turns and saunters up to the elevator bank, whistling. The second the doors ping open, Peter's body hits the floor.

I grab my jacket and follow. "And they say I'm dramatic."

Feliks spreads his hands wide in an *aw-shucks* gesture, a pistol with silencer clutched in his palm. "What can I say? I'm theatrical at heart."

I step over Peter's corpse. "Make up a trail. Lottery win, job offer overseas, romantic getaway—I don't care. Just make them disappear."

"Understood, *pakhan*."

"And make me a reservation for tonight."

"Sure. The usual place?"

"Yes." I stride into the elevator. "But make it for two."

Realization blooms in his eyes. "I see," he murmurs wickedly. "Should I wait up to drive you home?"

"I really don't give a fuck, Feliks."

I press the ground floor button. Feliks's shit-eating grin is the last thing I see before the doors close—but for once, he isn't wrong. I won't need a ride back tonight.

Ariel and I will be otherwise occupied.

12

ARIEL

"Jesus, Ariel. You look like the 'Before' picture in a Prozac ad." Gina's waiting at my desk with two Starbucks cups, a frown, and helpful compliments, as always.

"Thanks, friend." I collapse into my chair, sending a stack of unopened mail cascading to the floor. "I just had a heartwarming father-daughter chat. I said, *I want to be free.* He said, *Marry the worst man alive or watch everyone you love die*. You know, standard family stuff."

She shoves a quad espresso at me, no room for cream, sugar, or hope. Just the way I like it. "Lemme guess—you caved?"

"Ten days." I can barely bring myself to say it. Never before has an arbitrary length of time sounded so heinous and evil. "I have ten days to decide if I want to be Mrs. Bratva Barbie or sign your death warrant."

"*My* warrant?" she balks. "What'd I do?"

"You chose to be my friend in third grade. Should've known that was an unforgivable sin."

Gina snaps her fingers. "Dammit. Knew I should've picked Annie Clymer instead, even if she was an annoying horse girl." She spins my chair around, forcing me to face her. "So what's the play? Poison his borscht? Fake your death? Hop on a flight and parachute out the emergency exit over Darkest Peru?"

I stare at the article draft glowing accusingly on my screen—***Local Bakery's Cupcake Crusade Against Childhood Hunger.*** I'll always remember this one, I think. My last byline before becoming a mob wife.

"The play is I do my goddamn job."

For the next hour, I channel all my rage into typing. Every clack of the keyboard is a middle finger to Leander, to Sasha, to the universe. The column itself, however, is a little bit less heavy metal than that.

... The secret to owner Marisol Hernandez's delicious lavender honey mascarpone cupcakes? It all comes down to one special ingredient, she says: "Love."

I'm halfway through a paragraph on buttercream ratios when my phone buzzes.

Unknown Number.

An image loads—me and Sasha on the gala dance floor, his hand splayed possessively across my lower back. The caption reads: ***Looking forward to course two.***

The screen cracks against the wall before I realize I've thrown it.

"Whoa!" Gina dives under her desk. "What the actual—?"

"Wrong number," I rasp, staring at the shattered glass spiderwebbing across Sasha's smirking face when my phone finishes bouncing back toward me and settles at my feet. After a minute, the screen goes black.

But even when he's gone, I'm sick.

Fifteen years of running.

Six months of fetching coffee.

Ten days left before it all goes up in flames.

"There's gotta be a way out of this," Gina says.

I can only shake my head. "You should've seen my dad's face. He was… I don't even know what he was, Gee. If it was just him, then maybe I could get out of this. But there's Sasha, too. And Sasha is… well… If I don't know what my dad was, then I sure as hell don't know what Sasha may or may not be. And I'm terrified to find out."

"So it's roll over and die? Ask 'how high' when they tell you to jump? C'mon, Ari—you're a fighter. You've got more fire in you than that."

Angry tears stud my eyes as I shake my head once again. "I wish I did. But unless Sasha has a sudden change of heart, I'm stuck. He'd have to be the one to call things off. But even then—"

"Wait. Wait. *Hold the fucking phone,* girl." Gina's eyes light up. "Do you remember what Lora said about her and Ethan? How he ghosted her after she proposed?"

I frown. "I'm already engaged. Proposing isn't going to help.

"No, dummy. But think about it. She drove that guy away by being *too much. She* made *him* go running for the hills. And that's what you want, right?"

"… You've lost me."

"What I'm saying is that you need to be so utterly unbearable that even the Russian mob prince can't stomach you. Not for all the tea in China."

The idea crystallizes, sharp and dangerous as broken glass. "Make *him* dump *me*."

"Bingo." Gina leans forward, practically vibrating with glee. "Be clingy. Be psycho. Be the girl who names your future children on the first date and tells him about your recurring dream where you're both dolphins swimming through fields of cotton candy."

A laugh rips from my throat. "He'd rather shoot me."

"That's the point. Men like him want cool girls. Independent girls. Girls who don't need them." She ticks off on her fingers. "So be the exact opposite. Don't be cool; be needy. Don't be independent; be high maintenance. Make him realize marrying you would not be worth whatever deal he's trying to make with your father."

I want so badly to buy into this crazy scheme. But…

"You don't know Sasha." I rake my fingers through my hair. "He's not some fuckboi finance bro who'll run screaming from commitment. He's—" I lower my voice, glancing around the office. "He's dangerous, Gee."

Gina rolls her chair closer, undeterred. "Then we go nuclear. Stage one: constant contact. I'm talking fifty texts an hour minimum. Hearts, baby animal GIFs, those weird little animated stickers of bears doing yoga."

Despite everything, I snort. "I might drive myself insane."

"Stage two," she continues, warming to her theme, "social media assault. Tag him in every post. Write paragraph-long captions about your eternal love. Make one of those couple accounts—'*#SashaAndArielForever*.' Post badly edited photos of your faces morphed together to see what your babies would look like."

"He's not even on social—" I start, then stop. "Actually, that's perfect. Nothing says 'unhinged' like tagging a nonexistent account sixty times a day."

"Now, you're getting it!" Gina's practically bouncing. "Stage three: the pet names. The worse, the better. Schnookums. Babycakes. My little Bratva Bear."

I choke on my coffee. "Oh, God."

"Don't lose steam now because stage four might be the most important. The future planning. Get a wedding Pinterest board. Leave bridal magazines everywhere. Start referring to his apartment as 'our first home' and talk about where you're going to put the nursery."

I can see it all now. Every awful date I've ever had, every red flag I've ever dodged—weaponized. I can *become* them all.

"And," she continues, "under absolutely *no* circumstances do you make anything easy for him, ever. He'll have to work like a dog for a peck on the cheek. A hug? *Nuh-uh,* that's fourth date material at best. A kiss? In your dreams, buddy. You'll be old and gray before you lock lips. But the whole time, you look like a dime piece every single date. Buy out the whole stock of Honey Birdette and give him a little peek here and there. Drive him crazy and never, ever let him eat."

At this point, I'm cackling. "You're evil."

"I'm brilliant."

"You're both." I smile, and it feels like baring fangs. "But you know what? You're right. If Sasha Ozerov wants a wife, I'll give him one straight from his worst fucking nightmares."

"That's my girl." Gina raises her coffee in salute. "Operation Psycho Bride is a go. Just promise me one thing?"

"What?"

"If he doesn't crack, and you do end up married..." She grins wickedly. "I better be your maid of honor. I'll give the most emotionally inappropriate toast in wedding history. I'll tell everyone about that time in college when you—"

"Stop." I hold up a hand, laughing despite myself. "If this works, there won't be a wedding. And if it doesn't..." I swallow hard. "Well, I might need you to give that toast at my funeral instead."

"Please. You really think I'd let him kill you?" She pulls me into a fierce hug. "We've got this, Ariel. Ten days to make Sasha Ozerov regret ever hearing your name."

The flowers arrive an hour later like a declaration of war.

Two dozen black roses, their petals kissed with crimson edges like they've been dipped in blood. The card is simple.

Tonight. Le Bernardin. Eight o'clock sharp.

Wear something pretty...

unless you'd prefer I choose for you.

—S.O.

"Holy shit," Gina whispers, running her fingers over the thorns. "These are Midnight Supreme roses. They only grow in some secret Japanese greenhouse. You literally can't even buy them—they're invitation only."

Of course they are. Because Sasha Ozerov doesn't send grocery store bouquets. He sends impossible flowers, each petal screaming, *I own everything. I can have anything. And now, I'm coming for you.*

My hands shake as I read the card again. Eight o'clock. The first tick of my ten-day countdown to either submission or destruction.

"Perfect." I crumple the card in my fist. "This is perfect. What better place to start Operation Psycho Bride than a five-star restaurant?"

"Love it." Gina beams. "What are you gonna wear?"

I think of the bathroom at the Met. Of Sasha's hands sliding up my thighs, his teeth at my throat. Of how badly I wanted him before I knew who—what—he was.

"Something that'll make him remember what he will never, ever have again."

The countdown starts tonight. But Sasha Ozerov isn't the only one who knows how to play games.

Let's see how he likes dating a nightmare.

13

SASHA

One look at Ariel's dress and I know she'll be in my bed tonight.

Part of me wants to say fuck all this song and dance; let's get to the main event. But another part, a wiser part, counsels, *Patience, patience.* Half the fun is in the hunt. And this hunt will be short enough as it is. No point in rushing it along.

I lick my lips as I watch her emerge from the limo I sent. Red-tipped feathers on her dress catch the dying sunlight. A warning sign. Nature's way of saying, *Danger—Do Not Touch.*

Too bad I've never been good at following rules.

The dress hugs every curve like a second skin, setting my imagination on fire while revealing absolutely nothing at all. Not that I need much in the way of inspiration. She's covered from neck to collarbone, but I still have no problem picturing how easily I could grab Ariel by that delicate throat and teach her what happens to little girls who play with danger. Show her that no amount of demure smiling can hide the fact that she's *mine* now.

Because that's what this display is about, isn't it? It's an act of rebellion disguised as surrender.

The perfect daughter. The perfect date. The perfect wife-to-be.

I'm almost sad that she looks so meek, so submissive. I wanted more of an outright fight, if only so I could snarl in her ear, *Oh, sweetheart. You have no idea what you're getting yourself into.*

If she'd shown up in oversized sweats, at least I would've been justified in hauling her to the bathroom and shredding them off of her.

But fine. If she wants to yield this easily, I won't say no.

I extend my hand as she climbs the steps. When she's close enough, she places her fingers in mine.

Like a princess at a ball.

Like a lamb to the slaughter.

"Ms. Ward." I let my gaze strip her bare, watching pink bloom across her cheeks. "You look stunning."

A smile curves her lips—modest, timid, everything she wasn't at the gala. Everything I know she isn't. "Please. Call me Ariel."

"Ariel it is. I'm glad you could join me."

When I straighten to my full height, her eyes skitter away from mine, but not before I catch the heat in them. Those quick, darting glances tell me everything I need to know. Up my body, across my shoulders, to my face and away again.

Hungry. Desperate.

Good. The craving hasn't left me since our last encounter, either. Since I bandaged her hand and imagined wrapping it around my cock instead.

"Shall we eat?" I gesture toward the restaurant's doors, even though what I really want to say is, *Shall we stop pretending?*

Patience, Sasha. Patience.

I hold the door and guide her inside. The maître d' practically trips over himself at the sight of us. "Mr. Ozerov! We've been expecting you. Your usual table is right this—"

"We'll take the corner booth," Ariel interrupts.

Both the maître d' and I freeze. I turn first, but when I look at her, Ariel just smiles in the same easy, pleasant way she did when she first emerged from the car.

My gaze shifts to the maître d'. His face is pale and stricken. He knows as well as I do: No one contradicts me in my own kingdom. This is my territory, my empire in miniature, where everyone from the sommelier to the busboys understands exactly who holds the power.

Everyone but my date, it seems.

Her smile takes on a sharper edge, dripping saccharine poison. "Unless you'd prefer to stare at the scaly little lobsters in the fish tank all night long, darling?"

I nod once, teeth grinding. So be it. Let her have this small rebellion.

It'll make breaking her that much sweeter.

I give the man a slight nod and we're quickly shepherded in a different direction. The serving team hustles to transplant a crystal bucket over to this new table. It cradles a bottle of

Krug champagne, beads of condensation rolling down its neck like tears.

"With the compliments of the chef," the maître d' murmurs, bowing so low I half-expect his nose to scrape the floor. "Please enjoy your evening."

I help Ariel to her seat, watching her sink into the velvet cushions like she belongs there. Like a queen ascending her throne.

My queen—whether she likes it or not.

Her lips twist into that perfect smile again. "Who said chivalry is dead?"

"Not dead. Just unpopular nowadays." I settle into my own side of the booth, adjusting my tie. Her eyes track the movement carefully before she drags her glance away.

"Can't say I disagree. The last guy I dated took me to Chick-Fil-A."

The casual mention of another man touching what's now mine makes violence surge through my veins. I want to find this worthless piece of shit and explain exactly why that was a mistake. Preferably with my fists.

Patience, Sasha. Patience.

Instead, I grit my teeth in what could generously be called a smile. "I'm sure they can find a chicken to fry if the food here isn't to your liking."

Something hot and defiant flashes in her eyes—*there you are, little spitfire*—before that perfect mask slides back into place.

The server approaches with a respectful nod. "Sir, madam, it is a pleasure to have you joining us this evening. May I—"

"Five of those."

Ariel again. It's not that she's barking orders—on the contrary, her voice is so sweet and feminine and fucking *princess perfect* that it's a miracle I can even find it in me to be offended.

But something about the way she keeps lunging in just when I expect her to sit back and be waited upon pricks my irritation.

The server is every bit as taken aback as I am. "I'm sorry—five of what precisely, madam?"

"Those." She points a manicured nail rather rudely at the next table over. The couple there are both in evening attire that would've been "old school" a century ago. They must be pushing ninety years old at least. They blink at her in slow confusion.

"Five… osetra caviar portions?" the server struggles to clarify.

"Is there a problem with that?" she asks.

He shakes his head in a hurry, glancing over at me. "No, no. Of course not. I will be back momentarily with that." He's gone in a flash, leaving me to look at my date and wonder just what exactly is going through her brain.

"I intended to order for us," I rumble.

"I wouldn't want you to go through the trouble!" she says. "I mean, not that it's not *so* gentlemanly of you. What woman doesn't dream of a big, strong man to pull out chairs and order for her?" Her voice drips honey, but there's an ocean of vinegar underneath it. "How would I manage those things all by my dainty, ladylike lonesome?"

The challenge in her tone makes my dick throb. Makes me want to bend her over this table and show her exactly what kind of man she's dealing with.

But that would be... uncouth. And I am nothing if not a gentleman.

At least until the bedroom door closes.

"I lead an empire. I can handle ordering your dinner."

"Oh, an *empire,* hm?" She leans in and grins, all teeth and no warmth. "Tell me all about it. Got any big emperor's plans cooking? Parades? Grand balls? Maybe a big, round spaceship to destroy enemy planets?"

Something's off. The fire I saw in her eyes at the gala—the defiance that made me want to break her—it's here and there, present and gone, dancing around faster than I can place it. And when it does disappear, it's replaced by this sugar-sweet parody of fawning submission that sets my teeth on edge.

Was her stubbornness that night just an act? Or is *this* the act?

One thing's for certain: by the time this night is over, I'll strip away every mask she's wearing until there's nowhere for her to hide. I'll find the real Ariel Ward underneath.

And then I'll tame her properly.

People think romance is complicated, but it isn't. It's an equation, the simplest one of all: wine, dine, fuck. That three-step routine has won me way more hearts than I ever wanted, especially when all I was interested in was a night with the body that hosted them.

So why shouldn't Ariel be the same?

Why shouldn't she fall at my feet like every other woman before her?

Ten days is about nine and a half more than I need.

The waiter comes back with a heaping platter of caviar and sets it down in front of us. "Five portions of the osetra—"

"Oh, no, no, no," Ariel tuts sadly. "This isn't what I wanted! I meant *those.*" This time, she points at a completely different dish on a completely different table. The three blind mice wouldn't have missed by that far of a margin, but she shows no sign of confusion. Just that smile again.

I can't decide whether I want to laugh or fuck it out of her.

"Er… Ma'am, I just want to be sure I'm…"

"Those are tarts, right?" She eyes the man. "That's what I want! So sorry about the confusion!"

The server looks hopelessly at me. I shrug. If she wants to make a fool out of herself, I won't stop her. It doesn't change how this night will end: a moan in my ears, a ring on her finger, an army in my pocket.

In the meantime, I'll sip my champagne and wait.

She picks her nails absent-mindedly as the waiter once again vanishes into the kitchen in search of her tarts. To his credit, he doesn't take too long, though he brings backup this time. Another server to carry over two plates of hors d'oeuvres.

"Fig and goat cheese tarts," the poor bastard explains. "Paired with a glass of our best Chateau Pétrus. 1920 vintage. An excellent year."

The dish is a work of art: plump figs dripping with honey, goat cheese whipped into clouds, all of it paired with a

Merlot that's heaven on the palate. I wait for her to eat, if only because I want to see what ecstasy on her face looks like before I show her just how much more her body is capable of feeling.

But Ariel takes one delicate bite, then sets her fork down like it's burned her.

"Not to your taste?" I ask.

I shouldn't care what she thinks of the food. Shouldn't notice the way her throat works as she swallows.

Her smile is sugary enough to rot teeth. "I'm not really a fan of goat cheese."

Liar. There's no fucking chance that a Greek princess doesn't like goat cheese. Hell, she probably nursed on the shit from birth.

But fuck it. I won't waste time with this petty bullshit. If she wants to play this game, I'll let her. Let her pretend she isn't ravenous for more than just food.

I take a slow sip of wine, watching her over the rim of my glass. Her eyes follow every movement I make.

"What a shame," I remark, voice pitched low enough to make her shiver. "I had such plans for dessert."

Ariel shrugs and giggles like a wind-up Barbie doll. "Oh, no!" Then she signals for the waiter to come back over.

From there, it's like a fucking montage of pickiness.

A salad arrives: almonds and peas and the most inoffensive greens ever made. I've never met a woman who doesn't gorge on rabbit food. Surely she won't have anything to object to this time.

And yet…

"What now?"

"I have an almond allergy," she explains prettily.

No, you don't. I had a file put together on you. If you so much as sneezed at cats, Feliks would have found out. "Pity."

The voice in my head urging *Patience* is starting to grow hoarse.

The duck: "Oh, I'm *so* sorry," she says with a remorseful glance at the duck confit drizzled in cherry compote. "Duck reminds me too much of my childhood pet. I had a duckling named Sir Quacks-a-Lot."

Steak tartare: "Is the chef *trying* to give me parasites?"

Again and again, she dismisses everything brought to her, and again and again, I can't help but feel like something's off about this whole performance. The brattiness comes and goes like a tide, rising whenever the waiter approaches, falling when we're alone. Her body betrays what her mouth denies—the quick flash of her tongue when each new dish arrives, the white-knuckled grip on her wine glass every time I lean close.

I catch her staring at my hands as I slice through the tender meat of the short rib course. Her pupils blow wide when I bring the fork to my mouth, a flash of heat lightning in those green eyes before she remembers herself and looks away.

Oh, she's not immune. Not even close.

I spear another piece of perfectly-cooked wagyu, watching her push food around her plate like a child avoiding bedtime. "Something wrong with the sauce?" I ask as she scrapes it carefully off her fifth untouched dish.

She glances up through those thick lashes, radiating fake innocence like a nuclear reactor. "Just not a fan of mixing fruit with meat."

I set down my knife with deliberate care, metal clicking against bone china like a bullet being chambered.

Alright.

Fuck patience.

Time to end this little charade.

I signal the waiter. "Bring the lady's dish back to the kitchen. Remove the sauce."

Around us, the restaurant goes quiet. In the decade I've patronized this place, I've never sent back a dish. Ariel's cheeks flush pink as nearby diners turn to stare.

But she says nothing.

Maybe there's hope for the little filly after all.

When her new plate arrives, I watch her with dark amusement. "Better?"

She takes a bite, unable to refuse without making a scene. "Perfect," she manages, but her voice has gone husky.

I lean forward, close enough to catch the scent of peaches on her skin. Close enough to imagine tasting it. "I thought it might be." My voice drops lower, meant for her ears alone. "I always know exactly what a woman needs, even when she fights it."

The fork trembles slightly in her grip. She's not playing with her food anymore, and we both know why. Her little games have only made her more appetizing.

That's when the lightbulb finally goes off.

She isn't just trying to be difficult. She isn't turning her nose up at the food because she doesn't like it.

On the contrary... she's ready for dessert.

And so am I.

I catch her wrist as she reaches for another glass of wine. Her pulse flutters against my fingertips like a trapped bird.

"I want to show you something." The words come out rougher than intended.

"What kind of something?" she squeaks.

"The view from my penthouse. It's spectacular."

She hesitates just long enough to maintain her little charade of virtue. Just long enough to make me want to shred it to pieces.

"I'd like that." Her voice trembles. With desire or fear—at this point, I don't fucking care which. Both will get me what I want.

I rise and extend my hand. When she places her delicate fingers in my palm, they're shaking.

We cross the lobby and go to the elevator doors of the attached hotel. The doors slide shut with a soft *ding*. In here, shut close together, that smell of peaches is stronger than ever.

Something primitive unfurls in my chest. Something that wants to pin her against these walls and fuck her until she forgets every man who came before me.

But there's something else, too. Something that makes me wonder if I'm still the hunter here. If I ever was.

Then I dismiss it. She's a rabbit and I'm a wolf. What happens next will be messy, brutal, and brief. But it will get the job done—that's for fucking certain.

"Ten days" ends tonight.

14

ARIEL

Shit.

I do my best to keep my poker face on and shove my panic deep down. Because I am, in fact, panicking.

Going up to his penthouse was not part of the plan. I've been acting like a total brat all night. Why isn't Sasha running for the hills yet?

I was picky. I was annoying. I was snobby. I was rude.

So why does Sasha seem to think I'm DTF? And why is *he* DTF?

Where did I go wrong?

It'd be a lot easier to think if I actually *wasn't* DTF. As it is, all the blood is rushing south. I feel giddy, insane, flushed in a way I haven't felt in a long, long time. Haven't felt since—

Since a blue-eyed stranger fucked my brains out in a bathroom.

It's like we're picking up right where we left off.

I tried to wear this red dress like armor, like a mask, but the moment I saw him waiting outside the restaurant for me, five-alarm fire bells started ringing in every single cell of my body.

It's the hands.

No, it's the eyes.

Maybe the cologne.

Or is it the cut of his jaw, the angle of his shoulders, the rough edge of his voice whenever he purrs my name? He hasn't said it yet tonight, but if he growls *ptichka* in my ear, I might combust.

The elevator pings and the doors open. Sasha motions for me to get out first. Theoretically, that's chivalrous, but I know his kind too well. He's just cut off my last hope of escape. I could've let him go ahead and then button-mashed the elevator to send myself back to the ground floor.

Too late for that now.

Defeated, I step out. "Where is this, uhh—view?"

The sooner I see it, the sooner I can leave and celebrate my self-control with a cheeseburger. I was too busy sending everything back to the kitchen to actually eat. I'm starving.

"Patience," he says. "We have time for that."

"We" don't have anything. *He* has time; *I* have a ticking time bomb wired into the middle of my life, and I need to defuse it before everything I love goes *boom.*

The problem is that there's a part of me that wants to stay. Part of me wonders, *What if you just let it happen?* The memory of that bathroom haunts me like a fever dream. His hands on my skin, his breath in my ear. There was a raw, animal magnetism that pulled me toward him before I even knew his name. Chemistry doesn't begin to cover it. This is nuclear fusion—dangerous, explosive, capable of leveling cities.

Capable of destroying *me*.

I hate how much I crave him. I hate that even now, knowing what I know, fearing what I fear, my treacherous body still remembers his touch.

He's pursuing me for my family name. For the connections. For the empire I represent.

I need to remember that. I need to tattoo that truth onto my fucking soul.

He doesn't want *me*.

But a traitorous voice keeps whispering objections in the darkest corners of my mind. *If that's true, then why did he want you that night? Before he knew your name or your worth, when you were just a stranger in a bathroom—why did he look at you like you were everything he'd ever hungered for?*

I'm snapped out of my thoughts by the sight of the room. "Oh, my."

Gilded walls. Persian rug. A king-size canopy bed with sheer drapes. I was joking about the emperor thing earlier, but if I didn't know any better, I'd think Sasha beat up Louis XIV and stole his bedroom.

Get it together, dummy. You're gonna let him use a thousand-thread-count linen set like a pantydropper?

Right. The plan. Psycho Bride.

"So much for subtlety," I murmur.

He comes behind me, a wall of heat I can feel without having to turn around. "Subtlety is for men who aren't sure what they want." His breath grazes my neck. "I'm very sure."

I shudder and step away. "Your ego's soaking up all the oxygen in here. Let's crack a window."

Striding to the balcony doors, I try fiddling with the lock, but my hands are shaking and my brain is suddenly blank of every memory of which righty is tighty and if lefty is loosey or not.

The door refuses to open. With no other choice, I spin around to face him. Sasha is standing where I left him in the center of the room. Hands in his pockets, utterly bored, but with a gleam in his eye that doesn't do much to quell my shivers.

"Are you gonna stand there or are you gonna help me?"

He doesn't laugh. Doesn't blink. Just keeps staring at me like he wants a few seconds longer to memorize the exact shade of flush on my cheeks. "You're nervous."

"I'm bored," I correct in a shameless lie. "This whole 'brooding mobster' act is tired. Do you practice your smolder in the mirror? *'Oh, look at me, I'm Sasha Ozerov, I drink whiskey and murder people before brunch—'*"

He crosses the space between us instantly, effortlessly. A blur of black motion. His hand darts out and snares my wrist. "Careful, Ariel. You're not as funny as you think you are."

"And you're not as scary." I try to yank my arm back, but his grip tightens.

"No? Then why are you trembling?"

Because you're wildfire, and I'm gasoline.

His irises are so pale blue they're almost translucent. I look back as long as I dare before I wrench my gaze away. But he doesn't let me go far. The hand that's not cuffing my wrist comes up to redirect my face—gently, tenderly, almost reverently—back towards his.

"Breathe," he croons.

"I am."

"Yes, but you're doing it like you'll never get the chance to do it again."

He is not, strictly speaking, wrong. I let out a reluctant exhale, followed by a tentative sip of air. His fingers are burning on my cheek, resting there butterfly-light.

Another inhale. Another exhale. Slowly, my heart rate descends back toward something resembling normal.

Then his face gets closer. Closer. It takes me a long, dumb moment to understand the implications. To kiss me? Surely not. But here he comes, closer, more dangerous, closer, *closer*—

And then he lets go of my face, reaches past my waist, and undoes the latch of the balcony door.

The rush of December air is enough to extinguish all the Bad Idea Heat™ that was turning my insides to melted mush. I shiver, this time from the cold, and clutch my torso as goosebumps prickle up and down the backs of my arms.

Turning, I step out onto the balcony—

And my breath catches in my lungs.

New York glistens below like coins tossed into a fountain for good luck. Black and neon and silver and gold, motion and light everywhere, cars and people crawling the streets below.

You live in a city like this because it astonishes you every time. It does for me, at least. That's why I've never been able to bring myself to run quite as far as I should have.

Another blast of cold breeze makes the vista blur as tears prickle my eyes. But no sooner do I start to feel like a popsicle in Prada than Sasha once again comes up behind me. His arms cage me in as he grabs the wrought iron railing. Instantly, I relax, soaking up his warmth, even though I know it's poison.

"You like heights?" he asks.

"I like knowing I could jump if I had to."

A beat. His chest brushes against my back. "You say that like I wouldn't go after you."

The shiver that wracks me this time isn't from the cold. It's from the impossible fucking enigma of the man currently pinning me to the thin edge of one of the world's most expensive lookout points.

He's like one of those optical illusions: You look and you see two faces eye-to-eye. Then you blink and it's a vase. Faces, a vase, a good man, a bad man—it all blurs together and it's so hard to tell what's what or who's who or what's real or what's not or why I should or shouldn't let him do anything he wants with me.

"You'd chase me down there?" I gesture at the glittering streets below. "Through all that?"

"I'd burn this whole city to find you."

"That's not romantic; that's psychotic."

His laugh rumbles through his chest and into my spine. "They're one and the same, *ptichka*."

"Stop calling me that." I spin to face him, which is a mistake. Now, I'm trapped between his body and forty stories of nothing. "I'm not your little bird."

"No?" His eyes drop to my throat, where my pulse hammers against my skin. "You're certainly dressed like one. All these feathers. All this delicate silk."

The dress was supposed to be part of my strategy. I bought the most expensive thing I could find at Bergdorf's—yards of crimson-colored silk charmeuse that floats around my body, with white ostrich feathers trimming the high collar neckline.

But the way he's looking at me now makes me feel like I didn't dress to kill; I dressed to *be* killed.

His fingers trace one of the feathers, barely grazing my skin. "Did you wear this to tempt me? Or to torture me?"

"Maybe I didn't think of you even once while I got dressed. Ever think of that?"

He presses closer. "The restaurant is closed. The staff is gone. The city is asleep." His finger trails down my arm. "There's no one here but us, Ariel. No one to perform for."

His gaze drops to my mouth.

This is the game, I remind myself. *Let him think he's winning.*

I tilt my chin. "So what now, hm? You show me your bedroom? Your knife collection? Your taxidermied ex-girlfriends?"

"No." His thumb brushes my lower lip. "Now, you stop talking."

The kiss shouldn't surprise me, but it does. It isn't gentle. It's a claim—hot, hungry, all teeth and tongue and barely leashed violence.

What also surprises me is that I let him take it.

I fist his shirt, futilely clinging to my rapidly dissolving anger as my body arches into his with a different motivation entirely. He groans, the sound vibrating through me, and suddenly, I'm being lifted, my legs wrapping around his waist as he carries me to the table.

His hands are everywhere. My dress rips at the shoulder, his mouth following the tear, scorching a path down my neck. I gasp, nails raking his scalp. "Sasha—"

"Say it again," he growls against my skin.

"Sasha."

"Louder."

"Sasha."

He tears the other sleeve. Fabric slithers to the floor. His eyes lock on mine, black with want. "You're mine tonight, Ariel. Every gasp. Every scream. Mine."

I should push him away. I should knee him in the groin and run.

Instead, I kiss him again.

It's a mistake. He takes it as surrender, his hands sliding under my thighs, dragging me closer. His belt buckle digs into my stomach, a brand.

No. Not like this.

I wrench my mouth free. “Stop.”

He stills, chest heaving. “What?”

“I said stop.”

His laugh is harsh. “Your body says otherwise.”

“My body’s a liar.” I shove against him, but he doesn’t budge. “Get. Off.”

For a moment, I think he’ll refuse. Then he stands abruptly, leaving me cold.

“You’re playing a dangerous game, Ms. Ward,” he says, adjusting his cuffs with jerky movements.

I sit up, clutching my ruined dress. “You started it.”

“And you followed me here.”

“To your penthouse, not your bed.”

He stalks to the bar, pouring two fingers of vodka. “Then why come?”

“To prove a point.”

“Which is?”

I do the best I can to stand my ground on shaky legs. “That you don’t own me. That I can walk into your world and walk right out.”

He drains the glass in one go and sets it back down with a harsh *clink*. “Then do it. Walk out.”

“Watch me.” I grab my clutch, heading for the elevator.

He’s on me in three strides, backing me against the wall.

"What are you doing?" I breathe. "You told me to leave."

"I told you to try." His lips hover over mine. "So leave. Or kiss me."

I hate him.

I loathe him.

I kiss him.

This time, it's slower. Deeper. A freefall with no parachute. His hands frame my face, tender in a way that terrifies me. His tongue clashes with mine, playful, teasing, here and gone, sweet and skillful. I taste the tang of vodka and the sweetness of the fig tarts. When he pulls back, his breath ghosts my lips. "Stay."

Yes.

No.

Yes.

I wind my fingers through his hair, dragging him to the floor. The rug burns my knees, but I don't care. He yanks his shirt off, and I map the scars on his chest with my tongue. Each one is a story I'll never ask for.

The whole time, I tell myself I'm doing this as a power play. *Keep the upper hand. Play his game. Show him what he wants and then take it away before he gets it.*

The whole time, I'm lying.

His belt clatters open, his zipper rasps, and then his hands are under my thighs, pulling me astride him. "Ariel…"

His fingers dig into my hips. I rock against him, friction

burning through the lace of my underwear. He hisses, head falling back. "Fuck. You're—"

I cover his mouth with my hand. "Don't ruin it."

He nips my palm, eyes blazing, and flips us. The world spins. When he sits up, his teeth find my earlobe. "Tell me you want this."

"No."

"Liar." He grinds against me, and I choke on a moan. "Tell me."

"I want—"

Glass shatters.

We freeze, the sound jarring in the thick silence. But then I see it. Sasha's forgotten vodka glass, knocked from the table by our stumbling little dance. It lies in glittering shards across the floor.

It's the wakeup call I needed. *What's the prize for winning this game, Ari? How is this "pushing him away"? Aren't you going to end up just as broken as that?*

I scramble away from him, dress hanging off one shoulder. He reaches for me. "Ariel—"

I slap his hand away. "Don't touch me."

He sits back on his heels, chest still heaving. "It doesn't have to be like this."

"Like what? Like I'm being blackmailed into marriage by a monster?" I laugh, the sound sharp as the glass shards surrounding us. "That's exactly what this is."

His jaw ticks. "You came here willingly."

"To prove I could resist you." I stand on shaky legs. "And now, I will."

"Is that what you call this?" He gestures to the space between us, crackling with electricity and bad decisions dying to be made. "'Resistance'?"

"Let's call it a moment of temporary insanity." I grab my clutch from where it fell. "It won't happen again."

He rises in one fluid motion. "You're lying to yourself."

"So are you, if you think I'll ever be yours."

I hurry through the penthouse. The elevator opens at my touch. Small mercies. One second more in this place is a second too much.

"Ariel—"

I step inside and start jabbing the ground floor button. "Go to hell, Sasha."

His hand shoots out, stopping the doors before they can close. "You're forgetting something."

My self-respect? Yeah, I left it on your rug.

I bite my lip to hold back the words as he steps into my space, crowding me against the mirrored wall. "You're forgetting that I don't give up."

"There's a first time for everything."

"Not for that." He grabs my wrist and stares at me, hard and merciless, the blue at the heart of a flame. Then he lets go and steps away. "I'll see you soon."

The doors close on his smirk.

As soon as he's gone, all the fight dies in me. I slump against the mirror, trembling. My reflection mocks me—swollen lips, wild hair, a woman unraveling.

One day down, I think.

Nine to go.

15

ARIEL

"And that's it?" Gina balks. "He just let you leave?"

"Well, it's not like he could lock me inside." *Though a part of me almost, kinda, sorta wished he would.*

"Can't he?" she retorts. "He's a big, bad Bratva *pakhan.* Bet there's a lot of things he can do."

I take a sip of my triple chocolate mocha latte. After yesterday's lack of calories, I'm craving everything on the menu. *Any* menu, really. "I don't think he'd do that. Call me crazy, but he just… didn't give me that vibe. The 'lock you up and tie you down' vibe."

"Bummer," Gina sighs. "That's the best vibe there is."

I'm about to tell her that I'd prefer none of Sasha's vibes whatsoever, no matter how kinky, when Lora rushes into the café. "Sorry!" she gasps. "Traffic was insane. What'd I miss?"

"Ariel's still trying to shake off her bad boy billionaire," Gina informs her. It's the watered-down version, the one that doesn't mention my real identity, or *his* real identity, or why this union would be a career-ending move for me, or why refusing it might be a life-ending one. "Her dad wants her to marry him."

"Sweet baby Jesus!" Lora says in flabbergasted shock. "It's like men think we're back in the Fifties. I'm so sorry you have to deal with that, honey."

"It's okay. He's actually kind of hot."

"Gee!" I snap.

"It's the truth!"

"Huh," Lora muses. "Is he a bad guy?"

Technically, yes, but— "He's just not my type."

"But he's attractive?"

"Well, yes." *Unfortunately.*

"And rich?"

With drug money, but yeah. "Kind of."

She purses her lips, pensive. "You know I support you, right?"

Uh-oh. "Why am I feeling there's a 'but' at the end of this thought?"

"It's not a 'but'!" Lora quickly denies. "It's a… a 'well.'"

A "well." How comforting. I hope it's a deep one. I'd like to fall into it.

I slump forward in defeat. "Let's hear it."

Since earthworms have more backbone than Lora, the prospect of contradicting me puts a guilty expression on her face. If there's one thing Lora hates, it's conflict. "Well… it's just that he sounds kind of dreamy, doesn't he?"

More like nightmarey.

"Define 'dreamy,'" I tell her.

"Hot, rich, and famous," Gina fills in. "Bam. Triple threat."

I give her a fierce scowl. "Which side are you on again?"

"Oh, we're all on your side, honey!" Lora croons. "I just need a quick explainer… why *don't* you like this guy?"

"Well, he kind of… he…" There are plenty of ways to answer her question, but I find myself fumbling. *The first words I ever heard him speak were an order to commit cold-blooded murder* seems like a neat explanation, but it comes with even more questions I'd have to answer. "He just…"

"Kicks puppies," Gina cuts in. "For sport."

Lora gasps. "Oh my goodness!"

"He's also an advocate for baby seal clubbing. He has a bumper sticker and everything."

"What the hell?" I mouth in Gina's direction.

She pretends she doesn't see me. "Isn't it? Who in their right mind would hurt a baby ani— OW!"

I elbow Gina in the side, but Lora is locked in on the horrors.

"A monster, that's who," Lora decides. The joke seems to fly well over her head. "You're right, Ariel. This man is no good. You need to get rid of him."

Glad that's settled, at least. "That's the thing: I really tried last night. I was so rude, you guys."

"But *were* you?" Gina narrows her eyes. "I'm just asking because your threshold for 'rude' seems to be a bit…"

"Canadian?" Lora suggests.

Gina makes finger-guns. "Bingo."

I throw my hands up. "What does that even mean?"

Gina slaps her hands together. "Let's do a postmortem. Break down last night. Where do you think things went wrong?"

Aside from letting Mr. Big, Bad, and Brooding feel me up all over? "Hand to God," I say, "I have no idea. I did everything you're not supposed to do on a date: I was picky, passive-aggressive, thoughtless..."

"In what ways?"

"I didn't finish a single course," I say. "He took me to this fancy-schmancy French restaurant, and I pretended everything there sucked ass. Which it *so* didn't." I can still taste the single nibble of hors d'oeuvres I took.

God, goat cheese is to die for.

"So you were a spoiled bimbo?" Gina barks out a laugh. "Babe, I don't know if you've noticed, but those are the types of women that men like Sasha wife up by twenty-one. That's their brand."

"Then what am I supposed to do?!" I exclaim. "I'm out of ideas, guys."

"We don't need a new plan. Trophy wives have torpedoed empires with way less. Your game is just weak, Ward."

I'm about to swat Gina again when Lora's hand flutters up like an eager kindergartener. "I think I might have something." She leans in conspiratorially. "So last summer, I met this really sweet commodities trader at my sister's wedding. He had the most gorgeous green eyes, and when we danced, he told me all about his yacht in Sag Harbor."

"But you scared him off," Gina predicts, dunking a macaron in her coffee.

"No!" Lora protests. Then she wilts. "Well… maybe? I just got so excited. I made him a care package for our second date with his favorite snacks and a little photo album of pictures from our first date. And I might have mentioned that my Pinterest wedding board already had our couple aesthetic picked out…"

I wince. "Oh, Lora."

"I know! I know." She sighs dreamily. "But you should have seen his yacht, you guys. I already had names picked out for our future children. I was thinking Sebastian for a boy, after the boat. Get it? Like, *Sea*bastian?"

"Kill me," Gina mutters so only I can hear her.

Lora twirls her hair. "Anyway, he stopped answering my calls after I showed up at his CrossFit class with matching 'Soulmate' water bottles. And then at his office with chicken soup when I heard he had a cold. And then at his mom's house to introduce myself…"

Gina goes preternaturally still. "Wait. You're a genius."

Lora blinks. "I am?"

"Not on purpose, but yes." She leans over the table, a wicked grin smeared across her face. "Men want a hunt, Ari. Especially men like Sasha. So don't be a rabbit—be a werewolf."

I blink at her in confusion. "I do not follow."

She clutches my wrist, her bangles shaking. "We've been going about this all wrong! You don't just be a brat—you *mess* with him. Get him hot and bothered under that pretty Armani suit. Show up at his office all sexy librarian, bend low over his desk, whisper *exactly* where you want his hands in your best Jessica Rabbit voice—then peace out. No *adios,* no follow-through. Let him stew there with blue balls and a spreadsheet."

"At his *office*?" I squeak.

The thought terrifies me. I'm picturing corporate boardrooms filled with black leather riding crops and I really, truly feel like that's at least mostly accurate.

"At his office," Gina confirms. "Men's brains short-circuit when you invade their turf. Trust. I once gave a handjob to a VP in the Duane Reade stockroom during his lunch break and didn't even let him finish. He texted me sonnets for weeks."

Lora gasps. "Gina! That's cruelty."

"No, it's *science*."

I push my mug away. "You want me to… flirt. With Sasha. At work. Then bail."

"Correction: *Arouse,* don't just flirt. Then you tactically retreat. Then…" Gina mimes an explosion with her hands. "Capitalize on repressed Catholic guilt or whatever trauma he's lugging around."

"He's Russian Orthodox. I think."

"Potato, *kartofel'*."

Lora and I both stare at her blankly. She rolls her eyes. "That's Russian for— You know what? Never mind. My humor is wasted on this audience. My point is, dominance games are universal. So it's play to win or play to lose—but you're playing either way. Whether you like it or not."

I stare at my latte art—a collapsing tulip. Meanwhile, my mind starts playing movies for me. I imagine Sasha's scarred fingers drumming on a desk. The graveled hitch in his voice as the elevators closed.

"What if he… retaliates?" I ask timidly.

Gina scoffs. "Please. Bad boy or not, he's got a boardroom full of goons to look tough in front of. Worst case? He hauls you into a supply closet and eats you out 'til the cows come home. Best case?" She wiggles her brows. "He calls your dad and says, 'Sorry, sir, your daughter's a hazard to my productivity.'"

Lora folds her napkin into nervous origami. "It does sound a little… risqué…"

Risqué. That's a word for it.

Suicidal is another.

But Gina is right: Sasha is the one who set up the stakes of this game. I'm just the one stuck playing it.

So if he wants to take it this far?

Fine.

I can fight dirty, too.

16

SASHA

"What's that smell?"

Feliks, who's currently occupying himself by flicking his lighter on and off, on and off, again and a-fucking-gain because he knows it drives me batshit, shrugs his shoulders without looking at me.

Flick. "Dunno." *Flick.*

"You were supposed to get the cleaning crew in here," I growl.

"I did." *Flick.* "Twice." *Flick.*

"Then why does it still smell like blood?"

I glance at the seats across from my desk, the last place that Brian Fenner ever sat. To my eye, under the glare of the fluorescent lights in my office, it looks pristine. No gore, no stains, no signs that anything violent ever occurred there. It just looks like what it is: a damn chair.

But when I sniff, it smells like blood.

Flick.

"Put that fucking thing away before I shove it down your throat."

Feliks pockets the lighter with a smirk. "You're in a mood today."

My jaw clenches. Of course I'm in a fucking *mood.* I barely slept. Like it's done since the second those elevator doors closed, last night keeps replaying in my head: Ariel's feathers fluttering over my bedroom carpet. The tiny little gasps slipping through her lips. The soft edge of her panties when I—

For fuck's sake, get it together, man.

"Tell me about the cleanup," I bark. "Did anyone see anything?"

"Nah. Brian's body's already ash, and Peter…" Feliks stretches his legs out and yawns. "Let's just say the East River's got one more secret to keep."

I drum my fingers on the desk. The ring on my right hand catches the light—the same hand that touched her bare shoulder last night. That slid down her—

I'm gonna fucking lose it.

"The car?"

"Crushed and melted down at Igor's junkyard. No trace."

"Security footage?"

"Wiped clean."

"What about their phones? Computers?"

"All handled." He arches a brow. "I'm not a sensitive soul, boss, but you're starting to hurt my feelings today. It's almost like you don't trust me to do my job anymore. Or…" He grins shyly. "Is there something else on your mind?"

He's dangling bait, hoping I bite. But I wasn't born yesterday, and Feliks has been screwing with me since the day I dragged him out of that fucking Moscow ditch, so I'm used to his tactics.

"You keep saying they're clean, but I know a hole in the ground hiding a Serbian boy's body that might say otherwise."

Feliks has the gall to look offended. "Now, I really am gonna get my feelings hurt. Brian is—*was*—clean in that department, Sasha. Peter, too. They were crooks, but stupid, isolated ones. No Serbian influence whatsoever. We don't gotta get paranoid about this one."

"Paranoia keeps us alive, *brattan.*"

Feliks hesitates. "You sure you're okay, man? You seem…"

"I'm fine."

"Because if this is about—"

"It's not."

"But if it was, you know you could tell—"

The stapler I hurl misses his head by inches.

But, as reluctant as I am to admit it, he's not wrong. I grip the arms of my chair until my knuckles turn white and make myself exhale to calm down.

Because the stapler's not the only thing that missed by inches.

I had her there, *right fucking there,* moaning and mewling on the floor. A thin scrap of lace was the only thing keeping me from her.

Fuck knows her reluctance wasn't involved. She wanted it. She fucking wanted it just as bad as I did.

So why pull back? Why play these games?

And why can't I stop thinking about her?

I'm saved from having to answer those questions when a knock sounds on the door. "Come in," I call.

It opens and a man who looks utterly out of place in this prim and proper office building slips in. His face is haggard and tattooed, and his bald scalp is splashed with more of the same ink. He's not fit for polite society.

Bratva society, however, is exactly where he belongs.

"Something wrong, Yannik?" I ask.

He gulps and folds his hands behind his back. I've always appreciated that reaction. Something about cold-blooded killers tucking tail between their legs in front of you makes a man's inner warlord pleased.

"There's been a… a problem, sir. At one of the processing facilities."

I lean forward. "Which one?"

"Skillman Avenue, sir."

My jaw tightens. That's one of our smaller operations, but still. "What kind of problem?"

"Serbs." Yannik shifts his weight. "A handful of them showed up last night, swingin' baseball bats like fuckin' crazy. Started hassling our guys, demanding protection money."

I exchange a look with Feliks. This isn't the first time Serbian street thugs have tried marking their territory in our neighborhoods. Like dogs pissing on trees.

"Anyone hurt?"

"No, sir. But they did a number on the folks working. They're just low-level packagers, y'know? They get spooked by stuff like that."

I crack my neck. Finally, something to do besides sit around and think about— *Don't even go there.*

"Get Dmitri and Anton. We'll pay them a visit."

"Already called them," Feliks says, rising from his chair as he tucks his phone away. "They'll meet us downstairs."

I stand and reach for my coat. "Time to remind some people where they can and cannot stick their—"

Then, speaking of intrusive devils, the door bursts open.

And Ariel strides in, all of my distractions made manifest.

If that was all, I'd tell my secretary to take her to lunch and I'd keep going on my merry fucking way to bash some Serbian skulls in. My bride-to-be needs to learn her place.

But that's *not* all.

She's wearing glasses. Horn-rimmed frames perched on her nose, making her green eyes bigger, brighter. A crisp white button-down about three sizes too small and two buttons too low strains across her chest, tucked into a black pencil skirt that hugs every curve and barely kisses the tops of her knees. Her auburn hair is pulled back in a severe bun, with dainty little wisps escaping to frame her face.

My brain short-circuits.

"Mr. Ozerov." She pushes those glasses up her nose. "I hope I'm not interrupting anything important?"

Yannik gawks. Feliks coughs to hide his laugh.

I should be furious at this interruption. Should be thinking about those Serbs, about maintaining order, about bloodshed and business.

Instead, all I can think about is how much I want to mess up that perfect hair. About ripping that skirt to pieces so I can—

"Ms. Ward." My voice comes out rougher than intended. "This isn't a good time."

She blinks those big, green eyes at me from behind those fucking glasses. The picture of perfect innocence while I'm a dirty sinner about to fall off the wagon.

"I'm so sorry to interrupt. I—" Her hip bumps my desk as she leans over it, sending papers scattering, including Brian's file. "Oops! Clumsy me."

My jaw tightens as she bends to pick them up, giving me a perfect view down her shirt. The temperature in the room spikes out of nowhere. My collar suddenly feels tight, strangling me.

"You look tense, sweetheart." She runs a finger across my shoulder, curling it over my bicep. "Maybe you need a break? I was hoping we could have lunch together. I was just missing you so, so, so, *so* much today."

I catch Yannik's Adam's apple bobbing as he tries not to stare at her ass. Even Feliks can't keep his eyes off her legs.

I can't even blame them. My dick's hard enough to hammer fucking nails.

But I'll blame them anyway.

"Out," I spit. "All of you."

"But the Serbs—" Yannik starts.

"Handle it without me."

Feliks herds Yannik toward the door, throwing me a knowing smirk over his shoulder before pulling it shut. The click of the latch echoes in the sudden silence.

Then I turn on Ariel.

"What," I growl, "do you think you're doing?"

17

SASHA

The door clicks shut, sealing us in a silence thick enough to choke on. I don't move. Can't move. Not with her standing there, looking like every forbidden fantasy I've ever crushed beneath my boot.

The glasses. The shirt straining over her breasts. The skirt that should be illegal.

One nail in my coffin after the next.

My blood roars in my ears, a primal drumbeat. It's accompanied by voices saying things I can't let myself do.

Grab her.

Bend her.

Fucking take *her.*

Ariel tilts her head, lips curving into a coy smile. "You look tense, darling." She drags the word out like a blade, testing its edge against my patience.

It's fucking embarrassing how well it works.

"What are you doing here?" My voice is gravel, my fists clenched at my sides.

It's a rhetorical question; I know exactly what she's doing. But I want to hear her say it. I want her to admit this is a game, so I can tear it the fuck apart.

She shrugs. Her blouse slips just enough to reveal the lace strap of her bra. "Can't a fiancée visit her future husband at work?"

"You're not my fiancée yet."

"Oh, but I will be." She sashays closer, hips switching wildly with every step. "Ten days, right? Or nine now, I suppose. Might as well get acquainted until then."

Her scent hits me—jasmine and peaches, the same as that night in the bathroom. It floods my lungs, my throat, my skull. I'm drowning in it.

She stops inches from my desk, her hip brushing the edge. "You're not working, are you?" Her fingers trail over my closed laptop, painted nails tapping the lid. "Seems like you're just sitting here. Brooding. *Menacing*."

"'Menacing'?"

"Mm." She leans forward, bracing her hands on the desk. The blouse gapes, and I force my gaze to stay locked on hers, because if I peek down the cups of her bra again, I might implode. "All that scowling can't be good for your blood pressure."

"You're the one giving me a stroke."

Her laugh is low, honeyed. "Poor thing!" She straightens up and simpers out with that lower lip. "Maybe you need a distraction. A 'stroke' isn't such a bad idea, actually…"

I don't flinch when her palm lands on my tie, fingers toying with the silk. But my breath hitches, betraying me.

She notices—of course she does. Her smile sharpens.

"Careful, *ptichka*," I warn.

"Or what?" She tugs the tie, pulling me closer. Our faces are level now, her breath warm against my lips. "You'll... spank me?"

My hand twitches, itching to grab her, to flip her over the desk and show her exactly what happens to brats who play with fire. But I stay rooted, muscles coiled, letting her think she's in control.

For now.

"You're testing me," I growl.

"Testing what?" Her thumb brushes the hollow of my throat, right along the line of my scar. "Your self-control?"

"My mercy."

Ariel titters. "You don't know the meaning of the word."

Before I can retort, she swings a leg over me and settles into my lap. Her skirt rides up her thighs. My hands fly to her hips on instinct, gripping hard enough to bruise. She doesn't wince, though. Just grinds down, slow and deliberate, until my vision whites out. "Ariel, I—"

"Shh." She presses a finger to my lips. Her other hand slides up my chest, popping the top button of my shirt. Then the next. And the next. "You talk too much."

I could stop her. Should stop her. But her skin is fever-hot through the thin cotton of her blouse, her hips rolling in a rhythm that's fucking *obscene*. My cock aches, straining against my zipper, and she smirks like she knows. Like she's winning.

"You're not the only one who can play games, Sasha." Her nails scrape my collarbone. Soft, soft, and then *pang,* a scratch that draws blood. "You think you're so scary? So *untouchable*?" She leans in, her lips grazing my ear. "But I've seen you come undone. I've felt it."

Her teeth graze my earlobe and reality fractures. My hands slide up her back, memorizing each curve through silk. She arches into my touch like a cat, but when I try to capture her lips, she turns her head.

"Ah-ah." Her fingertip presses against my mouth again. "No kissing."

I growl. "Why not?"

"Because." She rocks her hips, drawing a groan from deep in my chest. "I make the rules today."

My laugh is dark, dangerous, delirious. "Since when?"

"Since… now." Her lips trail down my neck, tongue flicking out to taste the salt of my skin. But when I lean in, she pulls back just enough to deny me. "Hands above the waist, darling."

I grip her ass in defiance. "Make me."

She clicks her tongue and stills completely. "I could leave."

"You won't."

"Try me."

We lock eyes, neither willing to back down. Then slowly, deliberately, she starts to rise from my lap.

"Fine." I slide my hands up to her waist, surrendering. For now.

Her smile is pure sin as she settles back down. "Good boy."

My fingers dig into her ribs in warning, but she just laughs and goes back to work on my shirt buttons. Each new inch of exposed skin gets the same treatment—lips, teeth, tongue—while her hips maintain that maddening rhythm.

The air grows thick with want, with need, with the memory of that night in the bathroom. But every time I try to take control, to speed things up or draw her closer, she pulls back. Denies. Teases.

It's torture.

It's ecstasy.

It's driving me fucking insane.

Her nails rake down my chest, leaving angry red trails in their wake. "Getting frustrated?"

I catch her wrist, squeezing just hard enough to remind her who she's playing with. "You have no idea."

"Oh, I think I do." She leans in close, her breath hot against my lips. Close enough to taste, but not quite touching. "The question is... what are you going to do about it?"

My grip on her wrist tightens as the blood pounds through my veins. We're headed towards the point of no return.

"You're playing with fire, Ariel."

She shifts in my lap, and I bite back a groan. The friction is fucking killing me.

Her free hand meanders down my abs and toys with the buckle of my belt. "Hm. You sure seem to be enjoying it."

I capture her other wrist, but she just rolls her hips again, and my grip falters. My head falls back against the chair, a curse escaping through clenched teeth.

"Look at you," she purrs. "The big bad Bratva boss, coming apart because of little old me."

My eyes snap open—*when did I close them?*—to find her watching me with dark satisfaction.

She knows exactly what she's doing. How close I am to breaking.

Her weight shifts, and suddenly, she's standing. The loss of contact is the cruelest wakeup I've ever had.

"What—" My hands reach for her automatically, but she dances back, straightening her skirt.

"I didn't even realize how much of your time I was taking up!" She says it so innocently, with such a pure flutter of her eyelashes, that I almost buy it. "You did say you were busy, right? I didn't come here to interrupt. And besides…" Her tongue darts out to wet her lips. "I'm not that hungry, anyway."

Then she turns and, hips swaying, saunters out. Hips go left. Hips go right. Her hair goes back up in its neat little bun.

And the door goes *click* once more.

Gone. Just like that.

I stare at the empty doorway, my cock throbbing painfully against my zipper. My hands are still tingling from where they'd gripped her hips, her waist, her—

Fuck.

I haven't felt this raw, this exposed, since… since the bathroom, actually. Since I walked out on her, shaking with unspent lust and the gnawing certainty that I'd made a mistake.

Now, she's returned the favor, leaving me with the same bitter taste of what could have been. What almost was.

What I almost let happen.

I push myself up from the chair. The leather creaks beneath me. The room feels too small, too hot. The air is thick with her scent. *Peaches,* like I work in a fucking orchard now.

I stalk to the window, wishing I could wrench it open, but ripping my tie loose instead. Below, the city sprawls, a concrete jungle teeming with life. Usually, the view calms me. Reminds me of everything I've built, everything I control.

But today, it's a mockery. A reminder of how easily I can lose control. How quickly she can unravel me.

I slam my fist against the glass, the vibration jarring my teeth.

What the fuck was that?

It wasn't a seduction. Not exactly. It was a… a declaration of war. Not foreplay—a *power* play.

And I almost let her win. I almost forgot who I am, what I'm capable of.

Almost.

I turn, surveying the room. Her presence lingers everywhere

—in the scattered papers on my desk, in the faint scent of her perfume, in the throbbing ache of my frustrated cock.

I snatch up the laptop she'd toyed with and flip it open. The screen glows, illuminating the spreadsheet I'd been working on before she walked in. Before she turned my world upside down.

Serbian distribution routes. Profit margins. Logistics. The things that matter. The things I should be focused on.

Not the way her blouse strained over her breasts. Not the curve of her hip as she straddled me. Not the—

Fuck yet again.

I slam the laptop shut again. It's no use. I can't think. Can't focus. All I can see is her, perched on my desk like a queen on her throne, her eyes mocking me from behind those ridiculous glasses.

Ridiculous, yes. And yet… devastatingly effective.

Women have thrown themselves at me all my life. Models. Actresses. Heiresses. They've offered me everything—their bodies, their fortunes, their souls. But none of them have ever made me feel like this. Like *I'm* the one being hunted. Like *I'm* the prey.

It's infuriating. It's exhilarating.

It's very, very dangerous.

I pace the room, my mind racing. What is she playing? What does she want? Does *she* even know?

One thing's for certain: *I* know. I know what I want and what I'm playing for. I've known since the day my father wound that barbed wire around my neck and kept it there until the scar had set deep into my skin.

I have a business to run. An empire to protect.

And, apparently, a bride to tame.

Yes. *Tame*. That's the right word. She thinks she can control me. Thinks she can manipulate me with her games, her teasing.

I snarl, kicking my chair so it goes spinning across the room and thumps into the far wall. She's wrong. Dead wrong.

I'm the one in control here. I'm the one who calls the shots.

And I will not be played.

18

ARIEL

I did it.

The elevator ride up to my apartment feels infinite. My knees won't stop shaking. My skin hums. My breath comes in shallow bursts, like I just sprinted up ten flights instead of standing still in an airless box.

By the time I fumble my keys into the lock, my thighs are slick with rampant, ungodly horniness and my pulse is an electric current under my skin.

But I *did* it.

I won.

I finally get my door open, lunge inside, and throw it closed behind me like Sasha might be following behind me, ready to make good on my teasing. My purse and keys go clattering to the floor as I sink down to a seat, back to the floor, torn between laughing and screaming. The grin spreading across my face is downright goofy, but I can't stop it. I wouldn't even if I could.

"You're crazy," I whisper to myself. "I can't believe you just did that."

My phone starts tap-dancing in my purse. I pull it out to find Gina triple-messaging me.

GINA: ***So?***

GINA: ***... So??????***

GINA: ***SO??!?!?!?! Did you do it?!***

Good question. Did I? Did I just waltz into Sasha's office, dressed like a librarian porn star, in full view of his coworkers, and proceed to blue ball him until the veins stood out on his forehead like cables on the Brooklyn Bridge?

Yes, as a matter of fact, I did.

Pretty sure he's still drooling all over his laptop, I text back, giddy and delirious.

LFgggggggggg! is her immediate reply.

I want to shout from the rooftops, to throw open my window and let everyone in New York know that I, Ariel Ward, just got the better of the smug asshole commonly referred to as Sasha Ozerov.

Since that seems like a bad idea, I go with Plan B, which involves pressing my face into a throw pillow and screaming.

But even when I'm done with that, my body is still thrumming with restless energy. It's a heat that has nothing to do with the stifling New York summer and everything to do with the way Sasha looked at me when I straddled his lap.

Like he wanted to bury himself in me and never come out.

His eyes were huge, his hands tight, and his breath was a harsh rumble in his chest. He was one whispery moan away from spontaneous combustion.

I got him so fucking good.

Problem is… there might've been some collateral damage.

Namely, the raging inferno currently blazing between my thighs.

I kick off my heels and pad across the hardwood floor to my bedroom, the skirt of my *very* effective librarian costume rubbing around my thighs. It's probably wrinkled beyond repair, but honestly, who cares? It served its purpose. I ought to hang it in the rafters like an athlete's retired jersey.

I opt for another form of post-Sasha celebration: self-care.

The battery-operated kind.

I rummage through my nightstand drawer, pulling out my trusty vibrator. It's a sleek, rose-gold number that Gina gifted me last Christmas with a wink and the sage advice, *Never underestimate the power of a good buzz.*

Truer words have never been spoken.

I unzip and toss my skirt aside. The cool air of my window unit A/C is everything I've ever needed. Then I settle back against the pillows and flick my never-fails boyfriend to life.

Bzzz. My eyes drift closed.

In the black void behind them, two blue circles appear.

His face swims through the darkness. Of course it does. I'd normally try to force myself to revert to one of my old reliables—I mean, whomst among us hasn't borrowed Jason Momoa to get where she needs to go, right?—but given how insane this whole day has been, I just let it happen. Stealing Sasha for my own selfish pleasure kinda feels like yet another tally in the win column for me, anyway.

So he's there, hovering in the darkness. I reach out an imaginary hand and feel Sasha's imaginary stubble beneath my fingertips. I trace the line of his jaw, dropping to his throat, his collarbone, the valley between his pecs.

In my mind's eye, he's exactly as I left him: chewing the inside of his cheek, shirt unbuttoned, tie askew, skin feverish everywhere I touch.

Ms. Ward... he rumbles.

Who, me? I taunt back in my head. *You look upset, Sasha. Is something wrong?*

You're going to be the fucking death of me.

I laugh, both in my fantasy and out loud, because there are way too many hidden meanings in that sentence for it to be a smart thing to say out loud. I don't need the reminders of the stakes here; God knows I've spent enough time thinking about them as is.

What I need is for Dream Sasha to do what Real Sasha would never: *Let me use him how I need.*

I up the vibration. New sensations skitter through me as I tease aside the hem of my panties and touch it to my throbbing clit.

You stay right there, sir, I order him in my head, pushing back on his chest with one heel as I sit on his desk. He leans back in his office chair, legs spread wide. I shimmy my underwear down my thighs and let it dangle from my stiletto.

Then, with a playful *Oops,* I drop it in his lap. Sasha starts to reach for the lilac g-string, but I stop him with a toe to his wrist.

No, no, no, I scold. *Keep those hands right there. Yes, that's a good boy. Right on those armrests. Where I can see them and make sure you're not being naughty.*

Those taut muscles in his throat work hard. He's a fucking mess, and it's turning me into a mess, too. Hidden beneath the hem of my skirt, I'm so wet it's almost shameful.

But we still have so far yet to go.

Half of me is surprised that, even in my dreams, Sasha considers disobeying. The other half grins with satisfaction when he clamps down on the arms of his office chair as instructed and leans back. No part of me misses the muttered curse that slips between his perfect lips.

There are so many ways I could use you, I purr in my vision. I run a teasing finger up the inside of my calf, up my knee, until it disappears beneath my skirt. When I withdraw it, it's glistening with my desire.

I hold it out toward him. *I could let you taste me, if you wanted?*

His mouth parts and he arches his neck toward me. *Ariel, I—*

No, no, no! I tut again, shaking my head. *I don't think you should talk right now, either. Just sit there and be beautiful for me, mmkay?*

He does.

God fucking help me, he does.

Now, where was I? I look down at my sopping wet finger. *Oh! What a mess. Let me clean that up.*

Then, without ever looking away from him, I put it in my mouth.

Sasha's eyes go huge. Bluer than blue, but a dark kind, an ocean-deep kind. I don't think he'd be able to form words in Russian, English, or gibberish even if I did let him talk. He's on the verge of a feral growl and nothing else.

But, since this is my fantasy and I'm in charge, he stays silent.

I wonder with a giggle what it's costing him to obey.

That's better! I grin again. *So I was asking a question, wasn't I? I was considering all the ways I could use you. And there are so, so many options. My brain's spinning just thinking of them!*

I'm hamming it up and I know it, but sue me: shouldn't I get to act however I want in my own imagination? Sasha doesn't look like he minds, right?

I could hike this skirt up, wrap two hands in that curly mane of yours, and drag your face between my legs. I'd make such a mess of your beard, but you wouldn't be upset, would you? Nod your head if that'd be okay.

Sasha nods.

Or... Oh, I know! I could take those big, strong hands of yours and shape your fingers exactly how I want them. Just two of them, crooked like a question mark. I could slowly, slowly slide them inside me and make you sit perfectly still while I ride you until I get what's mine. Would you like that, Sasha?

Sasha nods again.

What else? Let's see. I could slide to my knees, unzip your pants, and take you into my mouth. I bet you'd be big. I bet you'd be hard. I bet you'd like that best of all.

His knuckles are white as he squeezes the chair. I increase the settings on my vibrator. It's a pulsing, whining groan now, and so am I, every joint in my back cracking as I arch up off the bed. My opened blouse flutters in the A/C's draft and I reach up with my free hand to tease one nipple into a perfect, painful point.

If I sat on you and rode you until you came inside me, would you like that?

If I bent for you and bucked back into you until you exploded everywhere, would you like that?

If I was yours and you were mine, if I used you and you used me, if we both stayed locked in here until the windows fogged and the desk was ruined and our clothes were nothing but a sweaty, ragged memory...

Tell me, Sasha, would you like that?

Would you like that?

Would you like that?

And then, right when the orgasm is so fucking close I can taste it on my tongue like a coming storm…

Someone knocks on the door.

"Goddammit!" I moan. All the almost-there tautness goes rushing out of me and I flop back on the mattress like a landed fish. I'm sweaty, achy, unsatisfied in the rudest possible way.

It almost makes me feel guilty for what I did to Sasha.

And I'm gonna kill Gina.

She always gets salty when I don't text her back. She once gave me a three-day silent treatment because I didn't heart-react to a GIF of a pair of otters hugging with the caption ***ugh, so us*** that she sent me at two A.M. It wouldn't be the first time she's dropped in on me unannounced to demand I watch the series of TikTok links she's sent.

I abandon the vibrator on the duvet so I don't forget to clean it later, throw on a bathrobe, and march irritably toward the door.

"Gee, I swear I'm gonna—"

But as I rip it open, I see it's not Gina. It's not Gina at all.

"Hello, *ptichka.*" Sasha's tie is still slung loose around his neck, exactly how I left it. "Miss me?"

19

ARIEL

There's a three-second delay between my eyes registering *Sasha* and my mouth catching up.

"What... How did—"

"You're not the only one who knows how to swing by without warning." He leans in, close enough for me to taste the mint on his breath. "Now, are you going to invite me in or not?"

I yank my robe tighter. The satin does exactly nothing to hide the fact I'm naked beneath it. "Not."

"Fair enough." He takes my wrist and pulls me into the hallway.

"Where are we— Jesus, I'm not dressed!"

"A shame." His gaze sweeps me head to toe, lingering on the strip of thigh my robe doesn't cover. "But it won't matter where we're going."

"And where is that?"

The elevator dings. Sasha tugs me inside. "You wanted to know who I am, right? Well, I'm showing you."

Twenty minutes later, we're deep in a part of the Bronx I've never been to before, parked outside a restaurant called *Babushka's Lap*. The neon sign flickers like a dying firefly.

Through the windows, I see plastic ferns, a countertop aquarium with a single listless goldfish, and a bulletin board papered over with ads from Russian newspapers.

Sasha strides in like he's home. When I follow him in, I see why.

An old woman behind the counter looks up, her creased face splitting into a grin as she cries out in pure joy, "Sashenka!" She rounds the counter faster than her cane should allow and grabs his face in her wrinkled hands. I'm stunned that he permits it. "How are you, *malchik?* Still handsome! Still scowling! Have you eaten?"

She doesn't wait for him to answer before she turns to me. "And you? Clearly not! You're skin and bones!" She swats Sasha on the arm and my eyes bulge at the fact that he doesn't immediately order her execution and public dismemberment. "Have you been starving this poor thing? She'll need fattening up if she's to survive you!"

Sasha chuckles and runs a hand through his hair. "Zoya, this is Ariel. Ariel, this is Zoya."

I keep my bathrobe clutched closed with one hand while I offer the other to the old woman to shake. Taking me by surprise, she sweeps me into a hug instead. I'm mortified, but she couldn't give a damn less.

"Any friend of Sasha is a friend of mine," she declares, oozing maternal warmth. "And any *girl*friend of his is even better."

My face goes beet red. Sasha makes no move to correct her.

She steps back, though she keeps both wrinkled hands plastered on my shoulders. "You are a beauty, dear! Let me put some food in your belly."

I keep blushing as I fumble to remember how adults make conversation with new acquaintances. Especially when that acquaintance doesn't even blink at Sasha showing up here with a woman in a robe. *Is this a regular thing he does?* "Is, uh— Am— Is this your restaurant?"

She cackles. "Mine? *Nyet,* girlie. This is Sasha's."

I nearly choke on my own tongue.

"It was my mother's," Sasha interjects, suddenly focused on arranging the salt and pepper shakers on a nearby table in military formation. "Zoya ran it for her. Took it over when she—when the time came."

Zoya's good eye twinkles, though the other is cloudy with cataracts. "Did my best not to run it into the ground. I know my way around a kitchen, don't be fooled. But I let Sashenka here deal with all the numbers and things." She waves a hand and laughs. "Now, come! Lots to eat. Lots of meat left to put on you, *malishka*."

I'm nearly speechless as she pinches my butt, loops a hand through my elbow, and then leads us into the kitchen, bathrobe and all.

Sasha follows behind. I could swear he's even smiling.

I'm so full I might die.

But Zoya does. Not. Stop.

The food keeps coming in endless courses: dumplings glistening with butter, borscht the color of fresh poppies, a bottle of vodka so cold it mists.

"I've never eaten so much in my life," I say for the fifteenth time. Zoya once again pretends she doesn't hear me. Instead, she tops off my shot glass with still more vodka.

"*Za lyubov!* For love!" she cries out as she throws hers back.

Sasha downs his in one swallow. I let mine sit.

For a lady who must be pushing at least eighty-five, she can put 'em back like a freaking pirate. Even with the ten thousand calories I've eaten, I'm woozy from the two shots she didn't let me talk my way out of.

Zoya sets the shot glass back down, mumbles something about "checking on inventory in the pantry," and disappears. I keep my eyes fixed on my plate, pushing food here and there with my fork. Sasha does the same.

"So." I brave a spoonful of soup. It's heaven—beets and dill and something smoky that reminds me of rainy days at my yia-yia's house, back when I was too young to know that Baba stashed us there for the weekends because he had "business" to attend to.

"So," he echoes back. It's barely a word. More of a grunt, really. Monosyllabic would be an improvement.

But after the day I've had, I'm gonna go insane if I'm forced to sit with my own thoughts. So I press on. "Your mom… She owned this spot?"

He nods, then tears a chunk of black bread with his teeth. "Yakov—my father—hated it. Called it a 'distraction.' My mother called it her soul. Maybe it was."

I tread carefully. "Is she…?"

"Dead."

"Right." *Duh, Ariel.* "I'm sorry for your—"

"Don't bother."

We lapse back into an awkward silence. The oven hisses as it cools, old gears settling back into place now that Zoya is mercifully done turning me into foie gras.

"Sashenka learned to cook here," Zoya announces as she bundles back in the room suddenly, making it painfully clear to all of us that she was eavesdropping the whole time. "Every Sunday, he'd knead dough until his arms shook. He's a better son than his father deserved, I'll tell you that much."

"Enough," Sasha snaps.

But Zoya's in storyteller mode now, and by the way she greeted us when we first entered, I'm thinking she might be the only person alive who can steamroll right over Sasha's direct orders and get away with it. She carries on, undeterred. "Fifteen years old, and already making *pelmeni* better than I ever have. Your mother wept the first time you made them, didn't she?"

His jaw flexes. "She cried because I used too much pepper."

"Oh, don't be so humble." She raps his forearm with a wooden spoon. "She cried because her little wolf learned gentleness."

The dumpling slips from my fork. *Gentleness* and *Sasha Ozerov* don't belong in the same sentence. Does not compute.

Zoya pats his cheek. "Ah, don't look so sour. She watches over you, your *mamochka*."

"Dead people don't watch anything."

"Says the boy who leaves lilies on her grave every month."

He stands abruptly, chair screeching. "I need air."

I'm almost relieved to see him go. I might need some air, too. Seeing Sasha interact with someone who clearly loves him, someone loud and fun and kind, has my brain scrambled. I don't know what to make of it.

But because Zoya is all of those things, she won't stand for Sasha being upset on his own. Without looking at me, she nudges me off my stool and towards the back door. I open my mouth to argue, but she shakes her head and winks.

Whatever she thinks I'm going to do out there, it won't make Sasha feel better. It'll probably make it worse. But I shuffle down the hallway and through the back door anyway.

The alley reeks of brine and garbage, but Sasha's leaning against the brick wall like it doesn't bother him. I hover by the dumpster, unsure whether to offer comforting words or a restraining order.

"Your *babushka*'s a chatty old bat," I say after an uncomfortable stretch. "I like her a lot."

"Not my *babushka.*" He doesn't look at me. "She was my nanny. Mother hired her when I was four."

"That's basically family."

"I wouldn't do Zoya the dishonor." His laugh is bitter. "Family is a knife you don't see coming."

The air shifts. This isn't mob philosophy anymore—this is personal. I step closer, drawn to him against my will. "What happened to her? Your mom, I mean."

Cold gray eyes meet mine. "You're a reporter. You tell me."

"I'm asking. Not interrogating. I'm off the clock, and anyway, I didn't bring my notepad." I make a show of patting my bathrobe's nonexistent pockets. It's a weak joke, though, and neither of us laugh.

A muscle jumps in his jaw. The scar along his throat pulses faintly under the flickering street lamp. I'm sure he's going to tell me to mind my own fucking business. And then—

"She jumped," Sasha says flatly. "From our apartment building. They said she left a note—***Forgive me***—sprayed with her favorite perfume. Not that I ever saw it."

My stomach curdles. "So you don't believe it."

He stares at something over my shoulder—a memory, a ghost. "When I found her, her hands… They were bruised. Broken fingers. Like she'd tried to…"

He lets it hang in the night air, unfinished.

"He killed her," I whisper. "Your father."

His gaze snaps to mine. "I don't want your pity, Ariel."

"I wasn't— I mean, I… I was just going to say that I can relate. I know how—"

"Bullshit." Something dangerous flashes in his eyes. He pushes off the wall, caging me against the damp bricks. "Your father sells daughters. Mine sold souls. Which is worse?"

The vodka on his breath mixes with his cologne. Cold as I am with only a bathrobe to keep me safe from the winter, my body arches into his heat. "Why are you telling me this?"

His thumb brushes my collarbone. "You want to play psychiatrist? Fine. Here's your diagnosis: I'm broken. Violent. *Unfit*." His lips ghost my earlobe. For the span of a breath, I let him pull me closer. Let his fingers skate up my arm, his gaze drop to my mouth. Let myself imagine how it would feel to help put Sasha Ozerov back together, one broken piece at a time…

Then I remember who I am. Who he is. Why we're here. I remember why I can't let myself keep falling into these daydreams, these nightmares, these twisted fantasies that he's anything but a monster pushing me to the ledge.

How come Mama never warned me the devil would look so good?

I twist free before Sasha's darkness swallows me whole. "We should go back inside," I murmur. "Zoya is making dessert."

Zoya doesn't say anything when we come back inside, just serves us honey cake drowned in sour cream. Sasha picks at his, the picture of brooding menace. But now, I see past the armor.

There's a boy in there somewhere. One who kneaded dough until his arms ached. Who leaves lilies on a grave. Who became exactly what his father made him.

"You're staring," he growls without looking up.

"Yeah. Trying to decide if you're more wolf or watchdog."

He leans back, assessing me. "And?"

I fork a bite of cake. "I'm thinking... *stray*."

His lip curls. Not quite a smile, but almost. He doesn't realize I've seen it. But for the briefest of moments, the mask slips.

I'm stupid enough to find it beautiful.

20

SASHA

An hour after taking Ariel back to her apartment, I find myself standing in a warehouse that reeks of gasoline and Serbian arrogance.

The flames have been put out, but the damage remains. Charred shipping containers slump like rotten teeth. Puddles of chemical runoff shimmer rainbow-slick under emergency lights. Half my shipment of pharmaceutical materials—the *legal* shipment, the one meant to keep DEA auditors off my ass—is ash.

"Third strike this month," Feliks mutters, kicking a melted pill bottle. "These *svolochi* aren't even trying to be sneaky anymore."

I crouch, dusting soot off a blackened ledger. The numbers swim—losses stacked on losses, alliances stretching thin. My father's smug face floats behind my eyelids. *This is what happens when you play house instead of war, boy. Pathetic.*

He's right.

I stand, crushing the ledger under my boot. "Get a cleanup crew. Dump anything salvageable at the Brooklyn docks. And find out who leaked the shipment route."

Feliks hesitates. "You think it's another rat?"

"I think stupidity is contagious." I stride past him, toward the corpse lying limbs akimbo on the loading dock.

The Serbian foot soldier, the only one we managed to snare today, can't be older than twenty. I toe the kid's shoulder, rolling him onto his back. Bullet between the eyes—clean work. My men know better than to leave a mess.

His jacket falls open, revealing a crude tattoo on his sternum—two-headed eagle, wings spread. The Serbian crest. Just in case I needed further proof of who's daring to fuck with what's mine.

"They're escalating," Feliks remarks as he joins me again.

"They're desperate." I straighten, wiping my hands on my coat. "Tell Viktor to triple the patrols. Shoot anything that moves."

"And if they hit the other warehouses?"

"Then you've failed."

Feliks's jaw twitches, but he nods and steps away to do as I commanded.

The drive back to Manhattan gives me too much time to think. Too much time to ponder the taste of honey cake still simmering on my tongue. Blood and honey, honey and blood—the two tastes mix and meld and mingle in my mouth, a perfect metaphor for the two irreconcilable halves of my life right now. They don't go together. They can't.

Only one can last.

Rain sheets down, blurring the skyline into a watercolor bruise. Memories flicker like a broken film reel—Ariel perched on my desk, cherry-red nails tapping my laptop. *Distracting.*

Pathetic.

I press the gas, swerving around a cab. Horns blare. Let them. These streets are mine. *Mine.*

My phone vibrates. Leander's name lights up the dash.

"*Malaka,*" I mutter. The last person I want to talk to right now, but one of the few I cannot afford to avoid. I answer via Bluetooth. "What?"

"Heard about the fire," he says by way of greeting. "Tsk-tsk. Hard to keep the lights on without friends, no?"

"I don't need friends. I need Serbian corpses."

"Ah, but corpses don't marry your daughters." A pause follows, thick with implication. "Speaking of which, how is my daughter? I worry still, Sasha. She is… troubled. Troubled by what happened. Troubled by Jasm—"

"I get it, Leander. She's fine. Everything is under control."

My grip tightens on the wheel. *Troubled.* Yes. The way she'd looked at me in that alley behind Zoya's—not with fear, but with pity. As if she'd peeled back my ribs and seen the rot inside.

"Hm."

"Ten days, Makris. That was the deal."

"Ten days," he agrees. "Very well. Keep me updated. We will put the Serbians where they belong—once the wedding date is set. Until then... well, take care."

The line goes dead.

I slam my fist against the steering wheel. *Take. Take. Take.* Take care, take heed, take cover. Isn't that what I've always done? I took my father's empire. Took his enemies' throats. Took and took until even the act of taking felt hollow.

But Ariel...

Am I doing the taking? Or is she?

I cut across three lanes, ignoring the symphony of middle fingers in my wake. She's not the only one trying to take from me. The Serbians are testing borders. My pill processing plants upstate were raided last week. Two dealers vanished in Queens—they're probably hogtied in some Balkan butcher shop while Serbian bastards carve them into ribbons.

Leander's docks are the only way to move product without Serbian interference. His cops. His judges. His *protection.* Once I have all that, this war will come to a swift and brutal end. The price to bring that all under my banner seemed so simple when I struck the deal.

A ring. A vow. A pretty bird to keep in my bed.

Nothing seems quite so simple anymore.

The memory of Ariel underneath me, gasping, clawing—it should disgust me. Or bore me, at the very least. Instead, it surges in my gut, hot and relentless and un-fucking-forgettable.

It takes, too. And takes. And takes.

By the time I reach the office, the rain has iced over into sleet. I shrug off my coat, the scars on my back pulling tight. Yakov's voice echoes. *Softness is a cancer. Cut it out. Cut her out.*

I need a drink to clear my head. But whiskey barely burns anymore. Even when I pour three fingers, drain it, pour three more—it doesn't touch the chaos raging in my skull.

This shit cannot continue. I need to do what I've always done: draw a line in the sand and defend it with my fucking life. The plan must remain the same as it was from the start:

Seduce. Marry. Control.

So if Ariel has decided that she wants to fuck with fire? So be it. I'll reduce her to cinders. Let her sob my name into Egyptian cotton. Let her claw my back raw. Let her trick her own body into mistaking lust for love.

But I won't *give* her love.

I can't.

Love is the first domino, and I turned my back on that the day I wrapped barbed wire around my father's throat and pulled.

I take out my phone and text her. Then I put it away. As I do, I see something: a single thread of auburn hair peeking out from under the couch.

I pick it up.

Then I put it in the trash where it belongs.

21

ARIEL

Why am I not surprised?

Sasha's text last night was a masterpiece in brevity. ***Noon tomorrow,*** plus a location pin. Someone ought to teach him how to form complete sentences one of these days.

I guess, technically speaking, this would count as one of our ten dates until death mercifully parts us, or whatever. As far as I'm concerned, it's nothing but a new battlefield for the same old war to continue.

What's worrying is that I'm less certain of my tactics than ever.

Yesterday's intrusion at his office was supposed to be my big offensive. It was supposed to put him in his place and change the tide of this whole shebang.

For a while, it did.

But then he showed up at my apartment. Even if he hadn't interrupted me mid-personal-time, it still would've felt like a changing of the guard. Like the terms of engagement had gotten completely flipped on their head.

Between Zoya, the restaurant, those whispered alleyway confessions as our clouded breath mingled in the winter air… Somewhere in the middle of all that, things shifted.

What things?

I'm not sure.

Where does that leave us?

Fuck if I know.

What comes next?

I guess I'll find out today at noon.

Sasha chose today's venue—an underground bathhouse hidden beneath a Tribeca art gallery—so of course it's all black marble and gold faucets and servers who float around like ballet dancers on ketamine. The kind of place that names its massage oils after the seven deadly sins and charges you five hundred bucks to whisper *gluttony* while rubbing juniper berries on your lower back.

I wish I could bring myself to hate it more than I do.

His assistant had emailed me a set of instructions after his so-blunt-it-could-barely-be-called-a-text message. ***Mr. Ozerov requests that you bring a swimsuit,*** she wrote.

Do I love being dressed from afar like a Barbie doll? No. No, I do not.

But did I listen? Sure did. In a manner of speaking.

Meaning I brought a bikini that makes dental floss look *thicc*.

And at the first opportunity, I intend to lose said bikini. Because fighting fair is for losers, and this is one fight I absolutely have to win.

"You're late," Sasha says when I stride into the dimly lit lounge. He's draped across a chaise, shirt already unbuttoned to reveal a slice of scarred chest, covered in wavering shadows cast by the actual, literal torch flickering in the sconce over his head. His blue eyes follow every step I take.

I drop my tote bag on the floor with a *thunk* loud enough to make the attendant wince. "You said noon. It's noon."

"It's 12:07."

"Close enough." I flop onto the adjacent chaise, letting my coat fall open just enough to flash the scandalous slash of spandex beneath. His gaze dips. Lingers.

I pretend not to notice.

A server materializes with two frosted glasses of cucumber water. Sasha takes his without looking. "Where's your swimsuit, *ptichka*?"

"You're looking at it." I cross my legs, letting the coat ride up to show that there's as much not-there on the bottom half as there is on the top.

He takes a slow sip. Ice clinks in his glass. "That's not a swimsuit. That's a health code violation."

"So arrest me, officer."

His jaw twitches.

We're off to a good start.

The attendant—a nervous twig of a man who introduces himself as Emil—emerges and ferries us back through a labyrinth of soaking pools and cedar saunas before landing at a private suite.

In here, the air is thick with eucalyptus, the walls shimmering with condensation. A single massage table dominates the center of the room, flanked by shelves of oils and salts and who the hell knows what else.

Emil starts babbling about hot stone therapy. "When we begin the treatment, you'll see how—"

"There will be no treatment today."

Emil and I both look at Sasha in utter confusion. "P-pardon, sir?" stammers the poor man.

Sasha answers him, but he's looking at me the whole time. "We don't need a masseuse. I'll handle this myself."

Then he ushers Emil out in a way that's both polite and undeniable at the same time. How he manages that little balancing act is a mystery to me, because I'm still gawking back and forth between the swiftly closing door and the lone massage table and all the implications resting upon it.

Then the door clicks shut.

And those implications start to feel very, very real.

I arch a brow as I try to hide my nervous gulp. "Handling it yourself, huh? Planning to drown me in mineral water?"

"Planning to see how long you last before begging." Sasha shrugs off his shirt. His scars are harsh in this light—ridges of ruined flesh carving highways across his shoulders, his abdomen, the serrated noose mark around his throat. A lifetime of violence etched into his skin.

My mouth goes dry.

He catches me staring. "See something you like?"

Blushing, I turn away. "Wouldn't you like to know?"

He plucks a glass jar of cream off the shelf and saunters closer to me. "Turn around."

"Excuse me?"

"You need protection from the steam." His voice drops. "Unless you'd prefer to burn…?"

Challenge flares in my veins. I shrug off my coat and let it pool at my feet.

His exhale is audible.

The bikini must be worse than he imagined—black lace triangles held together by fishing line and audacity. This moment is worse than I imagined, too. Even when I was putting it on in my apartment this morning, I was humming with anxious energy. I told myself it was all in the art of the tease. Show him what he can't have. Plant my flag in the ground.

Now, that plan feels flimsy and distant.

What's *not* so distant?

Sasha.

He's here and he's huge and he's looking right at me, waiting to see what I'll do next. Will I roll over and heel like the good little pet he wants me to be? Will I submit?

For a moment, I consider it. Maybe all this fighting is stupid. Maybe I should just give Sasha what he wants, give my dad what he wants. God knows it'd be less effort. Less headache and heartbreak.

Then I think four little words to myself:

What would Jasmine do?

And I have my answer.

I pivot in place and toss my hair over one shoulder. "I'm waiting, Lotion Boy."

For a second, I think he'll refuse. Then he dips two fingers into the jar, the cream glistening like liquid pearl.

"Get on the table."

Gulp again.

I climb up. The leather is soft and cool against my thighs. His shadow falls over me as he straddles the edge, his body heat every bit as hot as the steam billowing through the ceiling vents.

The first swipe of his fingers nearly undoes me. "Jesus!" I gasp.

"Close, but not quite."

The lotion's cold, but his hands are furnace-hot. He starts at my shoulders, kneading knots I didn't know I had, thumbs digging into the hollows of my collarbones. Every stroke is precise. Clinical. Infuriating.

I bite my lip to stifle a moan.

"Too much?" he purrs.

"Barely felt it," I lie.

His palms slide down my spine. Slow. Torturous. "Your body disagrees."

He's right—my skin's singing, nerve endings sparking under his touch. His fingers skate the edge of my bikini bottom, deliberately avoiding the cleft of my ass.

More teasing. More taunting.

I bury my face in the table's headrest. *Do not arch. Do not whimper. Do not—*

His thumb circles the dimple above my tailbone.

"*Sasha.*"

"Yes?" He says it all innocently. As if he isn't turning me into molten glass.

"Your technique sucks."

He chuckles, low and dark. "Still lying, I see."

The lotion eventually warms between his palms as he works my thighs. Higher. Higher. My breath hitches when his pinky brushes the knot at my hip. It'd be so terribly easy for him to undo it. Who knows if I'd even stop him? Maybe I'd *let* him undo it, undo me, undo this whole silly war I'm waging. It'd be a helluva lot easier than wearing myself to the bone trying to fight the inevitable.

Then he pulls back. "Your turn."

I jump to my feet so fast the room spins. "Come again?"

He holds out the jar. "Repayment."

Hell no. "I don't do back rubs."

"You do today." He stretches out on the table face up, all carved muscle and menace. The scars ripple as he folds his arms beneath his head. "But if you're scared, I understand."

The dare hangs between us.

Pride cometh before the fall, I think, scooping a dollop of cream. *But at least the road to hell will be well-moisturized.*

His skin is fire under my palms. I start at his shoulders, mimicking his detached technique. But with every flex of his muscles, every stifled groan, my resolve unravels a little bit farther.

My palms glide over Sasha's shoulders, the lotion turning his torso slick. Every ridge of muscle becomes a chance to lose whatever game we've found ourselves playing. I have to remind myself of the rules again and again.

Don't linger. Don't cave.

Make him hate you. Make him run.

"Harder," he rasps. "Or can those dainty hands not manage?"

I claw my nails in. "How's that?"

A low groan vibrates under my fingers. "Much, much better. A little pain makes the pleasure that much sweeter, doesn't it?"

Sweat beads at my temples. The steam coils around us, thickening the air until every breath feels like swallowing clouds. His scars gleam under my touch—raised, angry terrain. My fingertips hover over the one circling his neck before I pull away, ashamed.

I go back to the massage, and as I do, I try to make it a mechanical thing. I could be rubbing anything, right? Conditioning a leather couch, for instance. Bathing a dog. Completely non-sexual. No reason to get all hot and bothered.

Except, of course, for the literal heat. Sasha's heat, the steam's heat, my own heat bubbling up from somewhere deep between my thighs.

More heat blooms where my hand has found its way to splay across the bottom line of his abs. I watch in dumb shock as it goes lower. Lower. Low—

Nope, *too* low.

I try to wrench free, but he holds firm, guiding me over the swell of his—

"Sasha!"

"You're straying a little off the beaten path, Ariel." His eyes are bright, even as his face is framed by billowing steam. "A less humble man might even think you're after something."

I let out a derisive snort. "Putting yourself in the same sentence as 'humble' might be the most batshit thing you've done yet."

His other hand drifts to cup the back of my knee. "Oh, I've got lots more insanity you've never seen before."

"Keep it to yourself," I grit out. "Roll over."

Smirking, he does as I say. That's perfect—him facing away from me makes this easier. If I can't see his eyes, I can't be hypnotized by them, right?

But the fact that Sasha Ozerov just actually obeyed an instruction of mine immediately sends me hurtling back toward the fantasy I dreamed up in those feverish few minutes after the office invasion.

Keep those hands right there. Yes, that's a good boy. Right there, where I can see them and make sure you're not being naughty.

A full-body shiver commences.

It's not that I want to boss him around; if I had my way, there'd be thousands of miles between us, and I wouldn't give a damn about what he chose to do with his hands.

But there's something intoxicating about the idea. About him letting me be in charge.

Maybe it's because, percolating underneath the addictive high of that power fantasy, is the knowledge that it could end at any time. That if he wanted, he could rise up from the massage table, and *snap.*

Could go fucking feral.

Could pin me down and make me his and remind me that, at the end of the day, only one of us has ever truly held the upper hand.

And it's never, ever been me.

"Tell me about your first time."

His voice rips me out of my own head. "My *what?*"

"The first time you came undone." I look up to see he's still face-down, utterly at ease. Moisture beads in the crevice of his spine, pooling at each notch in the bone. "Was it alone or with someone? Quick and shameful? Or slow like sacrilege?"

"That's a little improper to ask a lady," I fumble.

"Only if that lady's scared of the truth." Sasha's hand, lolling off the table, grazes the inside of my ankle when I pass by.

I grimace as I dig an elbow into Sasha's lower back. I want a whimper of pain, but all I get is a contented sigh. "I was nineteen," I whisper. "Freshman year of college. There was a T.A. in my journalism ethics lecture with nice eyes. He kissed me in the library stacks and… Yeah. Kinda unfolded from there."

His palm hooks around my ankle and pulses, just once. "Was it everything you dreamed of?"

I consider lying. Men like Sasha are built one way: jealous. And wouldn't getting him riled up over the thought of this T.A. making me see stars be worth it? Wouldn't that get me where I want to go? *Handled merchandise*—surely he'd despise that kind of thing. He'd want a virginal bride who's never so much as locked eyes with a man before.

But he'd know.

He'd know I'm full of shit.

He'd know that Danny Moreno kissed nice but didn't know what he was doing with his fingers, and that I ended up walking out of those library stacks with a cramp and a headache and nothing even remotely close to a climax.

"No," I say shortly. "It wasn't."

"Mm." He's quiet for a moment. Then: "Did you hate yourself afterward?"

"Nope. I save all my hate for you," I retort. "Your turn. First time you killed a man."

His answer is immediate. "Twenty-two. Back alley in Grozny. Chechen smuggler, ventured too far onto our turf. I put the pistol right here—" He grabs my hand and guides it to the back of his head, where my fingers instinctively clutch the thicket of hair.

"And… bam?" I guess. "No more Mr. Smuggler?"

Sasha shakes his head. "It jammed. I used a broken bottle instead."

"Jesus." I shiver. "Do you regret it?"

"That's two questions. My turn again. How old were you the first time you came?"

"Thirteen. Who was the first girl you took to bed?"

"Marta. My father hired her for me. She taught me how to use my teeth properly." He turns his head to eye me. "She cried when I left Moscow."

"Adorable. Why don't you marry her instead?"

Sasha's hand darts out to loop around my waist and tether me close to the table. Slowly, slowly, he sits up, until we're eye-to-eye. "Because you are the only one I want."

He's iron around my hips, but even if I could leave, I'm not sure I would. Not when he's this close, when the steam is lassoed around us, when all these secrets feel like they can finally take their first breath of air in a long, long time.

"You don't want me. Not in any way that matters."

"Wrong. I want you in the only way that matters: utterly, completely, and permanently."

His face is still, eyes level, breath calm. But this close, I catch something I don't think he ever intended to show me: the faintest tremor in his hands.

He's not as in control as he pretends to be.

Something about that realization makes me salivate. I'm not the only one teetering some razor's edge between *What the fuck is happening* and *Why not let it?*

But the danger remains because Sasha is a hell of a lot more comfortable walking this tightrope than I am. *Utterly. Completely. Permanently.* Who can say things like that with a straight face? Who can lie like that?

Because it has to be a lie, doesn't it? Sasha doesn't want ME; he wants what I bring him. He doesn't want me; he wants what he can use me for.

He doesn't want me.

He can't want me.

He'll never want me.

"Your thoughts are deafening, Ariel." He reaches up to toy with a sweat-soaked lock of hair that's fallen over my face. He twists it in his fingers, then tucks it back up where it belongs.

I fumble for a bluff. "Just thinking of all the ways you're full of shit."

He laughs. "I'm an open book in every way that matters."

I laugh right back at him, because that's the biggest crock of shit I've ever heard. "You? 'Open'? All you do is hide, Sasha. You're literally a professional."

He rises from the table, brushing against me as he stands. "Maybe you're right. Fair is fair. I won't hide anything from you anymore."

He hooks his thumbs into the waistband of his swim trunks.

"Hold on—"

Too late. The trunks hit the floor.

My brain whites out.

He's... *crafted.* All hard lines and wicked intent. Michelangelo's dirtiest secret. My knees threaten mutiny.

And he's not even one percent shy of his nakedness. I keep my gaze far above the equator because that way lies temptation, and I've got plenty to deal with up top anyhow.

Sasha steps closer. I retreat. Closer. I retreat. "You're sweating."

"It's a sauna. We're literally in hell."

"Close enough for the difference not to matter," he agrees. He palms my waist, picks me up, and switches positions, so now, I'm hemmed in against the massage table by a naked, six-five giant.

"The real hell," he rasps, "is you pretending you don't want me as much as I want you."

Our mouths hover centimeters apart. "I don't—"

"One day, you'll learn to stop lying."

"I'm not—"

"No? Then why are you dripping for me, hm?"

I try to stop him again, but I'm too slow and too half-hearted and he's too much for me in all the important ways. His fingers are deft as they pluck the knots at the side of my bikini bottoms in one go.

My dental floss armor goes slithering to the floor.

Sasha leans in, his knee knocking mine apart, and his palm comes to cup my center. He peels it away a moment later and, without looking away from me, licks the heel of his hand.

"Tastes like the truth," he growls.

All I can do is whimper.

His hand returns to where I need it so fucking badly. He parts me, one thick finger sliding past the last resistance I have to offer. I reach out to grasp his shoulders for balance.

Slowly, still staring straight into my soul, Sasha pushes me onto the massage table, laying me out on my back. His hand is a slow pulse inside my throbbing pussy.

"Still hate me?" he growls down from where he towers above me.

"Yes." My nails score the underside of his wrist. "Despise you."

"Good." He adds a second finger. "Hate me louder."

"I h-ha… h-hate…"

"What's that? I can't hear you."

Something is building inside of me. Pressure condensing, heat rising, light coalescing like a Big Bang getting ready to birth whole new universes.

Sasha bends down. "Say it right to me, princess," he orders. "I want you to come with a curse on your lips."

I try. I swear to God I do. "F-f-fu—" But it won't work right; nothing will; nothing but Sasha's fingers spreading me open while my spine arches toward the ceiling. Fluttery mewls pour out of me, one on the heels of the next.

Sasha keeps going. He's panting, too. "Seven days left," he murmurs, lips grazing my ear. "That's what you wanted. But you're already halfway there, aren't you?"

"Go to *hell*—"

He bends down to ravage my mouth and swallow the curse, kissing me until the room spins. One hand fists my hair, angling my head to deepen the contact. The other pumps into me. Every atom in my body screams as I charge toward a breaking point that might just kill me.

Ploy backfiring in 3... 2...

A gong reverberates through the room.

Sasha freezes. So do I.

Emil's muffled voice floats through the door. "Mr. Ozerov? The next stage of your session is ready."

You cannot be serious. Inwardly, I'm not sure if I should be laughing, crying, sobbing, or shouting for joy.

Outwardly, my manic laugh echoes off the tiles. I sound giddy, insane. "Saved by the bell. Literally."

Sasha rests his forehead against mine, grip tightening on my hips. The war in his eyes mirrors the one in my chest—need versus control, fire versus ice.

"This isn't over," he vows.

"Feels pretty over from where I'm standing, er— Lying. Whatever."

His growl flays me raw as he steps back. "Keep telling yourself that. We'll see who believes it first."

He scoops my bikini up from the floor and drops it in my lap. Then he turns and strides out, shrugging into one of the waiting bathrobes as he goes.

The door slam reverberates down to my bones.

Alone, I sit up, knees hugged to my chest. The ghost of his hands brands my skin and my insides are moaning from the lack of release.

You're already halfway there, he accused. He was part right, part wrong. It's only day three—we still have a long way to go.

But my body's made a leap.

The rest of me wants so badly to follow.

22

SASHA

The spa door slams behind me. I don't look back. Don't slow down. Don't let myself think about the way her skin warmed under my palms or the fucking sound she made when my fingers passed so close to the cleft where her thigh met her hip. Sharp, short, and sweet, like a bullet to the gut.

Emil is going deeper into the bathhouse, but I'm headed in a different direction. "Sir?" he calls after me. "The plunge pools are this—"

"I won't be joining," I bark at him over my shoulder. "Tell Ms. Ward to stay as long as she pleases. Or not. I don't really give a fuck."

Then I'm gone, pushing through the doors. The valet scrambles to bring my car. His face is pale as he tosses me the keys and gets the hell out of my way. I peel out of the lot, tires screeching.

Through my windows, New York blurs into a smear of asphalt and steel—but all I see is *her*.

Ariel, sprawled on that table, defiance and desire warring in her eyes. Always fighting. Always running. Always, always lying.

I tell myself it's the untruths that have me so pissed off all of the sudden. The audacity to lie right to my face, again and again.

But that's not really it, is it? It's not that she isn't telling me the truth; it's that I *want* her to, so fucking badly.

I want to break her apart and see what makes her tick. No—I want her to beg me to do that. No, no, not that, either—I want her to show me voluntarily. That's conquering of a sort, isn't it? If she offered herself to me of her own free will, that's winning, right?

Fucking hell. We're barely a quarter of the way into this little probationary period and I'm already losing my goddamn mind.

Ten days. The number throbs in my skull like a bad hangover. It was supposed to be a speed bump at worst. Ten little days to turn a feisty brat into a simpering doll. I've done far more with far less.

But this... this shit is turning out to be far more complicated than it ever should've been.

Fuck knows there's plenty else that needs my attention. I should do the rounds of my territory. Should check the shipment from Odessa, interrogate the crew, remind them what happens to men who get sloppy.

But the thought of barking orders, of bloodstains on concrete, of business as usual—it curdles in my gut. I don't have the patience for that shit right now.

That's fortunate. Because, without meaning to, I've driven to Zoya's.

The restaurant's deliberately old school sign flickers, a middle finger to the sleek sushi bars and overpriced bistros gentrifying the block. I'll protect that sign, this place, with my last breath. My mother's laugh lives in these walls. Her ghost lingers in the flour-dusted counters, the dented pots, the stubborn refusal to die.

Zoya is at the register, counting cash with her one good eye. She doesn't look up when the bell jingles. "Sashenka. You look like hell."

"You're a vision, too, old woman."

She snorts, slamming the cash drawer shut. "Flattery will get you far with most women. Not me, though." But for all her tough talk, she's already shuffling toward the kitchen, waving her cane at a booth. "Sit. I'll make tea."

The place is empty—it's the 2 P.M. lull—so I slump into the same booth I hid under as a kid, back when I was still dodging my father's drunken backhands. The wood underside bears the knife marks where I carved my initials at fourteen, drunk on stolen vodka and rage.

Zoya returns with a chipped teapot and two glasses. She sets them down, fills both. "Drink."

The tea is bitter, brewed strong enough to raise ghosts. Just how I like it. She watches me swallow, her milky eye narrowing. "So. The girl."

"Who said anything about the girl?"

She points a withered finger right between my eyes. "Your

face tells me everything I need to know. You're letting her under your skin."

"I'm not letting her do anything."

"*Akh*, spare me the bullshit, *malchik*. I saw how you looked at her when you brought her here." She stabs that bony finger at my chest. "Heard your heart going *pitter-patter*, too. You're like a boy who found a stray pup and doesn't know whether to kick it or keep it."

My grip tightens on the cup until some of the tea sloshes over the edge. Steam rises from the puddle. "She's a means to an end. Nothing more."

Zoya leans in. "Your father said the same about your mother. Look how that ended."

The mention of him is a match to gasoline. I'm on my feet before I realize it, chair screeching. "Don't."

"Don't what? Don't remind you that love isn't a weakness?" She stands, too, trembling but relentless. "Your mother—Nataliya—she was strength itself. Soft hands, sharp mind. She kneaded dough while your father kneaded corpses. And you…" Her cane taps my shin, hard enough to bruise. "You're *her* son. Not his."

The air's too thick. The walls are too close. I stride to the kitchen, needing space, but her voice follows.

"You think closing your heart makes you safe? Makes you strong?" She laughs, a dry, hacking sound. "All it does is make you alone."

I brace myself against the stainless steel counter, head bowed. The kitchen smells of dill and burnt sugar—my mother's perfume. Her voice still whispers in the hum of the fridge, in the drip of the leaky faucet.

Moy malchik. My brave boy.

Zoya's hand settles on my back, light as a sparrow. "Sasha..."

I whirl on her. "What do you want from me? A confession? Fine. She's... infuriating. Reckless. Stubborn. She looks at me like I'm some broken thing she's determined to piece back together, even if it cuts her hands to shreds." Snarling, I turn back around so she can't see my face. "And I can't—*fuck*—I can't stop thinking about her. About what happens when the ten days are up. When the deal's done. When she realizes..."

"Realizes what?"

"That I'm exactly what she thinks I am." The admission hangs in the air, ugly and raw. "A monster. A killer. My father's son."

Zoya sighs, cupping my face. Her palms are rough, calloused from decades in this kitchen. "You listen to me, Sashenka. You are Nataliya's son. Her heart. Her kindness." Her thumb brushes the scar on my throat—the gift from Yakov that keeps on giving. "But kindness isn't a cage. It's a choice. Every day, you choose: armor or mercy. You've worn the armor long enough."

I pull away, throat tight. "Mercy gets you killed."

"So does loneliness." She grabs my arm, forcing me to meet her gaze. "Your mother chose love, even when it cost her everything. You think she'd want you to waste your life building walls instead of bridges?"

The old clock above the stove ticks. Somewhere, a pipe clangs.

“She’d want me to survive,” I mutter.

“Survive?” Zoya snorts. “You’re not surviving. You’re hiding.”

I pick up a knife from the butcher’s block and start flipping back and forth in my hand. Every revolution in the air, it catches the light and seems to glow for a moment. “The Serbians are circling. Leander’s commitment is wobbling. If I show weakness now—”

She smacks my shoulder and the knife goes clattering to the kitchen floor. “Since when is love weakness? *Bozhe moi*, you’re dense.” Zoya rummages in a nearby drawer, then pulls something out and slams it onto the counter: a rolling pin, chipped and aged. I recognize it immediately. “Your mother loved fiercely. Protected you. Protected me. Even when that *svoloch* Yakov took his pound of flesh to dissuade her from trying.” Her voice cracks. “You think her love made her weak? No. It made her dangerous. The kind of dangerous that outlives bullets and bastards alike.”

The rolling pin is the one my mother used—handle worn smooth by decades of fingerprints. Zoya shoves it into my hands. “You want to honor her? Then stop fighting your own heart. Let someone in before it’s too late.”

I stare at the rolling pin, at the ghost of my mother’s grip. *Let someone in. Let Ariel in.*

It’s fucking ludicrous.

Zoya pats my cheek. “Go. Before I start charging you rent.”

23

SASHA

My sleep that night is broken. Studded with dreams I can't shake away.

"Mommy!" A child runs up to a woman in a sweater dress, hugging her knees.

The woman laughs joyfully. "There's my little boy!" She lifts him up, groaning at the weight. "How was school?"

"Boring. I hate it."

"How about your classmates? Did you make friends today?"

"No." The child pouts, unhappy. And why wouldn't he? He's eight years old and thinks he knows what unhappiness looks like: a bad day at school, no one to play with. What could possibly be worse? "They all hate me. They say I'm dangerous."

The mother pauses. Despite knowing unhappiness far more intimately than her child, she still takes his feelings seriously. Always has, always will.

She sets him down and looks him in the eye. Her hand moves across his hair in a caress, so slow and sweet that no hug could ever compare. In time, the child will grow, but no one will ever touch him like this again. With kindness. Without expecting anything in return.

"You're my sweet boy. You could never hurt your friends."

"Easy for you to say. I don't have any."

She chuckles. "One day, you'll make so many friends. You'll find people who care about you, who love you for who you are."

"Will they want to play with me?"

She boops his nose three times, once for every word. "All. The. Time."

"Mom! That tickles!"

She scoops her child up again. "How about we go get some ice cream?"

"Really?!"

"Why not? We can call Tetya Zoya—"

"Not a fucking chance."

The mother freezes. The child in her arms does, too. "Yakov. You're home early."

"Clearly not a moment too soon." The man who spoke—a big, burly beast with a shaved head and an undertaker's black suit—strides up to the pair, temperatures plummeting in his wake. "What did I say about turning my son into a pussy? Into a ssyklo*? Huh?"*

"It's just ice cream." The mother's voice, so happy moments before, now trembles. "If you don't want him to have it, then fine, but—"

SLAP.

"MOMMY!"

The woman holds her cheek. Redness spreads, but she catches herself from falling. The child isn't mature enough to realize why—that his mother can't afford to fall. Not with him in her arms.

The man sneers. "'Mommy' this, 'Mommy' that. Did I sire a fucking daughter? Are you going to start wearing skirts now, boy?"

"Leave him alone. He's done nothing wrong."

"No, you're right. You *have."*

Another slap, this time across the other cheek. The woman's head snaps to the side.

"STOP!" the boy screams, his face tear-streaked now. "STOP HURTING HER!"

"So weak," the man spits in disgust. "Look at you. You're no son of mine."

Staggering, the woman sets her child down.

"Honey," she whispers, trying to keep her voice steady, "can you go play in your room for me?"

"No! I'm not leaving!"

"You have to." The boy stomps again, but the mother reaches out to soothe him. She strokes his hair, slow and sweet, and that finally seems to work. "Trust your mommy, okay? I won't be long. I'll join you."

"But—"

"Please." Her eyes are shining now. "For me."

The boy can't say no to that.

Slowly, he trudges away, sparing a single glare for the man who dared raise a hand to his mother.

Right now, he is too weak to do anything about it.

One day, he will make him pay.

At the age of nine, the child hasn't become strong yet.

But his father is impatient. He is cold, and rage, and everything his mother isn't. He claims he wants an heir worth his salt, and the boy is trying, he swears he is, but it's so hard when he doesn't even know what that means.

"You can't leave him here!" his mother is screaming. "He's a child! He'll freeze to death!"

"He won't if he's my heir."

"You're insane." She spits those words out like venom, like a scorpion desperately trying to sting for the first time in its life. But her target's too far, and the arms of the men holding her back are too strong.

Strength, weakness, who has it, who does not—it always comes down to that, doesn't it?

"Don't you have a heart? Don't you care about your son?"

"I care about the next pakhan.*" He slowly turns to the child, paying no heed to his small breaths misting the air. The woods, the wilderness—it's all just a test. And Yakov Ozerov will not accept failure. "If he can't even do this, then he wasn't fit to begin with."*

"He'll die, you asshole!"

"Then I'll just make another one."

More screaming. His father's men are struggling to hold her in place now. She's a wisp of a woman, Nataliya is, but a force of nature when it comes to protecting what's hers.

"You're delusional," she snarls. "I will never give you another child. Never."

With a dismissive wave of his hand, he orders his men to drag Nataliya away.

"Sasha!" she howls as they cart her off into the shadows. "SASHA!"

"Stop calling him that," the man barks after her. "His name's Aleksandr. Like the conqueror."

For a second, a deranged light shines in the pits of his cruel eyes as he stares down at the shuddering, terrified boy. Something that could almost be called pride.

Then he, too, turns and leaves.

That night, the boy named Sasha curls up at the foot of a tree. There's no fire—he doesn't know how to make one. Nobody taught him.

The leaves rustle behind him. The boy holds still, holds his breath, holds his fears right at the center of his chest. At this time of night, anything could be coming for him: a wolf, a bear, a monster.

Then, suddenly, warmth seeps into his back, a familiar smell hitting his nostrils like cookies on Christmas morning. "Mom?"

"I'm here, Sasha. I'm here."

The child turns. It's her—it's really her. "Mommy!" He hugs her fiercely. "How did you get away?"

His mother smiles. It's a little sad, a little broken, but a smile nonetheless. In the dark, her bruises look like shadows. "Mommy has her ways."

Only the next morning will the boy find out that she knocked out a guard, stole a car, and drove right back here in the night. Without a break, without rest.

But he doesn't know that yet.

"Mommy, I'm tired."

"I know. Let's get some sleep, shall we?" She cuddles her son close to her chest, a bubble of warmth against the cold, dark world around them.

The last thing he remembers is looking up at the sky: big, bright, beautiful, a quilt of stars overhead.

At that moment, he was happy.

In the morning, his father comes to get them.

He doesn't say anything. His mother doesn't, either.

But when the boy climbs into the car, right before his parents follow, he swears he hears his father hiss, close to his mother's ear, "You went too far."

"No, you *went too far," she hisses back. "You abandoned your son to die."*

"If you don't stop interfering with his training right fucking now—"

"What?" Her head snaps to the side, glaring daggers in her husband's eyes. "You'll kill me?"

For an endless moment, Yakov says nothing. "I'll protect my legacy," he answers in the end, cold, clipped. A block of ice shaped into a man. "Whatever it takes."

I thrash in my bed, trapped between sleep and wakefulness. The dreams won't end, no matter how much I want them to.

The boy runs out of his bedroom. "Mom!" he cries out. "Mom!" He calls and calls, but no one answers. "Mom! Mo—"

"Your mother is gone, Aleksandr. She isn't coming back."

The scene morphs. The home becomes a warehouse. The boy becomes a young man. Taller, stronger—but still not strong enough.

"Fight it," Yakov grits, the barbed wire in his hands tearing into his gloves as he tightens it around my throat. "For fuck's sake, fight it! What kind of heir are you?!"

Still not strong enough.

"Fight it! Fight it, goddammit!"

At seventeen, I finally am.

CRACK. Yakov's body falls to the ground. His neck skewed in the wrong direction. His heart slowing, slowing, stopped.

"Am I strong enough yet, Otets*?" I kick the body. "Am I strong enough yet?" Then I kick it again, and again, and again. "Am I strong enough yet, you fucking piece of shit?!"*

CRASH!

I wake up with a start. My head snaps towards the sound—it's the glass on my nightstand, shattered on the floor.

Water spreads everywhere. It fills the cracks in the hardwood floor, pooling like tears.

Belatedly, I realize my face is wet, too.

I wipe at it like it's filthy. "*Blyat'.* Fucking *ssyklo.*"

24

ARIEL

Gina's waving a lemon poppyseed muffin in front of my face like a dog treat. "Earth to Ariel. Hello? You're zonked and it's scaring me."

I blink, my fingers still absently tracing the dip of my spine where Sasha's hands had pressed into me yesterday.

Too much? he'd purred.

Barely felt it, I'd lied.

"Sorry. Just... thinking about work stuff."

"Bullshit. No article is that interesting. Especially not an article about bakeries." She leans in, nostrils flaring like a bloodhound. "You're doing the post-sexual-tension stare, and I sense some tea. I command thee to spill."

I duck so she doesn't see the blush pinking my cheeks, the same blush that's stayed stubbornly in place since I left the spa in self-loathing shame yesterday. "There's no tension. There's... annoyance." I stab the straw into my iced latte hard enough to crack the plastic lid. "I'm annoyed that he just dismissed the masseuse like that. Annoyed that he barks orders like a fucking drill sergeant all the time. Annoyed that—"

That when he pinned me to that table, steam curling around us like sin itself, I wanted to let him undo every stitch of my resolve.

Gina's smirk widens. "Annoyed that you didn't ride him into the sunset, you mean?"

The straw bends between my teeth. My mind briefly goes into replay mode: *Sasha's scarred torso glistening under spa lights, his grip on my hips firm enough to bruise. His breath hitching when I dragged my nails down his chest—*

"It was just a massage. He sucked. I've had better for ten bucks in Koreatown."

Lie. Such a big, fat, embarrassing whopper of a lie. It was the best massage of my entire life.

His technique had been devastating. Clinical at first, then deliberate. Punishing. A thumb pressed to the pulse point behind my knee. A knuckle dragged up the arch of my ankle. My body had turned traitor, arching into every touch like a fucking submissive.

Gina scoots closer. "Sucked *what*?"

I roll my eyes so hard I see my own prefrontal cortex. "You're not helping."

"I'm trying, but you gotta give some to get some, girl. Bratty first date? Backfired. Office tease? Backfired. Spa tease? Extra backfired." Gina's brows waggle. "Face it, Ariel—your repellent game is working about as well as a screen door on a submarine."

I slump, defeated. Gina's right. The office stunt? He'd looked at me like I was course number one at the Last Supper. The rude diner act? He'd sent dishes back without blinking. The spa? *Christ.* Let's not revisit the spa.

"We need a new strategy," I blurt. "He's like a horny Terminator. Nothing fazes him."

"Wrong." She leans forward, eyes glinting. "Everything fazes him. That's why he's still chasing. You're the first thing that hasn't fallen at his feet."

I flick a sugar packet at her. "Insightful. Got a plan or just commentary?"

"Glad you asked." She whips out her phone, pulling up a Pinterest board titled *How to Lose a Guy in 10 Hikes*. "We go full Basic Becky. Nature edition."

I'm dubious, to say the least. "Hiking? Gina, you and I walked the mile every single P.E. class from third grade to senior year. That's *horizontal,* and I still hated it. Now, you want me to go uphill?"

"That's my point exactly," she insists. "You were miserable for every single one of the twenty-three minutes it took us to walk that mile. Imagine how insufferable you'll be when there's elevation involved?"

My lips purse up as I think through the scenarios. "I'm not totally sure that's a compliment, but okay, fine. I guess I'm just not sold. We really think that some mildly irritating exercise is gonna work when literally nothing else has?"

Gina shrugs. "If you have better ideas, I'm all ears."

I press my forehead flat to the tabletop as I think. "I wish I could just stick him on the mountain and leave him there.

That way, I could— Wait." I bolt upright and look at Gina. "Are you thinking what I'm thinking?"

She grins wickedly. "I think I'm thinking exactly what you're thinking."

Perfectly in sync with each other, we chorus, *"Leave him there."*

It's simple.

It's genius.

Maybe this time, it'll actually work.

Or maybe not.

Two hours later, I'm standing in my closet, holding up a pair of sequined booty shorts that even a Vegas showgirl would side-eye. "This is insane."

"That's the point!" Gina's voice crackles through my AirPod. "We need distractions so he doesn't catch on. You're gonna be a glitter bomb in the wilderness. A peacock in REI."

I toss the shorts aside, reaching for a mesh crop top with strategic cutouts. "What if I get poison ivy on my… everything?"

"Then Sasha will carry you back to civilization and rub calamine lotion on your hoo-ha. It's a win-win."

"I hate you."

"Love you more. Now, don't forget the Bluetooth speaker in your Juicy Couture fanny pack. Have it on full blast the entire time."

"I'm getting less and less sure about this by the minute, Gee."

I can hear the hum of the microwave as she cooks herself a delicious, nutritious Instant Noodles dinner. "Funny enough, I'm getting more and more sure. It's foolproof. Men hate two things: being inconvenienced and Carly Rae Jepsen. All you have to do is blast your music, complain the whole time, and then strand him up there. Just like that, *boom,* engagement over."

"Let's hope so," I mumble.

"There's always the alternative."

I pause. "Which is…?"

"Complete one-eighty. You beg him to manhandle you over a fallen log. You drop to your knees and plead until he snaps and drags you into the bushes to feast on your—"

I hang up.

By dawn, my duffel bag looks like a Claire's boutique exploded inside it. I've got:

- A selfie stick with built-up ring light
- A portable speaker shaped like a daisy (preloaded with the *Barbie* soundtrack)
- Seven shades of lip gloss, all named after cocktails
- A "survival kit" containing glitter hand sanitizer and edible body glitter
- Stilettos spray-painted gold for maximum "hiking chic"

I stare at my reflection—hot pink athleisure set, rhinestone-studded visor, bronzer out the wazoo. The girl in the mirror looks like she's cosplaying a Bratz doll gone feral.

"You've got this," I tell the nervous woman in the glass. "Be unbearable. Be *unlovable.*"

As soon as I say it, my phone buzzes.

SASHA OZEROV: *Outside.*

Looking down, I see his SUV idling like a panther at the curb. My stomach flips.

But when I get downstairs and yank open the door, ready to deploy my absolute worst, Sasha's already got one hand braced on the headrest, his scarred neck craned to check oncoming traffic. His faded Henley rides up, revealing a sliver of abs—pale, ridged, there one second, gone the next.

He turns to look at me.

And for a millisecond, I'm back in that alley behind Zoya's, watching grief fracture his granite composure.

She jumped... Her hands were bruised...

"Are you going to stand there forever?" he snaps.

"Someone's grumpy." I toss my fanny pack onto his lap. "Carry this. It's vintage."

He doesn't move. Just lets the bag slide to the floor as I clamber in. His gaze stays fixated on the way my leggings strain at the thigh, the wobble of my stupid heels. When I'm finally seated, he sighs.

The engine roars.

So does my pulse.

No turning back now.

25

ARIEL

The trailhead sign mocks me in cheerful Comic Sans: ***Fun & Adventure Awaits! Stay on marked paths!***

I'm not so sure about the "fun" part.

As for adventure?

Well, some of us are about to venture a little farther than others.

I adjust my rhinestone-studded visor and crank my daisy-shaped speaker to max volume. Dua Lipa may be dancing the night away, but I'll be lucky if I make it out alive.

"Ready?" Sasha's leaning against a boulder, arms crossed, dressed like he's about to summit Everest in a henley and jeans. Meanwhile, I look like a disco ball threw up on a Lululemon clearance rack.

"Born ready," I lie, flicking dirt off my gold spray-painted stilettos. "Just… admiring nature's beauty before we embark."

His gaze drags down my neon-pink leggings, snagging on the bedazzled ***SNACKS*** pouch strapped to my thigh, which contains nothing but chewing gum. "You do know this is a mountain, not Coachella."

"Details, shmetails." I pull out my glitter-coated phone, angling for a duck-lipped selfie. "Woooo!"

And then we're off.

The first mile is all performative misery. I fake-stumble over pebbles, whine about nonexistent blisters, and serenade him with endless off-key renditions of *I'm Just Ken*.

But Sasha's reactions are… underwhelming. He hikes ahead, a shadow carved from granite, testosterone, and suppressed rage, offering only an occasional muttered retort.

That doesn't stop me from trying to push his buttons.

Mile 0.1: *Tripping dramatically over a twig:* "Who put all this wood out here?"

Mile 0.3: *Pulling out my phone*: "Wait, we need to document this for my new outdoor lifestyle blog. Should I use Valencia or Perpetua?"

Sasha: "Use airplane mode. Your battery's at 12%."

Mile 0.5: *Blasting "Toxic" through the daisy speaker:* "Sing with me! *'I'm slippin' under—'*"

Sasha, muttering: "This is what Judas hears in hell."

Mile 0.7: *Applying lip gloss mid-stride:* "Do you prefer 'Mojito Meltdown' or 'Cosmopolitan Crush'?"

Sasha, glancing at the sheer cliff drop beside us: "At this point, the sweet embrace of death."

Mile 0.9: *Stopping abruptly:* “Wait. Is that a *bear*?”

Sasha, not breaking stride: “Squirrel. Keep moving.”

Mile 1.0: *Collapsing onto a rock:* “I require hydration. And a pedicure. Not necessarily in that order.”

Sasha tosses me a canteen. “Drink.”

I take a sip and choke for real. “Is this *vodka*?!”

But it doesn’t take long for fake misery to become very, very real.

By mile three, my thighs are screaming. My Juicy Couture fanny pack digs into my ribs, and the edible glitter on my cleavage has fused with sweat into a dystopian shimmer.

Meanwhile, Sasha shows no signs of cracking.

Time to ramp things up.

“Wait!” I trudge to where he’s paused at a fork in the trail. The map I printed off Google—then spilled kombucha on—flutters in my grip. “We need to… uh… go left.”

He arches a brow. “Left leads to a ravine.”

“Exactly! Best views!”

“And where does right take us?”

“Bear mating grounds. Very dangerous. Much growling.”

His lips twitch. “You’re holding the map upside down.”

Shit. I take off down the trail at breakneck pace. If I’m lucky, that’s exactly what will happen. Sasha curses under his breath and chases after me, but I call back over my shoulder, “It’s a… topographic inversion. Modern cartography is really innovating these days.”

The only reason he doesn't grab my arm and drag me back to the main trail is because I'm dodging and weaving between trees and hanging vines. I'm grateful for the cover until, ten minutes later, we're bushwhacking through underbrush so thick that even the mosquitos look pissed. My stilettos snap. My speaker dies mid-*Single Ladies*. Sasha's shirt snags on a thorn and starts tearing at the hem, much like my sanity.

"This is your idea of a shortcut?" He swipes blood from a scratch on his jaw.

"Uh… YOLO?"

"YOLO," he repeats flatly. "Is that Greek for *I'm trying to get us killed*?"

The sun dips behind the peaks, scorching the sky in ruddy streaks. My phone's down to 2% battery. The ravine I swore would be breathtaking gapes below us, hungry and endless and filled mostly with dirt-covered rocks.

But when I turn around to pick up the proper trail again…

Oh.

Oh, no.

"We're lost," Sasha says, too calm.

"We're… adventuring!"

"Ariel."

"Exploring?"

He steps closer. Pine needles crunch under his boots like tiny bones. "Look at me."

I don't want to. His eyes will be icy. Disappointed. Terrifying.

But when I glance up, his gaze is… not that. On the contrary, it's more, like… curious. Amused? "You did this on purpose," he states flatly.

"Did what? Embrace the spontaneity of—"

"You wanted us stranded."

My mouth opens. Closes. *So much for selling the story, you dummy. Couldn't even pretend to be surprised?*

Then Sasha does something that actually does surprise me. He *laughs*.

It's a low, dangerous sound that curls my toes in their ruined heels. "Next time?" he advises. "Pick a mountain without cell towers."

He holds up his phone. The screen glows with a GPS dot pulsing safely on the main trail.

My stomach plummets. "You… knew?"

"I know you." He tucks the phone away. "Now, come. Sunset's in twenty. We need to find shelter before then."

"'Shelter'?" The word squeaks out. "B-but… we're going back, right?"

"Back where?" He gestures to the labyrinth of shadows swallowing the trail. "You led us three miles into nowhere, *ptichka*. We're staying put until dawn."

Nonononono.

No, sir.

No, ma'am.

This wasn't part of the plan. The plan was to strand *him,* not strand *both of us.*

But one look in Sasha's face says he's not joking.

Welp, alrighty then.

Unexpected outdoor sleepover with the man I'm dying to get away from, here we come.

We start the climb up the mountain in search of something resembling shelter. Sasha's phone flashlight beam cuts through the deepening gloom, exposing gnarled roots that claw at our ankles. I'm down to one heel; the other dangles from my hand like a wounded bird.

His back becomes the focus of my attention. Every muscle shifts and stretches with his stride. Shadows pool in the hollows of his shoulders. Keeping him in sight is the only reason I continue putting one foot in front of the other.

Focus, Ariel. Unlovable and unbearable, remember? Just because we've veered sliiightly off-course doesn't mean you abandon the whole plan.

When Sasha kneels to inspect a craggy rock formation for suitability, I stop and inspect him at the same time. Moonlight etches the scar around his neck into something else, something more.

"Here." He juts his chin at a shallow overhang. "Home sweet home."

"That's a *dirt floor cave.*"

"Your five-star suite awaits, princess. In you go."

Frowning, I hobble inside. If we're being honest, it's more of a lip in the rock than a cave. The space is barely big enough to sit without our knees touching.

Which they do. Immediately and unavoidably. He folds his brawny body next to mine and electricity crackles in the centimeter between his thigh and mine.

As I'm settling in, unstrapping my various packs and pouches, Sasha reaches down and pulls a knife from his boot.

I freeze.

Maybe my plan worked too well. I annoyed him to the point of homicide. This is where I die.

He stills, eyes narrowing. "You think I'd hurt you?"

"Wouldn't be the first time a man tried."

Something dark flits across his face. Then he moves in a blur so fast I can't help but scream. He raises the knife high…

… and then offers it to me butt-first. "Fine. You hold it, if it makes you feel safer."

I take it with trembling fingers. I may or may not be just a bit on edge right now.

"Th-thanks," I stammer. "I was just a little—"

"I'll be back."

"Wait! Sasha! Where are you—"

But he disappears without an answer, melting into the woods.

While he's gone, I try my best to recalibrate. It's just one night in the woods; what's the big deal? He can stay on his side of the Four Seasons Cave Resort and I'll stay on mine.

And if a few bug bites and a crick in my neck from using a rock as a pillow is all it takes to convince him I'm not worth this much hassle and buy my freedom, I'll pay that price every single time.

Seconds become minutes, though. My anxiety starts to creep back in. When I hear a thumping noise and crackling in the underbrush, I brandish the knife, ready to use it if—

"You should at least pretend you know which end to stick an enemy with," drawls Sasha as he reappears. He dumps an armful of wood on the ground in front of the cave.

I scowl at him. "I'd figure it out fast enough."

"Mm," is all he says. He starts building a fire with practiced ease.

I swear it's less than five minutes from the moment he starts until tiny little flames are consuming the pine straw kindling. Sasha sits back against the stone wall as the fire dances and grows.

"That was… mildly impressive," I admit, fiddling with the knife in my lap. "Who taught you that? Smokey the Bear?"

He stares into the heart of the fire, face wreathed in shadow. "My mother," he answers at last. "After…" His jaw clenches. "Bad nights."

The air shifts. Shrinks. Suddenly, Sasha's face tightens. I look over my shoulder like there might be a bear coming at us, pissed we stole his living room.

But there's nothing. "What? What is it?"

He shrugs off his shirt, revealing a thin thermal tank top underneath that clings to every ridge of muscle. "Arms up."

"Excuse me?"

"You're shivering."

"Am not!"

He steps closer. The cold bites harder. "Arms. Up."

In the end, it's not a choice. He's right—the sun is long gone and the air is cooling with every second that passes. My one-shoulder sports bra will not be doing much in the way of heat retention, unfortunately.

So I obey reluctantly. The henley engulfs me, smelling like cedar and recklessness. It's still warm from his skin.

Are you crazy?! Don't think about his skin! Don't think about—

"Hungry?" He pulls a protein bar from his pack.

"No." It's a lie, but if I let him clothe and feed me, I'm going to lose my head.

"Is it because it doesn't have glitter in it?" He toes the snack pouch on my thigh with his boot. "Or because it isn't bubblegum-flavored?"

I set my jaw. "Both."

He unwraps it, takes a deliberate bite. "Suit yourself."

Then he settles back against the rock.

I sit as far away as I can, anxious and jittery. Night falls fast here—no city glow to soften the edges. Stars punch through the blackness, brighter than I've ever seen them. Sasha tends the fire with a poking stick, his face completely impassive.

I huddle in his shirt, guilt in my stomach curdling and churning alongside something hotter.

"Why aren't you mad?" The words escape before I can stop them.

He glances up, firelight carving his face into something ancient. Feral. "Would you like me to be?"

"I mean, I'd understand if you were. I sabotaged this."

"And?"

"And… you should be furious! Yell! Threaten to leave me for the bears to eat!"

The fire crackles. His eyes hold mine. "I wouldn't do that."

I want to ask which part precisely he wouldn't do, but before I can, there's a loud boom—

And it starts to rain.

Not rain, actually—*pour*. The heavens crack open and let loose on us like this storm is personal. The fire is immediately snuffed out with a mournful sizzle.

I scoot backwards, but there's only so far to go. And besides, water leaks in from a crack in the ceiling, dripping ice-cold betrayal onto my scalp. It's been thirty seconds and my teeth are already chattering.

Sasha curses in Russian, yanking me against his chest. His heartbeat thunders through my cheek.

"Hypothermia," he barks over the storm. "Take off your clothes."

I snort. "Smooth. If you think that's gonna work, then—"

"They're wet. So it's either that or die of exposure. *Now*, Ariel."

We strip to our underwear, modesty sacrificed to survival. His tank top clings to every ridge of muscle, every old wound. My neon bralette feels absurd. Vulnerable.

He arranges our clothes near the dead fire, then pulls me back against him. I'm rigid as a plank of wood in his arms. Skin to skin, his breath hot on my nape, he murmurs, "Don't make this weird."

"You're literally spooning me in a cave."

"And you're shivering too hard to insult me properly. We're all suffering."

The rain continues to pour. His arms tighten. My mind scrambles for hatred—but my body…

My body remembers his hands in the steam room. His laugh at Zoya's. Blue eyes in an alleyway, saying things he'd clearly never said out loud before.

I try to hold out, but before long, I sink against his chest. Only because nuzzling into Sasha is the difference between life and death. It has nothing to do with the way his arms stay strong around me. Corded with muscle. Warm.

Safe.

Minutes or maybe hours later, the storm peters out. Through a gap in the foliage, we watch as the dark clouds roll on and the night sky reveals itself. I begin to regain feeling in my fingers and toes.

But the feeling of *This can't be real* remains, stronger than ever.

"Better?" His breath warms my ear.

No! I want to cry. *Worse. So much worse.*

Instead, I nod, throat tight. His heartbeat thuds against my spine, perfectly in sync with mine. Above us, through the opening in the treetops, the Milky Way bleeds across the sky, indifferent to our stupid, human messiness.

I focus on them, hoping I can forget, too.

"That one's Orion," I whisper, pointing.

"Mm." His chin brushes my hair.

"And there's Ursa Major. The Big Dipper."

I can feel his attention fix on me. "Who taught you that?"

"My sister. During… bad nights" I answer, in a funny-but-not-funny reversal of our conversation about the fire and his mother. "When my mom and dad were fighting a lot, we'd sneak out on the roof to stargaze. It was New York, so, y'know—not much in the way of stars. Mostly satellites and airplanes. But she'd make up constellations. And some nights—rare nights—we really could see stars."

His arms tighten. Silence stretches, swollen.

I'm half-naked against his chest, bearing my soul in the middle of the dark, deserted wilderness. Vulnerable in a way that's more terrifying than the storm.

"Tell me something real," I say suddenly. Whatever game this is, I'm losing. Badly. I need to even the score.

He stills. "Like what?"

"I don't know. Just, like, a secret. A memory. Something you've never told anyone."

The wind howls. Just when I think he'll shut me out, he speaks. "When I was twelve, my father locked me in a freezer for talking back." His voice is detached. Borderline lifeless. "Told me I could come out when I stopped crying."

My chest cracks. "Sasha..."

"I told you about the first time I killed a man. The smuggler in the alley. The jammed gun, the broken bottle. What I didn't tell you is that I threw up afterward. In an alley behind a kebab shop."

"Why are you telling me this?"

"You asked."

"But why *these* things?"

He's quiet so long, I'm sure that this time he really won't answer. Then—

"So that tomorrow, when you look at me again, you'll remember what I really am. Not the man who builds fires or holds you close to keep you warm. Not the man who lets you lead him on a wild goose chase up a mountain even when he knows that's exactly what you intended to do. I'm not that, Ariel. I'm something else."

I twist in his arms, searching his face. "What are you?"

"A monster."

The stars blur. "Sasha—"

"Sleep, Ariel." He tucks my head under his chin. "We're here 'til dawn."

I want to argue. To dissect every scar, every sin. To demand that he prove himself wrong. But his thumb strokes circles on my hip, and the fire's last sputtering embers paint him in gold. And suddenly, I'm a child again—terrified of the dark, clinging to the first warmth I've felt in years.

His breath evens.

His grip, though, never loosens.

And somewhere in the heart of the night, between the howl of coyotes and the rush of wind surging through the ravine, I realize the terrible, horrible, undeniable truth:

I don't want these ten days to end.

26

ARIEL

My list of *Do Not Do's* is growing worryingly long.

Do not dream of Sasha Ozerov.

Do not think of Sasha Ozerov.

For God's sake, do not even CONSIDER fantasizing about Sasha Ozerov. You'll summon him like Beetlejuice.

It's a good list. Very comprehensive.

Unfortunately, it's also useless.

Because all morning, ever since we tumbled down the mountain in the light of dawn and Sasha took me back to my apartment so I could hurriedly shower the cave dirt out of my hair and throw on a work outfit, thinking and dreaming and fantasizing about Sasha Ozerov is all I can do.

I stab at my laptop keys hard enough to crack the spacebar. *Focus, Ari. Work. Words. Journalism.* But all my brain is good for are ten-thousand word articles on the way his scar glowed ivory in the firelight, the broken-glass rasp of his voice saying "Sleep, *ptichka*."

I curse out loud as coffee sloshes over my "World's Okayest Reporter" mug. John's latest assignment—about a corgi who can skateboard—mocks me from the screen. My cursor blinks accusingly where I've typed "Sasha" instead of "Sparkie."

If Sparkie had been on that mountain this morning, he'd understand.

The descent was a blur of Sasha's grip steadying my waist, lifting me over tree roots, dawn breaking like an egg yolk over his stubbled jaw. He'd driven me home in silence, his Henley still draped over my shoulders. I'd wanted to fling it into the Hudson. Instead, it's now fermenting in my hamper, probably whispering treasonous things like, *Maybe some monsters have soft edges.*

Gina comes up beside me, snapping her gum. "You got beef with that corgi or something? You're staring at the screen like you're trying to put a hex on him."

"I'm—"

"Shut up!"

I blink at her. "Uh… pardon?"

"SOS," she hisses, jerking her chin toward the elevators. "Six o'clock. Code Red."

I turn slowly. I know what I'm going to see before I see it, but somehow, that does absolutely nothing to dampen the shock.

He's here.

Sasha Ozerov stands in the doorway of our grimy office, looking wildly out of place in a tailored charcoal suit, his scarred hands tucked casually in his pockets.

Every head in the room swivels toward him—editors pause mid-sip, interns drop highlighters, the sports guy chokes on his breakfast burrito.

What is he doing here? I mouth at Gina, panic rising.

She shrugs, eyes wide. "Dude's like a STD—shows up uninvited and ruins your week."

My first hope is that I can burrow beneath my desk like a meerkat and he'll leave me alone. But when I see motion in Editor John's office and realize just how bad it would be if Sasha nonchalantly asked my boss where he could find me, I bolt up and practically sprint towards him.

"You—!" I jab a finger at Sasha, then at the fire escape. "Out. *Now.*"

He raises an eyebrow, scanning the yellowed press clippings on the walls and the half-dead ficus by the copier. "Charming place you've got here. I—"

"Not. Another. Word."

I drag him by the elbow out onto the little fire escape landing. I'm mad, flushed, terrified, a million emotions all at once.

I whirl on him the door clangs shut. "Do you have any idea what happens when the *pakhan* of the Ozerov Bratva waltzes into a *newspaper office?*"

"They offer me coffee?" He leans against the concrete wall, all lazy, predatory confidence. "It was terrible, by the way. Tasted like motor oil."

"This isn't funny! I have a *career* here. A life that doesn't involve—" I gesture wildly at his entire existence.

"Criminal conspiracies? Midnight fireside chats? Me?" His mouth quirks. "Face it, *ptichka*. You're stuck with all three."

I press my palms to my eyelids. "I don't know why I bother. Just… God, make me understand. Why are you here?"

"You missed our morning check-in call."

"We don't *have* check-in calls!"

"We do now." He plucks a stray Post-It from my hair—a grocery list reading ***eggs, milk, self-respect***—and tucks it into his breast pocket. "Hungry?"

"I'd rather eat my laptop."

"Good. I know a place."

Fifteen minutes later, I'm squished beside Sasha on a splintered park bench, forcing a smile back at the street vendor who just handed him two dripping hot dogs.

"This is kidnapping," I mutter, watching him scrutinize the toxic green relish like it might be poison. "Not to mention terrible for my productivity. I have deadlines, you know? Actual journalism to do."

"Your editor assigned you a story about…" He squints at the mustard smeared on his thumb. "Canine athletes, was it?"

"It's a human interest piece!"

"It's a waste of your talent." He takes an experimental bite, pauses, then devours the rest in three brutal chomps. "Not bad."

I blink. "Have you… never had a hot dog before?"

"I don't normally eat food that touches pavement."

"It's *street meat*, Sasha. A New York rite of passage." I snatch the untouched second hot dog from his hand, biting off the tip with relish. Literally. "What'd you survive on as a kid? Caviar and death threats?"

"Vodka, mostly. Bullet casings. The occasional rat."

"Part of me doesn't think you're joking."

"Part of you might be right. But I'd believe in the joke if I were you—the reality is far uglier."

He says it like he's commenting on the weather—*cloudy with a chance of childhood trauma*. I stare at the half-eaten hot dog in my hand, suddenly nauseous.

"Hey." His knuckle brushes my wrist. "Eat. You're shaking."

"I'm contemplating."

"You're hypoglycemic." He nudges the food toward my lips. "Eat, or I'll force-feed you."

"Speaking of adjectives, you're insufferable."

"And you're stalling. Which is a verb, but true nonetheless."

I take a grudging bite. The pop of the mustard, the tang of onions—it's stupidly comforting. Sasha watches me chew with unsettling focus, like he's memorizing the way my jaw moves.

"What?" I lick ketchup from my lip.

"Nothing." He looks away, throat bobbing. "Doesn't matter."

Central Park unfurls around us, all golden-hour light and scampering squirrels. I'm suddenly antsy. You'd think that yesterday's hike debacle would've put me off of "walking" forever, but the thought of staying marooned on this park bench with Sasha is way too cutesy and anxiety-inducing for me.

"Walk?" I ask.

Sasha shrugs. "Sure."

We rise, toss our garbage, and fall into step on the winding path, our shadows stretching long and tangled ahead.

"This isn't a date," I announce to a passing poodle. "Just so you know. So everybody knows."

Sasha hums. "If it were, I'd have bought you better shoes."

I glance down at my scuffed ballet flats. "These are my daily drivers."

"They're falling apart."

"So's my will to live, but here we are."

His laugh is low and surprised. The sound does something dangerous to my ribcage. I start resolutely counting to one thousand in my head so it doesn't fill up with steam room thoughts instead.

We pass a busker playing Sinatra on a dented saxophone. Sasha tosses a hundred-dollar bill into his case without breaking stride.

"Showoff," I mutter.

"I prefer 'generous philanthropist.'"

"Funny. I'd default to 'dangerous sociopath.'"

He stops abruptly, turning to face me. "And yet you're not afraid of me."

It's not really a question. Nor is it wrong.

I lift my chin. "Should I be?"

"Most people are."

"Well, I'm not."

"Why?"

The truth sits sharp on my tongue: *Because I've seen you tender. Because Zoya said you carry lilies to your mother's grave. Because when you laugh the way you just did a moment ago, I forget to hate you.*

Obviously, me being the emotional coward that I am, I deflect. "Because you're secretly a Disney prince—a real softie, with a cupcake for a heart. I bet you have a song about repressed emotions and everything."

He steps closer. Our shoes nearly touch. "Is that what you fantasize about? Me serenading you with my feelings?"

My pulse thrums. "I don't fantasize about you."

Liar.

Dirty, rotten liar.

Liar liar pants on fire.

Didn't he warn you not to fib in front of him?

His gaze drops to my mouth as if he knows exactly what I'm thinking. "Pity. Wish I could say the same about you."

Oh, for the love of God. Why did he have to go and say something like that? Now, all I want to do, all I'm dying *to do, is ask him to tell me exactly what he dreams of. Is it me? The office? The spa? The gala bathroom? Something else, something new, something better, something worse? Is it wholesome or depraved? Is he in charge or am I? Does it end with fireworks, or does it end with one of us whimpering,* Please, don't leave me like this. Don't let me—

A group of joggers swerve around us, breaking the spell. I whirl away, hug myself, and start my count back over from zero. "We should head back."

"Why?"

"Because I shouldn't be here."

"Why?"

Because even that one word is enough to chip away at my resolve.

"Because this?" I explode as I gesture wildly between us. "This bullshit, this facade? It's not real! I mean, who are we kidding, Sasha? We all know what's happening here. Or at least, what's going to happen. You'll marry me, dismantle my father's empire, and toss me aside like yesterday's news. That's the deal, right? That's what I'm signing up for? At least have the balls to say it to my face."

His eyes cloud over. I wonder if I've gone too far.

"You think I want this?" His voice is gravel.

"I think you want *control*."

"And you?" He crowds me against a lamppost, ignoring the tourists snapping photos of Bow Bridge. "What do *you* want, Ariel?"

The words claw up my throat: *I want to un-know you. I want to stop wondering how your scars would feel under my lips. I want to stop pretending this is all a game, because if it is, I can't tell whether I'm winning or losing.*

"I want to go home," I whisper.

For one terrifying second, I think he'll kiss me. Instead, he steps back, jaw clenched. "As you wish."

The walk to the park exit is silent. My chest aches like I've swallowed broken glass. At the curb, his driver waits, engine purring.

Sasha opens the door. "I'll have Klaus take you—"

"I'll catch the subway."

"Ariel—"

"This wasn't a date," I say again, desperate to believe it.

He studies me—the smudged eyeliner, the mustard stain on my sleeve, the way I'm brandishing my purse in front of me like a shield.

"No," he agrees quietly. "It wasn't."

He gets in and shuts the door. The town car pulls away, leaving me watching taillights blur into crosstown traffic, until the hot dog in my stomach sours and the last of the sunlight dies.

27

ARIEL

"Riri! Over here!"

I rush across the road a split second before the light turns red. A car honks at me, but I don't even flip the driver off—that's how giddy I feel.

Because today, I finally get to see her.

"Mama!"

She hugs me tight, making me wobble from side to side. "My baby girl! It's been ages!"

One thing about Belle Ward that most people don't seem to clock until it's too late: she has a grip of steel. "Ow, ow, ow. Ribs alert."

"Sorry." She pulls away, her hands still firmly on my arms, that *Let-me-take-a-look-at-you* pose that parents do best. "God, you're so beautiful."

"You say that every time."

"Because it's true every time."

"That's just your rose-colored Mom Glasses talking."

She shakes her head, her smile as bright as summer. "Now, don't play coy. It's also your hair up in a— Hm, I know those braids. Dead giveaway. You heading to a date after this? Or coming from one?"

I blush. No matter what, her radar never fails. "It's not a date. It's…" *A date. Tell it like it is, Ariel. You can't sell bullshit to the woman who made you—she'll smell it a mile away.*

I try anyway. "The latter. Sort of. Not really."

"Mhmm. With a man?"

I stay silent.

"Just you and him?"

I stay silent some more.

"This isn't a trial, Riri. You can't plead the Fifth."

"I can try."

"Fine." She feigns indifference, her nose turned up to the skies. "We won't talk about your hot hunk of a boyfriend."

"Wait—how do you know he's a hunk?"

She smirks. "So he is a hunk! And hot! And your boyfriend!"

Fuck me. Played right into her hands. "He's not my *boyfriend,*" I grumble, ashamed of how easily I folded. "He's… something."

She nods sagely. "Great. Shall we toast to your 'something,' then? Perhaps with a nice cone of Pistachio Chocolate Dream?"

I close my eyes. I can already taste it—that milky, sugary perfection. "Fine, but only if you're treating."

"Of course. You're still being paid in leprechaun gold, aren't you?"

"Ouch, Mother. At least rub Sea Salt Caramel into that wound."

Laughing, she loops her arm through mine and we hit up the ice cream shop on the corner. Once we've got our cones of shame—four scoops and whipped cream, as if metabolism is just a river in Egypt—we head to the park. There's a family of ducks whose shenanigans we've been following religiously, and I'm starving for updates.

Also, for quality time with my mom.

We haven't had much of that since she left fifteen years ago, one week after Jasmine did. I saw her on weekends, sure, but it was never quite the same. Those first few months after the separation, I'd catch myself going to her room to ask her opinion about a dress, or help with homework.

Every time, I found it empty.

Every time, I bawled my eyes out.

Which is why, since then, I've been determined to make this work. No—*we* are. Mama wasn't any happier to be separated from me, and we quickly decided that, if we had to have less time together, we'd make every moment we *did* have count. In ways big and small. It's just my luck that today's regularly scheduled reunion is coming right on the heels of that definitely-not-a-date with Sasha.

"So," I start. "What's Quill Quackdashian been up to?"

"Oh, you have no idea. Last week, she took little Quortney for a swim around the islet. The poor baby kept falling over herself, it was so adorable. Total cuteness overload."

I palm my forehead. "Mom, that hasn't been a thing since, like, 2013."

"Well, I'm making it a thing again." She whips her hair and harrumphs. "Like 'epic fail.'"

"And *that* hasn't seen the light of day since the Financial Crisis."

"What can I say? I'm an old soul."

I shake my head, unable to suppress my laughter. The fact that Belle had me so early means all the memes of my childhood were also the memes of her late twenties to mid-thirties. Everything that's corny for me is still totally hip for her—including the word "hip."

"You're a very young soul, Mama."

"By all means, keep complimenting me. But it won't get you out of talking about your boyfriend. Or 'hunk,' as you so eloquently put it."

"*You're* the one who called him that."

"I was fishing, dear. And of course you'd land a hunk—you're my daughter." Her eyes dart to the lake. "Oh! Look! There's Quendall!"

We find a bench to sit on while we duck-watch. I'd never say it out loud, but I've missed this. Even though it hasn't really been that long. But I guess I'm still making up for lost time.

It's funny to see her like this, though: free and proud and utterly unfazed by how cruel life has been to her. A marriage ruined, one daughter gone, another in quasi-hiding—none of it has dimmed Belle Ward's shine. She's my hero, honestly.

"Wow. Look at her go," I remark.

"Right? Quortney can't swim for shit, but Quendall's a natural."

I scour the reeds, looking for the rest of the family. "Where's Quanye?"

"Who knows? Haven't seen him since the last time we were here together."

"Probably on tour, then."

"Probably." She turns her gaze back to me. "God, you really do look incredible. It's like you're glowing."

"I'm pregnant, actually."

She gives me a panicked look over before she thwacks my knee. "Oh, shut up. I almost believed you."

Then her eyes turn serious. "So, this hunk. Would he be this fake baby's daddy? Am I going to have to beat him up?"

"Mom!"

"It was just a question. Don't get all defensive." She squints at me. "You won't tell me anything voluntarily. Mama Bear's got no choice but to pull out her claws."

I roll my eyes. "There's nothing to spill. We're just… seeing where it goes." Which is a hell of a euphemism for *I'm trying to ditch him but he's trying to marry me and oh, by the way, it's all your ex-husband's fault.*

But I'm a journalist. I was taught to simplify.

"Is that code for 'fuck buddies'?"

I spit my ice cream through my nose. "Oh my God, Mom!"

"What? It's a fair question." She takes another bite of her cone. "Courtship rituals change with every generation. It's perfectly normal."

I sigh, slumping hard against the bench. "We're not 'fuck buddies.' We're more like..." I bury my face in my hands. "Why am I even telling you this?"

"Because I'm your mom and I'm awesome. Now, don't stop. You're more like...?"

I groan. This is all kinds of embarrassing. It's like I'm suddenly fourteen again and enduring the third degree about Nate from gym class. "We're just... circling."

"'Circling,'" she repeats.

"Yeah. Like, you know, vultures or something."

"That's awfully unromantic."

"You know what I mean."

"I assure you I do not."

"That's easy for you to say," I remind her acidly. "You got married within a year of dreamy courtship. Dad rented a white horse for the wedding, even though you were both broke. You're basically a fairy tale in a cocktail dress."

She shrugs. "I wouldn't have married for anything less. Even if it didn't give me a happily ever after, that doesn't mean it wasn't worth trying for. Love is always a leap."

My heart tugs at that. Of all people, Mom deserved that more than anyone: a fairy tale ending. I can't think of a single person who's more romantic than her, or who believes in True Love—capital T *and* L—with the same fervor. If my dream is to become a top notch reporter, hers has always been to be whisked away in a carriage with doves pulling the reins. To experience a romance for the ages, no matter the obstacles.

But Baba didn't give her that. He didn't make her a princess —he made her an empress. To an empire of shadows and darkness she knew nothing of and wanted no part in.

She tried to adjust. She really did. But tigers can't change their stripes, and people can't change their dreams.

Not even for the sake of someone they love.

"Honey, what's wrong?" Like always, Mom reads my mood shift immediately. "Is it something I said?"

"No, Mama, I—"

"You know I don't resent your father. It's all water under the bridge. And besides, he gave me you. That's the most important thing."

I shake my head and smile. It's a little bit sad, a little bit sweet, but that's our entire relationship in a nutshell. With our history, it's all we can do to focus on the good while leaving the bad in a dusty old box labeled *The Past — Do Not Open.*

"I just... I don't know if he's a good person. This hunk. I mean, he's good to me, but he's like..." I trail off, unable to finish that sentence.

"Like your father?"

"Please don't say it like that. It makes it sound so Freudian."

A cheeky smile plays on her lips. "You know, the problem with our marriage wasn't your father's... ahem, *activities.* It was that I didn't know about them. He kept it all a secret for so long that I just watched him change without knowing why. And he got to make that choice, but I didn't. If he'd discussed his plans with me, if he'd told me sooner... Who knows?"

Who knows? It's the biggest "What If" of my life: what if Dad had been honest? What if he'd made Mom a part of his world before his world consumed him?

Or what if he'd left it all behind? What if he'd given it up to work alongside her in that little hole-in-the-wall Greek restaurant she waitressed at? What if, eventually, he managed to buy it? What if they'd lived out a modest, happy life behind that counter?

How would our story have ended then? How would Jasmine's have ended?

But there's no answer. And the story isn't over yet, not quite. Despite everything, I know Mom still cares deeply for Dad. I know Dad feels the same. I hold no illusions, but who knows? With time, maybe...

Maybe your broken home might finally be mended.

Maybe your mom would get her happy ending.

And maybe your dad would remember what it was like to love you like a daughter instead of an asset.

That's why I can't tell her, even if it breaks my heart to lie to her. If Mama knew Baba was behind this, that he auctioned off my hand behind my back and threatened me into going along with it, she wouldn't stand for it. She'd get involved and she'd be fierce about it.

I can't let her do that. I can't let her burn that bridge for good.

And I definitely can't let her near any mafia business ever again. Not when she's been sober from the stuff for fifteen years straight.

"So what are you saying?" I slump, my gaze moving to the lake. The Quackdashian family is whole and well, teaching their ducklings to swim before the weather grows too cold. "If I know all the dirty details, then it's okay?"

"I'm saying there are no wrong choices, dear. Only different ones."

I glance up at the sky. Clouds are gathering fast, smooth and white and endless. This year, we might get a White Christmas yet.

And before then, I'll have to make my choice.

28

SASHA

Blood pools around this dead man's head like a macabre halo, seeping into the cracks of the concrete floor. To be frank, this ritual is getting a bit tiresome.

How many times am I going to stand over another dead Serbian until Dragan gets the message that this city is undeniably mine now? How many moles will I have to whack before the lesson is learned?

I toss down the tire iron I just used on him with a clatter. "Tell your boss this territory is mine," I snarl to the other man whimpering at my feet. His front teeth—what's left of them—glitter crimson in the dim light. "Next time he sends rats into my house, I'll mail your spines back in a jewelry box."

Feliks leans against the wall by the exit, chewing gum. "Ask him about the shipment."

I unbutton my ruined sleeves, rolling them past ink-dark wolves snarling up my forearms. "Rhetorical, brother. He's got nothing left to say."

The man gurgles. One hand claws toward my boot.

I crush his fingers under my heel.

Sighing, I turn my back on the mess and step out into the night for a breath of fresh air. Feliks comes with me as other Bratva soldiers fill in to clean up what I left behind.

"Cigarette?"

I shake my head. "I'm good."

He does a double-take. "Who are you and what have you done with my best friend?"

I bark out a harsh laugh as I take a seat on an abandoned milk crate. "Fuck if I know, man. Nothing seems like it used to anymore."

"Uh-oh. Them's contemplative words. You know what happens when we go down that road."

He's not wrong, but goddammit, I just can't help it lately. My thoughts churn and twist and morph in ways they've never done before.

My phone vibrates. I'm embarrassed by how quickly I whip it out of my pocket to look.

It's not Ariel, though. It's Zoya, demanding I pick up the borscht she made me before it expires. In the six years she's lived above that restaurant, her fridge has never worked, but she refuses to let me replace it.

"It's the girl, eh?" Feliks chimes in. "Ms. Front Page herself."

Three hours ago, Feliks held open his phone to show me Ariel's latest column. Front page of the Gazette's Metro section: ***Cantonese Dumpling Carts Standing Ground in the Shadow of Gentrification.*** Next to her byline is a photo of her leaning against a food truck, ink-smudge hair spilling over the collar of that ridiculous puffy jacket.

"You've been mum on the subject," he presses when I don't respond. "The people demand updates. How's the Capital-R Romance going? She asking you for dick pics yet?"

I roll my eyes. "Someone should teach you the meaning of the word 'subtlety.'"

"Nahhh," he demurs. "Life's too short to beat around the bush. Besides, it falls to me to pry the truth out of you. God knows everyone else is too scared to do it. So, let's hear it."

"No."

"C'mon, Sasha. You're doing that thing again."

"What thing?"

"The Jasmine thing." He pulls up an adjacent crate and takes a seat facing me. "Brother, do you forget I was there fifteen years ago? I know what you did. I know what it cost you. And here you are, doing the same thing again. Locking your heart in that little box because you think love makes you weak. Trying to be brutal to make up for the guilt of being human."

Motherfucker. Feliks is doing that serious face of his. He's such a fucking goof all the time that it's all the more powerful in those rare moments when he chooses to get somber. Makes him hard to deny.

The streetlight above us flickers. Somewhere in Chinatown, a car alarm wails.

I sigh. "Who died and made you my therapist?"

"Sarcasm won't get you out of this one, I'm afraid," he says sympathetically. "But fine—suit yourself. If you don't wanna open up, then maybe I'll just swoop in and show Ariel how a real man—"

I'm on him in a fucking instant, shoving him against the brick. His shoulder blades crunch the crumbling mortar. "You don't look at her." My thumb digs into his windpipe. "You don't talk about her. You don't *breathe* near her. Understood?"

Feliks grins from ear-to-ear. "Y'know, for someone who allegedly doesn't care, you've sure got a hard-on for this charade."

I release him, scowling at how easily I took his bait. I should know better. I *do* know better. But when it comes to Ariel, I just… react.

He coughs, rubbing his neck. "Make it make sense, Sash. If this is just a power play…"

Thunder growls above us. It *is* just a power play. It has to be. I need this to get Leander's loyalty. No bride means no alliance. No alliance means no victory. No victory means I spend the rest of my life exterminating Serbian rats in various filthy warehouses, fighting a war of attrition that leaves everyone worse off in the end.

"You ever think…" Feliks unwraps a new stick of gum and pops it into his mouth. "What if it was real?"

"'Real' is overrated. My father taught me that."

"Cool story. But you're not Yakov." He lobs the gum pack at my chest. "What I'm saying is, what if you stopped sabotaging this thing? What if you let yourself want her instead of scheming ahead of time how to survive losing her?"

A foggy chill soaks through my shirt.

"Or does that scare you too much?"

I stare at the puddle spreading around my boots. For a minute, I'm twelve years old again, knees bleeding through my school uniform. Father's voice rasping in my ear like rusted barbed wire. *Crying's for bitches and orphans. You'll be both if you don't shut up.*

I crush a stray piece of trash under my heel. "You're getting sentimental in your old age, man."

"Says the *ssyklo*."

The warehouse door clangs open and the cleanup team shuffles out with a pair of body bags. We watch them load both into the black van idling at the curb, then clamber in and drive away.

Feliks braces his hands on his knees. "I'll say one more thing and then I'm done, I swear. Jasmine made her choice. You gave her that. You think you're honoring her memory by martyring yourself on this shit?"

I say nothing. At my throat, my scar burns.

"It's been fifteen years," he says. "Let. Her. Go."

When I close my eyes, I see Ariel licking mustard off her thumb in the park. Lips chapped from the cold. Snowflakes caught in her lashes.

I see other things, too. *Endgame*. Wedding bells. Her in white lace, trembling as I slide a gold band onto her finger. Pretending it's only for the cameras.

Then what? What happens five years from now? Ten? Does the war you're fighting stain the hem of that pretty white dress? Does she start looking at you with hate in her eyes instead of lust? Or worse —what if she looks at you with love *in her eyes? Think you can handle that burden, Aleksandr?*

Feliks stands, joints popping. "You deserve a life, brother. Not just an empire."

"She'll destroy me if I do that," I whisper under my breath. I don't mean to say it out loud, but it just slips out.

I brace for what Feliks might say. He could mock me, belittle me, echo the voices in my head that are already doing the same thing.

Instead, he claps a hand on my shoulder and grins. "Maybe she will. But what a way to die."

29

ARIEL

Fuck.

Now, what?

Hiking with Sasha was supposed to be the final nail in *his* coffin. Me as my worst self, schlepping through the woods in designer heels and a sequined crop top, bitching about bugs and blisters until he snapped—that was supposed to do the trick.

Instead, it turned into… whatever that was. Lost. Cold. Huddled in his arms, drenched in rain, wondering why I wasn't quite as miserable as I should've been.

And what's worse? When the stars came out, so did the truth serum. *Orion, Ursa Major, The Big Dipper*—it was like my sister was at my side again for the briefest of moments.

There was no sarcasm when I told him how Jas and I used to sit out on the roof while Mama and Baba screamed at each other one story below. No bite. No snark. Just… sharing.

Central Park undid me further. That was more of the same. Or rather, more of the not-same: No agenda. No posturing. Just mustard on his thumb and a shockingly normal laugh. For one stupid, sunlit hour, we weren't at each other's throats.

We were just… *us*.

And that terrifies me more than any arranged marriage.

Mama's advice didn't help. "*There are no wrong choices; only different ones*," she said, licking ice cream off her spoon. As if hearts aren't just overripe peaches, bruised or bursting at the slightest pressure. Hers led her straight into Leander's bear trap. Mine keeps flip-flopping between wanting to shove Sasha off a cliff and wanting to shove him against the nearest flat surface.

I'm a reporter. I hunt truths for a living. So why can't I pin down the truth of him? Is he the monster he swears he is, or the man he seems to be when he thinks I'm not looking? Does he pluck lilies or break fingers?

Do I loathe him?

Or do I—God, I can't believe the words are even in my head right now—do I see a way I could one day *love* him?

But then I remember what happened to the women of my family. If I let Sasha in, will I end up a cautionary footnote, too? Will I be Jasmine—a ghost in the wind, a chalk outline where my sister should be? Will I become my mother, painting on a smile as the walls close in?

I'm not sure which scares me more: a lifetime bound to him… or a lifetime without this dizzying, dangerous high.

Today's date invite was as cryptic as the rest of them have been. A courier showed up at *The Gazette* offices with—get this—not a flower, but a fire-charred stick with a single leaf at the end. He handed me a note to go with it.

A memento from the mountain. Meet me at the New York Public Library. 7 PM.

Leave the glitter at home.

—Sasha

I knew, even as I left work early to go home and change, that it was a bad idea. I should've sent the courier back with a message that said, ***Shove this stick up your you-know-what.***

But I didn't.

Now, I'm here and Patience and Fortitude are judging me. The stone lions have seen a century of New Yorker's mistakes and regrets, but they seem to sigh as I climb the library steps.

Really? their frozen snarls say. *You're gonna make us watch you pretend to do this whole charade* again?

Speaking of judgmental faces, Sasha is leaning against a pillar, all black coat and sharp cheekbones. He's scrolling through his phone, but when he spots me, he slips the device into his pocket. His eyes do that thing—the slow drag from my scuffed Docs up to the messy topknot I spent twenty minutes making look careless.

"You're—"

"Late. Yes, I know. We do this song and dance every time. I am not a punctual person. You will have to get used to it."

A sudden breeze screams down the sidewalk. Acting on pure instinct—or maybe it's muscle memory from our sleepover on Mt. Regret—I step into Sasha to hide from the chill.

As if his body remembers too, he encircles me with both arms and plasters my cheek to his chest.

The wind passes.

One awkward millisecond later, we spring apart.

"It's December in New York," he says with a scowl as he surveys my outfit. "You didn't think a coat was appropriate?"

"That's rich coming from Mr. Funeral-Chic himself. Do you own anything that doesn't scream *'moody vampire'*?"

The corner of his mouth ticks up. But instead of more of his trademark withering condescension, he reaches out to pluck a stray eyelash from my cheek, holding it on his fingertip. "Make a wish."

I think for a second, then I blow it away. "Too late," I lie. "My wish lists are tapped out."

"Hm." His eyes rake over me in a way that makes me feel colder than any Manhattan winter breeze ever could. "Unfortunate. Because mine just came true."

Heat spreads through me, treacherous and sweet. I swat his hand away from my face. "How many women fall for that line?"

"None. You're my first. Feeling special yet?"

"Especially annoyed, maybe. But beyond that, it's just a cold, dead void where my heart should be."

I roll my eyes and turn my back on him to march up the

stairs, leaving Sasha in my rearview mirror, where he can't see the way my cheeks are burning red.

I step through the front doors and breathe in the sacred scent of old paper and lemon polish, a goofy smile spreading across my face.

God, I love this place. The vaulted ceilings, the golden light leaking through arched windows, the way every whispering footstep against the stone floors sounds like a secret being kept. Mama used to bring me and Jas here sometimes on rainy Sunday afternoons. We'd play for hours, reading and chasing each other up and down the reference aisles where it was quiet and no one minded two little girls being little girls for a while.

I miss those days.

I peek back at Sasha. He's doing the same thing I am: gazing up at the roof arching overhead, at the stacks of books running endlessly into the distance. He looks like he loves this place every bit as much as I do.

Which is exactly why I have to ruin it for him.

"So!" I spin around, nearly clotheslining a grad student carrying a teetering stack of Proust. "What's on today's agenda? You gonna show me the rare books collection? Read me sonnets by candlelight? Ooh, maybe we can play footsie under the—"

He grabs my elbow, steering me toward a spiral staircase. "You talk too much."

"Is this a preview of our marriage?" I muse sarcastically, just loud enough for a pair of old ladies shuffling by us to peer over in concern. "You dragging me hither and thither and telling me that women should be seen, not heard?"

"Christ, you're in rare form today," he mutters. "I'm trying to do a nice thing."

Sasha Ozerov and *nice things*—well, if that doesn't terrify me, nothing ever will. I suppress a head-to-toe shiver and silently repeat the only mantra that's going to get me through this fraudulent "date."

Remember to hate him.

I have to keep my eyes on the prize. I have to hate him. I have to chase him away so he doesn't sink his claws into my heart in a way that I can't undo.

I need to stick to the plan: be annoying, be unbearable, be unlovable.

Because Sasha Ozerov loving me might be the worst thing he could possibly do.

I yank free of his grasp and pull out my phone. "Hold on, I need to document this travesty for the 'Gram."

I snap a shameless selfie with the Murder Death Kill-Bot 3000 lurking in the background, making sure to frame his scowl nicely in the corner of the frame. Caption: ***When your arranged fiancé takes you to a library like he's not functionally illiterate. #mobwifelife #sendhelp***

"Ariel."

"Shh, I'm curating my existential crisis." I angle the camera lower, pouting. "Do I look more 'damsel in distress' or 'future corpse in a true crime podcast' here? It's a hard balance to strike."

But right as I'm about to snap the shot, the phone vanishes from my hand.

"Hey—!"

I turn just in time to see Sasha tuck it into his inner coat pocket. "When you're with me," he snarls, "you're *with* me."

A shiver rolls through me. I cover it with an eye-roll. "Wow, did you get that line from a Nineties rom-com? *You've Got Mail* called—it wants its toxic masculinity back."

He crowds me against a shelf labeled ***19th-Century Russian Literature***. Leather-bound Tolstoy digs into my spine as his breath tickles my ear.

For one terrifying, exhilarating second, I think he'll kiss me. Here. Now. In front of a wheezing librarian re-shelving books.

Instead, he reaches over my shoulder to pluck *Anna Karenina* off the shelf and hands it to me. "Read."

"Excuse me?"

"Page 763. Second paragraph." When I gape at him, he adds, "Unless you need me to sound out the big words for you."

"Asshole." But my skin is still flushed from *When you're with me, you're* with *me.* As much as I mocked it, something about that line *did* something to me.

I really would like to not inquire further as to why that is. I get the feeling it'll stir up a lot of stuff that's best left dormant.

So, grumbling, I flip to the page and start to read. My voice comes out shaky at first. *"'He stepped down, trying not to look long at her, as if she were the sun…'"*

Sasha leans in, rumbling the next line from memory. *"'… But he saw her, like the sun, even without looking.'"*

My throat goes dry. The air between us crackles, charged with something deeper than lust.

Something that tastes an awful lot like vulnerability.

He takes the book back, fingers brushing mine. They stroke down the spine like a lover. "My mother read this to me when I was seven. Only way she could get me to sit still."

The unprompted mention of his mom takes me off-guard. Historically speaking, that kind of thing has only come out under extreme duress and cover of darkness, and even then, he's reluctant to add details.

But now that I look closer, there's something… off about him today. Like he forgot to close a door in his personality. There's a softness… a way in.

I gulp. "Did it work? Did you sit still?"

He nods as he stares into the distance. "Yeah. For every word. I cried when Vronsky's horse died." A shadow passes over his face. "Then my father saw me doing it and he beat me until I stopped. After that, I didn't cry anymore."

I'm dumbstruck. But maybe that's a good thing. Some words aren't meant to be followed up by other words. How could they be? How can I respond to that? What could I possibly say that won't scare him off or shut him down—or worse, open up a matching can of worms in me?

I mean, I could tell him how quiet it was without Mama and Jasmine in my world. How hard was it to sit still without Mama's stories? How many tears did I shed?

And what did my own dad tell me when he caught me sobbing? *Stop crying, Ariana. Tears won't bring anyone back.*

If I don't know what to do with those memories of my own, I sure as hell don't know what to do with Sasha's. Or with this version of him, the one who knows Tolstoy by heart and mourns horses that only ever existed as words on a page. The one who lets the cracks in his armor show in front of the woman who's determined to shove him away.

I don't know. I don't know anything.

So I do what I've always done when faced with hard matters of the heart.

Deflect.

"Ah, I'm starting to see the full picture." I gesture to his entire... *everything*. "The brooding mobster thing is just daddy issues."

He snaps the book shut. "Careful."

"Or what? You'll have me whacked?" I push off the shelves, channeling Gina's most obnoxious Basic Becky voice and despising myself even as I do. "*Omigawd,* does that mean I get some of those cute concrete shoes? TikTok would *die*."

"You'll need better material if you want to scare me off." He starts walking, tossing words over his shoulder. "Though I'm curious—what's your master plan? Annoy me to death with pop culture references?"

"It's working so far!" I trot to keep up as he leads me into a secluded alcove. "... Right?"

He stops so abruptly that I run right into him. "I'm still here, aren't I?"

I frown as I step away, the smell of him swirling deep in my nose and brain. "Yes, you are. Unfortunately, so am... Wait, where are we?"

Sasha pushes open a heavy oak door with the library's seal carved into its center and ushers me inward.

I make it two steps before I freeze in my tracks.

I feel like I'm seeing something so beautiful it should be forbidden. Too many eyes on something this pretty would ruin it, as if every stare takes something away from the things it sees.

Golden afternoon light filters through leaded glass windows, catching dust motes in a slow waltz. As far as the eye can see, towering mahogany shelves stretch toward a coffered ceiling painted midnight blue, with constellations picked out in gold leaf. Velvet ropes cordon off cases displaying illuminated manuscripts—pages so delicate they look like they'll dissolve if I breathe too close.

I say nothing.

It's the kind of space that demands silence.

My fingertips ghost along the glass edge of a case containing a gorgeously gilded psalter. "How did you even…?"

"Patronage has its perks," Sasha says simply, lingering near the doorway.

I'm still not sure what to say. How did he know? Those memories of Mama and Jas, of running up and down the bookshelves and laughing… they're not the kinds of things I blab about casually. Like this room, I'm afraid that sharing them too loudly or too widely would make them crumble away.

So how the fuck did he know this would move me?

I turn and gawk at him. Hands shoved modestly in his

pockets, he meanders over to the study table in the center of the room, pulls out an upholstered chair, and sinks into it.

"Take all the time you'd like," he says. "Cry if you want, laugh, sing—it's ours for the evening."

Tears prickle in my eyes. Sasha watches me, silent. He doesn't smirk or prod. Just lets me feel the moment having its way with me.

And for as long as that moment lasts, I submit to it. I let the illusion shimmer: us as ordinary people, him as someone capable of tenderness.

Then I rip away and stride down the nearest set of stacks.

This is how monsters trap you, Ariel. Not with threats, but with the lethal poison of being seen.

I skitter my fingers down the spine of one book after the next, letting my heart rate even out. When I'm ready, I call over the shelves, "I never took you for such a bookworm romantic, Sasha. Next thing I know, you'll be throwing rocks at my window and reciting Rumi from memory."

"Would that work?"

"On a woman with weaker knees? Maybe. On me? I'd throw the rocks back at you."

Sasha laughs, then falls quiet. I keep wandering down the aisle. Something in me wants to touch all the books that aren't locked away behind display cages.

Stories have souls, Mama used to say. I want to feel every one pulsing beneath my fingertips.

The stained glass above us fractures the evening sunlight into jewel tones. As minutes pass and it dwindles, I become aware of a presence following me, though he stays one row away.

Until he doesn't.

I turn a corner and he's there, leaning against the shelves, eyeing me thoughtfully. He's abandoned his coat and cuffed his sleeves to the elbow, so I can see tattooed forearms folded across his chest.

"Your mother brought you here," he murmurs.

I whirl towards him. "How did you— Did my father tell you that?"

He doesn't even dodge the question, just ignores it entirely. Like I never said a word. "Have you ever thought about it? Being a parent?"

My heartbeat thuds in my chest. The way he says it implies… "Do I need to?"

Sasha doesn't answer for a few long breaths. When I turn back, he's still looking at me, as if to say, *You know you do.*

I start to sweat and stammer. "Th-that wasn't p-part of the…"

"Come on, Ariel. You know better than that. You know how these things work."

I clutch the nearest shelf for support, because my knees suddenly feel a little untrustworthy. "Just to be clear, you're talking about…?"

"You'll bear me an heir within the first two years. It's in the fine print, *ptichka.* Your father agreed."

I wheeze a deranged-sounding laugh.

"But I didn't. I recall signing exactly zero demonic pacts lately." My laugh comes shriller than intended. "What's next? Swear a blood oath at the altar? Brand me with your initials?"

Sasha reaches for me, but I lunge backward so his hand swipes through empty air. "Don't be dramatic. It's simple logistics. Leander needs heirs. So do I. It's in the contract."

With a mind of its own, my hand drifts to my stomach. I yank it away. "You're insane if you think I'm incubating your little crime lordlets."

"It's in the contract, Ariel."

Heat creeps up my neck. "Oh, please," I scoff. "Like you're not just making up all the rules as you go."

He steps into my space. "The contract stipulates—"

"Fuck your fucking contract, Sasha!"

The shout echoes, double-time, triple-time, until the ceiling finally swallows it without a trace.

Lowering my voice, I jab his chest. "You want a prop wife? Fine. But my uterus is a goddamn democracy. *I* decide whose babies I have. Not you. Not anyone else."

His gaze drops to my lips. "Careful. You're starting to sound like you're considering it."

I am.

That's the fucking problem.

His thumb brushes my inner wrist—chaste and yet devastating. Because inside, my mind is doing the devil's work in making this all sound so unbelievably *reasonable.*

It conjures forbidden images: Sasha's scarred hands cradling a swaddled newborn. Him bringing me coffee at 3 A.M. feedings. A triple chorus of laughter—him, me, and something that's a little bit of both of us—ringing loud in a backyard that doesn't reek of blood money.

Horror blooms under my ribs. "You're disgusting," I whisper.

He doesn't deny it. Nor does he look away. His eyes are sapphire blue in the gloom. "I told you a long time ago what I am, Ariel."

A monster. He said it. Multiple times. But no matter how hard I squint, the man in front of him does not match that description.

I see it then, the same thing I thought I saw earlier. That softness, that light, that way in. It's joined by something else, too: a flicker of want in his eyes that matches my own.

It's not just lust. It's deeper than that. Dumber.

Far more dangerous.

I twist free, fleeing toward the exit. Three steps. Five. Then my traitor feet stall and I come to a halt.

Sasha's reflection looms in the glass of the nearest display. A copy of the *Kama Sutra,* funny enough. The world's oldest babymaking how-to guide. "Ariel—"

"How are you even considering this? The things you've done…" My throat bobs. "The people you've hurt. And you want to bring a child into that?"

He sighs wearily. "Imagine how safe they'd be. Protected by both our families' reach."

My fingers curl. Fifteen years ago, Jas sat on our roof and said, *Baba wants me to marry. He says I have no choice.* Six weeks later, she was gone.

Now, Sasha stands here talking about *safety.* Where was he when she needed protecting? How can he say those words now?

His shadow blankets me. "You're afraid. I get that."

"Don't tell me what I am."

"You're wondering how this could possibly work."

"I said, don't tell me—"

"But you're hopeful, too, and that's maybe the worst thing you could be, because hope is the deepest cut and the slow bleed that would follow if you let it slice you open is what terrifies you most of all."

I shove back against his chest as he approaches me, but it's like pushing a brick wall. He comes closer instead of farther. I can't back up, either; I'm just pinned against a glass cage as Sasha looks down at me with the scariest light of all in his eyes: hope bright enough to match mine.

He cradles my face in his hands. "I didn't bring you here to frighten you, *ptichka.* I brought you here to show you it doesn't have to hurt."

"What doesn't?"

"Falling."

Then his mouth crashes into mine. It's not claiming; it's *erasing.* Rewriting every awkward fumble, every indifferent, unsatisfying blunder of my past and replacing it all with him,

him, him. His teeth catch my lip, pulling a ragged sound from my chest as his hands bracket my hips—anchoring me against history itself.

His kiss says, *Let me be the villain you deserve.*

My kiss replies, *Never.*

30

SASHA

The Beretta 92 clicks empty in my palm as I fire the last bullet. Five shots ripple through the abandoned warehouse—five targets meet their untimely demise.

I lower the gun to check my work. Not bad. Center mass on each silhouette.

Feliks whistles as the last shell casing clinks to concrete. "Not bad, *brattan*. You shoot like a man who's getting laid regularly."

I eject the magazine harder than necessary. "Impossible. Your mother moved to Miami."

He laughs, tossing me fresh ammo. "You wish you were that lucky. Mama Vasiliev would eat you alive." Slouching against the wall of the shooting stall, he squints at me. "But seriously, you've got that post-coital glow. Library date went well, *da?*"

I take my time loading in the new clip, racking a bullet into the chamber, squinting down the sight to check the alignment. The whole time, I do my damndest to ignore the thoughts crowding in my head.

Ariel's mouth going pliant under mine.

Her nails digging desperate half-moons into my shoulders.

Falling, I'd called it.

Bullshit.

This isn't normal gravity at work. This is getting sucked into a black hole.

"She's..." I look down the barrel, exhale, and fire. The target's head explodes. "... persistent."

Feliks snorts. "Persistent. Right. And Chernobyl was a minor electrical fire. Where do you two lovebirds go from here?"

"We're negotiating. Figuring things out."

"Ah, *negotiating.*" Feliks mimes jerking off to let me know what he thinks of that particular train of thought. "And then what? Holding hands in Central Park? Buying matching ***I <3 NY*** hoodies?"

I scowl at him, if only because the Central Park crack hits a little too close to home. "Do you know what happens to men who talk too much?"

"They get promoted to *pakhan*?"

"They get promoted to target practice."

Feliks just chuckles. He knows he's too valuable to kill. All I can do is scowl, give him the cold shoulder, and keep firing my feelings down-range.

Much to the dismay of my tattered paper targets, I burn through two more magazines before a text buzzes at my hip.

I holster the Beretta, already knowing it's her. She's been texting all day—photos of her work laptop, her lunch, a shot of her big toe mid-pedicure captioned ***Putting warpaint on.***

This time, it's an address in Queens. Followed by:

Change of plans tonight. Pick me up from my mom's place. 7 PM. Don't be late, Dracula.

P.S. If you're thinking of bringing flowers, I'd suggest bourbon instead. She's not a nun.

Feliks peers over my shoulder to snoop. "Uh-oh. Meeting Mama Makris? Better wear your good knuckle dusters."

"Shut up."

"Bring a fruit basket," he suggests. "Old ladies love pears. Shows you've got a sensitive side."

"I'll show you sensitivity." I shove the phone back in my pocket and nod at the mangled targets. "Clean this up. And tell the boys there's another shipment coming in tonight. I want the team ready to receive it."

He salutes with two fingers. "Aye-aye, Casanova."

From the outside, Belle Ward is no different than any of her neighbors. Her little house in Queens is quaint, small, humble. Bent gutter, stuffed with withered leaves. Bushes out front that have seen better days. It's all utterly forgettable.

I stand on the stoop at 6:58 P.M., adjusting my cuffs. I brought neither flowers nor bourbon. Just a Swiss Army knife in my pocket and the crushing sense that this is a terrible fucking idea.

Then the door creaks open, and Ariel's face appears in the gap.

"You're early," she says.

"You're filthy."

She swipes hair from her cheekbone, leaving a grease streak. "Mom's sink pipe burst last week. She just now told me. I've been telling her to let me fix the valve, but she's stubborn, and—"

I shoulder her out of the way and stride into the kitchen. Both of the cabinet doors beneath the sink have been propped open. When I kneel down, I see copper pipes gleaming dully under my phone's flashlight. The problem jumps out at me immediately.

"It's the gasket."

"How do you—*Ow!*"

She barely manages to catch the phone I tossed to her. Not my fault she's slow. "Hold the light."

For ten minutes, the only sounds are our breathing and the occasional curse as freezing water sprays my wrists.

Ariel's knee brushes my shoulder. "Why are you helping?"

"So you're not dripping sewage on my loafers."

"A gentleman as always," she mutters. She cranes her neck to check a clock on the far wall. "Hm. Weird. Mom was supposed to be back by now. She said she had to run to the grocery store."

The pipes groan as I twist the final coupling. "Try the water now."

She scrambles to turn on the faucet. After a brief belch, a healthy gush streams into her cupped hands. "Holy shit. You're like a Russian Bob Vila."

"Who?"

"He's a— Never mind." She hesitates. "Thanks, Sasha."

Before I can respond, the front door clicks.

"Ari? You still here? You didn't drown underneath the sink, did you? Goodness, the checkout aisle was—" Belle freezes, grocery bags dangling. Her eyes—which are Ariel's eyes, but weathered by older storms—dart between us.

Ariel steps forward. "Sasha, this is my mom. Mom, this is—"

"Ozerov." Belle sets the bags down slowly.

I wipe grease on my slacks before offering a hand. "Mrs. Makris."

"It's Ward." She ignores my hand and turns to her daughter instead. "Ari, the new lock on the basement door isn't latching. Could you…?"

Ariel throws me a warning look before vanishing down the hall.

Belle waits until her footsteps fade. Then she whirls on me.

"I know who you are." Her stare could flay skin.

"I assure you you don't." I lean against the wall, hands in my pockets, watching this five-foot nothing woman square up against a man who's killed hundreds without a drop of fear in her eyes.

I admire her fire. Makes sense that she's Ariel's mother.

"I know enough." Her knuckles whiten around her keys, as if she's considering gutting me with them. "More importantly, I know better, Mr. Ozerov. I've seen this before. The diamond cufflinks. The tailor-made charm. I *know* you."

The fraught tension in her face—that must be Leander's doing, as sure as the scars on my throat and back were left there by my father's hand. It ignites something in my chest that wishes it could reach back in time and erase this proud woman's suffering.

"I'm not here for anything like that, Ms. Ward. I promise."

Fuck me, what a funny thing to say. Just six days ago, that would've been a bold-faced lie. What is it now? A whole truth? Part of one? I don't know. Fucking hell, I just don't know.

Belle's eyes narrow. "You're good at this. Better than Leander ever was. You almost sound human when you lie."

I push off the wall. She doesn't flinch. "I don't lie."

"No? Then tell me why a man like you wants a life with her."

Because your ex-husband's shipping routes could end a war before it starts. That's the easy answer, the business answer. It dies in my throat.

Instead, I see Ari in the library—cheeks flushed, mouth bruised from mine, whispering, *This doesn't mean I like you* even as her body arched closer.

A twitch ripples through my left hand. I crush it against my thigh.

Belle catches the movement. Always watching. Head tilting to the side in curiosity, she asks, "You don't know, do you?"

"Your daughter's stubborn," I growl. "Annoying. Reckless with her sarcasm and her... *everything.*" The words come too fast, too raw. I clench my teeth, but the dam's cracked. "But when she looks at me?" My thumb grazes the scar at my throat. "She doesn't see a monster."

Belle stills. "And what does she see? No, better question: what do you see when you look at her?"

The basement door creaks downstairs. Ari's muffled curse floats up. "Stupid effing latch—"

Belle doesn't look away from me.

"A mirror," I answer quietly.

Her breath hitches. For the first time since she saw me in her home, her armor splinters—grief pooling in the cracks.

Then footsteps creak up the basement staircase, followed by Ariel's panting breath. The strain goes rushing out of the moment.

Belle grabs my wrist, her grip surprisingly strong. "If you hurt her—"

"I'll break myself first."

Yakov's voice in my head: *Too damn honest. Too damn weak.*

She searches my face. Then, a nod—sharp, reluctant. "Men like you don't know what to do with happy endings, Sasha Ozerov."

"We don't deserve them in the first place."

The basement door bangs open. Ariel strides in, scowling. "Hinges were installed upside down. Had to take the whole thing apart. What'd I miss?"

Belle releases me, smoothing her apron. "Nothing, sweetheart. Nothing at all. Now, come, Sasha—let me give you a tour."

She guides me around the house, the picture of a perfect hostess. The place itself is a time capsule. Faded lace doilies, framed photos of a younger Belle holding two dark-haired girls, a piano with sheet music yellowed at the edges.

"And that's that," she concludes when we return to the kitchen. "Not much to it."

"You have a beautiful home. Strangely enough, I mean it. It's so far from my world that I want to laugh out loud on seeing it. Mismatched cutlery in the drawers, but with fingerprints smudged into the metal that say it's been loved for so long. Watercolors she must've done herself hang on the walls.

It's a quiet, simple life, but a full one.

The shit makes my chest ache.

"Why, thank you," she says demurely. "Perfect timing, too. Dinner's almost done. Ariel, check the oven. Sasha—" She points to a rickety stepstool by the ceiling-high pantry. "Be a dear and fetch the bourbon? Top shelf."

I nod. "Of course, Ms. Ward."

The stool groans under my weight as I reach up to fetch the liquor. But up here, I'm eye level with the clock on the wall, and something occurs to me.

The hands haven't moved since I walked in.

Frowning, I lower myself down, set the bottle of bourbon on the counter, and approach it. A tiny, winding crack in the wooden surface is calling my name. With a fingertip, I lift the broken facade and peer inside.

Ach, it's all so wrong. Gears twisted, springs loose, mechanisms lolling like shreds of an open wound.

I immediately pluck it off the shelf and walk it over to the dining table. I peel off the shattered front piece, murmuring to the timepiece, *"Que t'est-il arrivé, mon ami?"*

Belle, bustling through the kitchen, freezes in place. "You speak French?"

"Enough to order wine and piss off waiters." I lift the clock carefully to peek underneath. "Ariel, hand me a screwdriver from the tool kit."

"Since when do you fix clocks?" she asks in amazement as she brings the tool over.

"Since never. But my mother… She had a knack for mending broken things."

Ariel is frowning as she watches me work, but Belle's face looks stricken, fragile, her hand covering her mouth. "Leander bought that for me on our honeymoon in Paris," she whispers hoarsely. "I broke it the day Jasmine left."

I freeze. A lot of things broke the day Jasmine left. I should know—I was there to send her off into the next life. But these women weren't where I was. There's a reason they don't know my face—only the consequences of the decisions I made.

"Give me twenty minutes and it'll work again."

"Oh, Sasha, you don't have to—"

"Twenty minutes."

Ariel watches me like I've sprouted horns. Belle keeps stirring the food on the stove, sipping bourbon, glancing furtively in my direction every minute as I dismantle the clock and begin to resuscitate it.

It's methodical work. Cleaning rusted gears. Realigning escapements. My mother's voice hums in my ear: *Careful, Sasha. Time is a jealous thing. It hates being mishandled.*

When the first chime rings out, crisp and clear, Belle's hand flies right back to her mouth.

Ariel gawks at the clock, then at me. "You… fixed it."

"Temporarily. It still needs proper restoration." I wipe grease on my handkerchief. "I know someone who can do a better job than I could."

Belle touches the polished wood, eyes bright. "You're full of surprises, Mr. Ozerov."

"So I've been told."

Ariel's still gaping. I lean close, inhaling her scent. "Close your mouth, *ptichka*. You'll catch flies."

She knees me under the table.

When dinner is over and the kitchen has been cleaned, Belle claps her hands and smiles. All traces of her shock when I repaired the clock are gone. Same with the fire with which she first greeted me. She's been nothing but pleasant since then, though I still catch her staring holes into the side of my face when she thinks I'm not paying attention.

"So!" she says. "Where are you taking my girl tonight?"

"Actually, Mama," interjects Ariel, "I'm the one taking Sasha out."

Belle's eyebrow floats up. "I stand corrected. What's in store?"

She bites her lip to stop from grinning. "It's a surprise."

"For both of us," I mutter. Ariel's been cagey all day long. Despite texting me nonstop, she's refused to divulge a single detail of tonight's activities.

"Trust me, you're gonna hate it," she warns with a cheeky elbow to the ribs.

"Well, just make sure you're home before you turn into a pumpkin, m'kay?" Belle wraps an arm around Ariel's waist and guides us to the door. She kisses Ariel's cheek and then turns to squint suspiciously at me. "As for you… I don't know what you'd turn into if you're out too late."

"A cloud of bats, if Bram Stoker is even remotely accurate." Ariel giggles when I pinch her side playfully.

"But," Belle continues, still talking to me, "it's no good for anyone to lurk about the city when it gets too late. For *anyone,* do you hear me?"

I nod as respectfully as I can, trying to put the proper assurances in the gesture. I want her to see what I feel—that the ground beneath Ariel and me is shifting. That things aren't what they seem.

That maybe men like me—or at least *one* man like me—might just figure out what to do with a happy ending after all.

"I hear you, Ms. Ward," I tell her. "Loud and clear."

~

We've been circling the block for damn near a half hour as Ariel's frown deepens and she counts the addresses again. "79… 81… 83… Oh, *there* it is!"

I growl in irritation. "Right. 85. Between 83 and 87. Who could've possibly known that's where it would be?"

"Oh, don't be a grump," she scolds, swatting my forearm. "Tonight's gonna be fun."

"Still keeping it a secret?"

"Until the last possible second," she confirms.

I park right in front of a fire hydrant. "What if someone tows you?" Ariel asks as she looks at the very clearly printed ***NO PARKING HERE*** sign looming from the sidewalk.

I laugh. "I would not like to be the man who tries something that stupid." Then I lock the car, tuck my keys in my pocket, and drape an arm around her shoulders. "Come on. 85, right? It's right…"

The voice drains out of me as I get close enough to read the sign hidden under the awning.

PRIVATE LAMAZE CLASSES, it reads in bold fuchsia print. ***MAMAS AND PAPAS IN TRAINING, ENTER HERE!***

I turn and look at Ariel. "What the hell did you cook up?"

31

ARIEL

I bite the inside of my cheek so hard I taste blood.

It's been hell trying not to laugh out loud the whole car ride here. Making it through the rest of this night without cackling might cost me a rib or two.

"C'mon," I say, tugging Sasha's arm to drag him up the stairs. "Aren't you the one who's always mad at me for being late?"

Inside, a wave of lavender hits me like a Sleepytime Tea grenade. Fake potted ferns flank a row of blue yoga mats. A bulletin board displays stock photos of beatific couples cradling potatoes in swaddles.

And there, at the front of the room, stands "Madame Giana" —a platinum blonde with thick magenta glasses and a Russian accent that sounds like Dracula with a head cold.

Gina doesn't do anything halfway. God help us all.

The whole plan, as per usual, was her idea. When I'd told her about Sasha's baby threat—because let's be real, what else could you really call it?—her eyes had bugged out of her head.

"Does he think you're an IVF test tube with legs? Is he even AWARE of what pregnancy does to the female body?" she'd crowed in fury.

"I'm guessing he has *some* idea. Do they teach female reproductive biology in mob boss school?"

Then she'd gotten that telltale wicked gleam in her eye. "They do now."

From there, everything had come together easily. She borrowed studio space from a friend, went wig shopping, and watched a YouTube video on Method acting so she could "get into character."

Which, apparently, looks like… this.

"Velcome, vvvelcome, to *Breathe, Push, Repeat*!" Gina trills, adjusting her wig. It lists violently to the left. "You are here for ze miracle of life, *da*?"

Sasha's grip tightens on my waist. "This is your surprise?"

"Like it? Thought we'd practice for our bundle of joy.: I bat my eyelashes. "Gotta make sure you know how to handle labor pains, right?"

His left eye twitches. Good. Precisely the reaction I wanted.

Madame Giana claps to draw our attention. She's added every single bracelet she owns, so any motion of her arms sounds like a snake made out of aluminum getting repeatedly Tasered.

"Ve begin vit pair bonding. First exercise: *empathy bellies*."

Sasha's already shaking his head. "No."

"Oh, yes." I shove a foam gut into his arms from the stack in the corner. The thing's the size of a beach ball, but Sasha is scowling at it like it's a live explosive. "Strap it on, Daddy-O."

I practically skip to the mat. Sasha looks at the thing like it personally offended him.

Then—slowly, reluctantly, but inevitably—he starts to shrug it on.

I really might tear an abdominal muscle keeping my laughter in. The sight of big, bad Sasha Ozerov, dressed to the nines as always in a crisp black shirt and gray suit pants, with a prosthetic baby belly Velcroed to his torso… it's just too much. I have to turn away so I don't erupt.

The half-hour that follows is more of the same. Gina—excuse me, *Madame Giana*—coaches us through synchronized breathing that makes me feel like a beached whale.

She keeps up a running train of commentary in that hideous Transylvanian accent the whole time. "More pelvis integration, Mr. Ozerov! As if you are trying to pass a vatermelon! He-hoo! He-hoo! Breathe, breathe, breathe!"

Sasha's glare could melt steel beams.

Does the session include "pelvic opening exercises" that wouldn't be out of place on a porn set? Yes, it absolutely does. Does it involve "partner-assisted stretching" for my adductors and groin? Why, that's in there, too!

But the true record scratch moment comes later. I'm sticky with sweat—more so from trying to contain my laughter than from the workout itself—when Gina puts on a dangerous smile that I know far too well.

"Last but not least," she croons, "we assume the birthing position."

"Oh," I blurt, "that won't be—"

"Down!" she screeches. She plants her talons into my shoulder and shoves me to my butt on the yoga mat. Then she turns on Sasha. "And you, Mr. Ozerov… behind. There, there." She jabs a nail at the space behind my back.

Sasha's scowl darkens. I wonder if he's going to outright refuse.

Then, slowly—like a jaguar lowering itself into a bath—he descends to a seat behind me. His thighs bracket my hips. Heat sinks through my jeans.

Gina picks up his hands and tries to put them on my belly. "Hands there. Hold her. *Protect* her. Protect your baby-to-be."

But he resists. His hands hover near my waist, a half-inch of very important space separating them from me. "If you don't touch me, she'll make us do it again," I hiss.

He growls. Another moment of wondering if this is all about to blow up in my face.

But then he does it. Presses his palms to my stomach. Gently, devotedly. His breath fans over the nape of my neck the exact same way.

Gentle.

Devoted.

Worship.

To make things even worse, Gina then drops a plastic baby onto my chest. "Skin-to-skin! Bond vit spawn!"

Sasha freezes as he gazes at it over my shoulder. The doll's painted eyelashes tickle my collarbone. His palm hovers over its lumpy back.

And for one stupid, suspended second, I glimpse it all—us, in some alternate universe. Him pressed against me in a hospital bed, sweat-damp and coaxing me on in proud Russian as a real baby wails. A baby with blue eyes and auburn hair. A little bit of him. A little bit of me.

My throat constricts.

His pinky grazes my neck. "This is absurd," he whispers.

"It's working, though." I tilt my head, catching his gaze. The classroom fades away and all I see is him. "Admit it. You're picturing me eight months pregnant. Huge. Raging. Demanding blinis at the ass crack of dawn. Then you demanding another five children right away."

"Never." His thumb traces the doll's spine. "I'd want six."

My heart lurches.

The smell of patchouli and way too much lavender clings to Sasha's suit as we stumble back onto the sidewalk. Madame Giana's cackle follows us out the studio door, muffled only when he slams it shut hard enough to rattle the hydrant next to his car.

Neither of us moves to leave.

Instead, both of us stand marooned on the sidewalk, awkwardly twisting in the wind. His hand drifts toward his collar to undo the top button like he's still suffocating under that foam belly. I watch his throat work—that angry scar, the faint stubble—and think absurdly of rocking chairs. Baby names. Brooklyn brownstones with too many stairs for a stroller, so he'd just pick it up—stroller, baby, mama—and carry us over the threshold himself.

Snap out of it, Ward.

"Hope you took notes," I mumble, kicking a pebble. "We'll have a pop quiz later."

Sasha just stares at the sky.

The streetlight above us buzzes. His keys jingle as he sighs. The sound reignites the phantom weight of his palms on my belly.

"What's wrong?" I ask. "You seem… bothered."

He drags his gaze down to me. As he does, his eyes soften—no, *melt*—and I see the man from the restaurant again. The one who looked at me like I was both the grenade that will kill him and the pin it came with.

Then he's stepping back, jaw steeled. "Nothing. I'm fine. Just tired."

I want to poke, to prod, to pry until he tells me what's really happening in his head. With a face that beautiful, it's sometimes hard to imagine him as a real person.

But he *is* real. I've seen it. I've felt it.

And I know what I just felt in that stupid room. I know he felt it, too.

My phone buzzes with Gina's victory emojis. ***Did he puke? Did he cry? Did we win?***

I bite back my reply as Sasha steps to the car and opens the door for me. ***Worse,*** I want to tell her. ***He almost acted human.***

32

SASHA

“Put the gloves on.”

“Aw, c’mon, Sash, I really don’t feel like—”

“Quit being a coward and put on the gloves, Feliks. I need to punch something and your face is the closest target I can reach.”

Feliks sighs, but he turns to the rack of gym equipment, plucks down his dusty pair of boxing mitts, and starts tugging them on.

I’m already laced up and ready. I’m still wearing the suit pants I wore to that fucking ridiculous Lamaze class, though I’ve stripped off the shirt and cast it aside, leaving my torso bare to the cold air whistling through the vents.

The gym is cold as a morgue, which is how I prefer it. Reminds me of the early days. Of the woods.

I bounce from foot to foot. “If you take any longer—”

"I'm coming, I'm coming," protests Feliks. "Fuck, impatience is not a virtue of yours."

He's not wrong. But if he'd seen my performance tonight, he might change his tune.

For sixty minutes, I was as Zen as it fucking gets. Patience oozed from every pore. As I cradled Ariel in my lap. Cupped that absurd prosthetic baby in my arms. Breathed in and out, the scent of Ariel filling my lungs with every inhale and stupid, stricken dreams of this being real rushing out with every exhale.

That's *patience.*

"Alright. Ready. Ready as I'll ever be, at least."

"'Bout fucking time."

I duck under the ropes and start shuffling around the ring, testing the air with jabs and uppercuts. I need to move and set these thoughts elsewhere.

I tried leaving them at Ariel's doorstep when I dropped her off after the class. She lingered on the sidewalk for a moment after I helped her out of the car. Almost like an invitation.

I wonder what would've happened if I'd taken her up on it.

Want to come inside for a sec?

Just a second. It'd be a bad idea to stay longer than that.

Of course, she would agree. *Very bad idea. Can't have that.*

Then we would have fucked like rabbits 'til the dawn rose.

That's how it goes in my head, at least. The fact that those fantasies are bubbling right below the surface, ready to surge out the second they spy a crack in my mental dam, is troubling. I don't even want to know what might be happening in Ariel's mind.

None of this is as simple as it was supposed to be. What ever happened to *Seduce. Marry. Control?* That was a simple, three-step process. Damn near foolproof.

The only fool left anymore is me.

I drop to the ground just in time to miss Feliks's fist coming to knock my skull off its moorings.

"*Blyat'*, you *mudak*—"

"You're the one who wanted to get feisty. Don't start throwing a hissy fit just because I got the ball rolling."

"I'm going to get your *skull* rolling momentarily," I snarl as I regain my bearings and advance on him.

Feliks laughs and slips one jab, then the next. But my low left hook buries itself in his gut, and the laughter comes wheezing out of him as he doubles over.

"You pay me too much to be a punching bag," he grumbles as he dances backwards and gets set up again.

"Correction: I pay you enough to be a punching bag whenever I need one."

His eyes gleam with that *Oh, shit, there's drama* mischief as he dodges and scoots backward to the far corner of the ring. "Uh-oh. You need a punching bag, hm? I take it The Love Boat hit some rough waters?"

I bite down and charge toward him again.

Rough waters? No, that's not it at all. The waters are too damn smooth, actually.

Maybe that's why I feel the need to make something bleed. Feliks or myself—so long as something gets a little bit broken tonight, my world will be back to the way it should be.

All this niceness, this lavender-scented domestic bliss? That's wrong. Way too fucking wrong.

Men like you don't know what to do with happy endings, Sasha Ozerov.

We don't deserve them in the first place.

The first round is pure exorcism. Every jab is another piece of that silly little dream getting shattered and bent beyond recognition. Feliks' right hook grazes my temple when I linger too long on the remembered weight of Ariel pressed between my thighs.

"Focus, boss," he pants, dancing back. Sweat glistens on his shaved head. "Or I'll have to tell your bride I beat you up."

I drive him into the ropes with an uppercut. "She's not my bride yet."

"Clock's ticking, though. What's left—four days, right?"

"Watch your fucking mouth."

The second round gets uglier. I let him land a body shot that knocks the wind out of my lungs, just to feel something that isn't the burn of my own shame. He pays for it with a nosebleed that splatters across the mat like Rorschach ink.

Feliks raises his face and grins like a madman. "You know your problem?" He catches my next punch in his mitt, leaning in close. "You're still swinging at your old man's ghost instead of looking at what's right in front of you."

I punch. I miss.

"That girl doesn't make you weak, Sasha. She makes you *hungry*. And hungry men?" He ducks me with a wet laugh. "They're the only ones who survive this shit."

I freeze mid-jab, knuckles hovering an inch from his ruined face.

The bell rings.

Neither of us moves.

Then, finally, I sneer in disgust, strip my gloves off, hurl them into the corner, and stalk away.

Feliks joins me outside a few minutes later. My courtyard is as silent as the Upper West Side ever gets. No birds or scurrying things to break up the noise; just the distant moan of the city at large.

"I should be getting paid extra for these counseling sessions," he remarks as he settles onto the bench at my side.

My sweat is almost frozen on my skin and my breath coalesces in silver mushroom clouds in front of my face. "Extra pay as a punching bag, extra pay as a therapist—you're going to bankrupt me if this keeps going, Vasiliev."

He chuckles and drapes an arm behind me. "I think it's moral bankruptcy you need to be worried about, *brattan*. You've already got enough money to last ten lifetimes."

I sigh and stroke my chin. He's right about that. He's right about too damn much tonight.

"I'm getting sick of your perceptiveness."

"Oh, the curse of being highly intelligent and extremely good-looking," he sighs. He gazes longingly into the distance. "And as if that's not enough of a burden to bear, I've also got this giant, swinging—"

He falls over laughing when I elbow him in the ribs.

But when he straightens up, his smile recedes. "I do mean it, though, in a way. Far be it from me to tell you to quit making money. You're good at it, and it keeps me swimming in caviar and Corvettes. But… there's more. There's other things."

"Is there?" I ask. I know what he's going to say, but I let him say it anyway.

"Love."

I squint at him blankly, waiting for a punchline. But Feliks just looks right back at me with a calm, level tranquility in his face.

"Love," I repeat.

"Love," he repeats.

"Love."

"Love, Sasha. The reason we're here at all."

"I'm here because my father fooled my mother into thinking he was quasi-human for long enough to knock her up. You're here because your mother dumped you in my lap when she got sick of looking at your ugly mug all the time. 'Love' had nothing to do with either case."

His mouth quirks up in a half-smile. The other half, though, remains downturned in contemplation. "You keep getting things twisted. I know you were joking when you said I was perceptive, but… Shit, man, sometimes I really do feel like you are failing to see what's right in front of your face. So things get forced on us. So circumstances sometimes dictate the cards we get to play. Does that mean you punt on the whole game and go cry about it?"

"Who's cry—"

"You are, in your own way. You cry with blood. You cry with spreadsheets. It's a little depraved and disturbing, if we're being honest, but hey, far be it from me to criticize another man's coping mechanisms. I'm just saying that I see *you,* Sasha Ozerov. I see what's in front of you. And I want you to see what I'm seeing." He slumps back against the bench. "That's it. Lecture over. I'm out of poetry for the night."

I brood as his words echo in caverns in my head that haven't seen light for a long time.

Love. He's wrong. He has to be. It's not that. It can't be.

But after the endless day I've had, I'm not going to find the flaws in his argument right now. I want to shower off this sweat and blood and go the fuck to sleep. Let tomorrow's Sasha take up the sword of *Love* and all its many ridiculous implications.

Before I go, though, I do what's become a ritual for six days and running.

"Check her detail."

Feliks lofts an eyebrow. "And by 'hers,' you mean…?"

"If you make me spell it out, I'm going to punch you in the face again."

"You barely even got me *once* tonight," he grumbles, but he fishes his phone out of his pocket and starts to do as I asked.

I look over his shoulder as he cues up the security footage being broadcast from the body cams attached to the men I have stationed outside Ariel's apartment.

Six feeds flicker to life, one for each of the Bratva soldiers guarding the block. I know the feeds by heart now. Every angle, fire hydrant, and bush lining the sidewalk in front of her building. Five of the feeds are empty.

But in the sixth…

Stands Ariel.

And she's not alone.

33

ARIEL

TWO HOURS EARLIER

I press my back against the brick wall of my building and watch Sasha's black Aston Martin disappear around the corner. My fingernails dig semi-circles into my palms. Every nerve ending under my skin crackles like live wires, still sparking from that godforsaken fake baby and Sasha's hands spanning my hips. All my oxytocin-drunk, oxygen-starved brain cells were screaming *kiss me, kiss me, KISS ME*—

"Fuck." I peel myself off the wall. The bright glass doors of my apartment beckon, but I set off in the opposite direction instead. The thought of going upstairs is depressing. It's gonna be empty and quiet up there, and house plants make for shitty company.

Besides, I feel like walking. *Motion is lotion,* as the overly peppy personal trainer that Gina drags me to every now and then likes to say.

Although the thought of lotion makes me think of Sasha and the spa room, and that makes my cheeks burn and my thighs clench, so maybe I'll stick to motion just being motion after all.

But motion for motion's sake is a good thing. Motion means going away from one thing and towards another, right? And that's what I'm trying to do.

Away from Sasha Ozerov. *Away* from my dad and all the many twisted things he'd like to shape my life into.

As for what I'm headed towards? Excellent question. Do not have an answer.

For now, lacking a true ethical north to orient myself, I head geographically west instead, cutting through Bedford-Stuyvesant with a vague plan of making it to see the East River sparkling in the night.

My reflection bounces off darkened boutique windows as I pass them—messy auburn ponytail, flushed cheeks, dreamy eyes gazing into a future that isn't really there. I look like I just sprinted through a romance novel.

"Get a grip, Ari. You're embarrassing yourself."

It's cold as all hell outside, but the remnant aura of Sasha's heat is keeping me warm enough not to mind. So is putting one foot in front of the other, again and again.

There's a nice rhythm to this, to walking. I'm pleasantly lulling myself to sleep with a thing that humans have been doing since we first descended from the trees.

Then my phone vibrates against my thigh. I yank it out, ready to scream profanities at whoever's interrupting my fragile grip on sanity.

But I crack a smile when I see the burly mustache lighting up the screen.

"Uncle Kosti? As in the one and only Konstantin Makris? To what do I owe the rare pleasure? You never call this late."

"My little night owl." His gruff chuckle crackles through the speaker. Static hisses between us—probably calling from one of his encrypted lines. As warm as his smiles are, he's still my father's brother, and with that DNA comes heaps and heaps of paranoia. "You think because I'm old, I go to bed with the pigeons?"

I lean against a dumpster, the metal frigid against my lower back. "You told me the Metamucil knocks you out by nine."

"Metamucil is for frightened little schoolgirls. I drink ouzo and piss excellence. Doctors hate me."

"And men fear you and women throw themselves at your feet, I'm sure."

I can hear his smile. "That's why you've always been my favorite niece, *koukla.* You know how to make this old man feel special."

"Is that why you called? To fish for compliments?"

"I'll never say no to them," he declares. "But… no. No, that's not why I called. I mean, yes, of course, I want simply to check on you. But, given… everything… well, there's no point keeping you in the dark. You've been given a big enough bite to chew on anyway. Unfairly so, in my opinion, but then again, that brother of mine has never given much of a rat's ass about my opinion in the first place."

I grip the edge of the dumpster for support. "Get to the point, Uncle Kosti. What's going on?"

He hesitates. "Your father is getting… cranky, Ari."

The scowl that rips across my face is withering. “Because I’m not spreading my legs fast enough for his favorite mobster? What happened to ‘ten days’?”

“Because his enemies are getting bold.” The playfulness bleeds out of his voice. “Serbians hit two of Sasha’s warehouses this week. They’ve begun sniffing around the Makris docks, too. Your wedding’s supposed to unite the families, shore up alliances… but every day you stall—”

“Is a day someone tries putting Leander and Sasha in early graves?” I kick a pebble into the dark. It pings off a fire hydrant and goes rolling into the nearest storm drain. “Let them. Maybe one’ll get lucky and solve all my problems.”

The silence throbs like a fresh bruise.

“You don’t mean that,” Kosti says finally.

Don’t I?

No. No, I don’t.

Not entirely, at least. The image of Sasha’s scarred knuckles cradling that plastic infant flashes behind my eyes. My thighs squeeze together of their own accord.

“I don’t know what I mean anymore.” I exhale and rub at my tired neck.

“Have these days changed nothing in your heart or your mind?”

“It’s not that. There’s… chemistry,” I admit through gritted teeth. “Doesn’t mean I want to be his Suzie Homemaker and baby manufacturing machine.”

“Chemistry.” Kosti snorts. “That’s what your mother called the tequila shots that led to you.”

"Gross."

"Ach, you're probably right. Sometimes, I forget you're my niece and I'm supposed to watch what I say to you. But Ari..."

He pauses again, long enough that I ask, "Yes?"

"If you... if you really don't want this... if you reach the end of these ten days and you truly, in your heart, in your soul, cannot go through with it... I will help you."

The pulse is thudding in every extremity of my body now. In the soles of my feet and the tips of my ears, I feel it.

Ba-boom. Ba-boom.

Cautiously, I ask, "What does that mean, Uncle Kosti?"

"It means I'm offering you an out, *koukla.*"

I still. A rat scuttles past my sandals, but I'm too dumbstruck by what my uncle is saying to even bother with a scream. "What kind of out?"

"Passports. Cash. New identity. If you say the word, I will erase you so completely that neither Leander nor even God will ever find you." His tone hardens. "But once you go... you don't come back. Not to New York. Not to your mother. Not even to my funeral. It's goodbye forever, darling."

The alley tilts. I cling to the dumpster's edge. "Jesus..."

"This life is..." Kosti coughs—a wet, rattling sound that makes my stomach drop. "It's a hungry beast, *koukla*. Doesn't matter if you're blood or not. You owe it flesh. Leander gave it Jasmine, but that didn't get him what he was after. So now, he'll feed it you."

Streetlights bleach the pavement bone-white in my vision. I just keep staring at a single piece of ancient gum stuck to the ground, blackened by Lord only knows how many sets of footprints. It's the only thing still tethering me to reality.

To say goodbye

"I need time," I whisper.

"You've got four days. Then even I can't help you. Take your time; think it through. I won't let you suffer needlessly. Talk soon, *koukla*."

He hangs up.

I stare at the phone. My lock screen is a selfie with Gina, the two of us smizing outside the Gazette. My chest constricts. If I run…

It'd mean goodbye to that.

It'd mean goodbye to everything I've scratched and clawed for: my crummy apartment, lattes for Sportswriter Steve, my Lois Lane pipe dreams. It'd mean goodbye to New York and to my Mama.

It'd mean goodbye forever to Sasha Ozerov.

Is that what I want anymore?

I turn around and start heading for home. Suddenly, all I want is to be amongst my things. My meager, stupid IKEA furniture and all the wobbles and unevenness that came from building it myself.

But I built it *myself,* dammit! Jas wasn't here to help me and Leander would sure as hell never bother, even if I was inclined to let him. I built this life myself, and it was *freedom,* and that's all I ever wanted.

I don't know how to give that up.

The alternative swims before my eyes: a veil blurring the sight of Sasha before me. *I do's,* murmured in the rasped baritone that sends shivers down my spine no matter how many times I hear it. That's terrifying. So are all the things that would come after it. Blue-eyed babies and baptisms in cathedrals cold enough to mist your breath. A place at Sasha's side as he waged war across the city.

Could I make that work? What would it take to accept that?

What if he looked at me like he did in the library when he said, *Falling doesn't have to hurt?*

What if he touched me like he did in the spa, his hands slick with lotion, his hips flush with mine?

What if he cuddled me like he did on the mountainside, or groaned for me like he did in his office, or settled his weight behind me while I brought his son or daughter into the world?

Would that really be so bad?

My feet are carrying me automatically, so I don't even realize I'm back on my block until I accidentally run headlong into someone right on the corner.

I grunt in shock and stumble backwards, but strong hands keep me from tumbling ass-over-teakettle on the frozen concrete.

"Whoa there!" an accented voice says, startled. "You came around that corner with some speed."

"I'm so sorry," I blurt as I orient myself. The cold is drawing up tears in my eyes, so I have to dig the heel of my hand into them until my vision clears up.

When it does, I see it's a man I've collided with. Late forties, maybe—just a few years older than Sasha, if I had to guess. Black hair shot through with silver and a beard to match. He's dressed nicely, in a long, camel hair jacket that sweeps just above his ankles, and his hands glisten with a set of silver rings. At his throat, through the gap in his black scarf, I see the upper half of a tattoo: a pair of eagle's heads, joined at the neck.

"It's quite alright, young lady." His eyes sweep over me. They're a dark espresso, almost black in the night. His nose bends left, then right, like it's been broken and reset so many times that he just shrugged and gave up on it ever aligning again. "Where are you off to in such a hurry?"

"Er, home," I say awkwardly. New York is full of weirdos, and you learn early on that it's best to politely but firmly disengage at the early possible opportunity and be on your merry way. Nothing good ever comes from fanning the flames.

The man's gaze flicks up to the building, then back down to me. "It's a nice home. Very safe."

The first prickles of *Something is wrong* start to crop up in my belly. After all, how does he know that this is where I live? I could've just been passing through.

"Y-yeah," I say. "It's nice. I'll just—"

"Hold on." His hands clamp on my shoulders, pinning me in place. "You look familiar."

I look at him. The scarf is halfway over his mouth and his felt newsboy cap is tugged low over his forehead, but even with all those obstacles, I'm fairly certain I've never seen this man in my life.

"I don't think we've ever met, sorry."

"No, no, we have," he insists. He's still not letting go, and his grip is starting to hurt. "It was a long time ago. Fifteen years or so. You don't remember me?"

Thud. Thud. My heartbeat is ratcheting up to concerning levels again. Those born-and-raised New Yorker Spidey senses are tingling that I should get the hell away from this creep, STAT.

"Nope. Sorry. And I really do need to go now, so if you could just—"

I knock his hands off me, duck under his outstretched arm, and do my best to bolt for the doors of my apartment.

I don't get far.

Before I even make it under the awning, a pair of hulking silhouettes separate from the shadows clustered in the nearby alleyway and scoop me up by the armpits. My feet pedal in the air like a toddler getting shunted into the bath against her will.

They carry me back and plop me down in front of the bearded man. He sighs and peels off his scarf. As he does, I see more of the tattoo on his chest and throat.

And with that, I remember.

Double-headed eagle inked across his torso. Silver rings. Eyes brown, no, black, no, blacker than black.

"I'm here for Jasmine." Darkening the doorstep like the bad guy in one of Mama's fairy tales.

"You can't have her!" I screamed, planting myself in front of her.

Baba peeled me away, hauled me upstairs, tossed me in my room. Jasmine could only watch.

We'd always known that arranged marriages were a possibility. But it had always seemed so abstract. What does "one day, you'll be wed off" mean to a little girl? Nothing, of course.

But little girls grow up. "One day" gets closer and closer.

And today was Jasmine's day.

An arranged marriage. The link between the Greek mob and the Serbians. Jasmine as the sacrificial lamb to make the whole thing come together. Did she want it? Who cared? None of the men striking the deals ever asked our opinion.

As I stood in my room in horror, I heard those same men thumping downstairs. Their voices felt like the earth shaking. I ran to the window and watched in blurry-eyed horror as my father and the bearded man carried Jasmine down the sidewalk. They put her in a black van. The door closed.

I never saw her again.

"Relax, *ptičica,*" he croons, brushing a stray hair out of my face. "I just want to talk."

34

ARIEL

Blood roars in my ears. His fingers dig into my jaw, tilting my face up toward the sickly glow of the streetlamp to expose my throat in a way that feels way too intentional for comfort. The acrid stench of his cologne—something musky and too-sweet, curdled by body heat—makes my stomach heave.

"Haven't you taken enough from me?!" I spit.

Dragan Vukovic's grin splits his brutal face like a scar. "Not even close."

One of his thugs yanks my head back by the ponytail. Stars burst behind my eyes. Dragan pulls out a syringe filled with murky liquid. My pulse goes atomic.

And then a black blur detonates the night.

"I'll kill any man who lays a finger on her."

Bone cracks. The arm holding my hair snaps like a tree branch in a hurricane. The thug screams, but Sasha's fist plows into his throat mid-shriek, silencing him.

The second enforcer's knife flashes, but Sasha pivots, seizing the guy's wrist and slamming it down on his own raised knee. A shard of bone pops through the skin.

"Bastard!" Dragan snarls, lunging for me.

True to his word, Sasha intercepts him before he lays a finger on me. His left hand fists in Dragan's beard while his right slams upward, knuckles burying into the Serb's breastbone in a sickening crunch. Dragan's eyes bulge.

Sasha shakes blood off his hands. It's not his.

"You don't touch her," he growls. "You *don't look* at her."

He headbutts Dragan. The cartilage in the Serb's earlier-broken nose definitively gives up the ghost. When Dragan drops to his knees, Sasha kicks his ribs in—once, twice—before slamming a boot into his chest. Vukovic skids five feet across the pavement.

I scramble backward until my spine hits cold brick. Sasha stalks toward Dragan. Each step echoes like a death knell.

Brass knuckles glint as he pulls them from his pocket. My breath hitches. "Wait, Sasha—"

He drives them into Dragan's mouth. Teeth skitter across asphalt like discarded Chiclets.

The Serbian gurgles, "Your gutter-whore mother would weep—"

Sasha raises his foot to stomp—but just before he reverses direction and brings an end to the Serbian boss's life, the crack of a gunshot rings out.

I look down the mouth of the alley to see half a dozen burly men charging towards us. Two of them have guns raised at Sasha.

Again, he moves faster than I thought possible. He lunges to me, scoops me up like I weigh nothing, and bundles me into his waiting car. I find myself hurled across the center console as he punches the gas and, with a wail of tires and burning rubber, we peel away down the street.

He drives for a while without saying anything. The only sound is his breathing as it slows.

His shoulders heave. Steam coils off his skin in the freezing air. Blood trickles down his wrist.

Finally, when we've gone far enough, he parks on the ground floor of an empty parking garage.

When he turns to me, I flinch.

Something awful and human flickers behind his ice-blue eyes.

"Ariel." Ragged. Hoarse.

His hands are on me before I can speak—palming my cheeks, tilting my face for damage.

The copper tang of carnage clings to him. I should be repulsed. Instead, I lean my face into his touch and let out the first sound I've made since this whole nightmare began.

"Sasha."

"Are you hurt?" His thumb dabs across my lip. Later, I'll realize it's where Dragan's ring split the skin. For now, all I feel is the heat of his touch.

I shake my head. He exhales sharply through his nose—a bull moments before the charge.

Then his mouth descends onto mine.

Fireworks detonate behind my closed lids. His kiss is brutal, aggressive, all teeth and desperation. He pulls me halfway onto him, his thigh slotting between mine. Breathing is optional. Survival is irrelevant. All I want is—

Suddenly, he breaks away like I bit him.

"Fucking hell." He pushes me into the passenger seat and leans back, pupils cranked wide open. One hand claws through his hair. The other fists against his mouth like he can shove the kiss he just gave me back in. "What the fuck am I—? *Blyat'.*"

My lip quivers. "Sasha—"

"Don't." He throws open his door and climbs out.

I follow suit, jogging around the front of the car to meet him. "Sasha—"

"I said *don't.*" He whirls on me, looking wilder than I've ever seen him before. His beard, his hair, his eyes are all positively feral. But it's the tremble in his mouth that undoes me.

I've never seen fear on him before. This is what it looks like.

But not fear for himself. Never, ever for himself.

I know without asking that this is fear for *me.*

"I thought he might have— I was afraid he was going to—" He breaks off and looks away, raising that hand to his mouth again like those words, too, can be repressed back into wherever they came from. "Fuck. *Fuck. Fuck!*"

I scream when he punches the brick pillar. I'm sure his hand will come away absolutely mangled, but it's a smear of mortar dust, not blood, that's left behind. He rips away in another circle, stops halfway, looks at me again. He looks possessed, like he doesn't know where to go or what to do with himself.

"I thought he was going to fucking kill you," he croaks. "And I realized as I came as fast as I could that if he did, he might as well kill me, too."

Then he turns and looks to a patch of shadows I can't see into. "Get her out of here, Feliks. I can't look at her anymore."

His second steps out, cigarette clamped between his lips, face unreadable. "Boss—"

"Now. Take her home. Lock her in the apartment. Post three men on the door."

Feliks sighs. Then he shifts his gaze from Sasha to me. He comes closer, though slowly, cautiously, as if I might get spooked if he moves too fast. Taking a grip on my elbow, he starts to steer me toward a car pulling up at the exit to the garage.

I shake him off. "Sasha, talk to me!"

He won't look at me. Won't even face my direction. "Get her away from me, Feliks."

I'm wobbling. It's a miracle I'm still upright. If it weren't for Feliks clamping me around the waist in brotherly fashion, I probably wouldn't be.

"Come on," he says softly. "Let's get you home."

Mute and stumbling like a zombie, I let Feliks turn me toward the exit. We shuffle slowly to the waiting car. He opens the door and helps me into the backseat, then closes it and takes his place up front.

As we peel away from the curb, piloted by a stone-faced man with Russian tattoos littering his scalp, I twist in my seat. Sasha stands amidst the concrete bones of the parking garage, backlit by a throbbing fluorescent pulse.

His mouth moves. I'm probably imagining things—hell, I must be—but I could swear he's saying to himself, *I thought for a moment I lost you.*

35

ARIEL

I don't want to smell like him anymore.

That's all I can think as Feliks escorts me up to my apartment and pushes me, kindly but irrevocably, inside. The door snicks closed and I know that it will not open until Sasha gives his approval.

But that's fine, because I'm headed straight for the shower. I strip off clothes as I go, leaving a trail of cold-sweat-soaked leggings, the twisted figure-eights of my underwear and sports bra, and my shoes kicked haphazardly against the hallway wall.

I don't wait for the water to warm up—I just jump right in, even though it feels like ice-tipped needles stabbing me. *I don't want to smell like him anymore.*

The million-dollar question, though, is this: Which "him" do I not want to smell like?

Because Sasha's scent *and* Dragan's scent are both clinging to my skin. Which one is it that's making me sick to my stomach?

I don't have it in me to suss out the culprit. I just scrub and scrub until my arms are pink and lemon-raspberry body wash is the only thing in my nose.

Even when I'm done and sitting on the foot of my bed, though, I keep thinking I catch whiffs of them.

Sasha's minty, cedar musk.

The smoky, acid tang of Dragan.

I shudder again and again, even though I've got a towel wrapped around my head, another around my torso, and the radiator heat cranked as high as it will go.

Every time I think I'm smelling Sasha, my insides quiver and my pulse roars in my ears.

Every time I think I'm smelling Dragan, I'm dragged back into a past I've spent fifteen years scrubbing out of my mind as desperately as I just scrubbed his touch off my throat.

Leander darkened my door. His under-eyes were baggy and purple, sagging low. I remember thinking that he looked like Eeyore. Winnie the Pooh's friend.

"She's gone," he told me, not moving from the door of my bedroom.

"I know she's gone," I spat back at him bitterly. "I watched her get fucking dragged out of here."

Cursing at age fifteen was new enough to still feel like it had some venom. Cursing at my dad was even newer than that. Leander wasn't the kind of father you hurled profanities at.

"No, neraïdoula mou. *I mean, she's* gone."

It took a moment for his words to sink in. When they did, the journal I was scribbling in fell from my hands. "Wh... what do... Baba, what are you talking about? Jas is— Jas is supposed to get married tomorrow."

He just shook his head. "The wedding is canceled. She's gone." Then he turned and stomped away down the hall, as if that explained that and nothing more needed to be said.

I stared at the dark rectangle of the empty doorway for a long, long time.

Memory's a funny thing. Easier to repress than people tend to think. I let myself erase Dragan Vukovic from the story, because as far as I was concerned, it wasn't him that killed Jasmine. Not really.

It was my father.

So when I ran from home, it felt like I was doing the worst thing that could be done to the man who'd done the worst thing that could be done to me: depriving him of the last daughter he had left.

For fifteen years, I've let myself believe that I was doing justice for Jasmine.

Now, I'm remembering that there are other bloody hands out there.

And they just tried to touch me.

Seeing him again... It's like my past was hitting me in the face. If that wasn't already insane and horrifying enough, my present then punched my past in the face. Rarely do metaphors appear quite so blunt and literal.

But there they were, two of the three men who've most defined my life, brawling it out in the street.

Then one of them scooped me up and took me to a chilly stone fortress to do what: kiss me like he'd never get to kiss me again? Then blast me with the coldest anger I've ever felt?

How is that *fair?*

So, no—I don't want to smell like Sasha, either. I'm furious with him. Terrified of him. In so many ways, he's back to being what he was when he first shook my hand at that gala: a mystery I have no interest in exploring any further.

I just can't. Some darknesses swallow you up and they will never, ever spit you back out.

I fall asleep like that, still turbaned and toweled.

I wake up hours later to my phone buzzing on my nightstand. I groan and peel myself off the damp sheets, then shuffle over to pick it up. When I see who's texted, my stomach curdles.

SASHA [9:47 A.M.]: ***I will be at your apartment in twenty minutes.***

SASHA [9:56 A.M.]: ***Eleven minutes away.***

SASHA [10:08 A.M.]: ***Knock-knock.***

SASHA [10:14 A.M.]: ***?***

The fact that he's texting me is shocking in and of itself. Does he really think we're going to keep going, after what happened last night?

No. The ten days bullshit is over with. I won't do this. I'm calling Kosti back and telling him to book the tickets. I'm leaving this place and I'm not coming back ever. I'll find a way to take Gina and my mom with me, but Sasha and Dragan and Leander and all these power-hungry men can go fuck themselves. Let them marry each other, for all I care.

My fingers tap out an angry response.

ARIEL [10:15 A.M.]: ***I'm sick. Not coming.***

His reply is immediate: ***Like hell you're not.***

I'm not doing this, either. This back-and-forth bickering. It's just too exhausting. I leave my phone on the nightstand, shed the towels and step into ratty sweatpants and a too-big tee, then make my way to the kitchen to start brewing tea. My head hurts like I guzzled liquor last night and my throat aches from walking and talking for so long in the cold. Earl Gray is just what the doctor ordered.

But just when the kettle is starting to whine, there's a knock at my door. I frown and go over. If it's Sasha, I'm gonna tell him to eat shit, and I'm sure as hell not opening the door for him.

But I peek through the eyehole to see that it's not Sasha. "Mr. DeMarco?" I ask, confused.

My building super is anxiously passing a key back and forth between his liver-spotted hands. "Hi, Ariel. You alright?"

"Uh, yeah, I'm fine. Are you? Is everything okay?"

"Yes, yes, yes," he says, still shuffling from foot to foot and rubbing that key in his palms. "Mind opening up? Quick question for you."

"I'm, uh…" I cast around for a plausible excuse. "Really would prefer not to. I'm not appropriately dressed."

"It'll be quick, dear, I promise. I've gotta hurry; told the wife I'd be back downstairs in a jiff."

I grimace. But the chain is latched and Mr. DeMarco is about five-foot-five on his best days, with a bum knee that makes climbing the stairs a marathon for him, so I'm not really worried about him doing anything crazy.

I undo the deadbolt and twist the knob. The door opens an inch, stretching the chain taut.

Mr. DeMarco looks at me apologetically. "I'm so sorry, dear. He said you were—"

Boom.

I scream and leap backwards as the door explodes inward. The chain bursts and broken links go flying everywhere.

Sasha fills the frame, brows knitted together into a single dark slash. He's in a black suit, black shirt, like he tripped and fell into an ink well on his way here.

His eyes lock onto my ***I Survived the Apocalypse and All I Got was This Stupid T-shirt*** tee, then the spoonful of peanut butter I'd been stress-eating straight from the jar.

"You *asshole!*" I snap. In the gap beneath his arm, I see Mr. DeMarco fleeing in terror down the hallway. "You just broke my door!"

"You tried to break our plans. It only felt right."

"We have no plans!" I want to tear my hair out. "This has all been a bunch of bullshit! Fuck ten days, Sasha. I'm not marrying you! I'm sure as shit not doing a single day more of these ridiculous dates with you. How could you possibly expect me to—"

"You're angry with me."

"Astute fucking observation," I seethe. "What gave it away?"

"Because of last night."

"Again, nothing gets past you."

He frowns again. "And you think that gives you the right to break your word to me."

"My—" Jaw, meet floor. Audacity, meet your master: Sasha Ozerov. "My *word*?!"

"You agreed to the deal, Ariel. Ten days. Ten dates. We have three to go. And I will not be denied."

Before I can begin to parse the logical holes in that crock of shit, Sasha is moving.

One stride. Two. My peanut butter spoon clatters to the floor as he hoists me over his shoulder like a sack of grain.

"Sasha— what the— PUT ME DOWN!" I hammer fists against his back, his shoulders, anywhere I can reach. My knee clips his ribs; he grunts but doesn't slow. "You can't just kidnap me because I ghosted you!"

He kicks the ruined apartment door shut behind us. "Already did."

The stairs rattle beneath his boots. I catch the flash of Mrs. Bernstein peeking through her door crack, her Yorkie's manic yaps chasing us down to the lobby. Señora Gutierrez from 3B actually crosses herself.

Outside, Sasha's black town car idles at the curb. Feliks is leaning against the hood with a to-go cup of coffee.

"I'll fix the door, don't you worry!" Feliks says cheerfully as he heads past us in the opposite direction, back toward my building.

I don't get the chance to respond before Sasha dumps me into the backseat. I scramble upright, glaring as he folds himself in beside me.

"You're insane," I spit.

His jaw pulses. "Eyes forward, Klaus."

The driver peels away from the curb.

"Where are we going, anyway?" I ask in disgust.

Sasha doesn't bother to look at me. "Shopping."

I guess Date #7 is a go after all.

36

ARIEL

"I have less than zero interest in shopping with you right now," I inform Sasha.

He doesn't turn his gaze from the window. "If I cared, that would be devastating."

"What kind of places does a guy like you even shop at? Whips & Chains 'R' Us?"

I'm aware that's not my most devastating burn ever, so I'm not surprised when he doesn't laugh. He does look at me, though.

And something in his expression gives me pause.

Sasha looks hangdog. Tired, in a lifelong sort of way. Still beautiful, but there's a sadness to it that grabs me by the throat for a second.

I shudder and look elsewhere. That's a dangerous trap and I will not be setting foot in it.

"We'll go wherever you like," he murmurs.

"Perfect. Walmart has a great line of granny panties I've been dying to try."

"On second thought," he says, the faintest hint of a laugh rippling through his voice, "we'll go where *I* like."

Le Petit Oiseau looks like Marie Antoinette's boudoir went apeshit with a Bond villain's credit card. Glass cases gleam with purses made from what I assume to be the hides of various endangered species. Chandeliers pour out of the ceiling overhead like it's' all one continuous waterfall, crystallized into place.

I feel guilty for besmirching their glistening tile with my peasant feet—to say nothing of my attire, which is ghastly. But Sasha strides past the glittering accessories toward a tall, stern woman in a black sheath dress with resting oligarch face.

She pales when she sees him. They exchange brief words in French—*I'll be damned; he really does speak it*—then both turn to look at me.

Sasha stays put. The woman marches over, her long legs chewing up the space between where she was and where I'm currently awkwardly marooned one step inside the entrance. "Mrs. Ozerova, it's a pleasure to make your—"

"Just Ariel," I interrupt with a gulp. Then, so as not to sound like a complete and total bitch, I add, "Please."

She hesitates. Her eyes flick to the side, as if she's looking at Sasha through the back of her skull. Then she nods crisply.

"Yes, of course. Ariel. My name is Yvonne. It would be a delight to assist you today."

I consider resisting. I could, in theory. Sasha is standing aloof in the rear of the store, hands holstered in his pockets, with a look of distant, utter disdain on his face. If I refused, I'd bet he'd just tighten his jaw and instruct the staff to bar the doors. Maybe I wouldn't be able to leave, but I wouldn't have to cooperate. It'd just be a Wild West standoff. Two gunslingers waiting for the other to crack.

But everything in this store really is stunningly beautiful. Ostrich leather, Peruvian cashmere—you can't look in any direction without seeing something so exquisitely made that it takes your breath away. My fingers itch to touch this dress and that scarf.

Jasmine would have loved it here.

We used to play dress-up when we were young, putting on our best dresses and clomping around in Mama's heels. Princesses at the ball, fairies flitting to and fro. I still remember her braiding my hair into fishtails for the first time, stepping back, and smiling. *You look beautiful, Ari.*

I force a smile to my face. "Great," I tell Yvonne. "Let's see what you've got."

She begins with a broad lap of the store to familiarize myself with the different sections. It's a guilty pleasure to let my fingers riffle over every single thing they can get close enough to touch. My eyes didn't fool me—it all really does feel incredible. Soft as clouds, sleek, gorgeous.

There are just two problems with that.

One, I'm not the kind of girl who can get away with rocking a gold lamé jumpsuit or a black crocodile trench coat. That's for movie stars and runway models, not for someone who still can't remember that there's no hard T at the end of "Yves St. Laurent."

Secondly, admitting I love this stuff would be giving Sasha what he wants. And after last night's eruption, I'm still hurting in a way that brings me back to the very first square he and I ever started on. I want to piss him off. I want to see that crack in his facade again, the one that made him kiss the hell out of me in the car. Not the one that made him bark at Feliks to "take me away."

Between those two issues, though, I think I can see a narrow way through. A way to get what I want—the opportunity to play dress-up again, even if it's just for an hour or two—while keeping him from his own grim, grimy, *you'll-do-as-I-say-and-you'll-like-it* satisfaction.

So it's back to the brattiness we go.

When the first circuit is completed, Yvonne looks at me. "Where would you like to begin, Mrs.— Pardon me, Ms. Ariel?"

I purse my lips and look around. Then I stroll toward a rack of beaded gowns, conveniently located within earshot of Sasha. "That one first," I say, pointing at a bruised purple evening gown with a ten-foot long train. "And the silver heels—no, the ones with the emerald straps. Actually, *all* the straps. Oh, and that kangaroo leather bag shaped like a swan. That'll be perfect."

Yvonne looks at me, then at Sasha.

Sasha looks at Yvonne, then away.

I pointedly look at no one.

"Whatever she wants," Sasha rumbles at last. He lights a cigarette by the three-way mirror. "It all goes on my account."

I grit my teeth. *Let's see how deep those pockets run.*

It's an absolute shitshow from then on. A never-ending clusterfuck of *this* and *that* and *three of those, please.* Chinchilla fur romper. Diamond-encrusted wedges. A sable stole that makes a PETA activist somewhere wake up from a dead sleep with their heart racing.

Sasha doesn't so much as bat an eye.

Every item goes up in front of him for perusal. I make sure the price tags are blindingly obvious, and I ask Yvonne again and again to announce as loud as she can what our running total is. We fly past five figures, past six, but even as two commas come into play, Sasha remains utterly unfazed. He takes a seat in an upholstered throne in the middle of the store. At one point, Yvonne approaches him. "This is quite a lot of items, Mr. Ozerov. Perhaps you'd like to—?"

"There was nothing ambiguous about 'whatever she wants,'" he snarls. "Whatever. She. Wants."

I redouble my efforts. For fuck's sake, all I want is to see the faintest hint of the human I know is inside of him. This blank detachment is the worst face he could possibly present. I'm dying to change it in any way I can.

And yes, I'd prefer the sweet Sasha, the Sasha who dotes on me, who laughs with me, who calls me *ptichka* in that rumbling bass voice that sounds like summer heat lightning. But if he won't give me that, I'll reach for the button I do know how to press.

Piss.

Him.

Off.

Four hours in, though, my plan is backfiring spectacularly. I've tried on another half a dozen ball gowns, twenty-plus pairs of progressively obscene stilettos, and a ruby-studded choker that made the security guard spasm and drool. Sasha watches it all from his velvet chair, legs splayed, smoke curling from his lips—unfazed as I morph from Golden Age starlet to Balkan trophy wife and back again.

Until I reach for the lingerie display.

Then, at last, his fingers go still.

"Ah!" Yvonne says when she sees where my attention has gone. "I admire your taste. Our newest collection just arrived."

I yank a scrap of crimson mesh from the rack. "This. And the leather harness. Oh, *especially* the harness."

Sasha's lighter clicks. I look at him and raise a questioning brow. "If you like," is all he says.

My frown curdles. That's progress—but I want *more.*

So I shrug. "I guess we won't know until I try it on, will we?"

Then, without waiting for his reaction, I turn and embark for the dressing rooms.

But unlike every other item I've tried on today, this one gives me pause. Inside the stall, I hold it up over my sweats. There's not much of it, all things considered. Red lace panties that loop over the hips, black leather garters that sit high on the thighs, all of it running up to connect to a complex maze of interwoven black leather straps that in turn flows into a leather collar with a tiny padlock at the throat.

It's outrageous. It's scandalous. It's gonna make Sasha go berserk.

Still, I hesitate. When I wore that slutty bikini to the spa, all I had in mind was to rile him up to break him down. It was pure and simple motivation. All day today, I've been telling myself that I'm right back on that same agenda.

But am I? Is it *riling* that I'm after, like I was just a few days ago?

I know without even having to risk a glance at my own embarrassed face in the mirror that it's not that. Not anymore.

Not *just* that, at least. What I want is to make him be honest with me. Be *authentic* with me. Is that so much to ask of a man who saved my life and bared his soul last night?

I don't know.

I guess we're about to find out.

Moving quickly before I lose the nerve, I strip off my PJs and chuck them aside. Then, using all the *Tab A into Slot B* expertise I gained from building the IKEA bookshelf, bedframe, and nightstand in my apartment, I assess the ins and outs of the lingerie and shimmy it into place. I do it without looking in the mirror so I can keep my composure. But when it's on and all my bits and bobs are adequately covered, there's nothing left to do but turn…

Oh, Jesus, Mary, Joseph. Throw in the Three Wise Men and the goats in the manger, too, while we're at it.

Because this is positively indecent.

The harness bites into my thighs. The mesh thong disappears between my butt cheeks. The padlock tinkles at my throat as I take in a deep, shuddering inhale.

I look like sex. I feel like a demon. Now, onto the main event.

What will Sasha think?

I stick my head out of the dressing room curtain. Yvonne spots me immediately and starts to hurry over, but I shake my head and point at Sasha instead. "Sweetheart," I call out in a cloyingly girlish voice that makes my own skin crawl. "Could you give me a hand, please?"

Sasha turns to look at me. His face is taut. "Can't you—"

"I need *you,*" I say. "This is a future husband kind of task."

His scowl darkens. But then he rises and starts to cross the room toward me.

I step back and let the curtain swish closed. My heartbeat is kicking up higher and higher. One-fifty. One-seventy. One-ninety. *2 Fast 2 Furious.* Any second now, that curtain is going to open, and neither heaven nor hell knows what's going to come next.

I hear his footsteps. It feels like the gala bathroom all over again—me trapped in a tiny little space, breathing hard, wondering what kind of man those footsteps belong to. *Thump, thump.* Closer. Closer.

They stop. I see the tips of his toes underneath the curtain's hem. Not oxblood, like before, but black. Black as sin.

Then the curtain rips open.

And there he is.

It occurs to me, not for the first or even the hundredth time, how beautiful he is. It's unfair, really. No one man should get to have hair that thick and eyes that blue. No one person should get to be so tall and so broad and so *there.* There's too much of him, too much width and depth. I feel overwhelmed. It's hard to breathe.

But it's his eyes that draw me in most of all.

Because they're looking at me like he's never seen anything quite so divine.

He's not saying anything, though. Just standing there, working his jaw side to side. His fist tightens on the swath of curtain in his grasp.

I finger-comb my hair into something approximating sex-messy. "Well? Will this properly degrade me at Bratva dinner parties?"

I brace myself for what has to be coming next. A crude remark, a *learn your place,* a scathing dismissal. Or maybe I'll get what I'm longing for: hope, heart, humanity.

What I get instead is this:

Nothing.

He turns to leave.

Before he can even finish his pivot, though, a word flies out of my mouth all on its own: "Coward."

Sasha pauses. The curtain is draped over him, not quite open, not quite closed. He doesn't turn back all the way, but he doesn't leave just yet, either.

So I press on. "You're a fucking coward. You know that? You think you're all big and tough because you have money and you hurt people. But one little kiss you didn't mean to give and you turn into a big, fucking coward."

All of my pent-up brattiness is turning into dirty fuel, getting channeled into something altogether different than what I thought I'd be doing today. I'm *hot,* seething from head to exposed toe. Barefoot and in lingerie and almost two feet shorter than this mute, brooding titan, but fuck it—I'll go to war with him if that's what he makes me do.

"You can't just save my life and then shut me out because it makes you a teensy bit uncomfortable!" I cry out. "I saw your face in that garage, Sasha. I *felt* you. And now, you're what—ashamed? Scared I'll figure out you're human under all that ice and steel?"

He faces me again and steps inside. The curtain swings closed.

"You don't know what you're talking about." Every vowel is saw-toothed.

"Bullshit," I spit. "You kissed me like you needed it more than you've ever needed anything. And guess what? I kissed you back in the exact same way! But you recoiled right after that in pure fucking terror. And today, you can't even look at me. Why? Because caring makes you weak? Because wanting me is inconvenient to your big empire-building plans?"

He strides forward and pins me back against the mirror. Our breaths fog the glass. "Wanting you is far more than 'inconvenient,' Ariel. It's fucking ruining me. Do you know that? How can you not *see that?"* His laugh, when it comes out, is utterly heart-wrenching. "I want you so much it's rotting my bones. Every second I'm with you, I want to bury myself in you until we both forget our own names. But wanting—" He presses his forehead to mine and exhales wearily. "Wanting is how men like me get people like you killed."

The confession hangs between us, every bit as fragile as the lace stretched across my ribs. I slide my hands up his chest. Feel his heartbeat cannoning against my palms.

"Then let me be the judge of what kills me."

"No." He shakes his head. "I won't risk that."

I swallow hard. The fire in me is still simmering, though. It knows there's something here to burn through, some thorny underbrush we can clear out of the way to let new things grow. "Why'd you come for me last night, Sasha?"

"You know why."

"Because my father would've slaughtered you if I died?"

"Because *I* would've slaughtered the world!" He surges up tall. His palms slam against the glass on either side of my head. "Is that what you want to hear? That seeing that Serb *mudak's* hands on you made me want to peel my own skin off? That I spent six hours parked outside your building last night because I couldn't fucking breathe until I was sure I saw your shadow move behind the blinds?"

His pupils swallow the last bits of blue left in him. "You asked me why I stopped kissing you in the car," he rasps. "It's because I *knew.* One taste, and I'd need another. Then another. Until you weren't just a means to an alliance—you were the fucking *air.*"

"So need me then, Sasha." My knuckles graze his split, scabbing knuckles. The site of the new scars he'll soon bear as the price for keeping me safe. "Need me like I need you."

He sucks in a breath. His face is close to mine again, so huge, so touchable. I reach up to touch it, and as I do, I nod. Just once, but all my heart goes into the gesture.

It's permission. It's salvation.

He takes it.

37

SASHA

Calling it a "kiss" feels inadequate. "Kissing" is what little boys and girls do on playground dares. This has nothing in common with a chaste peck of the lips, or a high school couple fumbling around in the backseat of their parents' car.

This is more like an asteroid hitting the fucking earth.

The red lace spiderwebbing across her collarbone tears in my fist. The sound shreds through the tiny room along with her gasp. My teeth find her bottom lip, bite hard enough to sting. She moans, loud and sloppy, and I smother it with my palm.

"Quiet," I growl against her spit-slick mouth. "Or they'll hear what a greedy little thing you are."

Ariel's hips jerk against mine. Through two layers of fabric, I feel how wet she is, smell the musk of her need. My cock throbs, trapped against my zipper like a caged beast.

"You're the one showing your hand," she pants, all defiance

and trembling limbs. Her nails score down my chest. "They already know what I am."

I spin her hard toward the mirror. Her palms slap against cool glass as I yank the harness straps down her thighs. "And what's that? What am I?"

She watches me through the reflection. "A man who breaks everything he touches."

The accusation tears through me, raw and true. I fist a hand in her hair, forcing her head back as my other hand clenches the flimsy lace between her legs. "Then why do you keep handing me the hammer?"

Her answer comes as a ragged cry when I rip the last of the lingerie off her completely. The leather straps pool at her ankles like bondage ropes. I kick them aside as my palm finds her bare pussy.

"Sasha—"

"Look." I tighten my grip on her hair, angling her face toward our reflection. My fingers glide through her, spreading her open, as her sweetness drips down my knuckles. "Look at what you do to me. What I do to you."

Her throat works as I slide two fingers inside. That perfect mouth falls open when I curl them just so. "You see? This?" I pump faster, thumb circling her clit with filthy, wet sounds. "This is what *wanting* looks like."

Ariel's shaking now, thighs trembling around my wrist. I watch drops of sweat slide between her shoulder blades, past the flush crawling up her neck. My cock aches—a persistent, primal drumbeat. But not yet. Not until…

"Come for me," I rasp against her ear. "Let them all hear."

Her back arches. "I can't—"

I bite the juncture of neck and shoulder as I shove her cheek against the glass and draw another whine out of her. "You can. You will." Every word is another crack of the whip she's begging me to use on her. "Show me how good you are."

She breaks open with a shattered cry I swallow with my palm. The convulsions around my fingers nearly undo me. I press her harder into the mirror to muffle the sounds, watching her mascara smear across the glass. Her whimpers vibrate through my hand.

When she slumps forward, I catch her against my chest. She's panting, those perfect tits heaving with every inhale. I tug the curtain aside—just a finger's width—and pause.

Voices float towards me. French syllables, sharp as stilettos—Yvonne and another client, three dressing rooms down. We're close enough to smell her Chanel No.5. She's close enough to hear every one of Ariel's hitched breaths.

Ariel goes rigid in my arms. I press my mouth to her damp hair. "Does it scare you? Being caught?"

"Not a bit."

I cluck my tongue. "Haven't I warned you about lying to me?"

"You do a lot of that," Ariel pants. "I think you're all talk."

I laugh cruelly, right in her face. "Pot, kettle. You've been thrashing at the reins since the minute we met. But you've been like *this—"* I reach out to cup her pussy, relishing how she moans and squirms, but not enough to actually get away from my touch. "—since the second you first heard me call you mine. Since the library, the spa, since the fucking gala bathroom. Dripping for me while you waste breathing calling me a bastard."

Her hand sneaks back, palming my cock through slacks. "I think you talk too much."

The challenge snaps something primal. I spin her again, back to the mirror, and shove her forward until her tits smear against the glass. The rasp of my zipper's downward drag echoes in the tiny space.

"Stay right fucking there." I bite the word into the nape of her neck as I release her and step back. "Don't move. Don't touch yourself."

She does as I say. Her reflection watches me strip—jacket hitting the floor, shirt following. When I'm bare-chested, I kneel behind her. My tongue licks a hot stripe from knee to thigh. She tastes like salt and poor decisions. Like every sin I've ever craved.

"You're insane," she whispers as my teeth sink into the soft flesh of her ass.

"And you're wetter than ever." I slide two fingers back into her heat. "What does that make you, Ariel?"

Her moan judders through the mirror when I add a third finger. The stretch makes her eyelids flutter. I watch her throat work as I pump slowly, carefully. "Answer me. It wasn't a rhetorical question."

"It makes me… d…d-des…"

"What's that?" I suckle her clit from behind for a moment, then let it fall from my lips. "I can't hear you."

"*Desperate*." Her hips jerk back. "Fuck—please—"

My free hand finds her throat. Not squeezing. Just… holding. A reminder. "Desperate for…?"

Her eyes meet mine in the glass. Defiance wars with hunger. Hunger wins. "You. Always you."

That guts me. Rips me wide open. I'm moving before I decide to—dragging her up by the throat, shoving her against the wall, her back to my front. Our mouths clash—a battle of teeth and tongues and broken growls. Her legs hitch around my hips. I shove my slacks down just enough, spit into my palm, stroke myself once. Her eyes find mine in the mirror—dark, hooded, *daring* me.

I slam home.

The mirror rattles. Her cry drowns in my mouth. For one suspended eternity, we're fused together—her heat strangling my cock, my hand bruising her thigh. Then she moves.

"*Sasha*."

My name becomes both prayer and profanity as she bucks back into me. I devour every sound, every twitch. When her head falls back against my shoulder, I crane around to nip the frantic pulse at her throat.

"That's it," I rasp against her skin. "Take what you need. Fucking use me."

Her hands reach up to fist in my hair and drag my mouth to hers. The kiss tastes like tears.

"Not using," she pants between thrusts. "Never using. *Wanting*. Fuck—!"

Her thighs clamp like a vice. An orgasm rips through her with a sob she buries against my palm. I hold still, shaking, letting her pulse around me. Letting her feel every inch I've claimed.

Gospodi pomiluy, she looks like a fucking goddess. My handprint, red and purple on her throat… Her tits bouncing with every thrust… My cock splitting her in two… The sweat and joyful tears and black, streaked makeup mingling on her face is the most beautiful painting I've ever seen.

"Please," she whimpers.

I tighten my grip. Her pulse drums against my palm. "Please what?"

"H-harder."

I snap my hips viciously. The mirror rattles. She chokes on a scream-turned-moan.

"You want them to know?" I hiss. "Want Yvonne to hear her precious merchandise getting fucked raw?"

Her cunt flutters. *Christ.* I drag her head back by the hair, exposing her throat. "Beg."

"Sasha—"

"Beg."

"Please—please don't stop—"

I release her throat to shove two fingers in her mouth. "Suck. Taste what you've done."

She moans around the digits, tongue swirling. I fuck her harder, angling deep. When her knees buckle, I catch her with an arm around her waist, never slowing. "That's it," I growl. "Take it. Take *me.*"

I can feel my own finish coming, but I'm nowhere near ready to be done with this fallen fucking angel. So I tear myself out of Ariel and I toss her on the velvet ottoman. Her legs part instinctively and I descend to my knees to feast on her pussy. Licking, fingering, consuming her like a dying man.

Her eyes roll back in her head as I keep devouring her clit and fingering her. "No. Don't you dare fucking look away. You look at me when you come, Ariel. For the rest of your life, it's my face you'll see when you come the fuck apart."

She obeys. Barely. But the overwhelm is tearing her face in half a dozen different directions. She looks almost broken as she murmurs, "Please—Sasha—I can't—"

"You can." My fingers spread her wider. "And you will."

I ignore Yvonne's concerned *"Everything alright in there?"* and suck harder.

Everything's fucking peachy, Yvonne.

When she comes, back arched like a bowstring, thighs crushing my head, I can only laugh. I don't give her long to soak in the aftermath, though. Instead, I rise and flip her onto all fours. I pull my belt free of my pants. In one quick motion, I loop it around her throat and tighten.

Ariel's eyes bulge. I can hardly blame her. Fucking in a public dressing room, with a belt around her throat—we're playing with fire, fucking on the razor's edge of what's dangerous and what will make her come harder than she's ever come in her whole cursed life.

But when I think about it, it all seems appropriate. This has been a bad idea from the start. What's the harm in pouring gasoline on a burning star?

What little is left of her composure dissolves when I crash into her again. One hand clamps on her waist; another holds the leather leash. Her elbows slide in our mingled mess as I fuck her from behind.

"Watch," I snarl, angling her face toward the mirror. My thumb digs into the purple bite mark on her ass. "Watch me wreck us both."

The first thrust punches air from her lungs. The second draws blood where her teeth split her lip. By the third, she's meeting me stroke for stroke—a frantic, filthy cadence.

"Fuck—" Her hand flies to my hip, nails digging. "Don't stop — Don't you fucking stop—"

I'm losing it. Not much longer left. I'm everywhere at once—hands on her breasts, teeth on her neck, cock buried to the hilt. The ottoman skids across the floor with every thrust. Lipstick tubes and price tags rain around us like confetti as I pull the belt tighter, tighter, tighter.

"Come with me," I demand, fingers finding her clit. I yank the belt fully taut. "Now."

She breaks first. I follow a heartbeat later, pistoning through her aftershocks until my release paints her dripping walls white. The roar I bury in her shoulder leaves teeth marks.

We collapse in a heap of limbs and gasping breaths. Fuck only knows how long we stay down there. As far as I'm concerned, it'd be fine if we never move again. I loosen the belt and let it slither aside.

Ariel exhales and trembles against my chest. I stroke her hair with shaking hands and worry that maybe we went too far. But as the shaking worsens, my concern does, too—until I realize it's not tears wracking her right now.

It's *laughter*.

"You're insane," she accuses again. "Absolutely crazy."

"I never pretended otherwise."

She turns in my arms. The trust in her gaze terrifies me more than any Serbian gun ever has. "It's not just sex, you know. Not for me."

My thumb traces her swollen lips. "I know. It's not for me, either. Not with you."

"Whatever comes next," she breathes against my mouth, "we face it honest. We face it together. Don't… don't hide from me anymore, okay?"

I look around at all the carnage: our clothes scattered in every corner, a shredded thong, the reddened outlines of my belt where it tightened around Ariel's throat as she sang such a pretty little song for me.

It's an utter disaster. It's perfectly us.

Then I look up. Through the skylight overhead, I see a soft, white snow has begun to fall.

The clerk stares at the armload of lingerie Ariel had "tried on." "Shall I… wrap these?"

"We'll take it all," I tell him.

Under her breath, Ariel adds, "It would be highly unethical to return it."

The afternoon sun hits my face as we exit. My grip tightens around her hand—not possessive, but *present*. Her grip tightens back in response.

Klaus lobs the bags into the trunk. "Sir, Feliks called. He asked me to inform you that you've got the Zimoy meeting in twenty—"

"Reschedule it."

"But the Albanians—"

"Reschedule it."

I help Ariel into the backseat, then follow her. When the door closes, she turns to me. "Sasha—"

"Not one word." I press my palm to her cheek and feel her sweet warmth seeping into me like honey. "Not yet. I just want to sit with you for a while."

The engine purrs to life. Somewhere beneath the musk of sex and leather, I smell other things.

Smoke.

Blood.

And the faintest hint of hope.

38

ARIEL

The morning light makes the gold shopping bags in my living room glow like radioactive waste. I press an ice cube wrapped in a dish towel against my inner thigh—which is bruised all to shit, courtesy of Sasha's teeth—and stare at the mountain of silk and lace spilling from yesterday's haul.

The image swims before my eyes and turns into something else: memories of my own face dissolving into one never-ending moan while Sasha fucked me from behind, his belt black around my throat, his hand clamping over my mouth...

Snap of it, for God's sake. I keep having these unholy sex flashbacks. My body has not forgotten the damage, either. I barely made it from bed to bathroom for a midnight pee, because the first two steps had me bowlegged like a cowboy.

Ruin is too clean a word for what Sasha did to me in that dressing room.

Not that I'm upset about it. It's pretty hard to get upset when you lose track of how many times you orgasm. There's maybe a tiny tinge of shame bubbling in me, if only because remembering how easily I begged for him to destroy me runs counter to my Greek Orthodox upbringing.

But that pales in the face of how good it felt to be *with* him. To be *for* him. To offer my body up to Sasha and have him claim it—not to use the way he'd use an object, but to consume like an offering at the altar.

I wanted so badly to be something that made him feel good.

Judging by the ring of bruises around my throat, I'm fairly sure I succeeded.

I leave my cup of tea in the kitchen to steep so I can go shower. But I'm barely two steps into the Naked Limp through my living room in that direction when keys jangle in the door (which, somehow, Feliks managed to fix in less than a day).

My heart swells. Is Sasha—?

"Honey, I'm home!" calls Gina as she butts into the door and pirouettes inside, her Doc Martens clomping on top of last week's unopened mail. "I brought you goodies, too. Cinnamon roll from Mazzola's and— Oh, sweet Jiminy Cricket."

She stops to ogle me. I can only wince, because I know exactly what she's seeing. I'm crouched in a bare-ass half-squat like a nudist hobgoblin, with a frozen dish towel cramped between my legs, as more than a million dollars' worth of haute couture forms a golden mountain on top of my couch. The sex-crazed hair, numerous hickeys, and lukewarm, Jell-O-like quality of my facial expressions are all self-explanatory.

"It's not what it looks like," I lie shamelessly, if poorly.

Gina raises a brow. "That walk of shame's looking more like a *hobble* of shame, girl. Did you even *pretend* to play hard to get?"

"It's not that! I, uh… fell."

"Mhmm. Onto his dick, maybe." She sets the baked goods down on my coffee table and scowls at me. "Ariel, you look like you just rode a Clydesdale bareback through Central Park. If you don't unload every single detail right this damn second, I'm going to scream."

"Gee, I—"

"I swear I will, so help me God. Three, two, one—"

"Okay! Okay! Okay, I— Shit, *ow*." Trying to lunge to stop my best friend from yodeling at the top of her lungs is even more painful than anticipated. I end up getting less than halfway there before collapsing in a wheezing pile on the couch.

Fortunately, Gina takes it as the sign of surrender that it is and sits next to me. She's even nice enough to drape a blanket on top of my body, so I'm not both naked *and* humiliated at the same time.

"The people are waiting, Ariel, and they want to know. Details are gold."

I bite my lip. "We… we… well, we had sex."

Gina rolls her eyes hard enough to alter gravitational fields. Then she plugs her ears and opens her mouth to start screaming again. "Ahh—!"

"Stop!" I snatch her wrist and drag her back to reality. "I'm going to tell you, I promise. But you really cannot scream like that. My neighbors all already think I'm into some very bizarre shit."

Gina eyes me warily. "Judging by the hickeys, I'd say they're not so far off."

My face reddens. But there's nowhere else to go from here, so I take a deep breath, then start to tell her everything.

"So this whole plan of ours..." Gina licks a whirl of cinnamon roll frosting off her fingertip. "Total dumpster fire, huh?"

"It's bad." I take a savage bite of croissant. "Call the fire department. Evacuate the city."

"Ari... I'm worried." Gina sighs and cups my hand between both of hers. "You're playing tag with tigers, babe. Very cute stripes. Very sharp teeth."

"It's not *that* bad," I protest.

"No, you're right," she agrees. "It's worse. Tell me something: When's the last time you filed a real story?"

"It's not my fault John keeps assigning me puff pieces!"

"It *is* your fault that you stopped asking for hard leads, though." Gina tenderly brushes a lock of hair that's escaped from my bun. "I just hate to see you losing yourself to something you swore you never wanted in the first place. I'm happy you're happy, I am. I just... I just want to know that you know what you're doing."

Yeah fucking right. I haven't known what I'm doing since the beginning. *Run, kicking and screaming; bite and claw if necessary*

—that's pretty much been the extent of a plan. Is it any wonder I ended up here when "borrow from Lora's bag of tricks" was the best tactic I could come up with?

"Maybe I don't, Gina. Maybe this was hopeless from the start."

"I know that Ariel Ward is not talking like that. My girl is a *fighter.* Not a quitter. And look, I'm not even saying you have to turn your back on him forever. It's just, like—knowledge is power, y'know? And I don't think you really know him yet. Like, *know him* know him." She purses her lips. "We don't have to throw the baby out with the bathwater. I say you test him."

I'm about to say, *Isn't that what we've been doing,* but before I can, she presses a finger to my lips. "Test the man behind the mask, Ariel. You want to know if there's a soul attached to that dick, and I don't blame you. So take him somewhere that'll give you a thumbs up or a thumbs down. What's he made of? Who is he *really?* Don't let your rose-colored glasses fool you. Maybe you like what you see and you end up riding into the sunset with this prince among men. Or..." She sighs and fixes me with one of her rarest, hardest looks. "Or maybe not."

She leaves it at that. We yap for a little while about what's going on in her life and at the office. Lighter fare, a palate cleanser. Then I get dressed—with her help, like I'm some Victorian lady who needs help zipping her own slacks—and we take the subway into work together.

She has a meeting, so we part ways with a promise to meet up for lunch. But on the journey to my desk, something catches my eye.

I stop in front of the community bulletin board. It's a riot of ads and flyers for yoga classes and lost cats. My real target is stuck in the bottom corner: a sun-bleached pamphlet for Safe Harbor Women's Shelter.

I'm reaching for it when Lora emerges from the supply closet behind me, arms piled high with reams of printer paper. I immediately change course and pluck a "private investigator for hire" flyer instead. ***Private Dick Will Do the Trick!*** it screams in bright green font.

Double entendres and questionable copywriting choices aside, it's not exactly the *nothing to see here* selection I was hoping for, in terms of making Lora keep going on her merry way. Sure enough, she pauses at my side.

"Oh, no! Did you lose something?" she asks.

"Er… no. Well, kind of. I'm…" Sighing, I pin P.I. Richard's flyer back to the board and point at what I was really interested in. "Have you ever heard of this place? Safe Harbor?"

I'm ready for any of the classic Lora responses. *Safe Harbor—is that, like, a boating club?* or *Shouldn't* all *women have shelter? Isn't that in the Constitution?*

What I'm less prepared for is how her face suddenly freezes. Her ever-present smile dies. "Yeah, I know it," she murmurs, which is probably the shortest and coldest sentence I've ever heard from her.

I'm surprised. I turn to face her, still jarred by how wrong that frown looks on her. This is glitter-snow-globe Lora, it's-always-sunny Lora. It's a crime against humanity for her not to giggle between every inhale and exhale.

She fidgets in place, her gaze dropping to the floor. "When I was… Like, for a little while, my mom and I lived there. While my daddy was… not being very nice. 'Too much beer' is the short version of the story."

It's funny how one little thing can change your whole view of a person. I suddenly feel hideously guilty for ever judging her, for ever laughing at her. *You're a bitch,* blares a voice in my head. It's not wrong.

I can see right here in my mind's eye her whole life, laid out like a completed puzzle. Wanting love, *begging* for love, and getting doors slammed in her face again and again.

No wonder she wants it so badly now.

No wonder we all do.

"Anyway," she says with a sniffle, "it's a nice place. There are a lot of really lovely women who work there. Why? Were you thinking of volunteering?"

"Kind of, actually, yeah." Gina's questions from this morning echo in my head again. *What's he made of? Who is he really?*

This is one way to find out.

39

ARIEL

Am I a bad person?

That's the question I'm asking myself over and over again as I stand outside on the sidewalk, waiting for Sasha. I've paced the same ten-foot stretch repeatedly to keep the circulation going in my fingers and toes. But the panicked thumping of my heart is doing plenty to keep the blood moving elsewhere.

There are a million reasons why the answer might be yes. I could be a bad person because I let a bad man do very bad things to me in a public place. I could be a bad person because I'm still holding out hope that that bad man isn't such a bad man after all. I could be a bad person because I'm bringing him to this place, Safe Harbor Women's Shelter, where bad-luck women go to escape bad situations in a world that's too bad to be kind to them elsewhere.

But I want so badly to be good.

And I want so badly to believe that Sasha can be good, too.

I keep looking up and down the street, waiting for one of Sasha's numerous blacked-out town cars to pull up and spit him out. No dice so far. But I shriek in surprise when I feel a gloved finger tap my shoulder.

My first thought is that Dragan is back for more. Instead, I spin around to see—

"Do not *ever* sneak up on me like that again!" I scold, smacking Sasha.

He laughs. "Good to see you, too." Then he grabs me and kisses me, and just like that, I already feel my sandcastle resolve start to crumble.

"I have to make a quick call," he informs me. "Go inside; I'll be right there." I don't miss how his eyes dart to the corner, the alley, and the nearby roofs in quick succession. I wonder, not for the first time, what it's like to be him. I've always run from stuff that hides in the shadows. Sasha? He shoots it.

But, with a sigh, I turn and do as he says.

The shelter's front door sticks when I push it, the bell jingling like a nervous laugh. It's a quiet space, but clean, with a cheerful plotted plant in one corner and a faded pink armchair across from a desk.

No one is behind the desk, though. I step up and crane my head around, trying to see if I can spy someone in the office beyond. "Hello?" I call. "Hi, is anyone there?"

I hear shuffling, a cough, and then a woman emerges from the office. She's got the sturdy build of someone who's spent a lifetime hoisting donation boxes and broken women. Her silver-streaked hair is twisted into a knot that defies gravity.

"You're early," she says—not rudely, but flat, straight, unvarnished. "Volunteer orientation isn't for another thirty minutes." Something about her face is still guarded, like she doesn't trust me.

Guilt curdles in my stomach. It's as if she can see my thoughts from when I was pacing outside. *Maybe I* am *a bad person. Maybe she sees it. Maybe I should just be straight up about the real reason why I'm here tonight: 'Hi, I'm using this place as a litmus test for my mobster fiancé's humanity. Please grade his performance on a curve.'*

Then she sighs, wipes her hands on her slacks, and offers one to me to shake. "I'm Elena Petrova. It's nice to meet you. We'll always welcome help here at Safe Harbor."

"Ariel." I smile back as I shake her hand. "It's really nice to meet you, too, Elena."

The front door bangs open while our hands are still entangled. Cold air sweeps in first, then Sasha. He fills the cramped doorway and my thoughts go loopy like they always do when I see him. Black overcoat swallowing his frame, leather gloves flexing as he adjusts the collar. He's a razor blade in a world of butter knives.

But is he a good one? screams the voice in my head. I tell it to STFU.

Sasha's gaze sweeps over the peeling ***EMPOWERMENT STARTS HERE*** poster taped to the wall before landing on me. When it does, he breaks into a crooked smile. "Hope I'm not too late."

"You're—"

"—exactly on time as always, Sashenka."

Ariel.exe has stopped working.

Because Elena is hugging him. Actually *hugging* him, her chapped lips pressing to his scarred cheek. "What a lovely surprise. Our guardian angel returneth."

They start jabbering back and forth in Russian. Meanwhile, my mind is short-circuiting. Guardian angel. Guardian *angel.* *Guardian* angel.

"Wh…what is happening?" I stammer.

The two of them turn to look at me. "You didn't tell her?" Elena arches a brow at Sasha as he shrugs out of his overcoat and hangs it up on the coat rack, as comfortable and familiar with the place as he is with his own home.

"Tell me *what*?" My voice comes out strangled.

Sasha grins as he rolls his cuffs up. "I help out here from time to time."

Elena snorts. "Don't let him sell you short. He funded the security system, the plumbing, the after-school program, and the dormitory remodel—and this wasn't just writing checks. I came in one night because I thought there was a robber—but it was just Sasha, slapping up drywall at 3 A.M." She plucks a pink onesie from an overstuffed donation box at her side and folds it gently. "He was in here last week, actually, paying for a woman's dental work after her husband knocked her teeth out."

Something fragile breaks in my chest. "Why?"

Sasha's jaw tightens. Behind him, through the office's smudged window, I watch snow begin to dust the Brooklyn streets.

Elena comes up to me and pats me on the shoulder. "I get the feeling that, tonight, you're going to learn what I've learned about Sasha Ozerov: Don't bother asking 'why.' Just take the man as he is. He gets awfully grumpy otherwise." She smiles once more, then walks toward the door that leads deeper into the center. "This way! We need hands in the donation room. Sasha Claus sent gifts."

I'm still dumbfounded as I trail along behind her. She spends ten minutes walking me through how items get catalogued and deposited in the various boxes for distribution, then leaves with a promise to come check in on us later.

We work in silence—Sasha sorts toys; I fold clothes. Every faded teddy bear looks like a grenade in his hands.

"Why didn't you tell me?" I ask after a while.

"You're the one who wanted to surprise me. I didn't want to ruin it."

"Yes, but I— I— Dammit, it's not fair that you keep turning the tables like this all the time!" I throw down a pair of toddler socks in a frustrated huff. "Just once, for one single, solitary time in my goddamn life, I'd like to seem like I know what I'm doing."

Sasha laughs bitterly as he stops sorting and turns to face me. "Ariel Ward, if you think for even a moment that I'm in charge of what's happening here, you're mistaken. I'm as helpless as you are."

A frown splits my face. "This feels like another trap."

He spreads his hands wide. "No traps here. No games, tricks, or bullshit. I didn't intend for any of this to happen the way it has. But…" He leans over and cups my fingers between his palms. "I'm not fighting it anymore, Ariel. I tried; I tried like fucking hell. But it failed. So I'm doing the only thing I can do now: seeing where it takes us."

I want to believe him. Truly, I do. I just… can't. Whether it's a lifetime of trauma, a genetic predisposition to paranoia, or some other third thing, I simply cannot let myself take Sasha Ozerov's words at face value.

Even when they're nice words.

Even when they're beautiful words.

"There's just no way you're not getting something out of this," I mumble. My face drops in burning shame even as I gesture around with a hand to encompass the whole shelter we're sitting in. I know I sound ridiculous—and I sure as hell feel that way, too. But I just have to press and poke until the truth is utterly undeniable.

"Like what?" he scoffs. "What could I possibly stand to gain from supporting a safe haven for people who have nowhere else to go?"

I shrug, face still aimed at the ground. "I know how people like you operate. You look for pretty fronts so you can clean your dirty money."

I have to stifle a scream when Sasha slams the donation box down. "Do not ever accuse me of that again." Dust motes swirl in the sudden silence. He grabs my face and makes me look at him. "You think I wipe ledgers here? With glitter glue and toddler socks? Or is it just that you think I'm so weak that I need to play charity to feel human?"

"I think I don't know you at all."

He stills. Beyond the thin drywall, where the women and children live in the dormitories that Sasha's money rebuilt, a child's laughter bubbles through—sweet, bright, completely alien in this bruised, battered world.

"You want my biography, Ariel, as if that will explain me. Since when do facts on a page explain a person? Are you summarizable? Does your fucking LinkedIn tell your story?"

I swallow hard. "I'm a reporter, Sasha. Is it so crazy that I want to know more?"

"It's not crazy." He catches my wrist. "It's just… incomplete."

"How can it be incomplete when there's nothing there at all? Sasha, I barely know the first thing about you—other than how you make me feel. Just give me something to tether that to. Give me a reason to believe I can trust this."

It's the closest I've come to admitting that things have changed, have *been* changing, between us. We're two days shy of the end of this crazy game, and I'm less certain than ever of anything at all.

Sasha's face smolders. Like this, in just a shirt and slacks, seated at a repurposed picnic table in this stale, quiet room, he almost looks human. The eyes, though, have seen things no one else was ever meant to see.

"You want a story? Fine. Here's a fucking story. My mother once begged my father to let her visit her cousins in Minsk. She grew up with them, as good as siblings, and all she wanted was to see them again." His voice grates like steel wool. "Do you know what he did? He hid her passport. Burned her letters. And when she tried to leave anyway, he broke her wrist." His hand clenches into a fist on his lap. "She didn't ask again after that."

For a brief, hallucinatory flicker, I see the face of the boy Sasha imposed over the man. I can imagine him running to his mother as she cradled that hurt wrist to her chest. I can hear how she sniffled to dry up her tears so she could tend to his instead. How she used her good hand to hold him close and tell him everything was going to be alright.

You wanted an answer, I laugh at myself in loathing. *Does this pass the test?*

I reach for him. If I can just touch him, that'll be the start of the apology he deserves. As soon as I feel his warmth, I can give up this stupid, silly game and let myself trust that the man in front of me, the man I've seen with my own two eyes, is no monster. He's not a saint, but he's not the beast I thought he was. He's… he's…

"Mr. Sasha!" A blur of neon leggings barrels into his legs just before my fingers make contact with Sasha's knee. "You came back!"

I spring backward to make room for the new entry. The girl who just ran in can't be older than five, her braids secured with mismatched butterfly clips. Sasha goes predator-still—then slowly crouches, beaming wildly as he lowers himself eye-level with her. "Anyusha. Where is your mother?"

"Talking to the lawyer lady." She thrusts a crayon drawing at him. Purple stick figures holding hands under a lopsided sun. One has bright blue eyes. "Look what I made! This is you and me at the park!"

"This can't possibly be right…" He takes the paper like it's made of blown glass. "There's no swing set!"

Anya giggles hysterically as he tickles her belly.

"Go add swings so I can push you higher than the trees, like I promised," he tells her.

"Come with me!" she pleads. Her eyes are huge and round, completely undeniable. I can feel my heart melting at the edges.

Sasha looks at me and I nod. "Go ahead," I murmur. "I'll be alright."

He rises and takes her hand. Well, sort of—her tiny fingers barely fit around his pinky. But he lets her lead him away through the door and into the room beyond, leaving me alone and wondering just what the hell I've gotten myself into.

The door clicks shut behind Sasha and Anya. I slump onto the bench, staring at the half-folded onesie in my hands. The fabric's worn thin at the knees. Some little girl will wear this until it disintegrates, and she'll never know the monster who paid for her safe place to sleep.

"He's good with the little ones, no?"

I startle. Elena leans against the doorframe, arms crossed, gazing at me.

"Seems like it," I mutter, folding the onesie into a tight square.

She hums, moving to sort through a box of battered board books. "You know, the first time he came here fifteen years ago, I thought he was casing the place. Big, rich man, scary man sniffing around my door? I nearly called the police."

My hands still. "What changed your mind?"

"The woman who came with him." Elena plucks a copy of *Goodnight Moon* from the box, thumbing its water-stained pages. "Her face was... how you say? A mosaic. Broken pieces glued with fear. Sasha carried her suitcase. When I asked if she needed sanctuary, he said, 'No. She needs a boat.'"

Jealousy licks my ribs. I hate myself for it. "His mistress?"

Elena barks a laugh. "His *conscience.* Her husband was a powerful man, a bad man." She sets the book aside and looks at me again. "Sasha showed up at their home in the middle of the night, put a gun to the husband's head, and made him let her go. Then he took her away. Last I heard, she's teaching violin in Marseille."

The onesie slips from my numb fingers. "Why?"

"Why does anyone do kindness?" Elena shrugs. "Maybe he saw his mother in her eyes. Maybe he simply felt like."

The jealousy is a feral thing inside me now. Still loathing how much it's affecting me, I can't help but whisper, "Did he love her?"

Elena's smile is pitying. "You think this is about romance? Think bigger, *solnyshka.*" She taps her temple. "The head, the heart—they speak different languages."

Footsteps echo in the hall. Elena straightens as Sasha reappears, Anya's giggles trailing behind him.

"That little princess is a tyrant in the making," he grumbles, but there's warmth in it.

My throat tightens. I want to ask about the woman from Marseille, about midnight drives and loaded guns pressed to abusive husbands' temples. I want to know if he kissed her goodbye at the docks, if her hands trembled when she thanked him for what he did.

Instead, I say, "You're good with her."

"Children are simple." He adjusts his hair. "They want safety. Swings. Teddy bears and cookies and for their fathers to stop coming home so angry."

"And you? What do you want?"

His gaze traps mine. "Do you still have to ask me that question, Ariel?"

At the sound of a door closing, I look up to see that Elena is gone. It's just us in here, Sasha and me, in this home of dreams that have been beaten but not yet killed.

Meanwhile, deep in the belly of Safe Harbor, the furnace kicks on with a groan. Somewhere closer, a mother sings a lullaby in soft Spanish. Sasha Ozerov sits amidst the chaos of discarded toys and secondhand hopes, smelling like snow and gunmetal, and I finally understand—

The monster isn't a mask. Neither is the man. They're the same person, split down the middle.

And I'm falling into the crack in between them.

40

ARIEL

"Your place, huh? Should I be flattered or concerned?"

Sasha looks at me and winks as the elevator doors start to open. "Terrified."

It's like seeing the penthouse through new eyes. Last time, I couldn't have been less concerned with the furniture or the man who picked it; I was mostly concerned about the location of the exits.

Now, though, I take my time looking around. Glass walls reveal Manhattan glittering like a spilled diamond necklace below, but the furniture belongs to a different century—ornate mahogany side tables, a velvet Chesterfield sofa aged to the color of dried blood. A bookshelf spans the entire west wall, crammed with titles in Russian, English, and what looks like Greek. How many languages does this man speak?!

"Decadent mobster or retired librarian?" I trail my fingers along a leatherbound edition of *Anna Karenina.* "It's hard to tell."

Sasha strips out of his coat and goes to pour himself a drink from the bar cart in the corner. "Just don't ask me if I've actually read them," he teases. "Some of those stories are long. You hungry? Thirsty?"

"Speaking of stories…" I turn to face him. "Elena told me about the first time she met you. The woman you saved, the one who's in Marseille now."

He stills, a vodka bottle frozen halfway to the crystal tumbler. For a second, I swear I see fear flicker in those mercury eyes. Then it's gone, replaced by his usual mocking nonchalance. "Eat first. We'll talk after."

"Afraid I'll lose my appetite?"

"Afraid I'll lose mine."

He strides into the kitchen. I follow in time to see him tying the leather strings of an apron. His hands are deft and his face relaxes as he chops and cooks. In a few short minutes, the air is filled with the sound and smell of sizzling oil. He starts setting plates in front of me. Blini smeared with caviar, beet soup so dark it looks like liquefied heartbeats, pillowy dumplings that burst with venison and guilt.

"What wise words did your mom have about food?" I ask as I try not to shovel dumplings in my mouth like I'm a trash compactor with legs. "Because if these are her recipes, I'll listen to anything she might've said."

"She said, 'The fatter the wife, the better your life.'"

My jaw drops with a shocked laugh. Sasha's eyes are twinkling, too, even when I chuck a dumpling at his head. "She did not say that!"

He snags the flying food right out of the air and pops it into his mouth, utterly unfazed. "I may be paraphrasing." Rubbing his hands on the dish towel, he adds, "These are her recipes, though. She had a gift."

"Yeah," I agree as the mood downshifts. "You can taste the love."

Sasha regards me, palms planted flat on the counter.

"What?" I ask. "You're staring."

"Observing," he corrects.

"Oh?" I lift my eyebrow. "Like what you see?"

His grin twitches. "More than you'll ever know."

"You're just buttering me up so I keep complimenting your cooking," I accuse, rapping the back of his knuckles with my fork.

"Shameless fishing for compliments is what gets me through the day, Ariel." He laughs and straightens up. "Stay here. I'll be right back."

"Where are you going?" I call after him as he vanishes down the hall.

His voice comes floating back. "I want to show you something."

I'm wringing my fingers in nervous silence, wondering if I've gone too far tonight. If I've pushed too deep into territory that has been very clearly marked as ***DO NOT TRESPASS.*** Sasha hasn't said anything about me trying to blindside him with the women's shelter thing. Part of that is because he effortlessly turned the tables there without even trying, but part of it also seems to be... acceptance? Like, he's acknowledging that there are parts of him he doesn't share with anyone, and that those are the parts I'm most interested in seeing, and he's maybe starting to warm to the idea of easing the restrictions and letting me in.

Or maybe not. Maybe that's just my hope talking.

He comes back into the kitchen a moment later with a thick volume in his grip. "Here." He thrusts it at me. "Take a look."

I'm frowning as I crack it open to the first page. It's a photo album. Blank leather cover, inside pages yellowed and crinkling.

But the first picture pasted inside stops my breath. A boy of maybe five straddles a bicycle too big for him, front wheel mangled beyond repair. His split lip blooms purple, but his grin could power the Eastern seaboard.

"You were *adorable,*" I gush. The bowl cut, the short shorts, the clear eyes, the irrepressible smile. I look up at the man version in front of me. "Wait—are you still fishing for compliments? Am I just falling into your ego trap?"

He chuckles and rolls his eyes. "Keep sassing and I'll take the book back."

"Over my dead body." I turn my back to him to shield it. Sasha is still chuckling as he plasters himself against me, his chin coming to rest on top of my head. "Keep going."

The next picture is even older than the first. Baby Sasha, swaddled like a burrito, with only his chubby cheeks peeking out. ***Aleksandr Ozerov—1 July 1986, 4.56kg.*** I do some quick math in my head and my jaw drops once again.

"You weighed more than *ten pounds* when you were born?!" I screech.

Sasha's laugh bounces his chin on top of my skull. "I was big."

"You were *fat*! Oh my God, Sasha, you must've killed your—" I freeze, even as the insensitive words are already halfway out of my mouth. Blanching, I change gears. "I'm so sorry. That's such a horrible way to— God, I'm an asshole. I'm sorry, Sasha."

His hand drifts up to graze my cheek from behind. "It's okay, Ariel. It's all okay."

But it's not okay. Because I turn the page and see eight-year-old Sasha with a black eye. The page after that has him in a leg cast. Then an ugly, puckered slice on his forearm, a grimace as he tries to run after a soccer ball. Another cast, another bandage. Page after page reveals a story written in bruises and blood. I see decades of Sasha's pain, preserved forever in Polaroid amber. Nataliya Ozerova appears ghost-like in the margins—a blurry figure drying tears in a ripped sundress, hands cupped around a candle in a blackout, pressing an ice pack to her son's eye while hers swells shut.

The last photo steals the air from my lungs. Nataliya stands before a quaint storefront with peeling gold letters: *Babushka's Lap.* Zoya's place. Her smile is sunlight through prison bars.

"That's—" My throat constricts. "She looks exactly like—"

Sasha reaches past me and snaps the album shut. "I think that's enough."

"Why show me this?"

"Because you wanted to know me. This is me."

"This *was* you," I correct. I turn to grab his wrist. He lets me take it, unresisting. "But a book of photographs and an asshole dad don't define you any more than a closet full of princess dresses and an asshole dad define me. I didn't want to be that anymore, so I stopped. You…" I look up at him, surprised that my eyes are filling with tears. "You don't have to be what he wanted you to be."

Sasha gazes down at me. It's impossible to say what he's thinking, what he's seeing. Do I look insane to him? Delusional? Or just plain stupid?

What I'm proposing is a complete and total rewrite of his entire life. His dad melted the soul of this little boy down and poured it into the mold of a monster. But fuck the mold. Outlines are only suggestions, right? I'm not the princess Leander wanted. Sasha doesn't have to be the beast Yakov intended for him to be.

We can find a different way.

… If he's willing to try.

Sasha's thumb passes over my cheekbone where a tear escaped without permission. His eyes burn through the fragile space between us. "You think it's that simple? Stop being what he made me?" The vodka on his breath is sweet fire. "Maybe you *are* delusional."

But there's no heat in it. Only wonder.

"Delusional's my middle name." My laugh cracks. "My parents couldn't decide between that, 'Disaster,' or 'Bad Decisions.'" I reach up to touch the scar around his throat, a question I've been too afraid to ask. He flinches—then stills, letting me trace the marbled skin.

"He did this," I whisper. Not a question.

"He tried."

Then he makes his move.

Not toward the exit. Not away from the truth. Toward *me.* Sasha's mouth crashes over mine like a storm surge—hot, desperate, inevitable. The photo album thuds to the floor, forgotten, and he picks me up to my feet.

We walk backward until my back hits cold glass as he pins me against the window. Manhattan winks below, a thousand judgmental eyes. I don't care. I bite his lower lip, swallow his growl.

"Watch," he rasps, wrenching my face toward the glittering abyss. "Watch what you do to me."

His reflection floats in the glass—eyes black with want, hands possessive on my hips. But it's *my* face that shocks me. Wild-haired, swollen-mouthed, *hungry.* I've never seen myself like this. So… uncontained.

His teeth find my earlobe. "You see it now? What you wake up in me?"

"I'm getting the idea." I rock into him, shameless, and feel his answering hardness. "Show me more."

Chaos unfolds in sharp, bright fragments. His buttons scatter. My blouse tears at the shoulder seam. He licks the exposed skin and murmurs, "That blush is my favorite color on you" when I shiver. All the while, the city stretches below us. We're in a snow globe of steel and sin, and Sasha's shaking it apart.

My palms flatten against the window. "You want answers?" His voice scrapes raw as he rips my pants down around my thighs. "I'll give you one."

The first thrust steals my breath. He sinks into me with a groan that unravels into Russian. I watch our reflection blur as he sets a punishing rhythm and the glass fogs with our panting.

"You're the only one, Ariel." His hand fists in my hair, tugging my head back to expose my throat. "The only one who *sees.*"

"Sasha—"

"No. Look." He smears the condensation with his palm, clearing a portal to the world below. "Look how high we are. How far you'd fall."

The duality guts me. Terror and tenderness. The way he pounds into me like vengeance, but cradles my hips like something precious. He's splitting me open in every way that matters.

"I'm not afraid of that," I lie.

He stills. Drags his thumb over the smudged lipstick at my mouth. "Then you're a fool." The next thrust is slow. Torturous. "You should run from this. From me."

"Then why don't you make me?"

He chuckles dark against my skin. A finger slides between my legs. Circles. Presses. My knees buckle, but he holds me up easily. "Because I'm a selfish bastard, and I can't let you go, even if that's the only thing left that could save you."

His teeth sink into my shoulder as I climax. The world blurs out, fireworks bursting behind my eyes. He follows me over the edge with a broken grunt.

When we're both spent, we slide down the glass into a puddle of tangled limbs and twisted clothes on the floor.

Sasha's heartbeat thrums against my spine, out of rhythm with the city's pulse below.

I count the sweat droplets tracking down the window. Five. Ten. Twenty. Fifty. A lifetime passes in the rise and fall of his chest.

"You asked me about the woman I helped. From the shelter."

I twist to face him. His gaze stays fixed on the ceiling.

"She was running from a bad man. Two of them, really." His thumb rubs absent circles on my hip. "She begged me to help her get out. Said she'd rather die than be another man's pawn." A muscle tics in his jaw. "So I gave her a new name. New life. Far from here. But she had to leave behind everything and everyone she knew."

Snow begins to fall past the window—silent flakes that dissolve the second they kiss the glass. I see the years etched in Sasha's face—the boy who learned his mother's recipes, the man who thought mercy made him weak. All the lives caught in his fists.

"Sometimes," I whisper, "isn't starting over a good thing?"

"Sometimes," he agrees. "But it's a hell of a price to pay."

I press my palm over his galloping heart. "Sasha… I'm starting to think I—"

He touches my lips. "Not yet. Don't say it yet."

We both know what *it* is. The word neither of us can survive. But when he kisses me again, soft as snowfall, I taste that word on his tongue.

For now, that's good enough.

41

ARIEL

I'm zipping up my knee-high boots when the knock comes. "Hold on!" I yell. I clomp like a horse to the door and pull it open.

Sasha is standing on the other side. He's winter incarnate. Snowflakes cling to the inky waves of his hair like diamond dust. The black cashmere scarf does nothing to soften that razor-blade jawline, only amplifies the brutal symmetry of his face. His coat—tailored, wool—hangs open, revealing a thick black sweater that looks like a really nice place for me to nuzzle my face for a while, if he'd let me.

"I said dress *warm,*" he tells me with an amused glance.

I scowl at him. "I'm wearing boots and a peacoat, and I brought gloves. What's not warm about that?"

He shrugs. "Paris is cold this time of year."

My hand freezes on the doorknob. "Paris, as in...?"

"Surprise!" Mama pops out from behind Sasha wearing a

beret she definitely just bought at the bodega downstairs. Her eyes are suspiciously shiny. "Road trip!"

"Plane trip," Sasha corrects. "Belle said she wanted to see Paris again." He shrugs a shoulder, but his eyes track my reaction like a hawk. Under his breath, he adds, "Leander took that from her. I'm giving it back."

I cross my arms and give him a feisty glare. I'm putting on a front because if I gave him a real glimpse at what this gesture is doing to my insides, we'd never make it out of my apartment. Mama would have to stand in the hallway while I showed Sasha just how much I appreciate his thoughtfulness. From my knees.

"You must think this is winning you a lot of brownie points, sir."

Sasha laughs. "If I wanted points," he purrs, stepping into my space, "I'd have gone about this in a much different way—and it would certainly not involve your mother." He kisses my forehead. "Besides, I'm getting something out of this, too. Paris has excellent champagne."

Something twists behind my ribs. Dangerous. Delicious. "What if I say no?"

"Then I'll fly there alone and drink it all myself." He tweaks my bottom lip with his thumb and grins. "But we're going to be late if you don't hurry up."

I'm still looking back and forth between the two of them, utterly baffled. "I just… I mean… *Paris?!*"

"Yes, Ariel. Paris." He steps inside to loop one arm around my waist and pick up my woefully inadequately packed duffel bag. "Hope you packed your thermal underwear."

At that, finally, I can give him a wicked grin. "Joke's on you," I tell him as Mama goes skipping down the aisle ahead of us, the sheer glee turning her into someone fifty years younger. "I didn't pack any underwear at all."

Sasha's strangled groan is exactly what I'd hoped for.

The plane hums all around us. Sasha is sprawled across from me in a cream leather seat, ankles crossed, flipping through a Russian architecture magazine like this is all just another day in his impossibly charmed life—which, I suppose, it is. At my side, Mom's glued to the window, tracing cloud shapes with her finger.

I can't remember the last time I felt so happy.

Sasha looks up. "If you're cold, Ms. Ward, there's a blanket beneath the seat right there. I could also have the attendant bring us tea, if you'd like a drink…?"

My mom laughs giddily. "Tea time at forty thousand feet sounds delightful. Thank you."

Nodding, Sasha rises and goes to talk to the cabin crew. As soon as he's a step away, Mama clutches my elbow and does the *squeeee* noise she's been emitting at regular intervals since we went wheels up. "This is so magical, Ari. Leander never—"

I can't help but wince. "Let's not compare them, Mama. Better yet, let's leave Baba out of it altogether."

"Why not?" She nods at Sasha, who's engaged in a rapid discussion with the flight attendant on how Belle takes her tea. "He listens. Leander just… took."

The plane lurches. My stomach drops faster than my common sense.

Six hours later, we're landing. Paris unfurls below us in a mille-feuille of ivory snow and amber streetlights. Wild curves, elegant streets, sugar-spun ice dangling from arches and spires. Mom still has her nose pressed to the window as she gasps again and again.

Sasha's hand finds mine, squeezes once, and lets go.

We step from the plane right into a waiting van, and from the van into the Four Seasons Hotel George V. Our suite occupies the entire top floor. Belle drifts through rooms trailed by soft "ohs," her fingertips brushing silk wallpaper and gilded door handles. When she disappears into her bedroom to unpack, I corner Sasha by the marble fireplace.

"What's this costing you?"

He tops off his cognac. "Less than you'd think."

"Bullshit." I grip his wrist. "Why are you doing this?"

Glass clinks as he sets the decanter down. Somewhere down the hall, Mom hums *La Vie En Rose*. "Because you deserve to see that it's a beautiful world, Ariel. And because your mother deserves better memories."

My throat tightens. "And you? What do you deserve?"

His smile could frost the Seine. "We're not here to talk about me."

Through the window, the Eiffel Tower glitters behind a veil

of falling snow—twenty thousand golden fireflies drunk on Christmas magic.

Sasha leans forward to kiss my temple. "C'mon. Let's go explore."

When Mama is ready, the three of us go downstairs and meander down streets dusted with glittering snowfall. Sasha doesn't let go of my hand for a second as we duck in and out of shops. By the time night descends, we're found our way to the foot of the Eiffel Tower. It looms overhead like a delicate iron finger pointing at the moon. I keep looking back and forth between it and my mom's retreating figure as she goes gallivanting off in search of pastries and coffee to ward away the cold. Even from here, I can see how she's still vibrating with joy.

A busker starts up with an accordion in one corner of the courtyard at the foot of the Tower. Grinning, Sasha twirls me in his arms and starts to slowly sway us back and forth. "Still think romance is dead?" he murmurs against my temple.

What a question.

I used to think romance was withered roses at a strip mall cemetery—all wilted clichés and empty gestures. But lately, I'm thinking differently. Because Sasha has blown romance's coffin open with a smolder and a simple kiss to the cheek. Romance is a bandaged hand in a bathroom. Romance is dragging my mom to Paris in a snowstorm because her eyes dimmed when she mentioned a time in her life things were simpler. It's brutal hands learning gentleness, Russian curses spilling like love poems between bites of sinfully good dumplings.

It's terrifying, this grenade of a feeling blooming in my chest —a kaleidoscope shrapnel of *what if.* What if it grows, a rose in this garden I thought was dead? What if it blossoms? What if we let it?

I gaze up at the man who taught me all of that. "I'd say it's showing signs of life."

His smile melts me. "There's that optimism I know and love."

I snort and butt my head into Sasha's chest as he spins me out and back in, the accordion player in the courtyard coaxing his instrument to wail soulfully into the night. "You're not exactly a ray of sunshine yourself, pal."

"The farthest thing from it," he agrees. "And yet you're here with me anyway. What does that make you?"

"Insane, probably."

"Most certainly. But what's light without some shadow, hm?" He winks. "Each one needs the other."

He gazes down at me as a violin player in the opposite corner of the courtyard starts up her playing. At first, the accordion player frowns. Then the violinist falls right into his rhythm. Two voices that don't belong together finding a tune that neither one anticipated. So much more beautiful than either one would've been alone.

And as the music swells, and as the night is chilly around us but I'm still warm in Sasha's arms, and as snow kisses my cheek and then Sasha does the same, and as one moment I never anticipated runs headlong into the next, and into the next, and into the next, I find myself looking up into blue eyes that I hated not so long ago and opening my mouth to say something that's been true for a while now but never *this* true, never *this* real, never *this* certain and undeniable deep in my chest:

"Sasha, I lo—"

His mouth smothers mine. It's a breathless kiss, and I'm almost panting when he breaks away. "I know I keep telling you not yet," he whispers, "but it's not because I— It's not because I can't— It's just… *Fuck*."

I brush my fingers against his lips. "It's okay," I whisper. "We'll know."

He nods. So many things seem caught behind the steel bars of his face, and it looks like he wants so badly to set them all free.

But not yet. Not now.

Soon, maybe.

He kisses me again, like we have an audience. Which, it turns out, we do—Japanese tourists are snapping photos while a street artist sketches our silhouette.

"Lots of Peeping Toms in Paris," I grumble.

Sasha chuckles right into my mouth. "Let them be."

Let them be. Let them watch and gawk and ogle. Let the whole city see how a monster holds his bride-to-be: one hand tangled in her hair, the other clutching her hip like she's the last life raft on the Titanic. Let that stubborn rose shove its way up through graveyard soil.

Mama comes back just as the song ends, mouth gaping wide with a yawn. "That's bedtime for me. Don't stay out too late, lovies." Her wink leaves scorch marks. "I'll find my own way back to the hotel, don't you worry." She pats Sasha's cheek, then mine, then goes dancing away into the night.

I watch her go. "She really is happy here," I say in amazement.

"Are you?"

I look up at Sasha and smile. "Yeah. I am."

42

ARIEL

Sasha makes love to me that night, slow and soft and tender. When I come in his arms, it feels like falling through clouds.

I fall asleep soon after, still warm from his touch. We wake at midnight to do it again, half-asleep and blindly fumbling through the dark, and again when dawn slants through the shutters.

His scars have never looked more beautiful to me than they do then. They're practically glowing, and I can't stop myself from tracing each one from start to finish. I save his throat for last. My fingers linger on the cut of his jaw, and when his Adam's apple bobs with a swallow, I smile.

What hurts is the crash landing back in reality.

Not the actual landing in New York—that goes smoothly, probably because Sasha would spike the pilot's head on a stake in his front yard if he so much as jostled Mama's tea the wrong way. But as soon as we step foot off the jet…

Pandemonium.

The first flash goes off like a bomb. The second, third, and fourth are like the moments in a war movie when the heroes realize suddenly that they're exposed and under enemy fire.

The voices follow, shrieking like zombie seagulls. I'm still dazed with sleep and trans-Atlantic brain fog, so I stop halfway down the jet's stairs and look back in terror at Sasha.

"*Blyat.*" His entire body tenses. His arm snakes around my waist, yanking me behind him. Meanwhile, from the horde on the tarmac, flashes erupt like landmines. At least two dozen ravenous paparazzi swarm us—shouting, jostling, iPhones thrust through the gaps in the thickets of arms all reaching toward us.

"Mr. Ozerov! Who's the lucky lady?"

"Is it true you're connected to the Brighton Beach shootings?"

"Ariel! Look here! How'd a nobody reporter bag the Butcher of Brooklyn?"

Sasha's fingers flex against my hip. I can feel the earthquake building in his chest. Mama, holding my hand, looks every bit as confused and terrified as I am.

"Keep moving," Sasha growls. Feliks shoves his way through the crowd to meet us at the bottom of the stairs, gripping Mom's arm to steer her through the chaos. But the pack follows us, rabid. They hedge closer, and closer, grabbing and plucking, until a beefy guy with a telephoto lens shoulder-checks me in his haste to reach Sasha.

That's when Sasha snaps.

He pivots so fast I get whiplash. One second, he's a marble statue; the next, he's got the photographer's collar in his fist, slamming him against a pillar in the hangar. The camera smashes against the floor and plastic shards go skittering across polished tiles.

"You touch her again," Sasha snarls, his scarred throat flexing with every word, "and I'll feed you your own fucking camera."

The photographer gurgles in Sasha's grip. "I-I'm sorry, man—"

"Not to me. Apologize to *her.*"

The man's bloodshot eyes dart to mine. "Miss—"

"Forget it," I choke out. My hands won't stop shaking. "Just let him go, Sasha. He's not worth it."

For a long, taut moment, I think he won't. Violence rolls off him in waves, that coiled Bratva rage I've only glimpsed in dark alleys and blood-slick boardrooms. Then he releases the man with a shove.

"If I see your face again…" He doesn't finish. He doesn't need to.

Feliks herds us toward the exit, barking orders in Russian at the security team who come charging up to surround us. The paparazzi fall back, cowed but still snapping shots from a safer distance. Sasha keeps his palm pressed between my shoulder blades, hot through my coat.

We hit the icy curb where three black SUVs idle. Sasha bundles my mom into the middle car. When I move to follow, he stops me.

"With me," he barks, steering me toward the lead vehicle.

I wrench free. "I'd rather ride with my mom."

"Ari—"

"That was..." I struggle to find the words. Not *scary*—I've seen too much of his world by now to be scared of him. But something about the whole scene has left me shaken, off-balance. "A lot."

His expression softens fractionally. He steps into me, all heat and cologne, and cups my face in his hands. His fingertips come away wet. I hadn't even realized I was crying.

"This is the world you're marrying into, Ariel. We don't apologize. We don't back down. Not when it comes to protecting what's ours."

"I know that. I do. It's just..." I gesture helplessly at the aftermath of chaos around us, my brain scrambling to make sense of what just happened. "I wasn't... I mean, I didn't think..."

"Stop. Breathe." I listen and he nods. "Good. Now, tell me what's going on in that head of yours."

"They were *everywhere*." The words tumble out of me in a torrent. "Like—like *vultures*, all those cameras—and they knew my name, Sasha. They knew who I was. How did they —?" My voice cracks. "I'm nobody. I'm just a reporter. But now, they're going to—" I break off as the full implications overwhelm me. I feel nauseous.

His eyes narrow. "Going to what?"

"Start digging." It comes out as barely more than a whisper. "About me. About... everything."

Understanding darkens his expression. He knows what I mean—about Leander, about my past, about all the secrets I've spent years burying.

"Let them try." His voice drops to that dangerous register that makes my spine tingle. "If anyone so much as whispers your name wrong, they answer to me."

I search his face, finding nothing but steel in those winter-blue eyes. "You make it sound so simple."

"Because it is." His fingers thread through my hair. "Your past is yours to tell or keep. Nobody gets to take that choice from you." He presses his forehead to mine, his next words barely a whisper. "I've buried worse secrets than yours, Ariel. Let me carry this weight for you."

Something in my chest cracks open at that—at the fierce tenderness in his voice, at the way he's offering not just protection, but partnership. My fingers curl into his shirt and cling there. He's the only solid thing left in a world gone sideways.

The car ride from the executive airport is silent. Sasha spends it glued to his phone, firing off curses while I stare out at the blur of the passing city. Everything feels sticky and wrong—like Paris was a dream and this is the noose dragging me back to reality.

Eventually, the SUV slows to a halt outside my apartment. Sasha hasn't stopped typing furiously on his phone, jaw clenched tight enough to crack molars. When I don't move, he glances up—impatient, harried, drenched in that bitter, smoky smell that clings to him after violence.

"Go inside," he orders. "I'm assigning a man to stay with you now. Feliks is sending extra security."

My fingers curl around the door handle. "That's it? Just 'go inside'?"

He doesn't answer for a moment. His thumb swipes across the screen. Orders go flying out somewhere in the cyber-ether: to kill someone, to hunt someone, every bit as violent and icily controlled as he was the first time I ever heard his voice. Finally, he looks up. "What? I'll see you later."

"Right. Yeah. Later."

Icy December wind slaps me across the face as I stumble onto the curb. Tires squeal before my door even slams shut. I watch the caravan peel away through a haze of exhaust, the hulking black vehicles shrinking to cockroach specks in the distance.

The security guy Sasha assigned—Yuri? Yakov? He tells me his name, but I don't catch it—falls into step beside me without a word. Somehow, his presence makes Sasha's absence feel all that much more palpable.

I'm two feet from the lobby doors when brakes shriek behind us. Heavy footsteps pound pavement.

I look up just in time to see a blue-eyed blur before Sasha crashes into me again. His arms band around my ribs, lifting me clear off my feet as he crushes his mouth to mine. The kiss tastes like regret, his teeth scraping my bottom lip hard enough to hurt.

"Little bird," he rasps against my cheek. His breath steams in the cold. "I'm sorry. I wasn't paying you enough attention."

My eyes are burning, so I look away. "I don't need it," I lie. "I can follow orders. Isn't that what a good mob wife does?"

But Sasha doesn't allow that. His gloved hand caresses my chin. "Look at me." When I still don't, he gives me a gentle shake. "Ari. Eyes here."

I blink up at him. Snowflakes catch in his lashes, crystalline against azure irises. The raw hunger in his gaze scorches through my winter layers.

"I will keep you safe," he says fiercely. "You are mine. You're still getting that ring. Still taking my name. And anyone who thinks they can come between us… They'll learn what Sasha Ozerov does to threats."

I shiver, not entirely from the cold. "Is that what I am now? A tactical vulnerability?"

"No." He walks us into the shadowy alcove beside the bodega, his security detail tactfully looking away to give us room. "You're what matters to me. The *only* thing that matters. That circus at the airport? That's my world testing us. My enemies sniffing for weakness. My allies judging if I'm strong enough to keep you." He pulls back just enough to meet my eyes. "But you are not some trophy on my mantelpiece. You're what I'm fighting for. Do you understand the difference?"

"I want to," I whimper. "I just spent so long trying to put this behind me, Sasha. For it to come back like this is terrifying. Fifteen years of running, and now, I'm front-page news because I'm stupid enough to…"

Love you. The unspoken words hang between us, fat and radioactive.

"You want to breathe," he says. "I get that. But the answer is this: Trust me. Let me strangle everything that suffocates you. Let me be the knife in your shadow. The wolf at your door." His forehead presses to mine. "I don't ask you to love this life, Ariel. Only to let me love you through it."

My heart is doing backflips. All this time, I've been seeing his violence as something to temper, to hide from. But maybe it's been his way of showing devotion all along—the wolf's teeth bared not *at* me, but *for* me.

"Okay," I whisper. "I'll try."

He kisses me again, slower this time, deep enough to make my toes curl in my boots. When he finally sets me down, his eyes are dark with promise.

Then he shrugs off his coat and settles it around my shoulders. The wool swallows me whole, rich with his mint-and-cedar scent.

"Keep that," he orders. "So you don't forget whose heat keeps you safe."

I watch him stride back to the idling SUV, my fingers buried in coat sleeves that dangle six inches past my fingertips. He pauses at the car door and shoots me that roguish grin over his shoulder.

He winks. Just that. Not a word with it, nor a gesture, but a wink that says everything he claims he's not ready to say quite yet.

Then the door slams. Tires scream. The cars disappear once more.

And I'm left to stand there in the middle of the sidewalk as snow falls around me in flurries, grinning like an idiot, wondering when hell froze over enough for me to fall in love with the devil.

43

SASHA

The first thing I notice when I wake is the silence.

No warm body curled against my chest. No soft snores puffing against my throat. Just stale air and pale winter light bleeding through the penthouse windows.

I roll over, hoping to find Ariel's indentation still pressed into the Egyptian cotton. My fist closes around cold emptiness instead. Just yesterday, I woke up in a different country, with her tangled around me. The pang of missing that is a knife to the gut.

I trace the barbed wire line around my throat. Her fingertips danced here yesterday. Not recoiling. Not calculating. *Loving.* As if my scars were constellations instead of proof that I'm irredeemably fucked-up.

Madness.

Further proof of my insanity comes when my fingers wander higher—and I realize I'm smiling. Fucking *smiling,* like a lovesick fool, as I stare at my bedroom ceiling and think about the broken little bird who fluttered into my life.

Molodets, *Sasha. How domestic you've become.*

Three months ago, I'd have bashed that paparazzo's head in and left him to gurgle and die on the tarmac, and I'd never have thought about it again. I wouldn't have even gotten angry.

But when I saw the fear on Ariel's face, the whitest, hottest rage I've ever felt ripped through me. And it was only her interference that kept me from tearing him limb from limb, then beating the rest of his colleagues with the bloody pieces.

Touch *her?* Touch what's mine?

I don't fucking think so.

It's a marvel how good it feels to fight *for* someone.

I sigh as I watch frost spiderweb across my windows. There's a phrase dancing in the recesses of my mind. Has been for a while now. So long as I think it in Russian, it feels safe enough, though only for a second. *Lyublyu tebya.* That's enormous in its own right, but bearable.

But translating those words… letting them be spoken aloud in a way where *she* could understand… I just don't fucking know. It's dangerous. Reckless. Everything Yakov beat out of me.

It feels less reckless if I let my eyes close and Ariel appear there, though. I've started collecting her quirks like precious little relics. The way her nose wrinkles when she's fibbing. How she snorts mid-laugh. The exact shade of pink her cheeks turn when she's trying not to come beneath me.

This is how hearts get cleaved open.

I sit up, knuckles white around the edge of the mattress. *Say it here,* ssyklo. *Say it now. There's no one here to hear you. You can say it like a fucking man—if you dare.*

I open my mouth.

And…

And…

… Almost.

I rise and step into the shower to start my day. But as I bask in hot water, that stupid smile still simmering in place, three syllables dangle on the tip of my tongue.

Almost.

My phone is vibrating when I step back out with a towel wrapped around my waist. Feliks's name flashes on the screen.

"Boss." Feliks clears his throat when I answer. "You need to see today's *Patriot Press.*"

I frown. It's not like him to bother me with such petty bullshit. "The fuck would I want that rag for?"

"Rag though it may be, they struck a nerve this time. Viral shit. People are talking, and it's only been on the newsstands for an hour. Front-page exposé on you."

I roll my eyes. "It's not the first time someone's tried to—"

"—They're talking about Ariel, too, Sasha."

There it is again. Rage. White-hot. Coursing from tips to toes. "Text me the link. Now."

The notification dings. My knuckles bleach around the device as I read the headline.

THE BUTCHER'S BABE: REPORTER ARIEL WARD EXPOSED AS CORRUPT MOB MISTRESS

Below the text: a blown-up photo of Ariel stumbling down the jet stairs, wide-eyed and disoriented. Beside that is a grainy shot of me slamming that photographer against the pillar. The byline credits some hack named Marty DiLaurentis.

"Call every fucking lawyer I own," I bark into the phone, already yanking on last night's slacks. "Shut down every vendor selling this trash. Burn every copy."

"I'm doing my best, man, but it's out of hand already. It's… everywhere, Sasha."

Ice floods my veins. I can picture Ariel now—hunched over her in her gloomy bedroom, watching her life implode through Twitter notifications. That fierce, fragile pride she guards like a fucking Fabergé egg crumbling to dust.

"Pick me up downstairs," I snap. "Ten minutes."

The city blurs outside the Bentley's tinted windows. Feliks hands me the hard copy of the tabloid without a word. I rip it open in disgust.

Page after page dissects Ariel's life: her job at the Gazette, her estrangement from Leander, even her goddamn college thesis on Watergate. They've spun every scrap of her identity into a sordid mob fairy tale.

We screech up to Ariel's building. I take the stairs two at a time, ignoring Yuri's greeting as I jam my key into her apartment lock.

The sight freezes me in the doorway.

Ariel sits cross-legged on the floor, surrounded by shredded newspaper. Her hair hangs in greasy curtains, face puffy and bare of makeup. A half-empty carton of Ben & Jerry's melts near her knee. When she looks up, the hollows under her eyes almost shatter me.

"Oh, goody." Her laugh cracks like old porcelain. "The Butcher is here."

I step over the debris, scanning for threats. But everything seems painfully domestic. Not so much as a throw pillow out of place. "Are you alright?"

"Oh, you know! I've been better." She cackles like she's losing her grip on reality. "Turns out reading five thousand words calling me 'Pseudo-Stalin's brainwashed concubine' really takes it out of a girl."

I crouch before her, grip her chin. "Didn't I tell you I'd keep you safe?"

"You've said a lot of things, Sasha." Up close, I see the red rims of her eyes. Dried tears meander down her cheeks and pool in her sarcastic, dimpled smile.

The bitterness in her voice sears worse than bullet wounds. I thought I could armor her. Instead, I've made her a target.

But I'm going to make this right.

"And I meant every fucking one of them." I rise and extend my hand. "Get up. We have somewhere to go."

Ariel frowns as she squints up at me. "What are you doing?"

"Erasing my mistakes."

The Patriot Press headquarters lies in a squalid corner of Long Island. It looks like what it is: a brewing pot of bullshit. Unfortunately for myself and Ariel, it's the exact flavor of bullshit that fools across the city and country love to swallow by the spoonful.

It's a two-part building. Half contains the offices of the editorial staff, while the other houses the printing presses.

"The factory side, Klaus," I order my driver. He pulls up outside the entrance and looks to me for further instruction.

"Stay close. And if you see a man named Marty DiLaurentis trying to run… smear him across the fucking grille."

Then I step out. Ariel follows.

The squeal of the doors announces our arrival. Workers freeze mid-motion, like roaches caught in sudden light, all of them watching warily to see what's happening.

A rat-faced man with squinty eyes comes up to me with a sneer. "Who're you, man? You can't just come in here and—"

He freezes when I brush him aside, reach behind him, and grab a crowbar lying propped against one of the pallets of today's issue waiting to be shipped out.

Then his jaw falls open when I turn and spear the crowbar into the grinding guts of the nearest rolling press.

An ear-splitting metallic scream rings out. It chews the crowbar halfway. Red lights and sirens go off as the machine moans, belches smoke, and finally slows to halt. One by one, the rest of the presses around us do the same.

Gone is the chugging, thudding grind of machinery.

Gone is the *thump* of stacks of this vile bullshit hitting the ground, one issue after the next.

In its place is stunned, baffled silence.

I turn to regard the dozens of workers watching me with huge eyes. "All of you," I announce, "need to get the fuck out of my building."

The rat-faced man starts spluttering. "Who the— What on— You're gonna have to pay for—"

I grab him by his shirt collar and hoist him against the wall. "I *did* pay for it," I snarl in his face. "As of fifteen minutes ago, the ground you're standing on is mine. The air you're breathing is mine. And if you're still here when I finish counting backwards from ten, I'm going to rip the beating heart out of your chest and call that 'mine,' too." I set him back on his feet and step away, dusting my hands against my pants. "That goes for all of you. Ten. Nine. Eight…"

By the time I reach five, the plant is empty.

Ariel and I are the last ones left in here. When only silence remains, she looks at me. "Sasha, what on…?"

"I told you I'd protect you, Ariel. This is how that looks." My knuckle tilts her chin toward the dead, still equipment. "This plant is mine now. Every lie they sold about you dies right here."

Her breath hitches. "You—you *bought* the paper?"

"Down to the last barrel of ink."

I pick up an issue still warm from the presses. Ariel flinches when I shred the front page with my bare hands. "The Bratva owns this place. Tomorrow's headline—" I scatter the strips of paper at her feet. "—will discuss your charity work.

Your Pulitzer-worthy bylines. It's ours to do with as we please."

Her throat bobs. She looks down at the ripped paper, then back up at me. Her voice is choked, half with tears, half with laughter. "Careful, Sasha. I'm almost starting to think you like me."

I take her hand. It's still cold and dead in mine, but it's warming, little by little. Through the open doors, I can see the plant workers fleeing to their cars as Feliks stalks around and tells them to run for their lives, cackling like a hyena.

I lead Ariel to the main press, its metallic jaws frozen mid-print cycle. "This machine spread today's filth. This is how we repay those favors."

Ariel eyes a nearby stack of papers. "Sasha—"

I rip the crowbar free of the first press I ruined and bring it down on the control panel. Sparks erupt and circuitry sizzles. "Let's see them call you a whore now."

She flinches at the crash. "Stop it! You're being insane!"

"Insane?" I kick a nearby paper spindle, sending rolls bouncing across the floor. "This is justice. You wanted to know the man you're marrying? Here he is!" I grab a Patriot employee ID from a desk and snap it between my fingers. "A beast who protects what's his!"

I lift her onto the dormant printing press, spreading her across the still-warm metal rollers. Her breath hitches as I yank down her jeans, fingers sliding through her dampness.

"Sasha..." Her nails dig into my shoulders. Everywhere we touch feels like a collision, like split atoms sparking nuclear winter.

There's nothing tender about our coupling. It's teeth and claws and ink-stained hands. The machinery groans beneath us, old gears protesting as we fuck like the world's ending—and maybe it is. Maybe this scorched-earth passion is all we'll ever have.

What if it is?

What if that's enough?

She comes with a ragged cry, back arching off the cold steel. I do the same a moment later. My roar echoes through the hollow carcass of the factory. Afterward, I let my forehead come to rest against hers, the acrid smell of solvents clinging to our skin.

Ariel brushes fingers through my hair. "You realize this makes us the trashiest cliché ever, right? Having hate sex on the ashes of our enemies?"

I lift my head, studying her smudged eyeliner and kiss-bruised mouth. "This wasn't hate, Ariel. Not even close."

44

ARIEL

The newsroom usually calms me. It's ASMR for journalism nerds: keyboard clatter, printer groans, the acidic tang of burnt coffee clinging to the back of my throat.

Today, though, it's all just making me think of sex.

Sasha driving into me as a printing press shudders beneath us.

Ink on my hands, smeared on his chest, as we fuck on top of lies.

No matter how many times I try to redirect to get actual work done, I keep ending up back in the same horny-ass headspace. Needless to say, not productive.

It doesn't help that I'm hiding. Instead of my normal cubicle, I'm balancing my laptop on my knees as I hide in the very back of a little-used conference room. I know my colleagues read the *Patriot Press*'s story, or at least heard enough about it to imagine the details. News junkies gonna news junkie, and what's better than hot, scandalous gossip about your coworkers?

But as long as I don't hear their whispers, I can pretend they aren't real. And as long as they aren't real, I can let Sasha's promise keep me sane.

I'll always protect what's mine.

He said it. He meant it. I can trust in that.

I'm elbow-deep in fact-checking Lora's piece on subway rats when a shadow falls across my desk. "Gina, I already told you, I'll—"

"*Koukla.*"

I jump hard enough to send my laptop flying. My uncle Kosti looms over me like a specter in a three-piece suit, reeking of cigar smoke and Acqua di Giò. His salt-and-pepper beard can't hide the tension around his mouth.

"You look like hell, darling."

I shudder and stand. "What are you doing here?"

He sets a cup of coffee down on the conference table. "Can't an uncle visit his favorite niece?"

"Not when you look like that." I frown. "What's wrong?"

He sighs and scratches uncomfortably at his beard as he looks around at the cluttered, lifeless conference room. "Let's go up to the roof to talk."

Winter wind claws at my cheeks as the door clangs shut behind us. Kosti paces the gravel-strewn rooftop, his oxfords crunching over pigeon droppings and stubbed-out cigarettes. Then he stops and turns to me.

"You need to leave, Ari."

I bark out a laugh. "You're my travel agent now? Where should I go? I hear Thailand is nice this time of year."

"This isn't a joke, *koukla.* I wish it was, but it's not."

My frown deepens. It's not like Uncle Kosti to be so serious. But the crow's feet in the corner of his eyes are drawn taut and the sad smile doesn't reach his eyes. He looks like he hasn't slept in days. "What's going on?" I ask quietly.

He just shakes his head. "The details don't matter."

"Of course they do!" I cry out. "God, I'm sick of everyone deciding things for me. My dad, you—can't someone just tell me about these fucking 'details' and let me make my own choices for once?"

Kosti grabs my shoulders, his grip bordering on painful. "Listen to me, Ari. There are things happening. Movements in the dark. Leander's making deals even I don't fully understand. And Sasha—"

"What about Sasha? Whatever's happening, he can handle it."

His jaw works. "This isn't about his strength; it's about yours. When things go *boom,* they don't give a damn about who gets caught in the blast. And the Serbs very much want to make things go boom. Do you understand? They're hunting, Ariel. Dragan Vukovic is hunting." He leans closer, voice dropping to a graveled whisper. "And your man is the prize buck in hunting season."

Fear sluices down my spine. I shake him off. "You're lying."

"I wouldn't do that to you." He pulls a manila envelope from his coat. Inside glints a Canadian passport bearing my face beside the name ***Emily Carter.*** A plane ticket flutters in the breeze—one-way to Ho Chi Minh City, Vietnam. "The last thing I want is to see you in a casket. After Jasmine… Well, an old man's heart can only take so much. I loved you girls like you were my own daughters. So let me protect you as if that's exactly what you were. If Leander won't…" His face hardens. "I will do what's right."

The world wobbles on its axis. For one dizzying moment, I see it—me, vanishing into some Vietnamese hostel in the jungle while Sasha burns. My fingers brush the passport's pebbled surface.

Two weeks ago, I would've kissed Kosti in sheer joy and started packing.

Now? Now, I see Sasha stabbing a crowbar in the maw of anything that would ever try to take a bit of me.

I see him in an apron, spooning sauce on top of *pelmeni.*

I see him glowing beneath Parisian lights as buskers played songs like the whole world conspired to make a moment perfect for us and us alone.

"Why now?" I ask.

Kosti's throat bobs. "Because I held you the day you were born. Because I couldn't save Jasmine. Don't make me bury another niece."

The heater next to us burps out sticky exhaust. "Uncle Kosti, Sasha's… different," I say. "He's not my father."

Kosti laughs bitterly. "No. He's worse. At least your father's evil is predictable."

I shove the envelope back into his chest. "You're wrong about him."

"Ari—"

"No. I've made my choice. You're wrong. He's not Leander. He's not Yakov, either. He's not a monster, Uncle. He's… trying. *We're* trying. And we're going to make it."

Kosti stares at me in disbelief. "Christ, Ariel. You're in love with him."

It's not a question. I open my mouth to deny it—default to sarcasm, deflection, *anything*—but the lie curdles on my tongue. Instead, I think of Lamaze class giggles smothered against his shoulder. Of him fixing Mom's broken clock and showing a little girl how to draw swing sets just so.

"Yes," I say proudly. "I am."

Kosti mutters something in Greek I haven't heard since Jasmine's empty casket funeral. Then he adds, "Love makes you stupid, Ariel. Stupid gets you dead."

"So does fear." My thumb finds the scar on my palm from the Met gala bathroom. "I spent fifteen years hiding. Look where that got me."

My uncle turns to light a cigarillo. The flame trembles in his cupped hands. When he faces me again, the lit tip makes the bags under his eyes look stark and purple.

"Things that once seemed solid are breaking. If your father's alliance with Sasha wobbles… " He exhales smoke like a dragon. "Sasha will choose his men. His power. Not you."

I grip the icy railing. Below us, taxis swarm like angry beetles. "You don't know him."

"Don't I?" His laugh rasps. "I was there when Leander made the deal. Your man didn't ask about your favorite color or whether you wanted kids. His first question was about shipping lanes."

I clench my teeth to ward off that old, familiar siren song in my head. The paranoia that my father cursed me with. "Things have changed."

"Nothing ever changes. Don't you know that? Wake up! Before you get hurt! This can end only one of two ways, Ariel: You lose your life, or you lose your soul."

Wind whips hair into my mouth. "Things change," I say again. "He's changed me. Let me change him, too."

Kosti's eyes glisten. He pulls me into a hug that feels, for the briefest moment, like old times. "Stubborn as your mother," he mutters into my hair. "But so it goes. When it all goes to hell, though... call me. The tickets will be ready for you."

45

ARIEL

I'm getting really sick of the on-the-nose metaphors.

As the stairwell door clicks shut behind me, I feel good about what I told Kosti. *You're wrong about him. He's not a monster.* But the first step down the stairs brings with it the first inkling of doubt.

Kosti's voice echoes between my ears: *You lose your life, or you lose your soul.*

I squeeze my eyes shut and clutch the railing for balance. No. Sasha is a good man. For fuck's sake, I've seen it! Bad men can't kiss you like that. Bad man can't cuddle you like that.

The next step down, though, comes with a question.

Why can't they?

After all, Sasha started this ten-day trial run with very clear goals: Do what he needed to do to break me. Sure enough, he's gotten what he wanted, didn't he? I'm putty in his hands now. I'm choosing him over my own uncle, for crying out loud. A man who held me the day I was born! I'm spitting in the face of that relationship for someone I've known for ten days because—*checks notes*—he's good in bed?!

Another step down. Another doubt. Another crumbling insistence that I chose the right path. By the time I hit the floor, I'm like what's left of a flower after too many rounds of *he loves me, he loves me not.* I feel frayed at the root.

With all the negative thoughts occupying my head, it takes me a second to realize what's strange down here. Then it clicks.

It's quiet.

The printers are still, the bullpen empty. I don't even hear the gurgle of the heaters pumping. Then someone clears their throat.

I turn to see John leaning against the hallway wall, arms folded over his chest. His tie is loose and his hair mussed, like he's been running his hands through it again and again in the throes of stress. The mustard stain on his cuffed sleeve makes me want to laugh and cry at the same time. It's the kind of thing you'd see on a sloppy child—but the expression on his face belongs to an executioner.

"My office, Ward. Now."

I gulp and follow.

The door hisses shut. John rounds his desk, then slaps something down on its surface. *The Patriot Press* masthead stares up at me in garish bold font. Beneath it, words and pictures I've already memorized.

...BUTCHER'S BABE...

...How a Mob Princess Infected NYC's Press Corps...

John collapses into his Aeron chair. It groans beneath his weight. "Here's the thing, Ariel."

Adrenaline sours my tongue. "I didn't realize you moonlighted at *TMZ* now. You want my side of the story? It's about—"

"Extortion, racketeering, conspiracy to distribute narcotics."

I stop short. "What?"

John tosses arrest records at me. ***OZEROV, SASHA*** is printed across the top. Blurry surveillance stills of Sasha exiting a Queens warehouse with blood splatters on his shirt. His scrawled signature on bank transfers moving nine figures into offshore accounts.

"Do you think this looks good for me, Ariel? For my paper?"

"John, I—"

He holds up a hand to silence me. "To be honest, I don't particularly give a shit about what you have to say. It might even make me legally culpable for something, which I assure you is the last thing I need."

"Please, John, it's just—"

"Stop. Ariel, just stop." He rises and plants his fists on his desk. "The legal shit is low on my list of worries. I'm worried about the *mob shit.* I worked the crime beat for twenty years. Did you forget that? I know how these guys operate. I've been to crime scenes that these fucks left behind. I'm still in therapy about it." His eyes are haunted, his cheeks gaunt. "One mobster's daughter? Another mobster's girl? You're a target. And as long as you work here, that means we're a target, too. For the sake of my paper and my staff, I can't allow that." He slides a termination letter across the desk. "All you have to do is sign to acknowledge it."

The pen John slaps down feels like a scalpel. The patient on the table?

My career.

Ariel Ward—Reporter. I worked so fucking hard for that title. I still remember doing "field work" my first semester in journalism school, interviewing a deli owner whose security camera had caught cops planting evidence. Rain soaked through my knockoff Blundstones as he chain-smoked Parliaments and laughed at my questions. *You the billionth kid who thinks she gonna change the world with a notepad?*

"No," I'd said, proud and defiant to a fault. "I just want to tell better stories than the ones the world makes up about us."

Two years later, John hired me straight out of j-school because I crashed the Gazette's holiday party wearing a dress made of rejection letters. That first byline is seared in my brain. ***Local Hero or Arsonist? The Strange Case of the Bodega Cat That Solved a Twenty-Year-Old Cold Case.*** Sixth page, but who cares? Mama framed it next to my preschool finger paintings.

She's the reason I'm here at all, actually. She taught me to love stories while we perched on the cracked vinyl stools of that Greek café. Our game was sacred: Mondays after school, two lemonades, one baklava to split.

I used to think those stories were real. Then, when I got a little older, I realized they were just to make me laugh. Now, I see that I was actually right the first time.

They *were* real. Because the man in the suit just might be a dark prince. There really may be a happy ending walking down the sidewalk.

We all wear masks. Book jackets that hide the story of our lives. It's not until you crack it open and start to read that you learn anything about anyone.

John taps the paper. "Whenever you're ready. Security is waiting to escort you out."

I put the tip of the pen to the paper, but then I hesitate. For a long moment, I consider what to write. I've been so many different people now that I'm starting to lose count. My past is littered with skins I've shed. I've been Leander's pawn, Jasmine's sister, Belle's daughter, Sasha's puppet. I've been Ariana Makris and Ariel Ward. So who am I now?

My choice in the end surprises me.

Ariel Ozerova.

Ariel Ward—Reporter dies without a byline. Just another mob story's bloody footnote. What comes next is anyone's guess.

He nods when it's done. "Your badge, please."

My fingers tremble as I tear the lanyard off and set it down on his desk. Then I rise to leave.

But the door bursts open before I reach it.

Gina's heel cracks marble as she storms in to hurl her own badge on John's desk. "Suck my entire feminist ass, you spineless sellout!"

Lora follows—shy, sweet Lora who orders decaf and colors her anxiety charts in lavender highlighter—tossing her badge after Gina's like a grenade. "Up yours!" she cries out, which is probably the meanest thing she's ever said aloud.

They both look at me. Gina winks. Lora flashes me a double thumbs-up.

I want to cry.

John sighs. "I take it the two of you are resigning in solidarity?"

"You take it right, you prick," Gina confirms. "Now, go fold the morning edition 'til it's all corners and shove it up your ass." She turns to me and smiles as big as she can. "Martini lunches for everyone. My treat."

We march out, chins held high, even as mine wobbles with tears I'm not yet ready to shed.

Down the street, we huddle on milk crates in a back alley. The owner, a friend of Gina's, brings us a handle of vodka, salted rim shots, and a trio of plastic cups.

I leave the cup aside and chug straight from the bottle. I feel like everything's upside down and inside-out right now. I'm supposed to pick who to trust, but how can I?

Kosti's right. Sasha's right. My father's right. Everyone's a little bit right and a whole lot wrong, and the only thing that matters is whose lie you choose to stand under when the sky finally caves in.

46

SASHA

The vodka in my glass catches the amber glow of desk lamps as I swirl it. Across the room, Marty DiLaurentis whimpers into the duct tape gagging him. His shabby chinos—already embarrassingly filthy—have been further ruined by the piss stains blooming down both thighs.

Feliks tosses another stack of documents onto the table between us. "Last of his accounts. Transferred everything to that shell corp in Belize, like you said."

I nod, tracing the laminated edge of Marty's *Patriot Press* badge. "And the wife?"

"Took the kids to her sister's in Poughkeepsie. Left him a Dear John letter that was honestly a little heartbreaking. I'd say she had the lion's share of the writing talent in that family, wouldn't you, Marty?" Feliks grins as he slaps the man on the shoulder. "Hey, wanna see her new Tinder profile? Swipe right for divorce!"

Marty makes a wet, gurgling sound.

I take my time finishing my drink. *Fuck,* it tastes good today. Even though the scent of Marty's fear is ripe in the air.

I crouch in front of his chair, meeting his bloodshot eyes.

"You wrote lies about my woman," I say softly.

He shakes his head, snot bubbling at the edges of the tape.

I rip the gag off.

"I didn't—I swear, I didn't know she—"

"Hush. You knew." I press my empty glass to his trembling lower lip. "You wanted clicks. Wanted to humiliate her. But here's the thing about sharpening your knife in public, motherfucker." The crystal cracks against his teeth. "Someone always comes for your throat."

Feliks tosses me a Zippo.

Marty screams when I flick it open.

A call comes as we're torching his apartment. Feliks answers, his face tightening as he listens. He gets about three seconds into the message before he turns to me with glee in his eyes.

"Sasha… you're not gonna believe this."

I pause, a gallon of gasoline in my hand. "You're no longer blacklisted at Spearmint Rhino?"

He grins. "Better. The Serbs are meeting in two hours—and *we know where.*"

I drop the can at once. "Tell me everything."

Salt spray from the harbor slicks the docks into a black mirror. Cranes loom like skeletons above us, casting shadows over tonight's target: a ship called *The Odyssey*. The scuttled cruiser lists in its dry dock cradle, exposing barnacles coating the underside. One porthole flickers dimly; the rest are dark.

It's seen better days. This whole place has. But the rust and rot have an epicenter, and it's exactly where these Serbian rats like to congregate.

At my side, Feliks adjusts his night vision goggles. "Thermals show twenty-three hostiles. All concentrated in the main bridge, right where that window is lit."

I check to my left and right. The darkness amongst the boatyard is filled with darker shadows amongst it. My Bratva, out in full force, bristling with enough guns to empty clips down every last Serbian throat.

"The exits?" I ask.

"Barred."

"Their boats?"

"Burned."

Finally, I let myself indulge in a grin. It's been a good fucking day already. And it's about to get even better. "Alright then," I say. "Give the order to move in."

Feliks murmurs into the radio clipped to his tactical vest.

Then the shadows descend on *The Odyssey.*

We move in tandem, boots silent on the gangplank. Nearly a hundred of my best killers, all thirsting for Serbian blood. This will be over quickly.

The first sentry dies with a knife in his trachea. The second barely turns before two silenced bullets rearrange his face.

Chaos blooms slowly, then all at once. By the time we hit the casino doors, the Serbs are scrambling. Dice and poker chips scatter as Dragan's lieutenants reach for weapons. A blonde in a sequin dress screams, champagne flute shattering.

I put a round between her companion's eyes. "Dragan! Come out, come out…"

He emerges from the VIP lounge, face a rictus of rage. Our last meeting wasn't kind to him—the bruises remain jarring and purple. But those piggish eyes still glint with the same cruelty that once made Jasmine tremble.

"Ozerov." He spits at my feet. "Here to finish stealing my wives and my city?"

I smile. "Just the city."

Gunfire erupts.

It's not a fight. It's a culling.

They're soft, these Serbs. My Bratva? We're wolves raised on broken glass and winter winds. Before I can give Dragan the death he deserves, a bald giant charges me. I sidestep and elbow his spine into splinters. Twin brothers fire Uzis blindly. I drop them with headshots so perfectly synced, their corpses collapse in unison.

But Dragan is elusive.

He takes advantage of my distraction to turn and run through a steel door, barring it behind him. It takes a few of my men with blowtorches to melt it open. By the time we're through, he's at the far end of a long hallway. The bullets we fire after him do nothing but score the metalwork. All that remains is his voice, floating down toward me, as he barks orders into his phone.

"... the helicopter, *budala*! Now, now!"

Slippery fucking mudak. I charge after him, followed by dozens of my men. We're too late, though. The helicopter is already lifting off when we burst out on the top of the bridge.

I stand beneath the downward draft and watch as that black bird lifts up and away. Dragan's face is pressed against the window, sneering at me.

I don't bother firing after him. I'd rather save my bullets for when I can press the barrel of my gun between his eyes and unload.

But I do watch as he goes. Until the chopper disappears into the smog over New Jersey, I keep my eyes locked on it.

Feliks joins me a few minutes later. Dusk is settling now, and sunset over the city has never looked more beautiful. "Anyone left?" I ask him.

He laughs. "As if I'd be that nice."

I nod in grim satisfaction. In some ways, it's a blessing that Dragan got away. Death is a mercy. This? A king stripped of crown, country, purpose? That's poetic justice. Besides, his death will come soon enough. When it does, I'll make sure I send him off in proper style.

I gaze at the Manhattan skyline. It's been a long time in the making—fifteen agonizing years—but now, I'm so close to achieving everything I've ever wanted.

I set out to call it my city. Who can deny that that's now exactly what it is? With the Serbs gutted and Leander's ports under my control, just as soon as I put that ring on Ariel's finger? It's over. It's finished.

I.

Fucking.

Win.

47

ARIEL

A fun thing about losing your mind is that you can make entertaining little games out of it, if you're creative enough. For example, I've been trying to time the bouncing of my knee to the hammering of my heart since the moment I first came straight to Sasha's penthouse and took a seat in the foyer. That stupid activity has kept me just barely on the right side of sane.

But I'm getting closer and closer to the tipping point. Every click of heels on tile makes my head snap up—a shitty Pavlovian response after three hours of false alarms. The security guard stopped making sympathetic eye contact around hour two.

Then he finally arrives.

Sasha bursts through the doors like a storm breaking. His tie is undone, sleeves rolled up to reveal corded forearms still speckled with… Is that blood or rust? Doesn't matter. All that matters is the way his eyes lock onto me the second he steps into the atrium.

I'm on my feet before I decide to move.

He catches me mid-collapse, his hands bracketing my ribs as I slam into him. The scent of gunpowder and sea salt clings to his collar. "Ariel," he murmurs into my hair, "what's wrong?"

The dam breaks.

"They fired me." The words come out mangled, my face pressed into his throat. "John said—he said I'm a liability now. That I'm your problem. And Gina and Lora quit and I—fuck, I *ruined* them—"

"Shh." He catches my tears with a kiss on each cheek. "Slow."

But I can't. It all spills out in a toxic geyser—the way John's mouth twisted in a sneer, the pitying stares from colleagues as security followed me out, Lora's shaky *Up yours!* as she handed over her press pass. "I spent years building that life," I choke. "And now, it's gone because I'm… because you're…"

His grip tightens. "Because you're mine."

"Because I'm falling right into the exact thing I ran from." I gulp. "I let myself get sucked back into this world. Let you—let my *father*—turn me into some… some *thing*. The exact same thing that happened to Jasmine! And for what? A ring? A penthouse? What happens when you decide I'm not worth the trouble anymore?"

"I would never do that," he growls.

"I know you say that, but how do I *know?*" I insist. "I didn't want this! Any of it! Do you know how hard I worked to get away from people like you? To be normal? To have a life where my work mattered more than my last name? But I can't even have that. It doesn't matter how far I run—the past always catches up to me. Always."

Sasha's quiet for a minute. Then he's steering me toward the elevators, his palm a brand between my shoulder blades. "Come."

"I don't want to go upstairs. I want—"

"You want answers? You'll get them. But not here." The elevator dings open. He crowds me into the corner and stabs the ***PH*** button. "We do this where walls don't have ears."

The ascent feels endless. Sasha's gaze never leaves mine. When we reach the top floor, he ushers me to the couch and sits me down, then kneels in front of me and holds my hands in his.

"You told me your mother used to tell you stories."

I want to tear out my hair. "What does that have to do with anything I just said?"

"Hear me out," he says. "You told me that, didn't you?"

"Yes. Fine. Yes, she did. Again, I don't see how—"

He holds up a hand. "That's why you became a reporter, right? You wanted to tell stories."

"I… Yes."

He regards me calmly, coolly. "Do you think that you have to have *that* job to tell stories?"

I frown. "I… Uh… I mean, it sort of depends on—"

But Sasha is shaking his head. "Wrong. All you need to tell stories is a story to tell, little bird. So fuck your editor. Fuck the *Gazette.* Tell any story you like. He didn't fire you, Ariel—he freed you."

I'm stunned into silence. Is he right?

For fifteen years, my whole identity has been built around ink-stained hands and press badges—a desperate hedge against the Makris blood in my veins. But Sasha's right. Stories don't require permission slips. Mama spun them from nothing but a stranger's face.

Truth doesn't need a byline. It only needs a teller.

"But just in case you're still feeling a little short on tools," Sasha says, "this might help."

He reaches into his pocket and pulls out a simple brass key, then hands it to me.

I hold it up to the light. It's simple, completely unadorned of anything that might give any indication as to what the hell it's for. "Am I supposed to guess, or…?"

He laughs. "*The Patriot Press* is yours."

I blink. And blink. And blink again.

Then: "Huh?"

Sasha rises, grinning from ear to ear like he's in on a joke that hasn't quite clicked for me yet. "You're a reporter. So go report. Expose whatever you want. Print whatever you want. *The Patriot Press* is yours, Ariel. Burn it down if you want, or build it into something that doesn't make you hate yourself in the morning."

I feel woozy. "You're… giving me a newspaper."

He nods. "I am."

"The one that *slandered* us."

"Yes." His mouth quirks. "It's poetic, no?"

I laugh—a hysterical sound. "You can't just buy my integrity back!"

"Integrity isn't a location, Ariel. It's not a byline or a business card." He steps closer, until our breaths tangle. "You think I don't see it? The fire in you? The need to rip the world open and make it account for itself?" His palm slides down to press over my racing heart. "That's not the Gazette. That's you. And I'd take a crowbar to every printing press in this city before I let them extinguish that flame."

I'm seated, but I still feel unstable enough that I'm worried about falling. Sasha sinks back to his knees in front of me and touches my hips. "I'm scared," I tell him.

"Good. That means you're on the right path."

"What if I fail?"

"You won't."

"What if I—?"

He silences me with a kiss. Not the hungry, devouring kind from the dressing room or the library. This is slow. Deliberate. A vote of confidence etched in heat and teeth.

When he pulls back, his forehead rests against mine. "You'll rage. You'll fight. You'll drag truth kicking and screaming into the light. And when the world pushes?" His hand slides into my hair, tilting my gaze up. "We'll push back harder."

The last thread of resistance snaps. I fist his shirt, pulling him down as I arch up. The kiss turns filthy, and I'm ready to follow it to its inevitable conclusion.

But before I can, he stands. "Come on. Let's go check out your new kingdom."

"Now? It's midnight!"

His grin is all wolf. "You think truth keeps business hours?"

Sasha kicks open the door marked ***EDITORIAL***, revealing a ghost town of abandoned desks. My fingers trail over Marty DiLaurentis's empty chair as Sasha spreads his arms wide.

"It's all yours," he announces.

I turn in a slow circle—the cracked whiteboards, the dusty computers, row after row of gravestone filing cabinets. Everything the light touches is mine.

"First order of business," I say, voice steadier than I feel. "We're changing the name."

Sasha leans against the doorframe, arms crossed. "To?"

I think for a moment, but when the answer comes to me, it's like it was always meant to happen like this. I meet his gaze. "The Phoenix."

Something warm flickers in his eyes. "Little birds rising from the ashes that made them. Fitting."

He bends down to kiss me, but when he starts to pull away, I grab his face. "Sasha… thank you. For believing in me."

I feel his grin in the kiss. "You made it impossible to do anything else." He pats my butt and then turns to go. "I'll let you get settled in. I won't be far, though. Call me if you need me."

I blow him a kiss as he leaves.

Outside, the world is quiet and still. But here, in this broken little kingdom of lies? Something new quickens.

I crack my knuckles, power up Marty's old computer, and start typing.

48

ARIEL

The offices of *The Phoenix* still look like the wrong end of a subway rat, but at least there's now a potted ficus in the corner.

In the newspaper business, we call that "progress."

I'm eyeballs-deep in rewiring a printer that predates the dinosaurs when Gina's voice slices through the hum of fluorescent lights. "Holy shit, Ward. You turned a trash fire into… a slightly less smoky trash fire."

I spin around, grease smeared across my cheek. Gina and Lora stand in the doorway holding cardboard boxes labeled ***GAZETTE CRAP*** in Sharpie. Lora's already got her sensible cardigan sleeves rolled up.

"First day of work and you're already late," I say, grinning.

Gina drops her box on an empty desk with a thud. "Traffic was a bear. Also, I stopped to flip off the Gazette building." She eyes the exposed wiring dangling from the ceiling. "Are we sure this place isn't gonna give us all tetanus?"

"Tetanus builds character." I wipe my hands on my jeans. "Welcome to *The Phoenix.* We've got Wi-Fi, questionable plumbing, and..." I gesture to the far wall where I've taped up my first front-page mock-up—a scorching exposé on city council kickbacks that John would never let me pursue. "Unbridled journalistic rage."

Lora peers at the headline. "You spelled 'embezzlement' wrong."

I blush. "I haven't hired a copy editor yet. We'll work on that."

With that, we dive in. I'd love to pretend that it's a fun, laugh-filled montage scored to some peppy pop song, but the reality is that it's a long, hard slog that makes little discernible progress no matter how much effort we throw at it. The truth of the matter is that *The Patriot Press* employees made their workspace into a reflection of their magazine: a pile of utter garbage.

The dumpster out back gets filled. Mold gets scrubbed away. Cockroaches are cursed out by Gina and then hit with lethal doses of what she calls her homemade *Get The Fuck Away From Me* spray. It's shockingly effective.

By the time the afternoon sun is slanting through the windows, we're all exhausted. But morale is surprisingly high. Turns out hard work is rewarding when you're doing it for your own higher calling.

As we're taking a break, Sasha strides in like he owns the place—which, I suppose, he technically does. Feliks trails behind him balancing three coffees and a box of donuts, and behind him come two-dozen or so Bratva men who look wildly out of place in a sea of cubicles.

"Wonderful," Gina mutters. "The emotionally constipated brigade is here."

Feliks plops the donuts onto Lora's desk. "Compliments of the management." His grin widens when Gina snags a cruller. "Careful, there. Those'll go straight to your hips."

Gina takes a massive, aggressive bite. "Good," she spits, crumbs flying from her mouth. "More of me to hate."

Sasha circles the room, inspecting my haphazard renovations. "You kept the bloodstain." He nods to a dark splotch near the supply closet.

"Charming, right?" I answer with a meek smile. "Gives the place… ambiance."

Lora edges away from the stain. "Whose blood do we think that is?"

"Former gossip columnist," Feliks says cheerfully. "Turns out writing about celebrity nip-slips doesn't prepare you for—"

"*Feliks,*" Sasha warns.

"—stress-induced paper cuts! Very tragic. But I'm sure he made a full recovery."

Gina snorts into her coffee. I catch the way Feliks's eyes linger on her laugh lines.

Sasha stops beside me, voice dropping. "You good, *ptichka?*"

His thumb brushes the printer grease on my jaw. I ignore the spark it sends down my spine and turn to pat the geriatric printer at my side. "Peachy. Just teaching this Nineties relic to respect its new queen."

"For its sake, I hope it learns quickly." The corner of his mouth twitches. "Do you need anything?"

"A time machine. And maybe a flamethrower."

"I'll see what I can do." He leans down to press a kiss to the top of my head. "Don't forget—dinner with your father tonight."

My gut clenches. Right. Can't wait to bread with the devil himself. In theory, it's date #9, and given how good things are between Sasha and me, it should be cause for celebration.

But that's exactly why I don't want to go: because things *are* going so well. Why ruin it with Leander, who's never seen a good thing he didn't want to ruin?

"I know," I tell Sasha, double-clutching his hand for moral support. "But we've still got an hour or so of daylight left. I'm gonna squeeze these worker bees for every ounce of effort I can get."

Sasha chuckles and cups my cheek. "I've taught you well. I brought more muscle for you to torture and they all know to do anything you ask. So have at 'em. I'll be back to check on you later."

I step up on a desk to speak over the assembled masses. I whistle with two fingers in my mouth to draw their attention, which works on Lora and all of the Bratva soldiers that Sasha brought to do my bidding.

Gina and Feliks, however, don't notice. They're deep in the midst of locking horns over what sounds like perhaps the most inane bullshit ever used as argument fodder.

"... Listen here, you Russian Ken doll," she snaps, "I told you that if you touch my Post-Its, I will end you."

"Big threats from a little woman," replies Feliks.

Gina whirls on him, her box braids swinging. “Keep laughing, Frosted Tips. I know twelve ways to kill a man with a ballpoint pen.”

“Don’t threaten me with a good time.” Feliks’s grin only stretches as he pushes off the wall.

I rub my temples and wonder idly if there might be a bottle of Xanax stashed in the supply closet somewhere. I’m less than one day into my new role as media mogul and I’m already daydreaming about setting the sprinkler system off. “Everyone shut up and gather ‘round. Now. Especially you two dummies.”

To my surprise, they all obey. Even the two hulking Bratva IT guys Sasha gifted me—Stefan and Pavel, who look like they bench-press SUVs between coding sessions—shuffle over from where they’d started picking apart the server room.

I clear my throat, suddenly nervous as thirty pairs of eyes settle on me. “Okay. Ground rules. One: This isn’t a mafia front. We’re a legitimate paper, which means no laundering money through classifieds. Two: If you’re carrying a gun, I don’t want to see it. Ever. Three: Lora’s in charge of layout. Question her choices, and you answer to me.”

Stefan raises a meaty hand. “What if enemy comes to shoot us? Do we still not show gun?”

“If someone storms in here shooting,” Feliks drawls before I can answer, “you have my permission to turn them into a colander. Happy, chief?”

Gina fake-coughs into her fist. “Kiss-ass.”

I point at him. “You, sir, are on thin ice. If there are no more questions, I'm gonna come around and start giving you tasks. Good? Great. Let's go."

The next hour descends into beautiful chaos. Lora transforms the production schedule into a color-coded masterpiece while arguing with Pavel the entire time. Gina badgers Feliks into fetching her another iced latte ("Three sugars, extra drizzle, or I'll revoke your kneecap privileges"), and I catch him slipping his number onto the cup sleeve.

"Subtle," I mutter as he saunters past my office.

Feliks winks. "You hired a pit bull. Someone's gotta tame her."

"She'll eat you alive," I warn.

"Promises, promises."

I could keep working all through the night. But the sun is finally dipping below the horizon and I've got dinner with Baba to go to. So when Gina comes to fetch me, I reluctantly concede defeat.

"Pack it up, Woodward," she says. "Your mobster prince is here to pick you up."

Sure enough, Sasha is leaning against the reception desk in a charcoal suit that should come with a warning label. His gaze flicks from my ink-stained hands to the messy bun I've secured with a pencil.

"Long day?" he asks when I approach.

"*You* try herding cats with PhDs in chaos theory." I nod toward Gina and Feliks, who are now engaged in a furious debate over... honestly, I've lost track.

Sasha checks his watch. "Dinner with your father's in two hours. You need time to change."

"Change?" I pluck at my stinky, sweaty tee. "You don't think my ***Sorry for Having Nice Tits and Correct Opinions*** shirt will fly with my father figure?"

"No, but not because it's wrong," Sasha teases, reaching around to pinch my ass. "Also, I brought you a dress."

I bat him away. "Control freak."

"You love it."

"I tolerate it."

The ride back to his penthouse is a blur of stolen kisses and wandering hands. By the time we're streaking through the marble foyer, my shirt's halfway over my head, which, according to Sasha, confirms at least one half of the text printed on the front.

I'm reaching for his belt when he stops me with a growl against my collarbone. "Later. We're already late."

"You started it!"

"And I'll finish it, too, if you're not careful." He nips my earlobe. "But dinner comes first."

He helps me shower—though his version of "helping" involves a vibrator and his tongue playing between my thighs—and then helps me step into the dress he bought.

It's black as sin and fits me like a dream. "*Bozhe moy*," he breathes when it's on and I give him a sassy twirl to show off.

"Too much?" I ask.

"Not nearly enough." He offers his arm. "Ready?"

I take it. "Let's go disappoint a patriarch."

His laugh echoes through the marble halls—dark, rich, and *mine.*

49

ARIEL

The black town car glides to a stop outside Leander's brownstone, and I'm hit with a memory so sharp it steals my breath—Jasmine squeezing my hand as we climbed these same stone steps twenty years ago, whispering *"Race you to the top!"* while our mother's laughter echoed behind us.

Now, there's only the click of Sasha's Oxfords against marble and the weight of his palm at the small of my back.

He knocks, then pauses at the top while we wait for the door to open. "Stay close," he murmurs against my temple. "Breathe. Squeeze my hand if you feel compelled to sink a knife in his kidney."

"Tempting." I force a smirk, adjusting the obsidian choker at my throat—Sasha's latest gift, cool and reassuring against my frenetic pulse. "But let's try words first. I hear they're civilized."

"Eh. Overrated."

Leander's butler—the same one from my childhood, Christos, now sporting a tragically bad combover—opens the door. "Sir. Madam." He bows low, then ushers us inside.

In the dining room, my father holds court at the head of an endless table. He rises from his throne and approaches us, arms spread wide. "There's my girl!"

My spine locks. "Baba. It's… good to see you, too."

His laugh could curdle milk. He nods to Sasha. "And you—keeping our princess out of trouble?"

"Trouble keeps finding her." Sasha pulls out my chair for me and helps me settle in. "But I'm… handling it." He takes the seat beside me. The candlelight catches the scar around his throat. "You look healthy, Leander."

"Ah, an old man does what he can to keep up with you youths." He takes a sip of his ouzo, then dabs at the corners of his mouth with a cloth napkin. "Eventually, though, he starts to wonder how much longer he can manage that. I'm finding that my clock is nearing its end."

I frown. For as long as I've known him, my father has been larger than life. Physically, temperamentally—nothing can topple him. But the longer I look now, the more I see signs of age. It's worsened since I stood in his office less than two weeks ago and watched his hands shake as he read me my fate.

Ten days. God, has it only been that long? He looks decades older. I see liver spots on his knuckles that weren't there before. When he goes for another drink, the liquid in the glass sloshes with tremors.

"We have lots to discuss," he says, clearing his throat. "But even though they say you're supposed to learn patience as you get older… Well, that lesson's just never stuck. So indulge my impatience and give me the simple answer first: Where do we stand?" His eyes shift from Sasha to me. "Either you're in, *neraïdoula mou,* or you're out."

Sasha stills beside me.

Leander arches a brow. "No?"

Blood thrums in my ears. Ten days pass before my mind's eye in one blurred flash. I see Sasha in Zoya's restaurant, hunched over borscht as he whispered about his mother's lullabies. Sasha buying a tabloid empire to spare me shame. Sasha with that child at the women's shelter, patiently watching her draw with crayon and telling her, *Yes, good, like that.*

Sasha Ozerov, the first man who's never asked me to be smaller. Softer. Less.

I clear my throat. "I'll marry him."

Silence.

Leander's glass pauses mid-sip. Sasha exhales roughly through his nose, like he'd been holding his breath until he heard my answer.

"Come again?" Leander purrs.

I lift my chin. "You wanted my answer? Here it is: *Yes*. To the wedding. To the alliance. To—" My voice cracks. I let it. "To everything."

Sasha's hand engulfs mine. At the far end of the table, Leander slowly sets down his ouzo. "You're certain? It wasn't long ago that you acted like I'd sentenced you to death."

"I'm certain," I tell him. "In fact..." I reach down to my place setting and pick up the steak knife that lies there gleaming.

The blade winks as I drag it across my palm. Blood wells in its wake, bright and burning.

"I swear." Blood drips down my wrist, welling over a scar that started this whole thing, in a bathroom that feels like a place from a dream. "On blood. On bones. On every silent grave that stands between us."

For a moment, Leander's mask slips. Some emotion I can't name etches itself into the cracks of his wrinkled facade.

Then it's gone.

"So it shall be," he murmurs. "Just like we always wanted."

The rest blurs—talk of security details, guest lists, which family jewels I'll wear to the engagement party on New Year's Eve where we'll announce everything to the world. Through it all, Sasha's thumb worries my bleeding palm, smearing our pact across skin.

Eventually, dinner ends and it's time to leave. We're almost to the foyer when Leander calls out, "Ariana."

I grit my teeth at the dead name, but I turn anyway.

He hesitates—just a flicker—before tossing me a velvet box. I stop short when I open it.

Inside glistens Mom's engagement ring, the emerald-cut diamond she hurled at his head the night she left. "She'd want you to have it," Baba mutters, suddenly fascinated by his cufflinks.

I snap the lid shut. "Thank you, Baba."

Then the door slams behind us. I make it halfway down the stoop before collapsing against Sasha, laughter and tears clotting my throat, woozy from the feeling of this momentous thing finally getting put behind me.

He crowds me against the limo, forehead pressed to mine. "*Ptichka.*" His mouth skims over my knuckles. "Why?"

I grab his lapels, dragging him closer. "Because you're the only man who'll never ask me to kneel."

His growl vibrates through my bones. The limo door opens and closes, sucking us in. Then there's only teeth and tongues and the delicious agony of finally, *finally* surrendering—not to my father, not to fate, but to the terrifying thrill of choosing my own gilded cage.

He chuckles, eyes flashing with mischief. "Careful what you wish for, Mrs. Ozerova. I'll have you on your knees by the end of the night."

The name should terrify me. Ten days ago, it would have.

Now, I can only smile up at him. "Do you promise?"

50

ARIEL

The limo's partition stays up.

Sasha's hands don't.

His teeth scrape my collarbone as he tears the slit in my dress wider, calloused palms mapping every shiver. "You looked like a queen in there," he rasps against my throat. "Cutting yourself open just to watch him bleed."

I claw at his belt. I've never hated anything more and I want it gone, gone, *gone.* The limo hits a pothole that throws me into his lap, which is fine, because that's where I was headed anyway. As I grind on him shamelessly, my head cocked back to cast moans up toward the ceiling, I whimper, "One of these days, you're going to stop talking so much and just *fuck me.*"

Sasha's growl sets me on fire. "You're going to regret saying that."

Then he shoves me onto all fours on the floor of the

limousine and hikes my dress up over my hips. He starts to eat me out from behind. I see instant stars.

Two fingers find their way inside me, pulsing and writhing as I do the exact same thing. "I'm gonna— I'm gonna—"

"Not yet, you're not." Sasha's hand clamps down on the back of my neck as he drags me upright and pushes me to my knees in front of him.

He frees his cock from his suit pants and pushes me down on it. I let him—no, I *beg* him to let me, because if I don't taste him right now then I might just fucking die.

My lips part around the slick head of him as I take him as deep as I can go. The moan when Sasha hits the back of my throat vibrates through me and into him, coaxing out a moan of his in response.

It's a drug. Hearing him moan like that, for me? Nothing and no one has ever made me feel better. *My* king. *My* man. He is my rabid wolf and I'm his little bird, and the rest of the world, as far as I'm concerned, can go fuck itself.

I suck on him, two hands gripping his shaft, until he pries me off with a wet *pop.* I know spit is dangling from my swollen lips and my makeup is probably running because "waterproof mascara" is the world's greatest lie, and if I had to guess, I'd say my carefully braided hair is now a shitshow, too.

But Sasha looks at me like I'm fucking holy.

"You, Ariel Ward, are the most beautiful thing I've ever seen."

Then he pushes me back down on his dick.

By the time Klaus parks outside Sasha's building, we've both brought each other right to the edge half a dozen times each.

I'm an utter mess and yet every nerve ending is singing songs I've never heard before. Sasha's growls keep getting deeper and darker.

He drags me through the lobby without breaking stride. The elevator doors barely shut before he's on me.

My back hits polished steel, his knee nudging my thighs apart as the numbers climb. 42. 57. 68. His teeth graze the claiming mark he left earlier this week, right above the choker. I palm his hardness through his pants.

"You're shaking," he observes.

"So are you."

The elevator dings. *Penthouse.*

He pulls me down the hallway by my hand, both of us laughing, our footsteps echoing through the vaulted space. Moonlight pools around the floating bed where he's taken me before—but tonight feels different. Final. A drumroll crescendo before the guillotine drops.

"Clothes off." He growls it against the shell of my ear, fingers already working the zipper of my dress. "Now."

I spin in his arms, pressing my half-bare back to his chest. "I'll need your help, Mr. Ozerov."

He takes his time dragging down the zipper. As if every new inch of skin revealed needs to be properly worshipped. By the time the dress is a puddle of black silk around my ankles, I'm a puddle in my own right.

I hear the clink of his belt hitting marble. The rustle of fabric. The wet heat of his mouth on my shoulder as his palms slide up my ribs to cup my breasts.

"Better?" he asks.

I arch into his touch, watching our reflection warp in the floor-to-ceiling windows. Two monsters silhouetted in lust. "Getting there."

"We've got a long way yet to go, *ptichka.*"

The possessive rasp undoes me. I turn, crashing our mouths together as we stagger toward the bed. His cock presses against my stomach, urgent and lethal as the rest of him.

I bite his lower lip hard enough to draw blood. "Say it again."

He spreads me across cold silk sheets, eyes glittering like icebergs in the dark. "*Ptichka.* My little bird. Mine. My wife. My queen. My vengeance made flesh." His tongue licks a stripe up my inner thigh. "Now, lie still while I worship what's mine."

I thread fingers through his hair—too hard, just how he likes it—as he drags the flat of his tongue over me. I revel in the way his groan vibrates against my clit. "You're… fucking… deranged."

His chuckle is pure sin. "But you'll scream for me anyway."

Then he pulls me on top of him. The first stroke is always the one I remember best. The last moment of clarity before the moments start melting together into one heat-soaked blur. But *this* first stroke—this moment, when his tip splits me open and then the rest of him slowly pushes in, stretching me wide, making me gasp and drool onto his chest…

This is one I'll remember forever.

He takes it slow at first, though I'll be damned if I know where he finds the self-control. Lord knows I left all of mine seventy stories below us.

But slow he goes. One stroke. Two. Savoring every millimeter of motion and friction and tightness. I'm bearing down on him as the first orgasm breaks over me like I'm being baptized into a new world. It's a splashing, relieving kind of thing and it consumes all of me.

Then he flips me beneath him and the speed picks up. Before long, his balls are slapping at me as each fuck spears deeper and deeper than ever before. I'm sweating, he's sweating, but when I lick a droplet from his scarred neck, it's as sweet as nectar to me.

Sasha can do no wrong now. When he puts me on my knees and fucks me from behind, it's perfect.

When I taste myself on his cock as he licks my pussy at the same time, it's perfect.

Whether he is behind me and beneath me and above me and within me, I'm just coming endlessly, no division between one orgasm and the next, just a long, breathless fugue that takes us higher and higher until at long last, with a guttural roar, Sasha says, "I'm almost there."

I lock my legs behind the small of his back and pull his forehead down to kiss against mine. Then, staring into the blue windows of his soul, I beg him, "Come in me, Sasha. Make me yours in every way that counts."

Then his mouth finds mine again, and sound becomes irrelevant.

Afterward, we lie sprawled in thousand-thread-count sheets that'll never be clean again. My head rests over the scar at his throat, rising and falling with each breath. He traces idle patterns on my hip.

"I have something for you," he says at last.

"I've taken everything I can possibly handle from you tonight," I say with a lilting laugh.

He tweaks my nose and follows it with a kiss. "You'll like this. I promise."

He slips from bed despite my protests and vanishes down the hall. When he pads back naked a moment later, he's holding an unmarked package wrapped in black velvet, with a red ribbon holding it together.

"I'm gonna guess it's not a pony."

Sasha laughs. "Not quite." Then he gives it to me.

I yank the ribbon. The lid falls away to reveal a book. Bound in supple black leather, title gold-embossed: ***A LITTLE BIRD TOLD ME.***

And beneath that… a byline.

By Ariel Ward.

My breath catches. *Holy shit.* Blank pages whisper as I flip through. Untouched. Unwritten. Waiting.

"You have so many stories to tell. But *your* story is the most important one of all. Your whole life, it's been written for you. Not anymore." He touches my chin to make me look up at him. "Write a better story. Write your story. *Our* story."

Words clog my throat. All I can do is stare at the space where the first words of my story will go when I'm ready to write it. Unmarked territory, all mine to conquer.

I look up at him. "I love you, Sasha."

It comes out before I can second-guess the instinct. Sasha goes statue-still. For one heart-stopping moment, I think I've miscalculated. That I picked the wrong moment. That "not yet" really meant "not ever." That this is where the fairy tale ends.

Then—

"Ariel Ward… I love you, too."

51

ARIEL

The next three days blur into a kaleidoscope of us.

Morning sunlight filters through bulletproof glass as Sasha hand-feeds me blini smeared with caviar off the blade of his knife. His free palm rests possessively on the swell of my ass, still sore from last night's adventures, which involved him lifting me onto the counter for a midnight snack that had nothing to do with food.

"Eat," he orders, black bathrobe hanging open to showcase the roadmap of bite marks I've left across his chest. "You'll need your strength."

That's the understatement of the year. It's a miracle that I'm still vertical—because we've spent that much time horizontal.

We've christened all of the rooms in his penthouse like we're on a holy mission to desecrate every possible flat surface. The shower flooded halfway through the fourth round of the morning when I spent a little too long teasing him from my knees. His office chair will carry a squeak for the rest of its life after I rode him through two back-to-back investor calls he barely pretended to pay attention to. Let us not speak of the bedroom, living room couch, or the armchair in the foyer.

It's not all sex, though. Gifts appear like offerings at my shrine: a first edition Brontë wrapped in silk, diamond earrings shaped like windblown feathers, a handmade leather holster for my pepper spray. He cooks me meals and reads Dostoevsky to me while I soak in his clawfoot tub. When we're too tired to make love again, he cuddles me in his arms and tells me stories about the tiny moments of stolen happiness he hoarded in his childhood.

The night before New Year's Eve, he traces constellations on my bare shoulder as snow parades past the windows. "You ever think about having kids?" he murmurs, breath warm against my ear. "Not because we have to—but because we *choose* to."

I go rigid. "Why? Trying to move up the timeline for your precious Bratva heir?"

"Don't be so combative, you little spitfire." His teeth close gently on my earlobe. "I was just wondering if you'd ever want a tiny you with my temper."

I flip to face him, knees bracketing his hips. Moonlight catches the silver in his stubble. "Watch yourself, Ozerov. That almost sounded romantic."

"You prefer transactional?" His hands slide up my thighs. "That's fine. I can work with transactional."

But when we crash back onto the pillows forty panting minutes later, he presses a kiss to my forehead so tender it cracks my ribs open.

We're perfect. He's perfect.

It's all so fucking perfect.

Which is why I don't see the blade coming.

New Year's Eve arrives with a blizzard. The Met's ballroom glitters like a snow globe shaken by God Himself. Ice sculptures drip tears and chandeliers weep diamonds. In every corner of the room, waiters circulate amongst the hundreds of guests: every crime lord, politician, and socialite that Sasha and my father, by virtue of this marriage treaty, have now cowed into utter submission.

I'm wearing the dress Sasha commissioned just for this: a blood-red Valentino with a neckline that dips to hell and back. The slit stops just shy of indecency.

Sasha's knuckles kiss my hip as we pause at the entrance. "Nervous?" he asks, lips grazing my ear.

"Of you? Never."

That's a lie. I'm nervous of everything tonight. Not just Sasha, but of all of this. In less than an hour, I'm supposed to pledge my forever to a man who once swore to break me or die trying? I'm supposed to announce an engagement to the world, just a few hundred feet from where Sasha first found me hyperventilating in a bathroom stall?

It's too neat and dainty. Too seamless. Full-circle moments are for celebrity memoirs, not for real life. I want to believe. I want so, so badly to believe in happily-ever-afters.

I've just been scarred too many times to fall for that again.

"Jesus," Gina breathes when she sees me. She's here as my other plus-one under protest, swathed in a silver pantsuit that makes her look like a shooting star. "You're sex on wheels, Ari."

"Look who's talking!" I cast around for our missing third wheel. "Where's Lora?"

Gina points with her champagne glass to a far corner of the room, where Lora, decked out in a pink ball gown with puffy, tulle sleeves, is deep in conversation with Pavel, the Bratva tech whiz Sasha assigned to work with us at The Phoenix. She's blushing shyly as she giggles at some joke of his.

"It's disgusting," Gina says flatly.

I smack her hand. "It's adorable."

She rolls her eyes, but then her gaze flits over my shoulder. "Speaking of disgusting..."

When I turn, I see Feliks sauntering in. Sasha even coerced him into wearing a tuxedo for the occasion, which is a miracle in and of itself. Honestly, he looks great. It's weird to see him not dressed in head to toe tactical gear, but the good kind of weird.

"You clean up nice, Regina," he remarks as he joins us, eyes raking up and down Gina.

"Call me that again and I'll castrate you here and now."

"You shouldn't talk so dirty in public," he croons. "Nor should you stare so much. Keep gawking and I might even start to think you've got a pulse under that ice queen act of yours."

"In your dreams, Vasiliev."

"Every night, *ogonyok.*"

I can't possibly roll my eyes hard enough to keep up with Mr. and Mrs. Romantic Denial here, so I turn around to find where Sasha might've snuck off to while they were bickering.

It takes me a moment to spot him and Baba talking by the piano. Both men are wearing smiles that, from this distance at least, look innocent enough. But beneath the surface…

Hush, you psycho. Don't look for things that aren't there, I tell myself. *This is normal now. This is what happily-ever-after looks like.*

My father has a hand clapped on Sasha's shoulder. But his free hand twitches toward his inner jacket pocket. He pulls out a silver pill case. Even from here, I see two tablets disappear under his tongue. His throat bobs with the dry swallow.

I'm still watching when Baba turns his head… and looks straight at me. When he does, his smile jitters, stutters, almost like a wince. Then he coughs and paints it back on in proper order again.

I shudder and pretend I didn't see that. I'm being absurdly paranoid; I know that. It's a big night and I'm understandably nervous. But I've got Sasha and Gina and Lora here to celebrate with me. Everything is great, grand, wonderful. Church bells soon to be ringing, fa-la-la, all that good stuff. It would be perfect if I just had my—

"Mama!"

With exquisite timing, my mom floats up to me like the fairy queen I always swore she was. The string of pearls at her throat—the first thing she bought herself after leaving Baba—glows beautifully underneath the chandeliers.

"You came," I breathe when she's close.

"Of course I came, silly goose!" She clutches my elbow and gives me a kiss on the cheek. "My baby is getting engaged. I wouldn't miss it for the world."

I don't miss the way her eyes flit toward the crowd before she reins them back in. She's uncomfortable here, and I get that more than anyone. But she came anyway. For me.

I love her so much it hurts.

"You look like a dream, Mama."

"Oh, nonsense. This dress was from the clearance rack at Dillard's, and my left eyeliner is half an inch lower than my right. *You're* the dream, sweetheart." Her lip starts to wobble as she reaches out to gently touch my cheek. "You look… you… Jasmine would've…" She cuts herself off.

"We don't have to go there." I squeeze her wrist. "Tonight's about fresh starts."

Her laugh sounds like shattered crystal. "Of course. My fierce girl." She tucks a loose curl behind my ear. "Just… be happy, okay? That's all I've ever wanted for you."

I recognize Sasha's heat at my back before I even turn to see it's him. His voice rumbles from over my shoulder. "Belle. You look stunning tonight."

"Such a charmer," she says.

"I prefer 'man moved by beauty.'"

"Did I say 'charmer'? I meant 'full of shit.'" Her face cracks into a smile as she pokes him in the ribs. "Said with love, of course."

Sasha returns her grin. "I'd expect nothing less."

Then Mama scowls as she wags that finger in his face. "This is a serious Mama Bear warning, though: Hands to self. If you smudge her lipstick before midnight, I'll come for you."

His thumb strokes the arch of my hip. "She's safe with me."

"Mm. I've heard that before." With a wink, Belle says something about shrimp puffs and goes skipping off.

The second she's out of earshot, Sasha's lips brush the hinge of my jaw. "What's eating you, *ptichka*?"

I do my best to keep my expression neutral. "Who says anything's eating me?"

Chuckling, Sasha taps the furrow between my brows. "This says so." Then he taps my chin. "This says so." He taps my fidgeting hands, my lip swollen from chewing on it. "And this, and this. All your tells are giving you away."

"Okay, I get it," I snap, knocking his hands away from my face. "You know me, I'm an open book, there are no such things as secrets when Sasha Ozerov is around."

His face darkens for a millisecond before the shade clears. "No," he rumbles. "No such things as secrets."

Sighing, I tilt into him, grounding myself in cedarwood cologne with my face against his chest. "Tell me this isn't the calm before the storm."

His chuckle rumbles against my spine. "You're *marrying* a storm, sweetheart. Best get used to it."

The hand on my hip slips lower. I arch instinctively, pulse fluttering under his palm.

"Do you trust me?" he murmurs.

I know my answer. It goes against logic. Against instinct. Against every survival gene I ever inherited from Baba...

Yes.

He laughs when he sees my worry lines ease. "That's what I thought."

A blast of microphone static silences the room. The string quartet dies mid-note as everyone in attendance turns in unison to see Baba stepping up onto the dais.

His smile is too wide, pupils swallowing the chilly gray of his eyes. "Ladies and gentlemen, friends and colleagues, thank you all for coming." He clears his throat. "It's a special night for me as a father. We're here to celebrate my daughter, Ariel—my last remaining jewel."

Whiskey sloshes over my knuckles as his hand trembles. It takes everything I have to hide my sneer. *Last remaining.* As if Jas is just another piece of broken jewelry he misplaced. Sasha's palm burns against the small of my back, steadying me.

"A man's legacy..." Baba once again reaches into his breast pocket and pulls out that silver case. Pills rattle as he dry-swallows two more. "A man's legacy is his children. And tonight, I give mine to a worthy—"

The mic squeals. Someone in the crowd coughs. My skin prickles as Baba sways, sweat glistening on his waxen face. This isn't the calculated monster who threatened me ten days ago—this is a marionette dangling from his last remaining string.

"Come," Sasha murmurs, steering me toward the stage. "Let's go give your father a hand."

I nod and we start to cut through the crowd in that direction. We're almost to the foot of the stage when I see him: Uncle Kosti, half-hidden behind an ice sculpture. My uncle's usually twinkling eyes are red-rimmed. When he sees me, he crooks a finger in my direction. *Hurry,* he mouths.

I hesitate. My father is on stage, listing badly to one side and murmuring something that the microphone can't catch. The crowd is murmuring, too, wondering what's happening.

So am I, to be honest. Why is Kosti looking like that? Why is he *hiding,* ducked out of sight, and waving his hands to me frantically?

Baba glances down from the stage and sees us waiting. He extends a hand. "Ariana… S-S-Sash…"

I wrench free of Sasha's grip. "Ari—" he growls.

But I'm already running toward the only man who ever felt like family.

When I reach Uncle Kosti, he grabs my arm hard enough to hurt. He reeks of sweat and his hair is badly mussed. "I can't do it, *koukla.* I can't let you go. Not without—not without *knowing.* I've been trying to-to-to protect you. But I—"

"Uncle Kosti, what's going on? Are you okay?"

His fingers dig into my arms. It feels freakishly wrong to see this horror painted on his face. "I got a call last night, Ariel. From Jasmine."

I recoil. Try to, at least. But my uncle doesn't release his death grip. "Jasmine's dead, Uncle Kosti."

"No, dammit. You're not listening! She's— I'm— *Gamoto,* just —Here." He fumbles with his phone, nearly dropping it before he manages to dump it in my hands.

A voicemail waits on the screen. I press play. A woman's voice crackles through the speaker.

It's a sweet voice. Soft, but not timid, and melodic despite the hint of an edge. Almost exactly as I remember—if I scrubbed fifteen years off the ghost in my memories.

"Hi. It's me. I don't have long—he always said calls home longer than a minute can be traced, so I want to keep it short. But... I saw the papers. The engagement announcement. She can't... You have to tell her not to do it. Tell her she can't trust him. He's doing it again, the same plan, the same... He said if I ever... She has to know that— And, Kosti... tell her I love her, too. Okay. That's it. I'm so sorry. I'm so—"

A hand reaches past me and snatches the phone away.

I turn to see those blue eyes I know so well.

Sasha's face isn't blank. Isn't cold. It's worse: resigned. Almost... *sad.* One look at him and I can see the whole horrible truth written there. Not every detail, but the bulk of it, the unbearable mass of it, like the hulking silhouette of something that'll break me if I see it eye-to-eye.

He said if I ever...

His thumb hovers over the voicemail. Deletes it.

She can't trust him...

His scar glints under chandelier light. The saw-toothed line of a father's cruelty.

He's doing it again.

My knees buckle. Sasha catches me, grip bruising. *"Ptichka—"*

"You *knew.*" The words shred my throat as surely as that

barbed wire did to Sasha's. "You knew she was alive. And you let me think— You let me believe—"

I can't finish the sentence. For ten days, I've told myself that he's not the man I thought he was.

I know better now.

52

SASHA

The world narrows to the fracture spreading across Ariel's face. Her lips part—not in a scream, but a silent shattering.

"Ari—"

She recoils from my outstretched hand. "Don't. *Don't.*" Her heel catches on the hem of that obscenely red dress as she stumbles back. "You let me mourn her. You let me *bury* her."

Her uncle grabs her elbow. "We need to go, *koukla. Now.*"

My instincts scream to break his wrist. My heart—that traitorous, atrophied muscle—keeps me rooted. "Ariel. Let me explain."

"Explain *what?*" Her laugh carves through me. "How you let me think I lost her? How you—*fuck*—" She presses shaking fingers to her mouth. "You knew. All this time. You *knew.*"

The ballroom's ambient murmur crescendos into a roar. Half of it is aimed at us. The other half flows in a different direction.

It's not until I look to the stage that I see why.

Dragan Vukovic is climbing the dais steps, his tailored tuxedo straining over shoulders still thick from years spent breaking bones in Belgrade's fighting pits. He drapes an arm around a gray-faced Leander's shoulders and beams.

"Ladies and gentlemen!" Dragan's voice booms through the mic. "What a touching family moment. Let's give the happy couple a round of applause!"

Leander sways beside him, pupils dilated wide. The pills, whatever they are, are no longer doing the trick. He looks like he's staring into the maw of a nightmare.

Ariel spins toward the stage. "Baba, don't—"

"Now, my friend, onto more important matters!" Dragan claps a meaty hand on Leander's shoulder. "I think it's time to tell them. Tell them all. Tell your *allies* what your precious future son-in-law did."

Leander's gaze locks with mine. His jaw works timidly, like the words taste repulsive on his tongue. "Sasha... helped... Jasmine..."

Dragan snatches the mic. "He helped your daughter fake her death! Framed *me* for her murder! All to steal your alliance!" Spittle flies as he jabs a finger at me. "This *svinja* played you! Played *all* of you!"

The crowd erupts.

In the midst of the mayhem, Ariel tries running toward the stage where Leander collapses to his knees in horror. "Baba!"

I catch her around the waist. "No."

She slams her stiletto into my shin. "Let me *go!*"

Leander crawls toward the edge of the dais, hand outstretched. "Ariana… *neraïdoula mou…*"

Dragan kicks him in the ribs. "You weak fucking prick. You swallowed his lies then. Swallow this bullet now."

"No!" Ariel is going feral in my arms, thrashing, screaming. "No. Baba! No—"

I'm dragging her backward when the shot rings out.

Leander jerks.

Croaks.

And topples into the orchestra pit.

Ariel's scream curdles my blood. Feliks shoves us behind a toppled table as doors burst open and Serbian soldiers begin to flood into the ballroom. Every last man, woman, and child in here is screaming or roaring, pulling out weapons, fleeing in whatever direction they can reach. "Sasha, we need to get the fuck out of here!"

"Get the others out, Feliks." I clamp a hand over Ariel's mouth, muffling her sobs. "Now."

She bites my palm. I feel the spurt of blood. "You *bastard.* This is your fault!" She's screaming, clawing, a wild thing unraveling in my arms. My grip tightens—not enough to bruise, never enough to hurt—but she twists like a gutshot animal.

"Listen to me!" I roar over the gunfire.

Her elbow cracks against my ribs. "You *lied!*"

Across the ballroom, Feliks drags Gina behind a marble column. Pavel's got Lora slung over his shoulder, sprinting for the service exit. Good. My men know their roles. But my role—the one that matters—is crumbling in real time beneath my hands.

Ariel bucks against me. "Let me *go* to him!"

"He's gone," I tell her. "Your father's gone, *ptichka.*"

She stills. For one second, I think she's finally hearing me. Then her palm cracks across my cheek.

"You don't get to call me that." Her eyes are twin supernovas —green fire collapsing into black voids. "You don't get to call me anything ever again."

A bullet shatters the ice swan beside us. Shrapnel peppers my neck.

"You want the truth?" I snarl, ducking us behind an overturned banquet table. Silverware skitters across the floor, dancing with the thunder of the crowd's panicked footsteps. "Your sister begged me to do what I did. Cried on her knees on that dock, terrified Dragan would track her down if I didn't set her free. Your father would've sold her back to that animal to keep his precious alliance. She had to die in order to be free."

Her breath hitches. "You don't know that."

"I saw the bruises!" The memory surges unbidden—Jasmine's trembling hands unbuttoning her blouse in that safehouse, mottled fingerprints circling her throat like a necklace as she showed me what he did. "You think I enjoyed lying to you? Letting you mourn? Don't you think I wanted to tell you? I tried to bring you as close as I could without risking her life. Ariel… *who do you think played the violin in Paris?*"

Another volley of gunfire. I count the shooters by the cadence—half a dozen Serbians ready and waiting. Dragan's voice booms over the din, rallying his men in that guttural mother tongue of his.

Ariel's fingers dig into my forearms as she sobs silently. "You could've told me."

"And risk your father finding out?" I crush her closer, shielding her body with mine as bullets chew through the table. "He'd have torn Europe apart to drag her back. Dragan, too. No one could know. This was the only way."

Her laugh scrapes raw. "The only way to manipulate everyone. To *use* us."

She's not wrong. I open my mouth—to apologize? To justify? —when a shadow looms behind her.

Instincts override thought. I spin us, taking the bullet meant for her heart.

The impact punches through my left shoulder. Ariel screams. The shooter—some Serbian grunt with a face like spoiled meat—smirks as he racks another round.

He doesn't get to fire it.

My pistol barks twice. His smirk dies with him.

"Sasha—" Ariel's hands flutter over the wound. "You're—"

"It doesn't matter." I shove her toward the service corridor. "Move!"

She stumbles, heels catching on her ruined dress. I catch her elbow, propelling us forward. Blood slicks my fingers—hers or mine or the Serbian's, I can't tell.

Her chest heaves. For a heartbeat, I see the girl from the bathroom stall—wide-eyed, trembling, so fucking alive that it hurt me to look at her.

Then her gaze hardens.

"Go to hell."

She knees me in the thigh. Not the groin—a mercy or a mistake, I'm not sure—and bolts.

"Ariel!"

Chaos swallows her. Society wives are busy trampling each other for the exits. Gunmen duel between ice sculptures. Somewhere, Feliks is shouting my name.

By the time I spot her again, Ariel is halfway up the grand staircase, scarlet train billowing behind her. She glances back once—hair tumbling from its pins, mascara bleeding down her cheeks—before vanishing out onto the mezzanine.

The wound in my shoulder screams as I give chase. Blood soaks my tuxedo jacket, warm and insistent.

Stupid girl. Reckless, stubborn, glorious girl.

Memories flash with every step. Her laughter in Zoya's kitchen. The way she'd bite her lip when pretending not to watch me work. That first time she fell asleep in my arms on that mountain, trusting me with her nightmares.

I follow the blood smears past shattered display cases. Tiffany diamonds glitter in the carpet like trapped stars.

"Ariel!"

Silence. Then—

"Stay away from me!"

Her voice comes from the Egyptian wing. I charge in that direction and find her crouched between two sarcophagi. The emergency lights paint her in hellish red. She's clutching a ceremonial dagger from the Cleopatra exhibit—twenty-dollar gift shop garbage, but sharp enough to hurt if she manages to stick me with it.

"Put it down." I step closer.

She brandishes the blade. "I mean it, Sasha."

"You won't use it."

"Try me."

We circle like wolves. Her back hits a display of canopic jars and sends them crashing to the ground. The dagger trembles in her grip, but her eyes never waver.

"You think I wanted this?" I snap. "You think I enjoyed lying awake, imagining your face when you found out?"

She shakes her head. "You don't get to play hero."

"I'm not. I'm the villain, remember? The monster who blackmails and manipulates and *lies.*"

I lunge. She's faster.

I manage to block the downward hurtling blade, but her other hand punches my wounded shoulder. White-hot agony blots out the world as I go staggering backwards. When my vision clears, she's at the emergency exit.

"Ariel—"

The door slams. The lock engages.

Through the wire-reinforced glass, I watch her run—barefoot, bleeding, beautiful—into the waiting storm.

53

SASHA

Blood on snow. Red on white. A trickling trail down alleys, like script on the ice, reading *Sasha Ozerov ran this way.*

I do what I can to cover my tracks, doubling back to lose the Serbian pursuers. It costs me precious seconds of chasing Ariel down, but if I'm dead, I'm no use to her. Fuck knows where Feliks is, where any of my men are. This is an unmitigated disaster.

But it's not the pain in my shoulder that's killing me, though my tuxedo jacket has fused to the wound with a mix of sweat and clotted blood. It's not the loss of the alliance that's darkening the edges of my vision.

It's her.

I can't see beyond the step in front of me and that frozen-still image of tears crystallizing in Ariel's eyes as she looked up at me and spat, *You knew.*

I knew.

Yes, I fucking knew.

I did what I did to *save* that poor girl. And yes, I did it for selfish fucking reasons, too. Framing Dragan for Jasmine's murder meant that Leander and the Greeks would never ally with the Serbians against me. I shored up my own empire, even though it's taken fifteen long years since then to convince Leander that backing me was the right play.

I was so close to the finish line. *Marry Ariel. Claim the docks. Profit from now until eternity.*

But I fucked up along the way.

And I know why.

Because I did everything my father warned me not to. I let my heart pull me from the path. I did what my mother did.

Jumped.

Fell.

Shattered.

Is it any wonder that it hurts so fucking badly?

How fitting that I've ended *here,* then. An ironic quirk of geography. The sign over the door gleams through the flurries of bone-chilling snow.

Babushka's Lap.

I kick the door open, bell jangling. More of my blood drips a Morse code trail across the linoleum as I stagger into the restaurant's kitchen like a ghost animating its own corpse.

Garlic and dill punch through the copper stench of my injury. Zoya looks up from her *solyanka,* cleaver poised over a head of cabbage. Her face tightens.

"Sadis." *Sit.*

I collapse onto a stainless steel prep table. "Don't mother me."

Her cleaver thunks into the cutting board. "If I don't, who else will?" She yanks open a drawer, retrieving vodka and a suture kit with practiced ease. "Shirt off."

The fabric peels away with a wet *schluck*. I have to bite my tongue so as not to roar in pain.

Zoya hisses through pursed lips when she sees the damage. "*Pizdets.* You never did do anything halfway, Sashenka. Did it go through?"

Rotating my shoulder sends white sparks across my vision. "Fuck. I think so."

She sloshes vodka over the wound. I clamp down on a scream.

"It's been a while since you limped in here, bleeding on my floor." Her tweezers probe the exit wound. "I was almost starting to enjoy the silence."

I can only grunt as fucking torture sears everywhere she extracts shrapnel.

"Where's your shadow?" Zoya sets the tweezers down, picks up needle and thread, and starts to sew the wound shut.

"Feliks can take care of himself."

"I wasn't talking about him."

I grab the vodka bottle she used as disinfectant and guzzle it. If it can clear bullet wounds, maybe it can clear away these fucking thoughts crowding my skull. And even if it can't, it burns less than Zoya's scrutiny.

"She's gone."

She squints at her handiwork, readjusts, and keeps going. The nip of needle going into my skin again and again feels like I'm being chewed alive.

"Gone?" she asks. "Or *gone*?"

The kitchen sways. I press a palm to the table. Steady. Always steady. "Does it matter?"

"Of course it fucking matters, you idiot!" Zoya slaps down the needle and jabs a finger in my face. "You come here—bleeding, shaking, smelling of her perfume—and pretend it doesn't matter? You think you are so tough, Aleksandr Ozerov. But I held you when you were *this big.*" Her hands span a loaf of bread's length. "When Yakov…"

"Don't."

"… would put cigarettes out on your arm for crying. I cleaned *this* wound, too, don't forget." Her finger jabs the scar across my throat. "I—"

The bottle shatters when I hurl it against the steel walk-in. Vodka dribbles down dented steel. "I said *don't.*"

Zoya couldn't be less intimidated. "Ach, well, I've never been a good listener."

"Being there for parts of it doesn't make you an expert on what I've survived. You know *nothing.*" I jump up and advance on her. The motion pulls free a few of her looser stitches, causing hot blood to drip down my arm.

She plants her fists on her hips and scowls at me. "I know this: When Yakov died, you came here. Do you remember? You sat in that exact seat. And do you know what you said that night, *malchik?*"

Our reflections hover in the reflective surface—her a smoking crater of a woman, me a bloodied shadow of a man.

"I said I'd piss on his grave."

"No." Zoya shakes her head. "You said, 'Now, she's safe.'"

I turn and sink back onto the wobbly stool. My head is throbbing in time with my shoulder now. Both hurt like hell. "*Blyat*," I spit at myself. "*Ssyklo.* Fucking *ssyklo.*"

Now, Zoya is the one who advances on me. "You, Sashenka, are a man who protects what he loves. Even if it means spilling your own blood to make it happen. So ask yourself: does this feel like it 'doesn't matter' to you?" She runs a finger through my pooled blood and holds it in front of my eyes. "This looks like blood to me, *malchik.* Do you regret spilling it for her?"

I press my forehead to the prep table surface and close my eyes. *Thump. Thump.* Pain, everywhere. "She hates me for what I hid, Zoya."

"So? Hate is just love that's still breathing." She cups the back of my head and sighs mournfully, the air whistling out of her in a long, sad stream.

"Nothing's left breathing, Zoya. Leander's dead. The alliance is dead. It's all fucking dead."

"*Nyet*, child. Nothing is truly dead until you give up on it. Do you think your *mamochka* is dead? Or is she here?" When I look up, I see Zoya spreading her arms wide to encompass the whole kitchen, the restaurant. "She's right here with us. In me. In you. And this Ariel… What you have with her is not dead unless you choose to let it die. Go to her. Beg. Grovel. *Live.*"

A guttural noise escapes me—part growl, part sob. "She'll shoot me on sight."

Zoya's smile curves like her cleaver. "So be ready to duck."

54

ARIEL

A rock through the window breaks it easily.

I climb through to get out of sight, off the street. But once I'm inside, I pause for a moment and look back.

The jagged shards of glass that didn't fall stick out of the opening like teeth. At my feet, the rest of them are a thousand tiny mirrors. In each one of them is an Ariel, and each of those Ariels is the same.

A fool.

An idiot.

A stupid, deluded dreamer in a stupid red dress who thought she could outrun her bloodline.

I tear my gaze away and look around me. It's strange to see the library at night. It was always bright and clean by day and magical by dusk. Now, though, the shadows are long and thick. Shelves lurk, huge, seeming almost to curve in over my head.

A cold breeze blows through the wrecked window. I shiver, wrap my arms around myself, and hurry in.

Pretty funny that I should end up here, right? This is where all stories come to die. When they're over, they get jailed in here and here they stay until the end of time.

My story is over. That fairy tale, that big, grand romance that Mama told me I deserved—it's about to be sealed up in a leatherbound coffin. I've got a great line to finish it off, whenever I get around to filling up those blank pages Sasha gave me:

And then no one lived ever after. Certainly not "happily."

I collapse into a study carrel, back pressed to walnut paneling. My hands won't stop shaking. Sasha's blood crusts under my nails from where I hit him.

Even funnier than my not-such-a-storybook ending is how I used to think I was Lois Lane. An intrepid reporter, a fearless heroine, a woman brave enough to take on the world and win. And, even though I fought it at first, I did truly come to think that Sasha might be my Superman.

But it turns out everyone is the same: liars, all the way down.

Him most of all. Liar. Fucking *liar.* Liar with his mother's eyes and his father's fists. Liar who hid my sister like a trump card. Liar who set my dad up to die on his knees in front of everyone he ever knew. Liar who made me love him in the gaps between truths.

He knew. Sasha *knew.* Sasha lied.

Artisan lies. Limited edition, bespoke deception.

Nausea crests in my stomach. I dig nails into my calves to stay silent.

Outside, the blizzard blurs the city into a chalk drawing. Somewhere out there, Sasha's probably stitching himself back together. Planning his next play. And I'm here, unraveling in the one place that ever made sense—amongst rows of bound truths, silent witnesses to all the sins we humans convince ourselves are for the greater good.

I press my cheek to a dusty copy of *The New York Times* from 1997 that someone left out on the desk. The headlines scream about Princess Di, stock markets, a world that kept spinning after other tragedies.

Why does it feel like this will be the one that halts it on its axis?

Or, actually, is it worse if it keeps spinning? *My* world might be over, but no one else will care. They'll just keep on going, falling in love, making babies, going to their sister's houses for Christmas to laugh together in warm living rooms and give each other neatly wrapped gifts. I'll be breaking into dark libraries and huddling my knees to my chest to ward off the cold.

I try to sleep. It goes poorly. Every time I close my eyes, I see Sasha there. He had ten days to convince me to marry him. And he did it. Against all odds, he fucking did it. I went from scratching and clawing to get away from him, to scratching and clawing to get *closer* to him.

And in those half-dreams, it's more scratching and clawing I'm doing. Only this time, I'm scratching and clawing at coffin lids closing over my face. At gilded cell bars clanking closed around me. At darkness descending like a rag held over my face until I can't breathe anymore.

Click goes the coffin.

Click goes the cage.

Click goes the…

Footstep?

I gasp awake and look to see a shadow standing in front of me. "I had a feeling this was the place," he says.

His voice wraps around me like barbed wire. I look away. I have to. If I look at him now, with snow still melting in his hair and blood crusted on his knuckles, I'll break.

"Go away, Sasha. For God's fucking sake, just leave me alone."

"No."

The single syllable vibrates through my ribcage. "Why not? Why the *fuck* not?" I cry out.

He waits until the echoes of my wail fade away into the library stacks. "You know why I'm here."

"To gloat? My dad is dead. You don't have to marry me and you still get everything you want."

He shakes his head. "No. Not everything."

I pry open my eyes. He's a step closer than he was. Enough to catch half a moonbeam peeking through the skylight. His blue eyes are bright, but his shirt is in bloody tatters and his posture is damn near broken.

"Don't," I tell him. "You don't get to do that. Not after lying to me about Jasmine. Not after I just watched my father get fucking executed. Not after letting me believe you weren't this… this *monster* who—"

"I *am* a monster." He catches my wrist when I try to shove him away. "But not that kind."

I pull free. The motion knocks a book off the cluttered desk. The thud of it landing on the floor reverberates through the cavernous room.

"You framed Dragan. Let my family grieve for a decade. For what? A fucking *alliance*?"

"For survival." His jaw ticks. "Same reason I did everything."

"Bullshit. You had a dozen chances to tell me the truth. On our dates. In Paris. Even when you—" The words get caught in my throat. *When you said you loved me.*

Sasha steps closer into my space, crowding me against the carrel wall. "Would you have believed me? That first night? The second? How about the third, Ariel? Would you have believed me then?"

"I don't know!" I lower my voice to a venomous hiss. "But you didn't even try. You just… You let me fall for a fairy tale."

His nostrils flare. "It wasn't all a lie."

"Wasn't it?" I gesture around us. "The library date? The spa? The goddamn *lingerie*? All part of the long con, right? Keep the little wife happy while you—"

He kisses me.

It's not like before—no slow burn, no teasing dominance. This is pain. Punishment. His teeth catch my lower lip hard enough to draw blood as his hands cage me against the wall. I bite back a whimper, nails digging into his biceps through the ruined tuxedo shirt.

When he pulls away, we're both shaking.

"*Eto ne lozh.*" His breath scalds my cheek. "None of that was a lie."

I swipe at my stinging mouth and spit, "Prove it."

"How?"

"Marry me."

He stills. "What?"

"Right now. No contracts. No witnesses. No political gain." I yank my mother's engagement ring off my finger and hold it up between us. "Just you and me in front of some city clerk who'll file the paperwork between coffee breaks."

His gaze drops to the ring. "Ariel—"

"If you mean it—if any of this was real—you'll do it." My voice cracks. "Otherwise, walk away from me and never look back."

He says nothing for a while. In the distant guts of the library, a clock ticks toward oblivion.

I watch the calculations flicker behind his eyes—the *pakhan* weighing risks, the boy raised by a tyrant recoiling from vulnerability.

"Give me time to make things—"

My heart shrivels to ash. "That's your answer then. At least it's an honest one."

"Ariel. Ariel, wait—"

He grabs for me again but I'm already moving, sprinting past fiction and romance and history and science. The library's rear exit looms ahead, winter light bleeding through frosted glass.

"Ya tebya lyublyu!"

The Russian stops me cold. I turn slowly. He's ten paces back, chest heaving, hair wild. A *tsar* brought to his knees.

"I love you," he repeats in English, raw as an open wound. "But marriage… It's not just vows. It's *power.* Over each other. Over everything."

I shake my head. "That's your father talking."

"He wasn't wrong."

"So that's it?" The exit sign blurs through my tears. "You'd rather be alone than risk someone having power over you?"

"I'd rather keep you safe!"

"From what? Yourself?"

"From the world I built. The one that killed your father tonight."

The words hang between us, poison gas in the musty air. I press a hand to my sternum, half-expecting to find a bullet hole.

"You think I don't know what this life costs?" My whisper is a hoarse croak. "I've been paying that price since I was eight years old, Sasha. But I was willing to pay it—for you. Because I thought… Because I thought you were worth it."

"*Ptichka.*" He takes a step forward. "Let me—"

"No, Sasha. You had your chance. Ten chances, actually. Now, you've ruined them all."

The door slams behind me with finality. Snow stings my cheeks as I stumble into the alley, but I don't look back. Can't.

Somewhere between the dumpsters and Fifth Avenue, the ring slips from my numb fingers. I don't stop to retrieve it.

Let the sewer rats have their shiny trophy.

Let it rot with the rest of his crown.

55

SASHA

I spit red onto the snow. It takes mere seconds for the fresh flurries to bury it. Another bloodstain for this godforsaken city to swallow forever.

Ariel's footsteps fade around the corner. Her scent lingers, though. *Peaches*. Always fucking peaches.

Pridi obratno ko mne, I want to roar. *Come back to me.*

But she won't. Not after this. And who could blame her? I thought I could play this game, balance these secrets, keep each one hidden from the next. But you can only juggle fire for so long before it sears your skin.

I press my forehead to the bricks of the building. When I glance down at my watch, I see with a hollow laugh that it's a minute past midnight. A new year. A fresh start. The city is blanketed with white snow like a clean, blank canvas for us to write a new story on.

But what story do we have left to write? Ariel is the reporter, not me. I've tried to bury everything, and look where that's gotten me: dripping cold blood in a dark, empty alley all by my fucking self.

Then metal clinks behind me, and I realize that I'm not by myself after all.

I turn too slow.

The first bullet catches me before I even hear the shot.

It spins me around like a fucking ballerina. I try to stagger, to stay upright, because a man on his back is a dead man. But my feet slip out from under me on the ice and I go sprawling with a pained grunt. Two more shots ring out. One in the gut, one in the thigh. Pain. So much fucking pain. My world coalesces to an inch-wide tunnel.

Into that tunnel of my vision steps Dragan. That smug Serbian bastard is grinning from ear to ear. Behind him, his goons fan out—Kalashnikovs slung low, faces hidden by balaclavas.

"Ozerov." Dragan's voice grates. "You look like shit."

"Likewise."

He kicks me in the injured thigh. I scream.

"Fifteen years, I waited," he sighs. "Fifteen years watching you think you'd gotten me so fucking good. You thought you were so *clever,* young Sasha. A clean swoop of the girl—and why would Leander believe me when I tried to tell him what had truly happened? No, no, of course not. Your story was so much prettier."

I want to tell him that nothing about this has ever been pretty. Barbed wire around my throat wasn't pretty. The bruises around Jasmine's weren't pretty, either. Even when I was handing her her life back, her face was streaked with horrified tears. *Where will I go? What will I do?*

That's for you to decide, I told her.

Dragan's face screws up and he kicks me again, this time in the torso. Ribs crack. Two? Three? It's hard to tell. All the pain is blending into a single inferno burning me alive.

"It's best that it ends this way," he decides. "I've never been much of one for speeches, so I'll leave it there, I think. Live like a dog, die like a dog. Gentlemen… hurt him."

I try to struggle up, but it's no use. They're on top of me before I can even draw a breath.

Boots. So many boots. They kick the ribs Dragan already broke. They stomp the bullet wounds until I'm screaming through clenched teeth. One *mudak* grinds his heel into my scar—the one around my neck—and suddenly, I'm twelve again, Dad's wire biting into my throat as he snarls, *Weak, weak, weak.*

So this is how it ends. Like my mother—dying in a broken mass of limbs on cold, hard ground. I give up the fight and wait for the city to swallow me, too.

Then, to my surprise:

"Enough." Dragan's voice cuts through the haze. "Put him against the wall."

They stop the beating to drag me upright and prop me against the alley bricks. Blood drips into my eyes, hot to the touch, but the rest of me is as cold as the grave.

Dragan squats down and lifts my sagging chin off my chest with one gloved hand so I have no choice but to look him in the eye. "You took everything from me. My reputation. My bride. My *empire.*" He pulls a knife from his coat—antique, curved. Ottoman steel. "Now, I take your heart."

He raises the blade.

But before he can bring it down—lights arc down the alley. Red and blue.

"Boss!" One of the Serbian goons nods toward the alley entrance. Headlights sweep across brick walls. "Five-O."

Dragan stands, wiping my blood on his slacks. "Bah! Give me your gun! I'll finish him before we go."

Police are shouting at the end of the alley as Dragan swipes a gun from one of his goons. The rest of the Serbians fire their weapons toward the cops to hold them at bay. Meanwhile, Dragan kisses the tip of the pistol to my forehead.

I can only laugh. Saved and condemned, saved and condemned, again and again… I'm sick of the carousel. *Just end it,* I think. *A man can only take so many rolls of the dice.*

Dragan's sneer deepens. His finger slides to the trigger. And…

Click.

Empty chamber.

I don't think; I just move. My hand finds the knife Dragan dropped and slashes blindly upward. The blade sinks into Dragan's groin. He screams. I yank it sideways, severing arteries, and roll as his goons open fire. Bullets stitch the wall where my head was.

Chaos.

Dragan shouts in Serbian. Tires screech. Cops descend.

Amidst it all, I crawl behind the dumpster, that knife still clutched in my bloody, shaking fingers. Dragan and his crew go sprinting to the far end of the alley and disappear from sight.

Snow falls.

Blood pools beneath me, steaming.

Get up.

My arms buckle.

Get up, ssyklo.

I claw at the dumpster, leaving red smears. Vertigo hits hard. The alley blurs—two dumpsters, four, eight.

Teeth chattering, I fumble for my phone. The screen is cracked. Blood makes the touchscreen glitch, but eventually, I get it to obey.

Feliks's number. Ringing. Ringing.

"Sasha? Sasha! Fuck, where are you?"

"Lib… Lib… Library…"

"Fuck. Hold on, I'm—"

The phone slips from my numb fingers before I can hear what he says. Darkness creeps in.

Not like this.

Ariel's face floats behind my eyelids—laughing in Paris, furious in the library, coming apart beneath me in that goddamn dressing room.

Ya tebya lyublyu.

I press a trembling hand to the gut wound, where I can feel the life draining away.

Pressure. Keep pressure.

Then a shadow falls over me.

"Oh, Sasha." Kosti Makris tsks, adjusting his cashmere scarf. "You don't look good."

He kicks the knife out of my hand. Then he crouches, tilting my chin up with a gloved hand. "Don't worry, my friend. I'll take care of you, just like you took care of my niece."

Blackness swallows me whole.

56

ARIEL

I make a vow as I run. Not the vow I thought I was going to make tonight, but a vow nonetheless.

I will leave Sasha Ozerov behind me.

Every step is an underscore on that promise. I'm gonna leave him behind me. All of him. Every kiss, every touch, every murmur he ever whispered in my ear when the lights were off and it was just the two of us pressed skin-to-skin beneath the sheets. It all stays in the past.

The snow stabs at my throat as I run. My breath comes in ragged clouds. I don't slow down until the library's silhouette fades behind me, swallowed by the iron-gray sky.

My right hand throbs. I glance down through frozen lashes to see blood trickling from a gash below my knuckles—courtesy of smashing through the library window.

God, I'm tired of life trying to stitch together these poetic circles. Doesn't it understand? Nothing is *neat.* Nothing is *whole.* It's all a broken, sobbing mess, and you never end up back where you started in a neat synchronicity—you end up worse off, every single time.

A neon sign glows through the blizzard ahead—CVS. Sanctuary. Perfect. I can shoplift a first aid kit and patch myself up.

The automatic doors wheeze open for me. Fluorescent lights buzz overhead, bleaching the aisles into a fever-dream haze. I grab a box of Band-Aids, hydrogen peroxide, and start to head for the bathroom.

Then freeze in front of the family planning shelf.

A pink box mocks me from the shelf. *Rapid Results!* it chirps. My stomach lurches. *It's just stress,* I tell myself. *Stress from dodging mobsters and playing fiancée to a human wrecking ball.* For ten days, my entire life has been a dumpster fire full of shit rolling downhill, so of course this weird, fluttery intuition of mine that says I should take the test, just to see, just to be sure… That's nonsense, right?

Right?

I grab the test.

In the bathroom, I fumble with the packaging, but my hands are slick with blood, so I drop it twice before I manage to tear the plastic free.

I pee, set the test on the sink, and count the seconds. Sixty. One hundred. A hundred twenty. I deliberately avoid the mirror. If I have it my way, I'll never see my reflection again.

I finish my own count right as the test's automatic timer starts to sing. I look down, and—

"No." I press a hand to my stomach. "No, no, *no*."

Two pink lines.

I brace myself against the sink, breathing through the vertigo. A baby. *His* baby.

Can't leave *that* behind, can I?

I smash the test into the trash.

Outside, the cold slaps me awake. I pull out my phone, fingers slipping on blood and snow. Kosti answers on the first ring. "Ari? Where are you? Are you—"

"I need the tickets." My voice cracks. "I'm leaving. Tonight."

TO BE CONTINUED

The story continues in
Book 2 of the Ozerov Bratva duet:
10 DAYS TO SURRENDER

ALSO BY NICOLE FOX

Litvinov Bratva

Inked Adonis

Inked Athena

Groza Bratva

Cashmere Cruelty

Cashmere Ruin

Kuznetsov Bratva

Emerald Malice

Emerald Vices

Novikov Bratva

Ivory Ashes

Ivory Oath

Egorov Bratva

Tangled Innocence

Tangled Decadence

Zakrevsky Bratva

Requiem of Sin

Sonata of Lies

Rhapsody of Pain

Bugrov Bratva

Midnight Purgatory

Midnight Sanctuary

Oryolov Bratva

Cruel Paradise

Cruel Promise

Pushkin Bratva

Cognac Villain

Cognac Vixen

Viktorov Bratva

Whiskey Poison

Whiskey Pain

Orlov Bratva

Champagne Venom

Champagne Wrath

Uvarov Bratva

Sapphire Scars

Sapphire Tears

Vlasov Bratva

Arrogant Monster

Arrogant Mistake

Zhukova Bratva

Tarnished Tyrant

Tarnished Queen

Stepanov Bratva

Satin Sinner

Satin Princess

Makarova Bratva

Shattered Altar

Shattered Cradle

Solovev Bratva

Ravaged Crown

Ravaged Throne

Vorobev Bratva

Velvet Devil

Velvet Angel

Romanoff Bratva

Immaculate Deception

Immaculate Corruption

Kovalyov Bratva

Gilded Cage

Gilded Tears

Jaded Soul

Jaded Devil

Ripped Veil

Ripped Lace

Mazzeo Mafia Duet

Liar's Lullaby (Book 1)

Sinner's Lullaby (Book 2)

Bratva Crime Syndicate

**Can be read in any order!*

Lies He Told Me

Scars He Gave Me

Sins He Taught Me

Belluci Mafia Trilogy

Corrupted Angel (Book 1)

Corrupted Queen (Book 2)

Corrupted Empire (Book 3)

De Maggio Mafia Duet

Devil in a Suit (Book 1)

Devil at the Altar (Book 2)

Kornilov Bratva Duet

Married to the Don (Book 1)

Til Death Do Us Part (Book 2)

Heirs to the Bratva Empire

**Can be read in any order!*

Kostya

Maksim

Andrei

Princes of Ravenlake Academy (Bully Romance)

**Can be read as standalones!*

Cruel Prep

Cruel Academy

Cruel Elite

Tsezar Bratva

Nightfall (Book 1)

Daybreak (Book 2)

Russian Crime Brotherhood

**Can be read in any order!*

Owned by the Mob Boss

Unprotected with the Mob Boss

Knocked Up by the Mob Boss

Sold to the Mob Boss

Stolen by the Mob Boss

Trapped with the Mob Boss

Volkov Bratva

Broken Vows (Book 1)

Broken Hope (Book 2)

Broken Sins *(standalone)*

Other Standalones

Vin: A Mafia Romance

Box Sets

Bratva Mob Bosses (Russian Crime Brotherhood Books 1-6)

Tsezar Bratva (Tsezar Bratva Duet Books 1-2)

Heirs to the Bratva Empire

The Mafia Dons Collection

The Don's Corruption